MW01434366

LADY ATHLYNE

Bram Stoker

VALANCOURT BOOKS
CHICAGO

Lady Athlyne by Bram Stoker
First published in 1908
First Valancourt Books edition, April 2007

This edition © 2007 by Valancourt Books

All rights reserved. The use of any part of this publication reproduced, transmitted in any form or by any means, electronic, mechanical, photocopying, recording, or otherwise, or stored in a retrieval system, without prior written consent of the publisher, may constitute an infringement of the copyright law.

Library of Congress Cataloging in Publication Data

Stoker, Bram, 1847-1912.
  Lady Athlyne / Bram Stoker. -- 1st Valancourt Books ed.
    p. cm.
  ISBN 0-9792332-4-0
  1. Love stories. gsafd 2. New York (N.Y.)--Fiction. 3. Scotland--Fiction. I. Title.
  PR6037.T617L339 2007
  823'.8--dc22
                                            2007001541

Published by Valancourt Books
P. O. Box 220511
Chicago, Illinois 60622

Typesetting by James D. Jenkins
Set in Dante MT

10 9 8 7 6 5 4 3 2 1

CONTENTS

CHAP.		PAGE
I.	ON THE "CRYPTIC"	1
II.	IN ITALY	15
III.	DE HOOGE'S SPRUIT	25
IV.	THE BIRD-CAGE	37
V.	AN ADVENTURE	45
VI.	TRUE HEART'S-CONTENT	55
VII.	A DISCUSSION	66
VIII.	"LOOK AT ME!"	80
IX.	THE CAR OF DESTINY	91
X.	A LETTER	103
XI.	THE BEAUTIFUL TWILIGHT	114
XII.	ECHO OF A TRAGEDY	126
XIII.	INSTINCTIVE PLANNING	139
XIV.	A BANQUET ON OLYMPUS	149
XV.	"STOP!"	162
XVI.	A PAINFUL JOURNEY	173
XVII.	THE SHERIFF	188
XVIII	PURSUIT	194
XIX.	DECLARATION OF WAR	206
XX.	KNOWLEDGE OF LAW	223
XXI.	APPLICATION OF LAW	235
XXII.	THE HATCHET BURIED	248
XXIII.	A HARMONY IN GRAY	259

LADY ATHLYNE

CHAPTER I

ON THE "CRYPTIC"

ON the forenoon of a day in February, 1899, the White Star S.S. *Cryptic* forced her way from Pier No. 48 out into the Hudson River through a mass of floating ice, which made a moving carpet over the whole river from Poughkeepsie to Sandy Hook. It was little wonder that the hearts of the outwardbound passengers were cheered with hope; outside on the wide ocean there must be somewhere clear skies and blue water, and perchance here and there a slant of sunshine. Come what might, however, it must be better than what they were leaving behind them in New York. For three whole weeks the great city had been beleaguered by cold; held besieged in the icy grip of a blizzard which, moving from northwest to south, had begun on the last day of January to devastate the central North American States. In one place, Breckenridge in Colorado, there fell in five days—and this on the top of an accumulation of six feet of snow—an additional forty-five inches. In the track swept by the cold wave, a thousand miles wide, record low temperatures were effected, ranging from 15° below zero in Indiana to 54° below at White River on the northern shore of Lake Superior.

In New York city the temperature had sunk to 6.2° below zero, the lowest ever recorded, and an extraordinary temperature for a city almost entirely surrounded by tidal currents. The city itself was in a helpless condition, paralyzed and impotent. The snow fell so fast that even the great snow-ploughs driven by the electric current on the tram lines could not keep the avenues clear. And the cold was so great that the street-clearing operations—in which eight thousand men with four thousand carts dumping some fifty thousand tons of snow daily into the river were concerned—had to be suspended. Neither men nor horses could endure the work. The "dead boat" which takes periodically the city's unclaimed corpses to Potter's Field on Hart's Island was twice beaten back and nearly wrecked;

it carried on the later voyage 161 corpses. Before its ghastly traffic could be resumed there were in the city mortuaries over a thousand bodies waiting sepulture. The "Scientific editor" of one of the great New York dailies computed that the blanket of snow which lay on the twenty-two square miles of Manhattan Island would form a solid wall a thousand feet high up the whole sixty feet width of Broadway in the two and a half miles between the Battery and Union Square, weighing some two and a half million tons. Needless to say the streets were almost impassable. In the chief thoroughfares were narrow passages heaped high with piled-up snow now nearly compact to ice. In places where the falling snow had drifted it reached to the level of, and sometimes above, the first floor windows.

As the *Cryptic* forced her way through the rustling masses of drifting ice the little company of passengers stood on deck watching at first the ferry-boats pounding and hammering their strenuous way into the docks formed by the floating guards or screens by whose aid they shouldered themselves to their landing stages; and later on, when the great ship following the wide circle of the steering buoys, opened up the entrance of Sandy Hook, the great circle around them of Arctic desolation. Away beyond the sweep of the river and ocean currents the sea was frozen and shimmering with a carpet of pure snow, whose luminous dreariness not even the pall of faint chill mist could subdue. Here and there, to north and south, were many vessels frozen in, spar and rope being roughly outlined with clinging snow. The hills of Long Island and Staten Island and the distant ranges of New Jersey stood out white and stark into the sky of steel.

All was grimly, deadly silent so that the throb of the engines, the rustle and clatter of the drifting ice-pack, as the great vessel, getting faster way as the current became more open, or the hard scrunch as she cut through some solid floating ice-field, sounded like something unnatural—some sound of the living amid a world of the dead.

When the Narrows had been reached and passed and the flag of smoke from the great chimney of the Standard Oil Refining Works lay far behind on the starboard quarter; when Fire Island was dropping down on the western horizon, all became changed as though the wand of some beneficent fairy had obliterated all that was ugly or noxious in its beneficent sweep. Sky and wave were blue;

the sun beamed out; and the white-breasted gulls sweeping above and around the ship seemed like the spirit of nature freed from the thrall of the Ice Queen. Naturally the spirits of the travellers rose. They too found their wings free; and the hum and clash of happy noises arose. Unconsciously there was a general unbending each to the other. All the stiffness which is apt to characterize a newly gathered company of travellers seemed to melt in the welcome sunshine; within an hour there was established an easiness of acquaintanceship generally to be found only towards the close of a voyage. The happiness coming with the sunshine and the open water, and the relief from the appalling gloom of the blizzard, had made the freed captives into friends.

At such moments like gravitates to like. The young to young; the grave to the grave; the pleasure-lovers to their kind; free sex to its free opposite. On the *Cryptic* the complement of passengers was so small that the choice of kinds was limited. In all there were only some thirty passengers. None but adventurous spirits, or those under stress of need, challenged a possible recurrence of Atlantic dangers which had marked the beginning of the month, when ship after ship of the giant liners arrived in port maimed and battered and listed with the weight of snow and frozen spray and fog which they carried.

Naturally the ladies were greatly in the minority. After all, travel is as a rule, men's work; and this was no time for pleasure trips. The dominant feeling on board on this subject was voiced in a phrase used in the Chart room where the Captain was genially pointing out the course to a tall, proud old man. The latter, with an uneasy gesture of stroking his long white moustache, which seemed to be a custom or habit at certain moments of emotion, said:

"And I quite agree with you, seh; I don't mind men travelling in any weather. That's man's share. But why in hell, seh, women want to go gallivantin' round the world in weather that would make any respectable dog want to lie quiet by the fireside, I don't know. Women should learn——" He was interrupted by a tall young girl who burst into the room without waiting for a reply to her breathless: "May I come in?"

"I saw you go in, Daddy, and I wanted to see the maps too; so I raced for all I was worth. And now I find I've come just in time to get another lesson about what women ought to do!" As she spoke she linked her arm in her father's with a fearlessness and security which showed that none of the natural sternness which was proclaimed in the old man's clear-cut face was specially reserved for her. She squeezed his arm in a loving way and looked up in his face saucily—the way of an affectionate young girl towards a father whom she loves and trusts. The old man pulled his arm away and put it round her shoulder. With a shrug which might if seen alone have denoted constraint, but with a look in the dark eyes and a glad tone in the strong voice which nullified it absolutely, he said to the Captain:

"Here comes my tyrant, Captain. Now I must behave myself."

The girl standing close to him went on in the same loving half-bantering way:

"Go on, Daddy! Tell us what women should learn!"

"They should learn, Miss Impudence, to respect their fathers!" Though he spoke lightly in a tone of banter and with a light of affection beaming in his eyes, the girl grew suddenly grave, and murmured quickly:

"That is not to be learned, Father. That is born with one, when the father is like mine!" Then turning to the Captain she went on:

"Did you ever hear of the Irishman who said: There's some subjects too sarious for jestin'; an' pitaties is wan iv them? I can't sauce my father, or chaff him, or be impudent—though I believe he *likes* me to be impudent—to him, when he talks of respect. He has killed men before now for want of that. But he won't kill me. He knows that my respect for him is as big as my love—and there isn't room for any more of either of them in me. Don't you Daddy?"

For answer the old man drew her closer to him; but he said nothing. Really there was no need for speech. The spirits and emotions of both were somewhat high strung in the sudden change to brightness from the gloom that had prevailed for weeks. At such times even the most staid are apt to be suddenly moved.

A diversion came from the Captain, a grave, formal man as indeed becomes one who has with him almost perpetually the responsibility of many hundreds of lives:

"Did I understand rightly, Colonel Ogilvie that you have *killed* men for such a cause?" The old gentleman lifted his shaggy white eyebrows in faint surprise, and answered slowly and with an easiness which only half hid an ineffable disdain:

"Why, cert'nly!" The simple acceptance of the truth left the Captain flabbergasted. He grew red and was beginning: "I thought"—when the girl who considered it possible that a quick quarrel might arise between the two strong men, interrupted:

"Perhaps Captain, you don't understand our part of the world. In Kentucky we still hold with the old laws of Honour which we sometimes hear are dead—or at any rate back numbers—in other countries. My father has fought duels all his life. The Ogilvies have been fighters way back to the time of the settlement by Lord Baltimore. My Cousin Dick tells me—for father never talks of them unless he has to—that they never forced quarrels for their own ends; though I must say that they are pretty touchy"—She was in turn interrupted by her father who said quickly:

"'Touchy' is the word, my girl, though I fear you use it too lightly. A man *should* be touchy where honour is concerned. For Honour is the first thing in all the world. What men should live for; what men should die for! To a gentleman there is nothing so holy. And if he can't fight for such a sacred thing, he does not deserve to have it. He does not know what it means."

Through the pause came the grave voice of the Captain, a valiant man who on state occasions wore on his right breast in accordance with the etiquette of the occasion the large gold medal of the Royal Humane Society:

"There are many things that men should fight for—and die for if need be. But I am bound to say that I don't hold that the chiefest among them is a personal grievance; even if it be on the subject of the measure of one's own self-respect." Noticing the coming frown on the Kentuckian's face, he went on a thought more quickly: "But, though I don't hold with duelling, Colonel Ogilvie, for any cause, I am bound to say that if a man thinks and believes that it is right to fight, then it becomes a duty which he should fulfil!"

For answer the Colonel held out his hand which the other took warmly. That handshake cemented a friendship of two strong men who understood each other well enough to tolerate the other's limitations.

"And I can tell you this, seh," said Colonel Ogilvie, "there are some men who want killing—want it badly!"

The girl glowed. She loved to see her father strong and triumphant; and when toleration was added to his other fine qualities, there was an added measure in her pride of him.

There came a tap on the panelling and the doorway was darkened by the figure of a buxom pleasant-faced woman, who spoke in a strong Irish accent:

"I big yer pardon, Miss Ogilvie, but yer Awnt is yellin' out for ye. She's thinkin' that now the wather's deep the ship is bound to go down in it; an' she sez she wants ye to be wid her whin the ind comes, as she's afeard to die alone!"

"That's very thoughtful of her! Judy was always an unselfish creature!" said the Colonel with an easy sarcasm. "Run along to her anyhow, little girl. That's the sort of fighting a woman has to do. And" turning to the Captain "by Ged, seh! she's got plenty of that sort of fighting between her cradle and her grave!" As she went out of the door, the girl said over her shoulder:

"That reminds me, daddy. Don't go on with that lecture of yours of what women should learn until I come back. Remember I'm only 'a child emerging into womanhood'—that's what you wrote to mother when you wouldn't let me travel to her alone. Some one might kill me I suppose, or steal me between this and Ischia. So it is well I should be forewarned, and so forearmed, at all points!"

The Captain looked after her admiringly; then turning to Colonel Ogilvie he said almost unconsciously—he had daughters of his own:

"I shouldn't be surprised if a lot want to steal her, Colonel. And I don't know but they'd be right!"

"I agree with you, by Ged, seh!" said the Colonel reflectively, as he looked after his daughter pacing with free strides along the deck with the stout little stewardess over whom she towered by a full head.

Miss Ogilvie found her aunt, Miss Judith Hayes, in her bunk. From the clothes hung round and laid, neatly folded, on the upper berth it was apparent that she had undressed as for the night. When the young girl realised this she said impulsively:

"Oh, Aunt Judy, I hope you are not ill. Do come up on deck. The sun is shining and it is such a change from the awful weather in New York. Do come, dear; it will do you good."

"I am not ill Joy—in the way you mean. Indeed I was never in better physical health in my life." She said this with grave primness. The girl laughed outright:

"Why on earth Aunt Judy, if you're well, do you go to bed at ten o'clock in the morning?" Miss Hayes was not angry; there was a momentary gleam in her eye as she said with a manifestedly exaggerated dignity:

"You forget my dear, that I am an old maid!"

"What has old-maidenhood to do with it? But anyhow you are not an old maid. You are only forty!"

"Not forty, Joy! *Only* forty, indeed! My dear child when that unhappy period comes a single lady is put on the shelf—out of reach of all masculine humanity. For my part I have made up my mind to climb up there, of my own accord, before the virginal undertakers come for me. I am in for it anyhow; and I want to play the game as well as I can."

Joy bent down and kissed her affectionately. Then taking her face between her strong young hands, and looking steadily in her eyes, she said:

"Aunt Judy you are not an old anything. You are a deal younger than I am. You mustn't get such ideas into your head. And even if you do you mustn't speak them. People would begin to believe you. What is forty anyhow!" The other answered sententiously:

"What is forty? Not old for a wife! Young for a widow! Death for a maid!"

"Really Aunt Judy" said the girl smiling "one would think you wish to be an old maid. Even I know better than that—and Father thinks I am younger and more ignorant than the yellow chick that has just pecked its way out of the shell. The woman has not yet been born—nor ever will be—who wants to be an old maid."

Judith Hayes raised herself on one elbow and said calmly:

"Or a young one, my dear!" Then as if pleased with her epigram she sank back on her pillow with a smile. Joy paused; she did not know what to say. A diversion came from the stewardess who had all the time stood in the doorway waiting for some sort of instructions:

"Bedad, Miss Hayes, it's to Ireland ye ought to come. A lovely young lady like yerself—for all yer jabber about an ould maid iv forty—wouldn't be let get beyant Queenstown, let alone the Mall in Cork. Bedad if ye was in Athlone its the shillelaghs that would be out an' the byes all fightin' for who'd get the hould on to ye first. Whisper me now, is it coddin' us ye be doin' or what?" Joy turned round to her, her face all dimpled with laughter, and said:

"That's the way to talk to her Mrs. O'Brien. You just take her in hand; and when we get to Queenstown find some nice big Irishman to carry her off."

"Bedad I will! An sorra the shtruggle she'd make agin it anyhow I'm thinkin'!" Aunt Judy laughed:

"Joy" she said "you'd better be careful yourself or maybe she'd put on some of her bachelor press-gang to abduct you."

"Don't you be onaisy about that ma'am," said Mrs. O'Brien quietly "I've fixed that already! When I seen Miss Joy come down the companion shtairs I sez to meself: 'There's only wan man in Ireland—an that's in all the wurrld—that's good enough for you, me darlin'. An he'll have you for sure or I'm a gandher!"

"Indeed!" said Joy, blushing in spite of herself. "And may I be permitted to know my ultimate destination in the way of matrimony? You won't think me inquisitive or presuming I trust." Her eyes were dancing with the fun of the thing. Mrs. O'Brien laughed heartily; a round, cheery, honest laugh which was infectious:

"Wid all the plisure in life Miss. Shure there's only the wan, an him the finest and beautifullest young man ye iver laid yer pritty eyes on. An him an Earrl, more betoken; wid more miles iv land iv his own then there does be pitaties in me ould father's houldin! Musha, he's the only wan that's at all fit to take yer swate self in his charge."

"H'm! Quite condescending of him I am sure. And now what may be his sponsorial and patronymic appellatives?" Mrs. O'Brien at once became grave. To an uneducated person, and more especially an Irish person, an unknown phrase is full of mystery. It makes the listener feel small and disconcerted, touching the personal pride which is so marked a characteristic of all degrees of the Irish race.

Joy, with the quick understanding which was not the least of her endowments, saw that she had made a mistake and hastened to set matters right before the chagrin had time to bite deep:

"Forgive me, but that was *my* fun. What I meant to ask are the name and title of my destined Lord and Master?" The stewardess answered heartily, the ruffle of her face softening into an amiable smile:

"Amn't I tellin' ye miss. Shure there is only the wan!"

"And who may he be?"

"Faix he may be anything. It's a King or a Kazer or an Imperor or a Czaar he'd be if I had the ordherin' iv it. But what he is is the Right Honourable the Earl av Athlyne. Lord Liftinant av the County iv Roscommon—an' a jool!"

"Oh, an Irishman!" said Miss Judy. Mrs. O'Brien snorted; her national pride was hurt:

"An Irishman! God be thanked he is. But me Lady, av it'll plaze ye betther he's an Englishman too, an' a Welshman an' a Scotchman as well! Oh, th' injustice t' Ireland. Him borrn in Roscommon, an yit a Scotchman they call him bekase his biggest title is Irish!"

"Mrs. O'Brien, that's all nonsense," said Miss Judy tartly. "We may be Americans; but we're not to be played for suckers for all that! How can a Scotchman have an Irish title?"

"That's all very well, Miss Hayes, yous Americans is very cliver; but yez don't know everything. An' I may be an ignorant ould fool; but I'm not so ignorant as ye think, ayther. Wasn't there a Scotchman thit was marrid on the granddaughther iv Quane Victory hersilf—An Errll begob, what owned the size iv a countthry in Scotland. An him all the time wid an Irish Errldom, till they turned him into a Sassenach be makin' him a Juke. Begorra! isn't it proud th' ould Laady should ha' been to git an Irishman iv any kind for the young girrl! Shure an isn't Athlyne as good as Fife any day. Hasn't he castles an' estates in Scotland an' England an' Wales, as well as in Ireland. Isn't he an ould Bar'n iv some kind in Scotland an him but a young man! Begob! av it's Ireland y' objict to ye can take him as Scotch—where they say he belongs an' where he chose to live whin he became a grown man, before he wint into th' Army!"

Somehow or other the announcement and even the grandiose manner of its making gave pleasure to Joy. After all, the compliment of the stewardess was an earnest one. She had chosen for her the best that she knew. What more could she do? With a sudden smile she made a sweeping curtsey, the English Presentation curtsey which all American girls are taught, and said:

"Let me convey to you the sincere thanks of the Countess of Athlyne! Aunt Judy do you feel proud of having a Peeress for a niece? Any time you wish to be presented you can call on the services of Lady Athlyne." She suddenly straightened herself to her full height as Mrs. O'Brien spoke with a sort of victorious howl:

"Hurroo! Now ye've done it. Ye've said the wurrds yerself; an' we all know what that manes!"

"What does it mean?" Joy spoke somewhat sharply, her face all aflame. It appeared that she had committed some unmaidenly indiscretion.

"It manes that it manes the same as if ye said 'yis!' to me gentleman when persooin' iv his shute. It's for all the wurrld the same as bein' marrid on to him!"

In spite of the ridiculousness of the statement Joy thrilled inwardly. Unconsciously she accepted the position of peeress thus thrust upon her.

After all, the Unknown has its own charms for the human heart. Those old Athenians who built the altars "To the Unknown God," did but put into classic phrase the aspirations of a people by units as well as in mass. Mrs. O'Brien's enthusiastic admiration laid seeds of some kind in the young girl's heart.

Her instinct was, however, not to talk of it; and as a protective measure she changed the conversation:

"But you haven't told me yet, Aunt Judy, why you went to bed in the morning because you pretend to be an old maid." The Irishwoman here struck in:

"I'm failin' to comprehind that meself too. If ye was a young wife now I could consave it, maybe. Or an ould widda-woman like meself that does have to be gettin' up in the night to kape company wid young weemin that doesn't like to die, alone . . ." she burst into hearty laughter in which Miss Judith Hayes joined. Joy took advantage of the general hilarity to try to persuade her aunt to come on deck. She finished her argument:

"And the Captain is such a nice man. He's just a wee bit too grave. I think he must be a widower." Aunt Judy made no immediate reply; but after some more conversation she said to the stewardess:

"I think I will get up Mrs. O'Brien. Perhaps a chair on deck in the sunshine will be better for me than staying down here. And, after all, if I have to die it will be better to die in the open than in a bed the size of a coffin!"

When Joy rejoined her father in the Chart-room she said to the Captain:

"That stewardess of yours is a dear!" He warmly acquiesced:

"She is really a most capable person; and all the ladies whom she attends grow to be quite fond of her. She is always kind and cheery and hearty and makes them forget that they are ill or afraid. When I took command of the *Cryptic* I asked the company to let her come with me."

"And quite right too, Captain. That brogue of hers is quite wonderful!"

"It is indeed. But, my dear young lady, its very perfection makes me doubt it. It is so thick and strong and ready, and the way she twists words into its strength and makes new ones to suit it give me an idea at times that it is partly put on. I sometimes think it is impossible that any one can be so absolutely and imperatively Irish as she is. However, it serves her in good stead; she can say, without offence, whatever she chooses in her own way to any one. She is a really clever woman and a kind one; and I have the greatest respect for her."

When Aunt Judy was left alone with the stewardess, she asked:

"Who is Lord Athlyne?—What kind of man is he? Where does he live?"

"Where does he live?—Why everywhere! In Athlyne for one, but a lot iv other places as well. He was brought up at the Castle where the ould Earrl always lived afther he lift Parlimint; and whin he was a boy he was the wildest young dare-devil iver ye seen. Faix, the County Roscommon itself wasn't big enough for him. When he was a young man he wint away shootin' lions and tigers and elephants and crocodiles and such like. Thin he wint into th' army an began to settle down. He has a whole lot av different houses, and he goes to them all be times. He says that no man has a right to be an intire absentee landlord—even when he's livin' in his own house!"

"But what sort of man is he personally?" she asked persistently. The Irishwoman's answer was direct and comprehensive:

"The bist!"

"How do you know that?"

"An' how do I know it! Amn't I a Roscommon woman, borrn, an' wan av the tinants? Wouldn't that be enough? But that's only the beginnin'. Shure wasn't I his fosther-mother, God bless him! Wasn't he like me own child when I tuk him to me breast whin his poor mother died the day he was borrn. Ah, Miss Hayes there's nothin' ye don't know about the child ye have given suck to. More, betoken, than if he was yer own child; for ye might be thinkin' too much of *him* an puttin' the bist consthruction on ivery little thing he iver done, just because he was yer own. Troth I didn't want any tellin' about Athlyne. The sweetest wean that iver a woman nursed; the tindherest hearted, wid the wee little hands upon me face an his rosebud av a mouth puttin' up to me for a kiss! An' yit the pride av him; more'n a King on his throne. An' th' indepindince! Him wantin' to walk an' run before he was able to shtand. An' ordherin' about the pig an' the gandher, let alone the dog. Shure the masterfullest man-child that iver was, and the masterfullest man that is. Sorra wan like him in the whole wide wurrld!"

"You seem to love him very much," said Miss Hayes with grave approval.

"In coorse I do! An' isn't it me own boy that was his fosther brother that loves him too. Whin the Lard wint out to fight the Boors, Mick wint wid him as his own body man until he was invalided home wid a bad knee; an' him a coachman now an' doin' nothin' but take his wages; And whin he kem to Liverpool to say good-bye when the *Cryptic* should come in I tould him to take care of his Masther. 'Av ye don't,' sez I, 'ye're no son iv mine, nor iv yer poor dear father, rest his sowl! Kape betune him an' any bullet that's comin' his way' I sez. An' wid that he laughed out loud in me face. 'That's good, mother,' sez he, 'an iv coorse I'd be proud to; but I'd like to set eyes on the man that'd dar to come betune Athlyne an' a bullet, or to prevint him cuttin' slices from aff iv the Boors wid his big cav-a-lary soord,' he sez. 'Begob,' he sez, 't'would be worse nor fightin' the Boors themselves to intherfere wid him whin he's set on his way!'"

"That's loyal stock! He's a Man, that son of yours!" said Miss Judy enthusiastically, forgetting her semi-cynical rôle of old maid in the ardour of the moment. The stewardess seeing that she had a good listener went on:

"And 'tis the thoughtful man he is. He niver writes to me, bekase he knows well I can't read. But he sends me five pounds every Christmas. On me birthday he gev me this, Lord love him!" She took a gold watch from her bosom and showed it with pride.

When she was dressed, Miss Hayes looked into the Library; and finding it empty took down the "de Brett," well thumbed by American use. Here is what she saw on looking up "Athlyne."

ATHLYNE EARL OF FITZGERALD

Calinus Patrick Richard Westerna Hardy Mowbray Fitz-Gerald 2nd Earl of Athlyne (in the Peerage of the United Kingdom). 2nd Viscount Roscommon (in the Peerage of Ireland). 30th Baron Ceann-da-Shail (in the Peerage of Scotland). b. 6 June 1875 s. 1886 ed. Eton and University of Dublin; is D. L. for Counties of Ross and Roscommon: J. P. for Counties of Wilts, Ross and Roscommon.

Patron of three livings:—Raphoon, New Sands, and Politore.

Seats. Ceann-da-Shail Castle and Castle of Elandonan in Ross-shire, Athlyne Castle C. Roscommon. Travy Manor, Gloucestershire and The Rock Beach, Cornwall, &c. &c. *Town Residence.* 40 St. James's Square S. W.

Clubs. Reform. Marlborough. United Service. Naval and Military. Garick. Arts. Bath &c.

Predecessors. Sir Calinus FitzGerald—descended from Calinus FitzGerald the first of the name settled in Ross-shire, to which he came from Ireland in the XII century—was created by Robert the Bruce Baron Ceann-da-Shail, 1314, and endowed with the Castle of Elandonan (Gift of the King) as the reward of a bold rally of the Northern troops at Bannockburn. Before his death in 1342 he built for himself a strongly fortified Castle on the Island of Ceann-da-Shail (from which his estate took its name) celebrated from time immemorial for a wonderful spring of water. The Barony has been held in direct descent with only two breaks. The first was in 1642 when direct male issue having failed through the death of the only son of Calinus the XXth Baron the Peerage and estates reverted to Robert Calinus e. s. of James, 2nd s. of Robert XVIII Baron. The second was in 1826 when, again through the early decease of an only son, the Barony reverted to Robert e. s. of Malcolm 2nd s. of Colin XXVII Baron. The father of this heritor, Malcolm FitzGerald, had settled in Ireland in 1782. There he had purchased a great estate fronting on the River Shannon in Roscommon on which he had built a castle, Athlyne. Malcolm FitzGerald entered the Parliament of the United Kingdom in 1805 and sat for 22 years when he was succeeded in Parliamentary honours by his son Robert on his coming of age in 1827. Robert held his seat until the creation of the Viscounty of Roscommon 1870. Three years after his retirement from the House of Commons he was raised to an Earldom—Athlyne.

When she went out on deck she found her niece taking with her father the beef tea which had just been brought round. She did not mention to Colonel Ogilvie the little joke about Lady Athlyne, and strange to say found that Joy to whom a joke or a secret was a matter of fungoid growth, multiplying and irrepressible, had not mentioned it either.

CHAPTER II

IN ITALY

DURING the voyage, which had its own vicissitudes, the joke was kept up amongst the three women. The stewardess, seeing that the two ladies only spoke of it in privacy, exemplified that discretion which the Captain had commended. Only once did she forget herself, but even then fortune was on her side. It was during a day when Joy was upset by a spell of heavy weather and had to keep her cabin. In the afternoon her father paid a visit to her; and Mrs. O'Brien in reporting progress to him said that "her Ladyship" was now on the road to recovery and would be on deck very shortly. Colonel Ogilvie made quite a lot of the error which he read in his own way. He said to his sister-in-law as they paced the deck together:

"Capital woman that stewardess! There is a natural deference and respect in her manner which you do not always find in people of her class. Will you oblige me, Judy, by seeing, when the voyage is over, that she gets an extra honorarium!" Judy promised, and deftly turned the conversation; she felt that she was on dangerous ground.

Judith Hayes called herself an old maid, not believing it to be true; but all the same there was in her make-up a distinctive trait of it: the manner in which she regarded a romance. Up to lately, romance however unlikely or improbable, had a personal bearing; it did not occur to her that it might not drift in her direction. But now she felt unconsciously that such romance must have other objective than herself. The possibility, therefore, of a romance for Joy whom she very sincerely loved was a thing to be cherished. She could see, as well as feel, that her niece by keeping it a secret from her father had taken the matter with at least a phase of seriousness. This alone was sufficient to feed her own imaginings; and in the glow her sympathies quickened. She had instinctively at the beginning determined not to spoil sport; now it became a conscious intention.

Mrs. O'Brien, too, in her own way helped to further the matter. She felt that she had a good audience for her little anecdotes of the child whose infancy she had fostered, and towards whom in his completed manhood she had a sort of almost idolatrous devotion. Seeing the girl so sympathetic and listening so patiently, she too began to see something like the beginnings of a fact. And so the game went merrily on.

The telegrams at Queenstown were not very reassuring, and Colonel Ogilvie and his party pressed on at once to Sorrento whence his wife had moved on the completion of her series of baths at Ischia. Naturally the whole of the little party was depressed, until on arrival they found Mrs. Ogilvie, who was something of a valetudinarian, much better than they expected. The arrival of her husband and daughter and sister seemed to complete her cure; she brightened up at once, and even after a few days began to enjoy herself.

One day after lunch as she drove along the road to Amalfi with Judith and Joy—the Colonel was lazy that day and preferred to sit on the terrace over the sea and smoke—she began to ask all the details of the journey. Judy who had not had a chance of speaking alone with safety began to tell the little secret. Her method of commencement was abrupt, and somewhat startling to the convalescent:

"We've got a husband for Joy, at last!"

"Gracious!" said Mrs. Ogilvie. "What do you mean, Judy? Is this one of your pranks?"

"Prank indeed!" she answered back, tossing her head. "A real live lord! A belted Earl if you please—whatever that may mean."

"Is this true, Joy?" said her mother beaming anxiously on her—if such a combination is understandable. Joy took her hand and stroked it lovingly:

"Do you think, Mother dear, that if there was such a thing I should leave you all this time in ignorance of it. It is only a jest made up by the stewardess who attended us on the *Cryptic*. Aunt Judy seems to have taken it all in; I think dear you had better ask her; she seems to know all about it—which is certainly more than I do."

"And how did this common woman dare to jest on such a subject. I don't think Judy that this would have happened had I been with her myself!"

"Oh my dear, get off that high horse. There's nothing to be alarmed about. The stewardess—who is a most worthy and attentive person——"

"She is a dear!" interrupted Joy.

"—took such a fancy to Joy that she said there was only 'wan' in all the world who was worthy of her—a young nobleman to whom she had been foster-mother. It was certainly meant as a very true compliment, and I am bound to say that if the young man merits a hundredth part of all she said of him there's certainly no cause of offence in the mere mentioning his name."

"What is his name?" There was a shade of anxiety in the mother's voice.

"Lord Athlyne!"

"The Earl of Athlyne!" said Joy speaking without thought. Then she turned quickly away to hide her blushing.

"I—I—I really don't understand!" said Mrs. Ogilvie, looking around helplessly. Then with the shadow of a shade of annoyance in her voice she went on:

"I really think that in a serious matter of this kind I should have been consulted. But I seem not to count for anything any more. Colonel Ogilvie has not even mentioned the matter to me. I think I ought to have some say in anything of importance relating to my little girl."

"Lord bless the woman!" said Aunt Judy throwing up her hands and lifting her eyes. "Sally dear don't you comprehend that this was all a joke. We never saw this young Lord, never heard of him till the stewardess mentioned him; and as for him he doesn't know or care whether there is such a person in the world as Joy Ogilvie——" The mother interrupted hotly—it seemed want of respect to her child:

"Then he ought to care. I'd like to know who he is to consider himself so high and mighty that even my little girl isn't . . . Oh! I have no patience with him."

There was silence in the carriage. Mrs. Ogilvie had come to the end of her remonstrance, and both the others were afraid to speak. It was all so supremely ridiculous. And yet the mother was taking it all so seriously that respect for her forbade laughter. The road was here steep and the horses were laboriously climbing their way. Presently Judy turned to Joy saying:

"Wouldn't you like to look at the view from the edge of the cliff?" As she spoke she looked meaningly at her niece who took the hint and got down.

When she was out of earshot and the driver had stopped the horses Judy turned to her sister and said with a quiet, incisive directness quite at variance with all her previous moods:

"Sally dear I want to speak a moment to you quite frankly and, believe me, very earnestly. I know you don't usually credit me with much earnestness; but this is about Joy, and that is always earnest with me." All the motherhood in Mrs. Ogilvie answered to the call. She sat up with eager intensity, receptive to the full and without any disturbing chagrin. Judy went on:

"You have been thinking of your 'little girl'—and actually speaking of her as such. That is the worst of mothers—their one fault. With them time seems to stand still. The world goes flying by them, but in their eyes the child remains the same. Gold hair or black turns to white, wrinkles come, knees totter and steps become unsteady; but the child goes on—still, in the mother's eyes, dressing dolls and chasing butterflies. They don't even seem to realise facts when the child puts her own baby into the grandmother's arms. Look round for a moment where Joy is standing there outlined against that Moorish tower on the edge of the cliff. Tell me what do you see?"

"I see my dear, beautiful little girl!" said the mother faintly.

"Hm!" said Judy defiantly. "That's not exactly what I see. I agree with the 'dear' and 'beautiful'; she's all that and a thousand times more."

"Tell me what you do see, Judy!" said the mother in a whisper as she laid a gentle hand imploringly on her sister's arm. She was trembling slightly. Judy took her hand and stroked it tenderly. "I know!" she said gently "I know. I know!" The mother took heart from her tenderness and said in an imploring whisper:

"Be gentle with me, Judy. She is all I have; and I fear her passing away from me."

"Not that—not yet at all events!" she answered quickly. "The time is coming no doubt. But it is because we should be ready for it that I want to speak. We at least ought to know the exact truth!"

"The exact truth . . . Oh Judy . . . !"

"Don't be frightened, dear. There is nothing to fear. The truth is all love and goodness. But my dear we are all but mortal after all, and the way to keep right is to think truly."

"Tell me exactly what you see! Tell me everything no matter how small. I shall perhaps understand better that way!"

Judy paused a while, looking at the young girl lovingly. Then she spoke in a level absent voice as though unconsciously.

"I don't see a child—now. I see a young woman of twenty; and a fine well-grown young woman at that. Look at her figure, straight and clean as a young pine. Type of figure that is the most alluring of all to men; what the French call *fausse maigre*. She has great gray eyes as deep as the sky or the sea; eyes that can drag the soul out of a man's body and throw it down beneath her dainty feet. I may be an old maid; but I know that much anyhow. Her hair is black—that isn't black, but with a softness that black cannot give. Her skin is like ivory seen in the sunset. Her mouth is like a crimson rosebud. Her teeth are like pearls, and her ears like pink shell. Her head is poised on her graceful neck like a lily on its stem. Her nose is a fine aquiline—that means power and determination. Her forehead can wrinkle—that means thought, and may mean misery. Her hands are long and fine; patrician hands that can endure—and suffer. Sally, there is there the making of a splendid woman and of a noble life; she is not out of her girlhood yet, but she is very near it. Ignorance is no use to her. She *will* understand; and then she will take her own course. She has feeling deep and strong in the very marrow of her bones. Ah! my dear, and she has passion too. Passion that can make or mar. That woman will do anything for love. She can believe and trust. And when she believes and trusts she will hold the man as her master; put him up on a pedestal and be content to sit at his feet and worship—and obey . . . She . . ."

Here the mother struck in with surprised consternation "How on earth do you know all this?" Judy turned towards her with a light in her eyes which her sister had never seen there:

"How do I know it! Because she is of my blood and yours. Have I not seen a lot of it in you in our babyhood. Have I not gone through it all myself—the longing part of it—the wishing and hoping and praying and suffering. Do you think Sally that I have arrived at old maidhood without knowing what a young maid thinks and feels; without having any share of the torture that women must bear in some form or another. I know it all as well as though it was all fresh before me instead of a lurid memory. Ah, my dear she has all our nature—and her father's too. And he never learned the restraint that we had to learn—and practice. When she is face to face with passion she may find herself constrained to take it as he has always done: for life or death!" . . . She paused a moment, panting with the intensity of her feeling. Then she went on more quietly:

"Sally, isn't it wiser to let her, in her youth and ignorance of herself and the world, break herself in to passion and romance. It would be hard to get a safer object for sentimental affection than a man she never saw and is never likely to meet. After all, he is only an idea; at best a dream. In good time he will pass out of her mind and give place to something more real. But in the meantime she will have learned—learned to understand, to find herself." Then she sat silent till Joy turned round and began to walk towards them. At this the mother said quietly:

"Thank you, dear Judy. I think I understand. You are quite right, and I am glad you told me."

That journey round the Sorrentine Peninsula became a part of Joy's life. It was not merely that every moment was a new pleasure, a fresh delight to the eye; her heart was in some mysterious way beginning to be afire. Hitherto her thoughts of that abstract creation, Lord Athlyne, had been impersonal: an objective of her own unconscious desires, rather than a definite individuality. Up to now, though he had been often in her thoughts, he had never taken shape there. The image was so inchoate, indefinite, vague and nebulous. She had never tried or even wished to find for him in her imagination features or form. But now she had begun to picture him in various ways. As she stood beside the Moorish tower looking down across the rugged slope of rock and oleander at the wrinkled sea beneath, his image seemed to flit before the eyes of her soul in kaleidoscopic form. It was an instance of true feminine receptivity, the form did not matter, she was content to accept the Man.

The cause—the sudden cause of this change was her mother's attitude. She had accepted him as a reality and had not hesitated to condemn him as though he was a conscious participant in what had passed. Joy had found herself placed in a position in which she had to hear him unfairly treated, without being able to make any kind of protest. It was too ridiculous to argue. What on earth could her mother know about him that she should take it for granted that he had done wrong? He who had never seen her or even heard of her! He who was the very last man in the world to be wanting to a woman in the way of respect—of tenderness—of love. . . . Here she started and looked around cautiously as one does who is suspicious of being watched. For it flashed across her all at once that she knew no more of him than did her mother. As yet he was only an abstraction; and her mother's conception of him differed from hers. And as she thought, and thought truly for she was a clever girl, she began to realise that she had all along been clothing an abstract individuality with her own wishes and dreams—and hopes. . . . The last thought brought her up sharply. With a quick shake of the head she threw aside for the present all thoughts on the subject, and impulsively went back to the carriage.

There were however a few root thoughts left which *would* not be thrown aside. They could not be, for they were fixed in her womanhood. Another woman had accepted her dream as a reality; and now, as that reality was her doing, he was her own man. And he was misunderstood and blamed and unfairly treated! It was her duty to protect him!

Had Aunt Judy been aware of her logical process and its conclusion she could have expressed it thus:

"Hm! a man in her mind.—*Her* man. Her duty to protest. . . . We all know what that means. He's only in her mind at present . . . Hm!"

The whole day was spent on the road, for the beauty was such that the stoppages were endless. Joy, with the new-arisen soul which took her out of her own thoughts, found delight in every moment. She could hardly contain her rapture as fresh vistas of beauty burst upon her. When the curve of the promontory began to cut off the view of Vesuvius and the plain seaward of it, she got out of the carriage and ran back to where she could have a full view. Underneath her lay the wonderful scene of matchless beauty. To the right rose Vesuvius a mass of warm colour, with its cinder cone staring boldly into the blue sky, a faint cloud hanging over it like a flag. Below it was the sloping plain dotted with trees and villas and villages, articulated in the clear air like a miniature map. Then the great curve of the bay, the sapphire sea marked clearly on the outline of the coast from Ischia which rose like a jewel from a jewel.

Past Naples, a clustering mass with San Martino standing nobly out and the great fortress crowning grimly the hill above it. Past Portici and the buried Herculaneum; till getting closer the roofs and trees and gardens seemed to run up to where she stood. To the left, a silhouette of splendid soft purple, rose the island of Capri from the sea of sapphire which seemed to quiver in the sunshine. Long she looked, and then closing her eyes to prove that the lovely image still held in the darkness, she turned with a long sigh of ecstasy and walked slowly to the waiting carriage.

Again and again she stooped, till at last she made up her mind to walk altogether until she should get tired. The driver took his cue from her movements when to stop and when to go on.

The road round the Peninsula runs high up the mountain side with mostly a steep precipice to seaward and on the other hand towering rocks. But such rocks! And so clad with the finest vegetation! Rocks rich in colour and quaint in shape; with jagged points and deep crevices in which earth could gather and where trees and shrubs and flowers could cling. High over-head hung here and there a beautiful stone-pine with red twisted trunk and spreading branches. Fig and lemon trees rose in the sheltered angles, the long yellow shoots of the new branches of the lemon cutting into the air like lances. Elsewhere beech and chestnut, oak and palm. Trailing over the rock, both seaward and landward, creepers of soft green and pink. And above all, high up on the skyline, the semi-transparent, smoke-coloured foliage of the olives that crowned the slopes.

Then the towns! Maggiore and Amalfi quaint close-drawn irregular relics of a more turbulent age, climbing up the chasms in the hillside. Narrow streets, so steep as to look impossible to traffic. Queer houses of all sorts of irregular design and variety of stone. Small windows, high doors, steep, rugged irregularly-sloping steps as though time and some mighty force had shaken the very rock on which they were built. Joy felt as though she could stay there for ever, and that each day would be a dream, and each fresh exploration a time of delight. In her secret heart of hearts she registered a vow that if ever she should go on a wedding journey it should be to there.

At Amalfi they had tea, and then made up their minds that they would drive on to Salerno and there take train home; for it would be time to travel quick when so long a journey had been taken.

When they were at the end of the peninsula a sudden storm came on. For awhile they had seen far out at sea a dark cloud gathering, but it was so far away that they did not think it would affect them. The driver knew and began to make ready, for there was no escaping from it. He turned his horses' heads to the rock and wedged up the wheels of the carriage with heavy stones so that in case the horses should get frightened their plunging could not be too harmful.

Heavier and heavier grew the cloud out at sea, and as it grew denser it moved landward. Its grey changed to dark blue and then to a rich purple, almost black. A keen coldness presaged a coming storm.

There was stillness all round the mountain road; a positive desolation of silence from which even the wondrous beauty of the scene could not distract the mind. Joy absolutely refused to sit in the carriage which was now properly hooded. She threw on the cloak which she had brought with her and stood out on the open road where she could enjoy the scene undisturbed by human proximity. As she stood, the velvet black cloud was rent by a blinding sheet of lightning which seemed for a moment to be shaped like a fiery tree, roots upward in the sky. Close following came such a mighty peal of thunder that her heart shook. Ordinarily Joy was not timorous, and for thunder she had no fear. But this was simply terrific; it seemed to burst right over her head and to roll around her in a prolonged titanic roar. She was about to run to the carriage when she heard the shrieks of fear from the two women; the driver was on his knees on the road praying. Joy felt that all she could do to help her mother and aunt would be to keep calm—as calm as she could. So she moved her hand and called out cheerfully:

"Don't be afraid! It is all right; the lightning has passed us!" As she spoke the rain came down in torrents. It was tropical; in a few seconds the open road was running like a river, ankle deep. By the exercise of her will the girl's courage had risen. She could now actually enjoy what was before her. Far out to sea the black cloud still hung, but it was broken up in great masses which seemed to dip into the sea. It was almost as dark as night; so dark that the expanse became lit by the lightning flashes. In one of these she saw three separate water-spouts. The sea appeared to have risen as the cloud sank, and now were far apart three great whirling pillars like hour-glasses. And then, wonder of wonders, without turning her head but only her eyes she could see away to the left a whole world of green expanse backed up by the mountains of Calabria. With each second the sinking sun brought into view some new hilltop flaming in the glow. A little way in front of her at the southern side of the peninsula the copper dome of the church at Vietri glowed like a ball of fire. Away to the south on the edge of the sea rose the many columns of the majestic ruins of Psestum, standing still and solemn as if untouchable by stress of storm or time.

Joy stood entranced, as though the eyes of her soul had opened on a new world. She hardly dared to breathe. The pelting of the rainstorm, the rush of the water round her feet, the crash and roar of the thunder or the hissing glare of the lightning did not move or disturb her. It was all a sort of baptism into a new life.

Joy Ogilvie, like all persons of emotional nature, had quick sympathy with natural forces and the moods of nature. The experience of the day, based on the superlative beauty around her, had waked all the emotional nature within her. Naples is always at spring time; and the young heart finding naturally its place amongst the things that germinate and develop unconsciously, swayed with and was swayed by the impulses of her sex. Beauty and manhood had twin position in her virgin breast.

Aunt Judy's insight or prophesy was being realised quicker than she thought. Joy's sex had found her out!

CHAPTER III

DE HOOGE'S SPRUIT

In Italy Joy Ogilvie learned to the full, consciously and unconsciously, all the lessons which a younger civilisation can learn from an elder. To the sympathetic there are lessons in everything; every spot that a stranger foot has pressed has something to teach. Especially to one coming from the rush of strenuous life, which is the note of America, the old-world calm and luxury of repose have lessons in toleration which can hardly be otherwise acquired. In the great battle of life we do not match ourselves against individuals but against nations and epochs; and when it is finally borne in on us that others, fashioned as we ourselves and with the same strength and ambitions and limitations, have lived and died and left no individual mark through the gathering centuries, we can, without sacrifice of personal pride, be content to humbly take each his place.

The month spent at and round Naples had been a never-ending dream of delight; and this period of quiescence told on her naturally sensuous nature. Already she had accepted the idea of a man worthy of love; and the time went to the strengthening of the image. There was a subtle satisfactoriness in the received idea; the wealth of her nature had found a market—of a kind. That is to say: she was satisfied to export, and that was the end of her thoughts—for the present. Importation might come later,

"The mind's Rialto hath its merchandise."

None of the family ever alluded to Lord Athlyne in the presence of her father. Each in her own way knew that he would not like the idea; and so the secret—it had by this very reticence grown to be a secret by now—was kept.

On the voyage back to New York Joy's interest in Lord Athlyne became revived by the surroundings. They had not been able to secure cabins in the *Cryptic*; and so had come by the Hamburg-American Line from Southampton. By this time Aunt Judy's interest in the matter had begun to wane. To her it had been chiefly a jest, with just that spice of earnest which came from the effect which she supposed the episode would have on Joy's life. As Joy did not ever allude to the matter she had almost ceased to remember it.

It was Joy's duty—she thought of it as her privilege—to make her father's morning cocktail which he always took before breakfast. One morning it was brought by Judy. Colonel Ogilvie thanking her asked why he had the privilege of her ministration. Unthinkingly she answered: "Oh it's all right. The Countess made it herself, but she asked me to take it to you as she is feeling the rolling of the ship and wants to keep in bed."

"The who?" asked the Colonel his brows wrinkled in wonder. "What Countess? I did not know we had one on board."

"Lady Athlyne of course. Oh!" she had suddenly recollected herself. As she saw she was in for an explanation she faced the situation boldly and went on:

"That is the name you know, that we call Joy."

"The name you call Joy—the Countess! Lady Athlyne! What on earth do you mean, Judy? I don't understand." In a laughing, offhand way, full of false merriment she tried to explain, her brother-in-law listening the while with increasing gravity. When she had done he said quietly:

"Is this one of your jokes, Judy; or did this Countess make two cocktails?" He stopped and then added: "Forgive me I should not have said that. But is it a joke, dear?"

"Not a bit!" she answered spiritedly. "That is, this particular occasion is not a joke. It is the whole thing that is that."

"A joke to take ... Is there a real man of the name of the Earl of Athlyne?"

"I believe so," she said this faintly; she had an idea of what was coming.

"Then Judith I should like some rational explanation of how you come to couple my daughter's name in such a way with that of a strange man. It is not seemly to say the least of it. Does my daughter allow this to be done?"

"Oh Colonel, it is only a joke amongst ourselves. I hope you won't make too much of it."

"Too much of it! I couldn't make enough of it! If the damned fellow was here I'd shoot him!"

"But, my God, the man doesn't know anything about it; no more than you did a minute ago." Miss Judith was really alarmed; she knew the Colonel. He waved his hand as though dismissing her from the argument:

"Don't worry yourself, my dear: this is a matter amongst men. We know how to deal with such things!" He said no more on the subject, but talked during breakfast as usual. When he rose to go on deck Judy followed him timidly. When they were away from the few already on deck she touched him on the arm.

"Give me just a minute?" she entreated.

"A score if you like, my dear!" he answered heartily as he led her to a seat in a sheltered corner behind the saloon skylight, and sat beside her. "What is it?"

"Lucius you have always been very good to me. All these years that I have lived in your house as your very sister you never had a word for me that wasn't kind . . ." He interrupted her, laying his hand on hers which was on the arm of her deck chair:

"Why else, my dear Judy! You and I have always been the best of friends. And my dear you have never brought anything but sunshine and sweetness into the house. Your merriment has kept care away from us whenever he tried to show his nose . . . Why my dear what is it? There! You mustn't cry!" As he spoke he had taken out a folded silk pocket-handkerchief and was very tenderly wiping her eyes. Judy went on sobbing a little at moments:

"I have always tried to make happiness, and I have never troubled you with asking favours, have I?"

"No need to ask, Judy. All I have is yours just as it is Sally's or Joy's." Suddenly she smiled, her eyes still gleaming with recent tears:

"I am asking a favour now—by way of a change. Lucius on my *honour*—and I know no greater oath with you than that—this has been a perfectly harmless piece of fun. It arose from a remark of that nice Irish stewardess on the *Cryptic* that no one was good enough to marry Joy except one man: the young nobleman whom she had nursed. And she really came to believe that it would come off. She says she has some sort of foreknowledge of things." The Colonel smiled:

"Granted all this, my dear; what is it you want me to do?"

"To do nothing!" she answered quickly. Then she went with some hesitation:

"Lucius you are so determined when you take up an idea, and I know you are not pleased with this little joke. You are mixing it up with honour—the honour that you fight about; and if you go on, it may cause pain to us all. We are only a pack of women, after all, and you mustn't be hard on us."

"Judy, my dear, I am never hard on a woman, am I?"

"No! Indeed you're not," she avowed heartily. "You're the very incarnation of sweetness, and gentleness, and tenderness, and chivalry with them . . . But then you take it out of the men that cross you!"

"That's as a gentleman should be I take it" he said, reflectively, unconsciously stroking his white moustache. Then he said briskly:

"Now Judy seriously tell me what you wish me to do or not to do. I must have *some* kind of clue to your wishes, you know." As she was silent for the moment he went on gravely. "I think I understand, my dear. Be quite content, I take it all for a joke and a joke between us it shall remain. But I must speak to Joy about it. There are some things which if used as subjects for jokes lead to misunderstandings. Be quite easy in your mind. You know I love my daughter too well to give her a moment's pain that I can spare her. Thank you Judy for speaking to me. I might have misunderstood and gone perhaps too far. But you know how sensitive—'touchy' Joy calls it—about my name and my family I am; and I hope you will always bear that in mind. And besides my dear, there is the other gentleman to be considered. He too, may have a word to say. As he is a nobleman he ought to be additionally scrupulous about any misuse of his name; and of course I should have to resent any implication made by him against any member of my family!"

"Good Lord!" said Judy to herself, as he stood up and left her with his usual courtly bow. "What a family to deal with. This poor little joke is as apt to end in bloodshed as not. The Colonel is on the war-path already; I can see that by his stateliness!"

Colonel Ogilvie thought over the matter for a whole day before he spoke to Joy; he was always very grave and serious regarding subjects involving honour and duty.

Joy knew that he had something on his mind from his abstraction, and rather kept out of his way. This was not on her own account for she had no idea that she was involved in the matter, but simply because it was her habit to sympathise with him and to think of and for him. She was just a little surprised when the next afternoon he said to her as they stood together at the back of the wheel-house over the screw, the quietest place on the ship for a talk:

"Joy dear, I want you to listen to me a minute."

"Yes, Daddy!"

"About that joke you had on the *Cryptic.*"

"Yes, Daddy." She was blushing furiously; she understood now.

"My dear, I don't object to your having any little harmless romance of that kind. I don't suppose it would make any difference if I did. A young girl will have her dreaming quite independent of her old daddy. Isn't it so, little girl?"

"I suppose so, dear Daddy, since you say it." She nestled up close to him comfortably as she spoke: this was nicer talk than she expected.

"But there is one thing that you must be careful about: There must be no names!"

"How do you mean, Daddy?"

"I gather that there has been a joke amongst some of you as to calling you the Countess or Lady Athlyne, or some of that kind of foolishness. My dear child, that is not right. You are not the Countess, nor Lady Athlyne, nor Lady anything. A name my dear when it is an honourable one is a very precious possession. A woman must cherish the name she does possess as a part of her honour."

"I am proud of my name, Father, very, very proud of it; and I always shall be!" She had drawn herself upright and had something of her father's splendid personal pride. The very use of the word 'Father' instead of 'Daddy' showed that she was conscious of formality.

"Quite right, little girl. That is your name now; and will in a way always be. But you may marry you know; and then your husband's name will be your name, and you will on your side be the guardian of his honour. We must never trifle with a name, dear. Those people who go under an alias are to my mind the worst of criminals."

"Isn't that rather strong, Daddy, when murder and burglary and theft and wife-beating and cheating at cards are about!" She felt that she was through the narrow place now and could go back to her raillery. But her father was quite grave. He walked up and down a few paces as though arranging his thoughts and words. When he spoke he did so carefully and deliberately:

"Not so, little girl. These, however bad they may be, are individual offences and are punished by law. But a false name—even in jest, my dear—is an offence against society generally, and hurts and offends every one. And in addition it is every one of the sins you have named; and all the others in the calendar as well."

"How on earth do you make out that, Daddy?"

"Take them in order as you mentioned them. Murder, burglary, theft, wife-beating, cheating at cards! What is murder? Killing without justification! Does not one who approaches another in false guise kill something? The murderer takes the life; the other kills what is often more than life: self respect, belief in human nature, faith. One only kills the body; but the other kills the soul. Burglary and theft are the same offence differently expressed; theft is the meaner crime that is all. Well, disguise is the thief's method. Sometimes he relies on absence of others, sometimes on darkness, sometimes on a mask, sometimes on the appearance or identity of some one else. But he never deals with the normal condition of things; pretence of some kind must always be his aid. The man, therefore, who relies on pretence, when he knows that the truth would be his undoing, is a thief."

"Daddy you argue as well as a Philadelphia lawyer!"

"I don't believe much in lawyers!" said the old man dryly. "As to wife-beating!"

"I'm afraid you've struck a snag there, Daddy! There isn't much pretence about that crime, anyhow!"

"Not at all, my dear. That comes within the category of murder. The man who descends to that abominable crime would kill the woman if he dared. He is a coward as well as a murderer, and should be killed like a mad dog!"

"Bravo! Daddy. I wish there was a man like you to deal with them in every county. But how about cheating at cards. *That's* a poser, I think!"

"No trouble about that, Joy. It *is* cheating at cards."

"How do you argue that out, Daddy?"

"Any game of cards is a game of honour. So many cards, so much skill in playing them according to the recognised rules of the game; and, over all, a general belief in the honour of all the players. I have seen a man shot across a handkerchief—in honourable duel, my dear—for hesitating markedly at poker when he stood pat on a 'full house.' That was pretence, and against the laws of honour; and he paid for it with his life."

Joy wrinkled her brows; "I see it's quite wrong, father, but I don't quite see how it fits into the argument," she said.

"That is simple enough, daughter. As I say, it is a pretence. Don't you see that after all a game of cards is a simple thing compared with the social life of which it is only an occasional episode. If a man,—or a woman either, Joy—misleads another it must be with some intention to deceive. And in that deception, and by means of it, there is some gain—something he or she desires and couldn't otherwise get. Isn't that plain enough!"

"All right, Father; I quite see. I understand now what you mean. I did not ever look at things in quite that way. Thank you very much, dear, for warning me so kindly too. I'll stop the joke, and not allow it to go on—so far as I can stop it."

"How do you mean? Does anyone else know it?"

"I may have written to one or two girls at home, Daddy. You know girls are always fond of such foolishness."

"Had you not better write to them and tell them not to mention it."

"Good Gracious! Why you dear, old goose of a Daddy it is evident you don't know girls. That would be the very way to make things buzz. Oh no! we'll simply drop it; and they'll soon forget it. I may have to tell them something else, though, to draw them away from it."

"Hm!" said her father. She looked at him with a sly archness:

"I suppose, Daddy, it wouldn't do to have it that an Italian Grand Duke proposed for me—to you of course!"

"Certainly not, Miss Impudence! I'm not to be drawn into any of your foolish girls' chatter. There, run away and let me smoke in peace!" She turned away, but came back.

"Am I forgiven, Daddy?"

"Forgiven! Lord bless the child, why there's nothing to forgive. I only caution. I know well that my little girl is clear grit, straight through; and I trust her as I do myself. Why Joy, darling" he put his arm affectionately round her shoulder "you are my little girl! The only one I have or ever shall have; and so, God willing, you shall be to me to the end."

"Thank you dear, dear Daddy. And I pray so too. I shall always be your little girl to you and shall come to you to cheer you or to be comforted myself. Mother has of late taken to treating me like a grown-up which she always keeps firing off at me so that I don't know whether I am myself or not. But whatever I am to anyone else, I never shall be anything to you but your 'little girl!'"

And that compact was sealed then and there with a kiss.

Nine months later whilst Colonel Ogilvie was in the library of his own house, "Air" in Airlville, Joy came in and closed the door carefully; she came close and whispered:

"Am I still your little girl, Daddy?"

"Always my dear! always!"

"Then you don't mind having a secret with me?"

"*Mind* my dear! I love it. What is it you want to tell me?" She took a folded newspaper from her pocket and handed it to him, saying:

"I came across this in the New York *Tribune*. Read it!" Colonel Ogilvie turned it over with a rueful look as he said:

"The whole of it!"

"Oh Daddy, don't be tiresome; of course not." Her father's face brightened:

"Then you read what you want me to know. Your eyes are better than mine!" Joy at once began to read:

"From our own Correspondent, Capetown. Some details of the lamentable occurrence at de Hooge's Spruit which was heliographed from the front yesterday have now come to hand. It appears that a battery of field artillery was ordered to proceed from Bloomgroot to Neswick escorted by a Squadron of mixed troops taken from the Scottish Horse and the Mounted Yeoman. When they had begun to cross the river, which here runs so rapidly that great care has to be observed lest the horses should be swept away, a terrific fusillade from an entrenched force of overwhelming numbers was opened on them. Colonel Seawright who commanded ordered a retreat until the disposition of the enemy could be ascertained. But before the manœuvre could be effected the British force was half wiped out. Accurate fire had been concentrated on the artillery horses, and as the guns were all on the river bank ready for the crossing it was impossible to rescue them. Gallant efforts were made by the gunners and the cavalry escort, but in the face of the hail of bullets the only result was a terrible addition to the list of killed and wounded. Seeing that the ground was partly clear, a number of Boers crept out of cover and tried to reach the guns. At this our troops made another gallant effort and the Boers disappeared. Still it was almost hopeless to try to save the guns. One only of the battery was saved and this by as gallant an effort on the part of one young officer as has been as yet recorded in the war. Captain Lord Athlyne." Here Joy looked up for an instant and saw a frown suddenly darken her father's brow—"who was tentatively in command of a yeomanry troop took a great coil of rope one end of which was held by some of his men. When he was ready he rode for the guns at a racing pace, loosing the rope as he went. It was a miracle that he came through the terrific fire aimed at him by the Boer sharp-shooters. Having gained the last gun, behind which there was a momentary shelter, he attached the end of the rope. Then mounting again he swept like a hurricane across the zone of fire. There was a wild cheer from the British, and a number of horsemen began to ride out whilst the firing ran along the front of the waiting line. But the instant the rope was attached the men began to pull and the gun actually raced along the open space. In the middle of his ride home the gallant Irishman's cap was knocked off by a bullet. He reined up his charger, dismounted and picked up the cap *and dusted it* with his handkerchief before again mounting. Despite their wounds and the chagrin of defeat the whole force cheered him as he swept into the lines.

"Daddy I call that something like a man! Don't you?" Her colour was high and her eyes were blazing. She looked happy when her father echoed her enthusiasm:

"I do! daughter. That was the action of a gallant gentleman!" There was a silence of perhaps half a minute. Then Colonel Ogilvie spoke:

"But why, my dear, did you tell this to *me?*"

"I had to tell some one, Daddy. It is too splendid to enjoy all one's self; and I was afraid if I told Mother she might not understand—she's only a woman you know, and might put a wrong construction on my telling her, and so worry herself about me. And I didn't dare to tell Aunt Judy, for she's so chock full of romance that she would have simply gone crazy and chaffed me out of all reason.

There is no holding back Aunt Judy when she is chasing after a romance! And besides, Daddy dear" here she took his arm and looked up in his face "I wanted you to know that Lord Athlyne is a gentleman." Her father frowned:

"Why should I know—or care?"

"Not on your own part Daddy—but—but only because I want you to. It is hard to explain, but I think you took a prejudice against him from the first; and you see it makes it less awkward to be coupled with a man's name, when the name and the man are good ones." The Colonel's frown was this time one of puzzlement.

"I'm afraid I don't understand. You never saw the man. Why should you dislike less to be coupled with him because he did a brave thing? Besides, the whole thing is mere nonsense."

"Of course it is, Daddy. All nonsense. But it is better to be good nonsense than bad nonsense!"

"Look here daughter—my little girl—I'm afraid you have got or may get too fond of thinking of that fellow. Take care!"

"Oh, that's all right, Daddy. He is only an abstraction to me. But somehow he interests me. Don't you be worrying about me. I promise you solemnly that I will tell you everything I hear about him. Then you can gauge my feelings, and keep tab of my folly."

"All right; little girl! There can't be anything very dangerous when you tell your father all about it."

It was three months before Joy mentioned the name of Lord Athlyne again to her father. One morning she came to him as he sat smoking in the garden at Air. Her eyes were glistening, and she walked slowly and dejectedly. In her hand she held a copy of the New York *Tribune*. She held it out, pointing with her finger to a passage.

"Read it for me, little girl!" In answer she said with a break in her voice:

"You read it, Daddy. Don't make me. It hurts me; and I should only break down. It is only a dream I know; but it is a sad dream and is over all too soon!" Colonel Ogilvie read the passage which was an account of the fighting at Durk River in which numbers of the British were carried away by the rapid stream, the hale and those wounded by the terrible fire of the Boers alike. The list of the missing was headed by a name he knew.

"Major the Earl of Athlyne, of the Irish Hussars."

The old gentleman rose up as stiff as at the salute and raised his hat reverently as he said:

"A very gallant gentleman. My heart is with you, my little girl! A dream it may have been; but a sad ending to any dream!"

A week after Joy sought her father again, in the garden. This time her step was buoyant, her face radiant, and her eyes bright. The moment her father saw he felt that it had something to do with what he called in his own mind "that infernal fellow." When she was close to him she said in a low voice that thrilled:

"He is not dead, Daddy. He was wounded and carried down the river and was captured by the Boers and taken up to Pretoria. They have put him in the Birdcage. Beasts! It's all here in the *Tribune.*"

Colonel Ogilvie was distinctly annoyed. When he could look on Lord Athlyne as dead he could admire his bravery, and even tolerate the existence that had been. But this chopping and changing—this being dead and coming to life again—was disturbing. What sort of fellow was he that couldn't make up his mind on any subject? Couldn't he remain dead like a gentleman? He had died like one; wasn't that enough! Joy saw that he was not pleased. She was too glad for the moment to take her father's attitude to heart; but every instinct in her told her not to remain. So she laid the paper on his knee and said quietly:

"I'll leave it with you, Daddy. You can read it yourself; it's worth reading. You are glad, I know, because your little girl is glad that there is one more brave man in the world."

Just as she was going her father called her back. When she was close he said in a kindly manner but with great gravity:

"No more mentioning names now, little girl!" She put her finger to her lip as registering a vow of secrecy. Then she blew a kiss at him and tripped away.

CHAPTER IV

THE BIRD-CAGE

The "Bird-cage" at Pretoria was the enclosure wherein the captured British officers were imprisoned during the second quarter of the year 1900. Here at the beginning of May two men were talking quietly as they lay on the bare ground in the centre of the compound. The Bird-cage was no home of luxury; but the men who had perforce to live in it tried to make the best of things, and grumbling was tacitly discountenanced. These two had become particular chums. For more than a month they had talked over everything which seemed of interest. At first of course it was the war and all connected with it which interested them most. They were full of hope; for though six months of constant reverses were behind them they could not doubt that Time and General Roberts would prevail. These two items of expected success were in addition to the British Army generally and the British soldier's belief in it. When every battle or engagement which either of them had been in had been fought over again, and when their knowledge of other engagements and skirmishes had come to an end they fell back on sport. This subject held out for some time. The memories of both were copious of pleasant days and interesting episodes; and hopes ran high of repetitions and variations when the war should be over and the Boers reduced to that acquiescence in British methods and that loyalty to the British flag which British pride now demanded. Then "woman" had its turn, and every flirtation with the bounds of memory was recalled, without names or identification marks.

Then, when they knew each other better, they talked of the future in this respect. Young men, whatever exceptions these may be, are very sentimental. They are at once imaginative and reticent. Unlike girls their bashfulness is internal. The opening of their hearts, even in a measure, to each other in this respect was the crowning of their confidence. At this time they were occasionally getting letters. These had of course gone through the hands of the censor and their virginity thus destroyed; but the craving of all the prisoners for news of any kind, from home or elsewhere, was such that every letter received became in a measure common property. Even from intimate letters from their own womenkind parts were read out that had any colourable bearing on public matters. A few days before one of the men had a letter from his wife who was in Capetown; a letter which though it was nothing but a letter of affection from a loving wife, was before the day was over read by every man in the place. It had puzzled the husband at first, for though it was in his wife's writing the manner of it was not hers. It was much more carefully written than was her wont. Then it dawned on him that it had a meaning. He thought over it, till in a flash he saw it all. It was written by her, but she had copied it for some one else and signed it. The passage of the letter that now most interested him read:

"I do so long to see you, my darling, that if I do not see you before, I am going to ask to be allowed to come up to Pretoria and see you there if I may, if it is only a glimpse through that horrid barbed wire netting that we hear of. You remember my birthday is on Waterloo day; and I am promising myself, as my birthday treat, a glimpse of the face of my dear husband."

It did not do to assemble together, for the eyes of the jailors were sharp and an organized meeting of the prisoners was suspicious and meant the tightening of bonds. So one by one he talked with his fellows, telling them what he thought and always imploring them to maintain the appearance of listless indifference which they had amongst themselves decided was the attitude best calculated to avert suspicion. Some did not at first understand the cryptic meaning; but the general belief was that it was a warning that the capture of Pretoria was expected not later than the fifteenth of June. This created enormous hopes. Thenceforth all the talk in private was as to what each would do when the relief came.

To-day the conversation was mainly about Athlyne's affairs. He had been unfolding plans to his friend Captain Vachell of the Yeomanry and the latter asked him suddenly:

"By the way, Athlyne, are you married."

"What!—Me married! Lord bless you man, no! Why do you ask?"

"I gathered so from what you have been saying just now. Don't be offended at my asking; but I have a special purpose."

"I'm not a bit offended; why should I be? Why do you ask me?"

"That's what I want to tell you. But old chap this is a delicate subject and I want to clear the ground first. It is wiser." Athlyne sat up:

"Look here, Vachell, this is getting interesting. Clear away!" The other hesitated and then said suddenly:

"You never went through a ceremony of marriage, or what professed to be one, with anyone I suppose? I really do ask pardon for this."

"Honestly, Vachell, I'm not that sort of man. I have lots of sins on me; more than my fair share perhaps. But whatever I have done has been above board." The other went on with dogged persistence:

"You will understand when I explain why I ask; but this is your matter, not mine, and I want to avoid making matters still more complicated. That is of course if there should be any complication that you may have overlooked or forgotten."

"Good God! man, a marriage is not a thing a man could overlook or forget."

"Oh that's all right with a real marriage; or even with a mock marriage if a man didn't make a practice of it. But there might be some woman, with whom one had some kind of intrigue or irregular union, who might take advantage of it to place herself in better position. Such things have been you know, old chap!" he added sententiously. Athlyne laughed.

"Far be it from me to say what a woman might or might not do if she took it into her pretty head; but I don't think there's any woman who would, or who would ever think she had the right to, do that with me. There are women, lots of them I am afraid, who answer the bill on the irregular union or intrigue side; but I should certainly be astonished if any of them ever set out to claim a right. Now I have made a clean breast of it. Won't you tell me what all this is about?" The other looked at him steadily, as though to see how he took it, as he answered:

"There is, I am told, a woman in New York who is passing herself off as your wife!"

Athlyne sprang to his feet and cried out:

"What!"

"That's what I took it to mean! By the way—" this was said as if it was a sudden idea "I take it that your mother is not alive. I had it in my mind that she died shortly after you were born?"

"Unhappily that is so!"

"There is no dowager Countess?"

"Not for more than thirty years. Why?"

"The letter says 'Countess of Athlyne.' I took it to be your wife."

"Let me see the letter." He held out his hand. Vachell took from his pocket—the only private storage a man had in the Bird-cage—an envelope which he handed to his comrade, who took from it a torn fragment of a letter. He read it then turned it over. As he did so his eyes lit up; he had seen his own name. He read it over several times, then he looked up:

"Have you read it?"

"Yes. I was told to do so."

"All right! Then we can discuss it together. He read it out loud:

"So Athlyne is married. At least I take it so, for there is a woman in New York, I am told, who calls herself the Countess of Athlyne. I know nothing of her only this: a casual remark made in a gossipy letter."

"Now tell me, Vachell, can you throw any light on this?"

"Not on the subject but only on the way it has come to you. I had better tell you all I know from the beginning." Athlyne nodded, he went on:

"Whilst we were in the trenches at Volks Spruit waiting for the attack to sound, Meldon and I were together—you remember Meldon of the Connaught Fusiliers?"

"Well! We often hunted together."

"He asked me that if anything should happen to him I would look over his things and send them home, and so forth. I promised, but I asked him why he so cast down about the fight that was coming; was it a presentiment or anything of that kind. 'Not a bit,' he said, 'it's not spiritualism but logic! You see it's about my turn next. All our lot have been wiped out, going up the line in sequence. Rawson, my junior, was last; and now I come on. And there is a message I want you to carry on in case I'm done for. You will find among my papers an envelope directed to Lord Athlyne. It has only a scrap of paper in it so I had better explain. The last time I saw Ebbfleet of the Guards—in Hospital just before he died—he asked me to take the message. 'You know Athlyne' he said 'I got a letter saying a woman in New York was calling herself his wife, and as I know he is not married I think it only right that he should know of this. It will put him on his guard.' Well you know poor Meldon went under at Sandaal; and so I took over the message. When you and I met up here I thought we were in for a long spell and as we couldn't do anything I came to the conclusion that there was no use giving you one more unpleasant thing to think of and grind your teeth over. But now that we know Bobs and Kitchener are coming up before long I want to hand over to you. It is evident that they expect us to be ready to help the force from within when they come, or else they wouldn't run the chance of telling us. Four thousand men, even without arms, are not to be despised in a scrimmage. If the wily Boer tumbles to it they will take us up the mountains in several sections, and I may not have another chance."

"That is all you know of the matter I take it?"

"Absolutely! Of course should I hear anything more I shall at once let you know. Though frankly I don't see how that can be; both men who sent the message are dead. I haven't the faintest idea of who sent the original report. Of course, old chap, I am mum on the subject unless you ever tell me to speak."

"Thanks, old man. I fancy there won't be much time for looking after private affairs for a good spell to come after we have shifted our quarters. There will be a devil of a lot of clearing up when the house changes hands and continues to 'run under new management,' as Bung says."

All that had been spoken of came off as arranged by the various parties. On the fifth of June Roberts took Pretoria in his victorious march. Mafeking and Ladysmith had been relieved, and Johannesberg had fallen. Now, Kruger and the remainder of his forces were hurrying into the Lydenburg mountains to make what stand they could; and not the least keen of their foes were those who had been their guests in the Bird-cage. Athlyne rejoined his regiment and was under Buller's command till the routed army escaped into Portuguese territory. Then he was sent by Kitchener along the ranges of block houses whose segregations slowly brought the war to an end.

When his turn came for going home three years had elapsed. London and his club claimed him for his spells of his short leave, for there was still much work to be done with his regiment. When he began to tire of the long round of work and distractions he commenced to think seriously of a visit to America.

His experience of the war had sobered him down. He was now thirty-two years of age, the time when most men, who have not arrived there already, think seriously of settling down to matrimony. In other respects he wanted to be free. He was tired of obeying orders; even of giving them. The war was over and Britain was at peace with the world. Had there been still fighting going on anywhere such thought would not have occurred to him; he would still have wanted to be in the thick of it. But the long months of waiting and inactivity, the endless routine, the impossibility of doing anything which would have an immediate effect; all these things had worn out much of his patience, and stirred the natural restlessness of his disposition. At home there seemed no prospect of following soldiering in the way he wished: some form in which excitement had a part. Indeed the whole scheme of War and Army seemed to be shaping themselves on lines unfamiliar to him. The idea of the old devil-may-care life which had first attracted him and of which he had had a taste did not any longer exist, or, if it existed it was not for him. Outside actual fighting the life of a soldier was not now to consist of a series of seasonable amusements. And even if it did the very routine of amusements not only did not satisfy him, but became irksome. What, after all, he thought, was to a grown man a life of games in succession. Polo and cricket, fishing, shooting, hunting in due course; racquets and tennis, yachting and racing were all very well individually. But they did not seem to lead anywhere.

In fact such pastimes now seemed inadequate to a man who had been actively taking a part in the biggest game of them all, war!

When once the idea had come to him it never left him. Each new disappointment, the unfulfilled expectation of interest, drove it further and further home. There was everywhere a lack of his old companions; always a crowd of new faces. The girls he had known and liked because they were likable, had got married within the few years of his absence. The matrons had made fresh companionships which held possession. Bridge had arisen as a new society fetish which drew to itself the interests and time of all. A new order of "South African Millionaires" had arisen who by their wealth and extravagance had set at defiance the old order of social caste, and largely changed the whole scheme of existing values.

When he fled away from London he found something of the same changes elsewhere. In the stir of war, and even in the long weariness of waiting which followed it, the whirling along of the great world was, if not forgotten, unthought of. The daily work and the daily interest were so personal and so absorbing that abstract thinking was not.

In the country, of course, the changes were less, but they were more marked. The few years had their full tally of loss; of death, and decay. The eyes that saw them were so far fresh eyes, that unchecked memory had not a perpetual ease of comparison.

For a while he tried hard to find a fresh interest in his work. But here again was change with which he could feel neither sympathy nor toleration. Great schemes of reform were on foot; schemes of organization, of recruiting, of training. The ranks in the Service, of which he had experience, were becoming more mechanical than ever. Had he by this time acquired higher rank in the army it is possible that he would have entered with ardour into the new conditions. He was fitted for such; young, and energetic, and daring. Those in the Cabinet or in the Army Council have material for exercising broader views of the machinery of war, and to the eyes of such many things which looked at in detail seem wrong or foolish stand out in their true national importance.

His dissatisfaction with the army changes was the last straw. He took it into his head that in future the army had no place for him. The idea multiplied day by day with an ever-increasing exasperation. At last his mind was definitely made up. He sent in his papers; and in due time retired.

It is generally the way with human beings that they expect some radical change in themselves and their surroundings to follow close on some voluntary act. They cannot understand, at once at all events, that the "eternal verities" are eternal. "I may die but the grass will grow" says Tennyson in one of his songs. And this is the whole story in epitome. After all, what is one life, howsoever perfect or noble it may be, in the great moving world of fact. The great Globe floats in a sea of logic which encompasses it about everywhere. What is ordained is ordained to an end, and no puny hopes or fears or wishes of an individual can sway or change its course. Conclusions follow premises, results follow causes. We rebel against facts and conditions because they are facts and conditions. Then for some new whim or purpose entirely our own we take a new step—forward or backward it matters not—and lo! we expect the whole world with its million years of slow working up to that particular moment to change too.

This belief that things *must* change in accordance with our desires has its base deep down in our nature. At the lowest depth it is founded on Vanity. We are so important to ourselves that we cannot but think that that importance is sustained through all creation.

For a little while Lord Athlyne tried to persuade himself that now, at last, he was enjoying freedom. No more parades or early hours; no more orderly rooms or mess dinners, or duties at functions; no more of the bald, stale conventionalities of an occupation which had lost its charm. He expected each day to be now joyous with the realization of ancient hopes.

But the expectations were not realized. The days seemed longer than ever, and he actually yearned for something to fill up his time. Naturally his thoughts turned, as in the case of sportsmen they ever do, on big game. The idea took him and he began to plan out in his mind where he would go. Africa for lions? No! no! He had had enough of Africa to last him for some time. India for tigers; the Rockies for bear?

Happy thought. Bear would just suit. He could put in two things: look up that woman in New York who claimed to be his wife and silence her. He wouldn't like such an idea to go abroad in case he should ever marry. Then he would go on to the Rockies or Colorado and have a turn at the grizzlies.

He went straightway into the reading room of the club he was in and began to study Bradshaw.

At last he had found a new interest in life. For a week he devoted himself to the work in hand, until his whole sporting outfit was prepared. Then he began to think of the other quest; and the more he thought of it the more it puzzled him.

CHAPTER V

AN ADVENTURE

WITH regard to his quest after his alleged wife the first conclusion Lord Athlyne came to was that he must go incognito—"under an alias" he expressed it to himself. Otherwise he would give warning of his presence, and that was the very thing which he wished to avoid. The woman must be an unscrupulous one or she would not have entered on such a scheme of fraud; and she would naturally be quick to protect herself by concealment or flight. An ordinary individual would have left such an investigation to his solicitors who would have procured the services of local detectives. But then Athlyne was not an ordinary individual. He liked to do things for himself in most matters which interested him; and in this case there was so distinctly a personal bearing that he would not have been satisfied to leave it to any one else.

When, however, he began to work out details of his alias he found that he had landed in a perfect hornet's nest of difficulties. The mere matter of clothing and luggage was, he found, almost enough to turn his hair prematurely grey. What was the use of taking a false name when his true one was engraved on the brass plates of his portmanteaux and bags so that every porter would know everything about him within five minutes of his arrival; the chambermaid and laundress would see the marking of his linen. He very soon found that he would have to set about this branch of his effort very systematically if he did not want to give himself away hopelessly even before he started. He had already come to the conclusion that he must not take a valet with him. It would be quite enough to support an alias amongst his equals, whose habits and breeding had at least a certain amount of reticence, without running the risk of the world of servants who were much more inquisitive than their employers and much more skilled in matters of suspicion and detection.

First he had to decide on the name, and to get familiar with it in all sorts of ways; speaking, writing, and hearing it spoken. The latter he could only effect by hearing his own voice; he was conscious that he must, for some time at all events, be open to the danger of a surprise. He shrank in a certain way from using a name not his own; so he salved his conscience by selecting two of the simplest of his many names. Thus he became for his own purposes Richard Hardy. He fixed his domicile as "Sands End," a small place in the middle of Wiltshire which he had inherited from his mother. It was too small to be included in his 'list of seats' in Debrett, and thus answered his purpose. Then he got quite fresh store of linen from a new shop and had it marked 'R.Hardy' or 'R.H.' He bought new trunks and kit of all kinds. He had them marked with the same letters, and sent to a lodging which he had taken for the purpose under his new name. He had cards printed and got plain notepaper as he had to avoid a crest. Then he found that all his sporting things, which had already been packed, had to be unpacked and overhauled lest the real name should remain anywhere. When all this was done, and it took weeks to complete, he began to feel an unmitigated fraud and a thorough scoundrel. To a man who takes honour to be a part of a gentleman's equipment any form of dissimulation must always be obnoxious.

One person alone he took into his confidence: his solicitor. It was necessary that he should have a bank account opened in New York. Also that in case of any unforeseen accident it would be at least advisable to be able to explain his actions. When the solicitor remonstrated he explained his purpose and made a special request that he should not be subjected to any opposition. "I go to protect myself" he said. The other shrugged his shoulders and remained silent. He arranged before he terminated the interview that his letters should be sent to him under cover to his new name at his bankers in New York. In due time an account for a large sum was opened there. Then, when all was as complete as he could think of, he took a cabin in one of the French boats as he thought that in a foreign ship he would run less risk of running up against some acquaintance than would be likely on a British or American vessel.

He had hardly got clear of land when he began to realize in what a false position he had placed himself. He felt that any acquaintanceship which he could make might possibly lead to some imbroglio. To those who took him in good faith and made friends he must either reveal his purpose or accept a false position from which he might never be able to extricate himself. As the former was impossible, without creating a suspicion which would destroy his purpose, he had to take chance for the latter. The result was that he had to be aloof and unresponsive to any of the proffered friendlinesses of the voyage; and seeing this the other passengers did not press friendliness on him or even repeat their overtures. He felt this acutely, for he had been always in the habit of making friends. Such is one of the delights of travel, as all know who have been about the world. Those who once "rub shoulders" in a casual way often make acquaintanceships which ripen into friendship and are life-long. Perhaps this is from the fact that in such cases each is taken from the first on his personal merits. There being no foreknowledge there cannot be any premeditation of purpose of gain of any kind. Like meets like, recognises natural kinship; and union is the result.

When after a somewhat tedious and uneventful voyage he landed in New York he was altogether in a disappointed and a discontented frame of mind. The acute cause of this was the filling up of the immigration paper which is so exhaustive as to details as to become inquisitorial. The answering of each question seemed to him like telling a lie—as indeed it was. As, however, he had nothing to declare and was without obvious objection he had no trouble. The only effect from the Customs examination that he noticed on himself was that when he drove out of the gates he felt somewhat as he had done when he passed from the prison pen at Pretoria into the cheering ranks of the victorious British army. He was lucky enough to escape from the ranks of the journalists who make copy out of any stranger of distinction who lands. His name was not sufficiently striking to even attract attention. He took quiet rooms high up in the "Manhattan," and for two days kept his own company.

The third day he went out. He walked through street after street; took trolley-cars now and again; went "up town" and "down town" on the road. Crossed the ferries to New Jersey and Long Island. Lunched at Martin's and dined at Delmonico's; and returned to his hotel without having made so far as he knew a step towards discovery. The only thing which he brought back was a slight knowledge of local geography. He had seen something of New York—from the streets; but except to ask his way from policemen or for food from foreign waiters he had not spoken to anybody.

The next few days he spent in walking about the streets. In summing up this afternoon he came to the conclusion that there was, for him, nothing so bad in Pretoria. All the time he felt with increasing force that he was a fraud, and constantly found himself evolving schemes as to how he could shed his incognito. The question of clubs alone made him unhappy. He had always been a clubbable man; in London he belonged to a number of the best. Whenever he had been in any city where there was a club its doors had always through the forethought of some friend been thrown open to him. Here was a city so full of those masculine refuges that it might be called the "City of Clubs." In every fashionable street was at least one, palatial places where men who were of the great circle met their friends. And yet he felt like the Peri outside the gates of Paradise. The feeling grew on him that he could not enter any one of them, even if he got the chance. How could he explain to men that he was not what he seemed—what he professed to be. Clubland is in some ways to men holy ground. Here they can afford to be natural—to be true. Except the club laws, written or unwritten, there is no conventional demand. As a man who had grown old knowing little of any other life put it; "In a club you can afford not to lie." (It is to be presumed, by the way, that the speaker did not take a part in the conversations regarding episodes of fishing or *bonnes fortunes!*)

He could not see any way in which he could even *begin* to make his inquiry; or he could get honestly within any house he had seen. He became sorry he had ever thought of making the inquiry himself—that he had ever come at all. Dimly at the back of his thoughts was an intention to go back to London, resume his proper name, and then perhaps return in an upright way—as a gentleman should. Still he was a masterful man and did not like giving up. . . He thought a ride would do him good; it would clear his mind and freshen him up. A horseman is never lonely so long as he has a horse.

He asked the hotel clerk where he would get one. The man gave him several addresses. Then he added:

"By the way do you want to buy or only to hire?"

"Either. I should buy if I could get something exceptionally good."

"Then take my advice. Go up to Seventh Avenue right at the top near the Park. There is an auction there this morning of fine horses. You will I daresay get what you want; but you will doubtless have to pay for it."

"I don't mind that!" he smiled as he spoke; he did not remember that he had smiled since he left London. The very prospect of a horse brightened him up.

Before going to the Auction he called at the bank and drew out a handsome sum. In horse buying ready money is often a matter of importance.

At the Horse Exchange there was a good show, some of the horses being of real excellence. Prices ran high for these, and competition was spirited. But he got what he wanted: a big "Blue Grass" thoroughbred well up to his weight. His warranty was complete. The Auctioneer at his request brought to him presently a livery man on whom he might, he said, depend; and with him he arranged for the proper keeping of the horse.

For a few days Athlyne was really happy. His horse was as good as it looked, and had evidently been trained by some one who understood him. His mouth was as fine as possible and he realized an inflexion of the voice. Lord Athlyne rode well, and he knew it; and the horse knew it too from the first moment when his hand touched the bridle. After the first ride up the Riverside Drive the two became understanding friends.

The effect of the exercise on Lord Athlyne was to do away with his intention of trying to discover the identity of the offending lady. He would start soon for the Rockies and get after the grizzlies. Or better still he would go home, shake off his alias, and return—a free man.

On the Sunday afternoon he went for a ride in the direction he liked best, up the Riverside Drive. He went quietly till he got near the University where there was a long stretch of proper riding ground. There he let the black horse go, and the noble beast went along at a splendid pace. It was still a little early, and though there were a good many pedestrians there were but few persons in carriages or "horsebacking" and so the "ride" was fairly free. Horse and man were a noble pair. The one jet black, full of fire and mettle, every movement charged with power and grace; the other tall and slim, hard as nails with his long spell of South African soldiering, sitting like a centaur. Man and horse together moved as one. All eyes were turned on them as they swept by, with admiring glances from both women and men, each in their respective ways. Two park policemen, a sergeant and a roundsman, both finely mounted, were jogging quietly along. As the black horse came dashing up the roundsman said:

"Shall I stop him, sergeant?" The other looked on admiringly and answered quietly:

"Guess not! 'Twould be a burnin' shame to stop them two. An there won't be any need neyther, *they* know what they're doin, Halloran. They ain't goin' to ride down nobody. Did ye iver see a finer seat. I'd bet that's an English cavalry man. Look at the spring of him. Be the Lord I'd like to be in his shoes this minute!"

Amongst the few riders Athlyne passed on his course were an old man and a young woman. The man tall with a big white moustache, a haughty bearing, and steely eyes under shaggy white brows. The girl tall and slim and graceful with black hair and big gray eyes. Both were fairly well mounted, but the girl's mare was restive and shying at anything. As the black horse came thundering along she had to use considerable skill and force to keep her from bolting. Athlyne had just time for a passing glance as he swept by; but in that instant the face and figure became photographed on his memory. The girl turned and looked after him; she was in the receptive period of her young womanhood when every man has a charm, and when such a noble figure as was now presented is a power. With a sigh she turned and said to her companion:

"That is the horse that we saw sold at the Horse Exchange. I was jealous of whoever bought it then. I'm not now; a man who can ride like that deserves him. Daddy, don't you think he is something like what a man ought to be? I do!"

"You're right, little girl! But you'd better not say things like that to any one else but me; they mightn't understand!" Joy made no answer but she smiled to herself. During the hour or two that followed she chatted happily with her father. They had occasional canters and gallops until the road got too crowded when they went along more sedately. Whenever her father suggested turning homeward she always pleaded for one more turn:

"Just one more, Daddy. It is so delightful here; and the river is so lovely." Of course she had her way. The old man found more true happiness in pleasing her than in any other way. In her heart, though she did not tell her father for she felt that even he mightn't understand, she had a wish that the man on the black horse would return the same way. She had a feeling that he would.

After his gallop Athlyne went quietly along the road past Grant's Tomb and followed the course of the Drive. Here the road descended, circling round the elevation on which the Tomb is erected. Below it is the valley of some old watercourse into the Hudson. This valley has been bridged by a viaduct over which the Drive continues its course up the side of the river for many miles. To-day however, it was necessary to make a detour, descend the steep on the hither side of the valley and rise up the other side. Some settlement had affected the base of the up-river end of the bridge and it had given way. The rock on which New York is based is of a very soft nature, and rots slowly away, so that now and again a whole front of a house will slide down a slope, the underlying rock having perished. Not long before, this had actually happened to a group of houses in Park Row. Now the bridge had fallen away; the road ended abruptly, and below lay a great shapeless mass of twisted metal and stone. The near end of the viaduct was barred off with wooden rails, and in the centre was a great board with a warning that the thoroughfare was closed.

Athlyne rode up as far as the Up-Town Club, sat for awhile amongst the trees on the river bank and thought of many things. Amongst these of the girl with the gray eyes who looked so admiringly at his horse—or himself. Perhaps he accepted the latter alternative, for as his thoughts ran he smiled and stroked his big moustache.

When he rode towards town again he kept a sharp look out, unconsciously slackening speed when any old man and young woman riding together came in sight. He had ascended the eastern side of the valley, over which lay the broken viaduct, and commenced to traverse the curved slope leading up to Grant's Tomb when he heard a sudden shouting on the road in front and saw a rush of people to both sides and up the steps to the Tomb. An instant after a mounted constable appeared urging his horse to a gallop as he cried out:

"Clear the road! Clear the road! It's a run-a-way!" Instinctively Athlyne drew to the roadside, a double purpose in his mind; to keep the way clear as directed, and to be able to render assistance if possible. The noise and cries drew closer and there was on the hard road a thunder of many hoof strokes. Then round the curve swept a brown mare dashing madly in a frenzied gallop—the neck stretched out and the eyes flaming. The woman who rode her, a tall girl with black hair and great gray eyes, sat easily, holding her reins so as to be able to use them when the time should come. She was in full possession of herself. She did not look frightened, though her face was very pale. Behind her but a little way off came two mounted policemen and the old man with the big white moustache. Other men variously mounted came hurrying in the background; beyond them a whole long series of horse vehicles and motor cars.

As he saw her Athlyne's heart leaped. This was the girl whose face had attracted him; his time had come quicker than he had dared to hope. He shook his reins and started his horse, spurring him with his heels as he did so. If he was to be of service he should be able to keep at least equal pace; and that would require a quick start, for the runaway was going at a great pace.

And then a great fear fell on him, not for himself but for the girl. He knew what perhaps she did not, that the viaduct was broken, and that her course lay down the steep roadway to the bottom of the little valley. He rode in earnest now; the sloping curved road was so short that if he was to stop the mare the effort should be made at once. He rode close by her, his powerful horse keeping pace almost without an effort, and said quietly to the girl:

"Try to hold her in if ever so little, there is a steep road which you must go down. The viaduct is broken and the road barred."

"I can't," she said "she has the bit and I am powerless."

He struck his heels sharply and the black horse bounded forward. The girl saw the movement and understood:

"Take care" she said quickly "One policeman tried that and was thrown over, he may be killed." As she spoke, the words died on her lips; they had rounded the curve and the danger ahead lay open to them. It was a choice of evils: a dash down the steep incline with a maddened mare, or a crash against the barrier cutting off the viaduct.

But the woman had no choice; the maddened mare took her own course. Down the curving slope she dashed and went straight for the barrier. This was made of heavy balks of timber below, but the rails above were light. These she broke through as she leaped; hurling a cloud of broken rails and splinters right and left. The girl had nerved herself to the effort when she had seen what was coming and held up as at a jump on the hunting field.

The moment that Athlyne had realized the situation he too was ready. Seeing that the mare was making for the right side of the barrier he went for the left, and they leaped together. The instant they had landed on the other side he was ready and rode alongside the mare. Ahead of them was the chasm—with death beneath. The girl saw it and her pale face grew ashy white. Athlyne, riding level and holding his reins in his left hand, hurriedly cried:

"Loose your stirrup and when I get my arm round you take hold of my collar with your left hand. Then try to jump to me as I pull you towards me."

The girl loosened her boot from the stirrup and let go her rein, bending towards him as his arm went round her waist and catching his collar as directed.

"Go!" he cried and she sprang towards him as well as she could. He drew her towards him with all his strength, and in a second the girl was landed on the pommel of his saddle. She knew what she had to do: to leave his right hand free, so she clasped both her arms round his neck. He pulled at his reins with all his might—it was two lives now—and cried to the horse. The noble animal seemed to understand and threw himself back on his haunches.

He stopped only a few yards from the open chasm, into which the mare went with a wild rush.

Athlyne slid from the saddle, holding the girl in his arms. As the terrible danger came to an end her eyes closed and she sank senseless to the ground.

Then the deluge!

Through the barrier, which appeared to melt away before them, came a rush of people. Some were on horseback, some on foot, others in buggies, carriages, motor cars. Foremost came Colonel

Ogilvie who leaped the broken barrier; then after him a policeman whose horse had manifestly been trained to timber. At last several mounted police fearing that some terrible accident might occur from the crowding on the viaduct ranged themselves in front of the opening and protected it till the coming of a sufficient number of policemen, on foot and panting, had arrived to hold it.

Colonel Ogilvie threw himself from his horse and knelt down beside Joy. When he saw that she was only fainting he stood up and lifted his hat to her rescuer:

"I don't know how to thank you, sir," he said in a voice broken with emotion. "'Twas a gallant act! Some day, when you have children of your own, you may understand what it is to me!" Athlyne who was kneeling, still holding up Joy's head, said in the disconnected way usual to such circumstances:

"Do not mention it! It has been a pleasure to me to be of any service," and so forth. Then, seeing signs in the girl's face of returning animation, he said aloud so as to divert some of the attention:

"Has any one seen after the mare? The poor brute must be mangled, if it has not been killed; it ought to be put out of pain."

The poor brute was indeed a pitiable sight; there was a sigh of relief from the crowd round it down below when a policeman put it out of pain with a revolver shot.

Seeing that the lady was now recovering and in the charge of her father, Athlyne wanted to get away. He hated all such fuss and publicity. He could not let her go lest she should be hurt, but he signed to her father who took his place; then he arose. The girl's eyelids quivered and she gave a heavy sigh. Then the eyes opened and she stared wildly at the sea of faces around her. She seemed to recall everything in an instant, and with a shudder and a violent movement sprang to her feet.

"Where is he?" she said anxiously. Then, recovering her full presence of mind and seeing her father, she turned to him and putting her arms round him began to cry on his shoulder.

CHAPTER VI

TRUE HEART'S-CONTENT

ATHLYNE's one idea was now to get away quickly. The crowd was gathering closely and were beginning to ask questions. One big, intelligent-looking sergeant of police had out his note-book.

"May I ask your name, sorr?"

"Is that necessary, my good man?"

"Well, we have to report, sorr, but" this he said with a confidential look "it mayn't be necessary to make it public. You see, the lady's all right, and no one is goin' to make trouble over a dead horse. Though why any man would want to keep his name out of the papers for a deed like *that*, bates me!" Athlyne beckoned him aside; they leaned against the parapet with their faces towards the river. He had by now taken out his pocket-book and handed the sergeant a bill with a yellow back. The man's eyes opened when he saw it; and there was more than respect in his voice as he said: "Thank you very much, sorr! Be sure I'll do all I can. An' I don't know that we can't pull it off nayther; but ye must look out for them blasted kodaks!"

"All right sergeant. I'm much obliged for the hint. By the way wasn't one of your men tumbled over?"

"Yes, sorr; but I'm tould he wasn't hurt, only a bruise or two an' the skin from off iv his nose."

"Good! You'll tell the lady, she is sure to be distressed about him. Give him this for me, please. And here is my card. I am at the Manhattan."

"Thank you again, sorr. 'Tis mighty kind of ye. An' sorr if I may make so bould. If ye want not to be in all the papers to-morra betther not ride back. There'll be a million kodaks on the Boulevard." Just then a tall man raised his hat to Colonel Ogilvie and said:

"My motor is here, sir, and I shall be very happy if you will use it for the lady. The chauffeur will leave you where you wish."

"Thank you exceedingly. I shall be very grateful. I dare say I can get somebody to bring my horse to the stables; I couldn't leave my daughter alone after such a shock."

"I'll see to it, sorr," said the sergeant, who had come close. Colonel Ogilvie gave him his card and said:

"We are at the Holland House. Come up and see me some time to-morrow morning. I have some gratitude to express to you and your men!"

Whilst this conversation was going on a slim young man came up to Athlyne and raising his hat said:

"Can I do anything for you, sir. It will be a pleasure I assure you." Athlyne summed him up a glance as a soldier.

"Thanks, old fellow," he said, impulsively holding out his hand. "You're a soldier aren't you—a cavalry man?"

"No. Field Artillery 27th Battery. But we're all cavalry at West Point. I knew you were a soldier when I saw you ride—let alone what you did. What can I do?"

"If it wouldn't trouble you too much I wish you'd get some one to bring my horse to the Exchange in Seventh Avenue. You see I want to avoid all this fuss and kodaking."

"I should love to; what a noble animal he is. But I shan't send him. If you don't mind I'll ride him myself. Catch me missing a ride on a horse like that. May I come and see you after."

"Delighted. Manhattan Hotel." They bowed and parted. Athlyne went to Colonel Ogilvie, he felt it would be indecorous to leave without a word.

"I hope your daughter is all right, sir."

"Thanks to you, my brave friend. I am Colonel Ogilvie of Airlville. Joy this is Mr.——" Athlyne felt in an instant like a cad. He realised now, in all its force, the evil of deception. Silently he handed his card. "Mr. Hardy" her father said. Joy held out her hand and he took it.

"I'm not able to thank you, now and here!" she said, raising to him her glorious grey eyes. He mumbled out a few words in reply and raised his hat to part. As he was turning away Joy whispered to her father:

"Daddy, won't you ask him to come to see us. Mother will want to thank him too. Ask him to come to dinner to-night."

"My dear, you will be far too upset. Better——"

"Nonsense, Daddy dear. I'm all right now. Indeed, dear, it will seem strange if you don't, after what he has done for—for you, Daddy dear—and for me."

In his own formal and kindly way Colonel Ogilvie gave the invitation. Athlyne answered with equal kindly ceremony; and they parted.

By this time the stranger's motor had been taken in through the broken barrier. Colonel Ogilvie insisted that their host should not leave them, and they drove off together.

In the public excitement at their going Athlyne escaped unnoticed. He took the street at right angles and shortly got a downtown West-End Avenue car.

An hour later he had a call from his military friend, who announced himself as "Lootenant R. Flinders Breckenridge." Athlyne had now made up his mind how to meet him. He said at once:

"I am going to try your patience, old chap, and perhaps your friendship; but I want you to keep a secret. I can't deceive a comrade; and we military men are that to each other all the world over. I am here under a false name. I had reasons for keeping my identity concealed as I came for a special purpose. So I want you to bear with me and keep even that much a secret between you and me."

"That's all right!" said the boy with a hearty smile. "On my honour I'll keep your secret as my own."

"And when I can I'll write and let you know!" And so a friendship began.

"Mr. Hardy" left word at the desk that he would not see any one, especially any newspaper man. But on the Riverside Drive the kodaks had been hard at work; the black horse was recognised, and the morning papers had many execrable likenesses of Lootenant Breckenridge as he appeared galloping.

In the hall of the Holland House Lord Athlyne found Colonel Ogilvie waiting for him with that old-fashioned hospitality which is still to be found in the South. He cordially greeted his guest, and when they had come from the elevator took his arm to lead him into his own suite. Athlyne was quite touched with the greeting extended to him. He had not for years been in the way of receiving anything of the nature of family affection. But now when his host's warmth was followed by a tearful gratitude on the part of his wife which found expression of a quick bending forward and kissing the hand which she held in hers—to the great consternation of the owner thereof—he was sensible of feeling foolish.

"Oh, pray! pray!" he said, and then remained silent; for what could he do but submit gracefully to such an overt outcome of the feelings of a grateful mother. Joy was a girl in whom were the elements of passion; was it strange that the same emotional yeast worked in her as in her mother's nature.

The introduction to Miss Judith Hayes was a relief. She too felt strongly; no less strongly when she realised that the valiant stranger was so handsome and of so distinguished an appearance. But after all the matter was not so vitally close to her. An aunt, howsoever loving her nature may be, cannot be actuated by the overwhelming impulses of motherhood. This very difference, however, made speech easier; she it was who of all the grateful little party gave best verbal expression to her feelings. In frank phrases, touched with the native warmth of her heart and emphasised by the admiring glances of her fine eyes, she told him of the gratitude which they all felt for his gallant rescue of her dear niece. She finished up with an uncontrollable sob as she said:

"If it hadn't been for your bravery and resource and strength there would be no more sorrowful band of poor souls in all the wide world than—than" she turned her head and walked over to the window. Athlyne could see that for quite a minute or two afterwards her shoulders shook. When at last she did turn round, her glassy eyes but ill accorded with her incisive humorous phrases or her ringing laugh. The effect on Athlyne was peculiar; without analysing the intellectual process too closely, he felt in his mind with a secret exultation that he had "found an ally." It may have been the soldier instinct, to which he had been so long accustomed, working in his mind; or it may have had another basis. Anyhow he was content.

His meeting with Joy surprised whilst it satisfied them both. They looked into each other's eyes for an instant, and to them both the whole world became crystal. The "whole world" to them both— their world—the only world that was to them at that moment, that ever could be, that had been since the ordination of things. This is the true heart's-content. It is the rapture of hearts, the communion of souls. Passion may later burn the rapture into fixed belief, as the furnace fixes the painted design on the potter's clay; but in that first moment of eyes looking into answering eyes is the dawn of love— the coming together of those twin halves of a perfect soul which was at once the conception and realisation of Platonic belief.

At dinner Athlyne was placed between Mrs. Ogilvie and Joy, Colonel Ogilvie being next his daughter and Miss Hayes next her sister. Thus Aunt Judy, being opposite both her niece and the guest, could watch them both without seeming to stare. In the early part of the dinner she was abnormally, for her, silent; but later on, when she felt that things were going dully with some of the party, she manifested her usual buoyancy of spirits. She had in the meantime come to certain conclusions of her own.

Somehow there was an air of constraint over all the party, but in different ways and from different causes. Athlyne was ill at ease because they all made so much of him; and as he was painfully conscious of his false position in accepting the hospitality of such persons under an alias, their kindness only emphasised to him his own chagrin. Colonel Ogilvie conscious, rather by instinct than from any definite word or action, that his guest was more reticent than he would have thought a young man would be under the circumstances, was rather inclined to resent it. The Ogilvies had from the earliest times been very important people in their own place; and many generations of them had grown up to the understanding that their friendship, even their acquaintance, was an honour. Now when he had asked into his family circle a young man known personally to him only by his visiting card and by the fact that he had saved his daughter's life— very gallantly it was true—he found his friendly interest in his new acquaintance was not received with equal heartiness. The truth was that Athlyne was afraid. He felt instinctively that he was not his own master whilst those great grey eyes were upon him—most certainly not when he was looking into the mystery of their depths. And so he feared lest he should become confused and weave himself into a further tangle of falseness. In the background of his own mind he knew what he wished—what he intended; that this beautiful grey-eyed girl should become his wife. He knew that he must first get clear of his false position; and he was determined at any cost not to let anything interfere with this. At first Colonel Ogilvie's allusions to his home and his place in the world were purely kindly; he thought it only right, under the circumstances of his great obligation, to show such an interest as a man of his age might with another so much his junior. But he could not help feeling that though his guest's manner was all that was winning and that though his words were adequate there was no loosening of the strings of self-possession. Such a thing was new to the Colonel, and new things, especially those that he could not understand, were not pleasing to him. Still, the man was his guest; and only a few hours before had rendered him the greatest service that one could to another. He must not let him, therefore, feel that there was any constraint on his part. And so he acted what was to him an unfamiliar part; that of an exuberant man.

Joy was constrained, for with her deep knowledge of her father's character she saw that he was upset by something; and, as that something could only be in connection with the guest, she was uneasy. She knew well what her opinion of that guest was; and she had a feeling of what her hopes would be, dare she give them a voice. But that must be postponed—till when she should be alone. In the meantime she wanted to enjoy every moment when that guest was by her side. And now her breast was stirred with some vague uneasiness.

Mrs. Ogilvie had her own disturbing cause. She could not but see that her daughter was very much absorbed in this strange gentleman whom she had not ever even seen till that afternoon, and she wanted to know more of him before she could allow matters to become more definite. She knew that he was brave and she could see that he was a gentleman and a handsome one. But still—A mother's heart has its own anxieties about her child. And this mother knew that her child was of no common nature, but had her own share of passions which might lead her into unhappiness. Too well from herself she knew the urging of a passionate nature. Joy had not been tested yet, as she had herself been. She had not yet heard that call of sex which can alter a woman's whole life.

As to Judy her sympathy with romance in any form and her love for Joy acted like the two ingredients in a seidlitz-powder. Each by itself was placid and innocuous, but when united there was a boiling over. It needed no spirit come from the grave, or from anywhere else, to tell her of the power which this handsome, gallant, young man had already over her niece. A single lifting of the girl's eyes with that adorable look which no habit of convenience could restrain; a single lifting or falling of the silky black lashes; a single sympathetic movement of the beautiful mouth in its receptive mood as she took in her companion's meaning told her all these things and a hundred others—told her a story which brought back heart-aching reminiscence of her own youth. She was not jealous, not a particle—honestly and truly. But after all, life is a serious thing, serious to look back on, though it seems easy enough to look forward to. The heart knoweth its own bitterness. "A sorrow's crown of sorrow is remembering happier things."

So far, as to possibilities. Judith was much too clever and too sympathetic a person to go wrong as to facts on which they were based. She was a natural physiognomist, like other animals who have learned to trust their instincts; and within a very few minutes had satisfied herself as to the worthiness of "Joy's man"—that is how she tabulated him in her own mind. She felt quite satisfied as to her own judgment, not always the case with her. In her own mind, living as she had done for so long in a little world of her own thoughts, she was in the habit of arguing out things just as she would were she talking with some one else, a man for preference. She always wanted to know the truth, even if she did not use it. She had once said to her sister when they were considering how they should act with regard to a scandal in a neighbouring family:

"Well, Sally, it's all very well not being inquisitive; but you know, my dear, we can't begin to lie properly till we know what we are to lie about. There's nothing so destructive of after happiness—no kindliness so full of pitfalls, as a useless lie."

Now, her argument ran:

"You can't be all wrong about a man. You have thought too much on the subject not to be able to form an opinion. And even if your old maid's instinct—for you are an old maid, my dear, despite your saying that you are so to prove that you are not—warps your judgment in favour of the man. The pride that is in that man's features never came out of merely one or two generations of command. It takes a couple of centuries at any rate to put *that* stamp on a face. He is bold—well we know that from to-day's work; he is courtly—a man doesn't do nice things unconsciously, unless it has been his habit. He's in love with Joy—no doubt about that; and small blame to him for it. He's in her father's house, an honoured guest as he should be. He's sitting next to her and she's looking straight into his soul with those big lamps of eyes of hers. He saved her life a few hours ago, and now he can see—if he's not a fool and he's not that whatever else he may be—that she adores him—and yet he's not at his ease. . . What is it? What does it mean? For Joy's sake I must find that out. I may have to lie a bit; but at least I'll know what I am doing!"

With this object in view she took, when the charm of the meeting began to lose its lustre, the conversation in hand herself. She felt that the time had come. Well she understood when she saw on Colonel Ogilvie's face the very faintest shade of a shadow of that dark look which in earlier years had meant trouble for some one. "Lucius is thinking!" was the way she put it to herself. To a woman of her bringing up, the acts of the men of the family, and especially of its head, were not within the women's sphere. In the old slave-owning families there was perpetuated something of the spirit of subordination—some survival of old feudal principle. This was especially so in everything relating to quarrels or fighting. It was not women's work, and women were trained not to take any part in it, not even to manifest any concern. Indeed the free-spirited Judy having lived so many years in that particular atmosphere, before being able to look round her in wider communities, compared the dominance of view of a man in his own family life to that of a cock who lords it over the farmyard, struts about masterfully, and summons his household round him with no other purpose than his own will. Woman-like she was content to yield herself to the situation.

"We're all the same," she once said to a farmer's wife, "women or hens. When the master clucks we come!"

As it was quite apparent to her that both her sister and brother-in-law were uneasy, she began to take on herself the responsibility of action, even if it should have to be followed by the odium.

"What's the use of being an old maid if you can't do *something!*" she said to herself as a sort of rallying cry to her own nerves. Such gathering of one's courage is not uncommon; it is, in unusual circumstances, to many men and to most women. It does not as a rule apply to professional or accustomed duties. To the soldier, the lawyer, the engineer, the man of commerce, each as such, the faculties which wait on the intelligence are already braced by habit. And to the woman in her hours of social self-consciousness the same applies. When a woman puts on her best frock she is armed and ready as completely as is the cavalry man with the thunder of the squadron behind him; as the artillery man when "Action!" has been sounded. Ordinarily Miss Judith was equal to all demands made on her; now she was engaging in a matter in which she did not thoroughly understand either the purpose or the end. Now she spoke:

"Have you been staying long in New York Mr. Hardy?" At the moment Athlyne was talking with his hostess and did not seem to hear; but Joy heard and said gently: "Mr. Hardy!" He turned suddenly red, even to his ears.

"I beg your pardon, I didn't . . . " There he stopped, suddenly realizing that he had almost betrayed himself. The fact was that he heard the question but forgot for an instant the part he was playing. His ears had been tuned to the music of Joy's voice, and he did not wake at once to the less welcome sound. Partly it was of course due to the fact that as yet he had heard but little of Aunt Judy's speech; her intentional silence had a drawback as well as an advantage. He stopped his explanation just in time to save suspicion from the rest of the family, but not from Judy, who having an intention of her own was alert to everything. She made a mental note to be afterwards excogitated: "I didn't"—what?

She repeated the question. He answered with what nonchalance he could:

"No. Only a few days."

"Do you remain long?"

"I am sorry to say that I cannot. I had promised myself a few weeks after grizzlies; but that has to be foregone for the present. Something has happened which requires my going back at once. But I hope to renew my visit before long." He was pleased with himself for the verbal accuracy of the statement, and this reassured him.

"What a pity you have to give up your hunting," said Colonel Ogilvie, heartily. "You would find it really excellent sport. I haven't had any of it for twenty years; but I'd dearly like to have another turn at it if I could."

"What boat do you go by?" asked Mrs. Ogilvie.

"By the French boat. The *Mignonette* which sails on Saturday." He answered with confidence for he had spent a quarter of an hour looking it up before he had dressed; and had already posted a letter to the Office asking to have the best cabin open kept for him.

"What a pity," said Joy. "We are going on the *Graphic* on the Wednesday after; you might have come with us." She coloured up as she became conscious of the dead silence—lasting for a few seconds—of the rest of the party.

"H'm!" said the Colonel.

"Perhaps dear, Mr. Hardy has reasons of his own for choosing his own route," said Mrs. Ogilvie, determined that her daughter should not appear to be too ardent in pressing the new acquaintanceship.

Athlyne hastened to set matters right, as well as he could. He knew from his own bringing up that such a request should come rather from the parents than from the girl herself; but he understood and tried to protect her. He addressed himself therefore to Mrs. Ogilvie and not her daughter as he spoke:

"It would I assure you, be a delight to me to go on your ship. But unhappily it would not be possible. Some business matters, not altogether my own, are dependent on my arriving in England. If I had only known that you were going—Indeed I may say," he added with a smile which all three women accepted as "winning" "that if I had known, to begin with, that such delightful people existed . . . But until that . . . that accident I had no such knowledge. I must not say that 'happy' accident for it was fraught with such danger to one whom you hold dear. But, that apart, it *was* a happy accident to me that has given me the opportunity of making friends whom I already value so highly!" This was for him quite a long speech; he breathed more freely when it was over.

When the ladies had gone, he and his host had a long chat over their cigars. He was now more at ease, and as the conversation was all about sport and horses, matters in which he was thoroughly at home, he could speak more freely and more naturally than he had yet done. There was not any personal element which would require him to be on guard and so cause constraint. The result was that

Colonel Ogilvie got quite over his stiffness and began to warm to his genial influence.

It was quite a sign of his existing attitude that he now took on himself to say just what he had reprehended in his daughter:

"I am really sorry you can't come on the *Graphic* with us. It would make the voyage a new pleasure for us all!" As he spoke he took the young man's arm in a most friendly way; and to Joy's secret delight, they came in this wise into the drawing-room.

CHAPTER VII

A DISCUSSION

ON reflection Lord Athlyne was glad that circumstances had not allowed him to travel on the *Graphic* with his new friends. At first he felt horribly disappointed; as if Fate had in a measure checkmated him. Had he known that the Ogilvies were to travel on the White Star boat he could have easily arranged his plans. The voyage would in some ways—*one* way—have been delightful. Well he knew that; but as he should have to keep up his alias he would have been in a perpetual state of anxiety and humiliation.

This feeling made it easier for him therefore to come to a definite conclusion regarding his journey home: he would keep to himself, as far as possible, during the journey and try to get at the earliest possible moment out of his present humiliating position. Under any ordinary circumstances he would have gone to Colonel Ogilvie and told him frankly of the state of matters, relying on his good feeling to understand and sympathise with his difficulty. Had there been opportunity for reflection he would have done so; but all was so hurried at the scene of the accident that there had not been time for thought. He had accepted of necessity the invitation to dinner. Then, or before going to the Holland House would have been his chance. But again the Colonel meeting him and taking him at once to his family made present explanation difficult. Dinner finished him. When first on the Drive he had seen Joy he had thought her a beautiful girl. The act of rescuing her had made her of the supremest interest to him. But it was not till he had sat beside her and looked into her eyes that he felt that love had come. No man could look into those beautiful eyes and remain untouched. But this man, heart-hungry and naturally susceptible after some years of campaigning, fell madly in love. His very soul had gone down into the depths of those unfathomable eyes, and come back purified and sweetened—like the smoke drawn through the rose-water of a hookah. Every instant that he sat beside her the spell grew upon him. Joy was a woman in whom the sex-instinct was very strong. She was woman all over; type of woman who seems to draw man to her as the magnet draws the steel. Athlyne was a very masculine person and therefore peculiarly sensitive to the influence. That deep thinking young madman who committed suicide at twenty-three, Otto Weininger, was probably right in that wonderful guess of his as to the probable solution of the problem of sex. All men and all women, according to him, have in themselves the cells of both sexes; and the accredited masculinity or femininity of the individual is determined by the multiplication and development of these cells. Thus the ideal man is entirely or almost entirely masculine, and the ideal woman is entirely or almost entirely feminine. Each individual must have a preponderance, be it ever so little, of the cells of its own sex; and the attraction of each individual to the other sex depends upon its place in the scale between the highest and the lowest grade of sex. The most masculine man draws the most feminine woman, and *vice versa;* and so down the scale till close to the border line is the great mass of persons who, having only development of a few of the qualities of sex, are easily satisfied to mate with any one. This is the true principle of selection which is one of the most important of Nature's laws; one which holds in the lower as well as in the higher orders of life, zoological and botanical as well as human. It accounts for the way in which such a vast number of persons are content to make marriages and even liaisons, which others, higher strung, are actually unable to understand.

As yet, of course, Joy being a young woman had not her power developed. Such an unconscious power takes in the course of its development its own time. Instinct is a directing principle, and obedience can be given to it in many different ways. With Joy its course had been slow, the growth of time alone. Up to now there had been no disturbing element in her life; most of her years had been spent in a quiet house in a quiet neighbourhood where there were but few inhabitants of her own class; and where, therefore, the percentage of eligible men was small. There was even to her, as there must be to any girl like her, certain protecting oppositions. She was at once practical and sentimental, sensuous and dainty. Her taste was her first line of defence to the attacks of the baser qualities of her own nature. Nothing could appeal to her thoroughly which did not answer widely divergent conditions. Aunt Judy had summed her up well in saying that she would, if she ever fell in love, give herself absolutely. But it must be the right man to whom she did so give herself; one who must comply with all the conditions which she had laid down for herself. A girl of her upbringing—with a father and mother who adored her each in special way; with an aunt who represented impulsive youth all the more actively because she professed the staidness of age which is without hope; and with no intimate relationships or friendships of the male kind—had not only a leaning to, but a conviction of romance as a prime factor of life. "Life" was to her not that which is, but that which is to be. As the world of the present, where such thoughts are, is not one which is lit and coloured by love, the world of the future is the World of Love. The Fairy Prince who is to bring so much happiness—when he comes—is no mere casual visitor to feminine childhood. He is as real to the child's imagination as the things of her waking life, though his nodding plume has little in common with the material things which surround her. As she grows older so does he change form, coming more into harmony with living fact; till at last in some lofty moment, whose memory is a treasure for after life, the ideal and the real merge in one.

To Joy the hour had come. The Prince Charming who had swept across her path in such heroic fashion was all that she had ever longed for. He was tall and strong and handsome and brave. He was a gentleman with all a gentleman's refined ways. He had taste and daintiness, though they were expressed in masculine ways. He too had love and passion. How could she not know it who had seen—had felt—his soul sink into the deeps of her eyes, where mermaid-like her own soul peeping from behind the foliage of the deep had smiled on him to lead him on. How could she forget that strong arm which was thrown around her waist and which tore her from her saddle just in time to save her from a horrible death. How could she forget the seconds when she hung on to him for life, her arms clasped around his neck.

Whilst he was beside her at dinner she was in an ecstasy. Every fibre of her being quivered in response to his. And yet, such is the influence of teaching and convention, all this did not detract from her outward calm. When the ladies had left the table she had gone out with her arm round Aunt Judy's waist as was the convention of the time, and her smile had not lost its frank geniality. But in very truth she did not feel like smiling. She would have given anything to have stolen away to her own room and have lain on her bed, face down, and have thought, and thought, and thought. The whole thing had come on her so suddenly. Even the little preparation which she had had at the auction—the beautiful horse and the fine-looking masterful man who had bought him—did not seem to count. As he had swept past her in the Drive, man and horse seen singly seemed superb; but together a dream. Still there was nothing to fix it in her mind. There needs some personal quality to fix a dream; just as the painter requires a mordant to hold his colours to the canvas. But such luxury of thought would have to be postponed. It would come, of course—later in the night when there would be loneliness and silence. So she had to contain herself, and wait.

When "Mr. Hardy" came back to the drawing-room arm in arm with her father her heart thrilled. It seemed like a promise of hope if not hope itself. Aunt Judy, ever watchful, saw and understood. To her seeing eyes and understanding nature there was no mistaking the meaning of the girl's unconscious pantomime—those impulsive expressions of thought made through the nerves: the eager half turning of the ear to catch the sound of the opening of the dining room door and the passing of the feet in the passage way; the uplifting of the head as the drawing-room door began to open; the glad look in the eyes and the quick intake of the breath as she saw the attitude of the two men, each to the other.

As he came in Athlyne looked at her; a look that seemed to lay any ghost of a doubt in her mind. She was glad when he went straight across the room and began to talk with her mother. She was content to wait till when, having done his social duties, he would find his way to her. Mrs. Ogilvie had much to say and detained him, Judy thought, unduly; but Joy gave no possible sign of impatience. When in due course he spoke a few words to Judy herself that estimable young lady managed to find something to say to her sister.

When the guest was at last beside her in her corner of the room Joy felt that all was right and becoming. No matter how willing a woman may be to take steps to the accomplishment of her own wishes, it is an added pleasure to her when she is the objective of man rather than his pursuer. Even the placid pussy-cat when her thoughts tend to flirtation runs—slowly—from her mate until she sees that he notices her going. Then she stops and sings to him—in her own manner of music—as he approaches.

The two young people did not use many words in their speech; such seemed inadequate for what they had to say. Suffice it that what they did say was thoroughly understood.

Athlyne did not prolong his stay, much as he would have enjoyed staying. He felt that it would be better, in every way, if he did not enforce his first opportunity. Mrs. Ogilvie very graciously hoped that he would manage to make them a visit before sailing. Joy said nothing—in words. He had a little conversation with Colonel Ogilvie who was standing away from the rest and leaning on the chimney piece.

When he had gone Joy said good-night to them all; she felt that at present she *could* not talk the little commonplaces of affectionate life; and she could not bear to hear "him" discussed. If that acute reasoner on causes and effects in the female mind, Aunt Judy, had been able to permeate her heart and brain she would at once have understood that simple way of accepting a man's personality—simulacrum. What need is there to differentiate when there is but one. Names are given as aids to memory; and at times memory ceases to be an important matter.

The next evening after dinner "Mr. Hardy" became the subject of conversation, and Joy was not comfortable. She knew that there must be divergent views regarding any one, and was content to let them all have their own opinions. She had hers. Indeed she would not have been wholly content to hear him praised even up to the perfection which she allowed him. He was by far too personal a possession of her own to share even community of feeling regarding him with any one.

In the night that had passed her own feeling had grown, multiplied; the feelings of the others had changed too, but in a different way. The glamour which had become for her intensified had for them been lost in the exactness of perspective. Perhaps it was that Joy's night had been different from theirs. To her had come all the evils of reaction. Now and again with wearing recurrency came the exciting memories of the day; but always with that kaleidoscopic inconsistency which is the condition of dreaming. The brains of most people are not accustomed to self-analysis, else we should perhaps more widely understand that this very inconsistency is mere reproduction. Whilst we think we do not think that we are thinking, and memory does not adjust our thoughts to comparison. But, all the time, our thoughts are really errant; reflections of the night, which seem to be exaggerations or caricatures, are but just surveys taken from an altitude which is not our own. In the day time thought is too often initiated by carnal or material considerations. Selfishness, and need, and ambition, and anxiety are bases on which thought is built in working and waking hours. But in the dark and freedom of the night the mind borrows the wings of the soul and soars away from the body which is held down by all its weighty restraints. It is perhaps in such moments that we realise that passion, however earthly may be its exciting-cause, is in itself an attribute or emanation of the Soul. Over and over again did Joy live through the mad moments of that ride towards death. Over and over again did that heroic figure sweep up beside her out of the great unknown. She began to understand now whence came her calmness and quickness of apprehension as she realised his presence—the presence of a man who dominated her—even whose horse in the easiness of its calm intention outstripped the wildness of her own maddened steed. Here again the abstract mind was working truly; the horse had its own proper place in her memories of the heroic deed. Over and over again did that strong hand and arm seize her; and over and over again did her body sway to him and yield itself to the clasp, so that at his command it went to him as though of its own volition. And then, over and over again, came the remembrance of the poor mad mare disappearing over the edge; of the sickening crash from below and the wild scream of agony; of the confused rush and whirl; of the crowding in of people; of the vista of moving carriages and crowds down the curve of the road. And then all kept fading away into a blind half consciousness of the strong arm supporting her and her wearied head resting on his shoulder. . . .

This evening Mrs. Ogilvie was very quietly inclined to be tearful. She too had had a bad night; constant wakings from vague apprehensions, horrible imaginings of unknown dangers; dread that she could not localise or specify. Altogether she was upset, something as one is in the low stage following an attack of hysteria; nervous, weak, apprehensive, inclined to misunderstand things on the melancholy side.

Colonel Ogilvie was in that state of mind following a high pressure, which is a masculine reaction. He was very hard to please about anything. His wife always thought of this nervous and intellectual condition as "one of Lucius's humours," to others she said "the Colonel is worried about something." Judy called it: "one of his tantrums." This however did not affect his manner, outwardly. At such times he was perhaps even more precise than usual in his observance of the little etiquettes and courtesies of social life. It had perhaps been unfortunate that his household was exclusively female, for want of opposition rather encouraged the tendency. In his club or amongst men such irritation or ill feeling as he had found more outward expression; and the need to keep himself so that standard of personal hearing which his own self esteem had set, perpetually recalled him to himself. But at home, this, though it would not have been possible for a stranger to find fault with any part of his manner or bearing, still kept the rest of the family in a sort of hushed self-surrender. Even Judy the daring kept her natural exuberance in control at such times and was content to rest in unnoticed quiet. Joy knew well the storm signals and effaced herself as far as possible; she loved her father too well and respected him too much to do or say anything which might cause him disquiet or tend to lower him in his own eyes.

Judy on this as on other occasions maintained a strictly neutral position. But her wits were keener and her eyes more observant even than usual on that very account. She did not know the cause of her brother-in-law's disturbance, but she understood it all the same. Few things there are which lead so directly to the elucidation of truth as a clever, unselfish woman on the watch.

Silence rather than speech was the order of the day, and the talking, such as it was, began with Colonel Ogilvie. Men when they are carrying out a settled intention or policy can be more silent than women; their nerves are stronger and their nature more fixed. But in the casual matters of life they are children in the hands of women. Here were three women, all of them clever, all of them attached to the man and all respecting him; but they had only to remain neutral, each in her individual way, and let him overcome the *vis inertia* as well as he could. He could not but be aware that the subject of the guest of last evening had been tacitly avoided. He had been conscious of such in his own case, and with the egotism which was so marked a part of his own character he took it for granted that the avoidance was with the others due to the same cause as with himself. It was therefore with something like complacency—if such a thing could be synchronous with irritability, even if one of the two be in a latent condition—that he began on the deferred subject:

"I am afraid that our guest last night did not enjoy himself!" There was silence for a few seconds. Then each of the three listeners, feeling that some remark must be made by some one, spoke suddenly and simultaneously:

"Why, Lucius, what do you mean?"

"You surprise me, Colonel!"

"Is that so, Daddy!"

He waited deliberately before saying more; he had been thinking over the subject and knew what he wanted to say. Then he spoke with an air of settled conviction:

"Yes, my dear!" He spoke to Joy alone, and thus, to all three, unconsciously gave away his purpose. "I thought so at the time, and to-day, whenever I have considered the matter, the conviction has increased." Mrs. Ogilvie, seeing on her daughter's face a certain hardening of the muscles, took it for granted that it was some form of chagrin; in a protective spirit she tried to make that matter right:

"My dear Lucius, I really cannot see how you arrive at such a conclusion. It seemed to me that the young man was in rather an exalted condition of happiness. I could not help noticing the way he kept looking at Joy. And indeed no wonder after the gallant way he had saved her life." She added the last sentence as a subtle way of reminding her husband that they were all under obligation to the young gentleman. Moreover there was in her heart as a mother—and all mothers are the same in this respect—that feeling of pride in her daughter which demands that all men shall be attracted by her charms. No matter how detrimental a man may be, nor how determined she is that his suit shall not be finally successful, a mother considers it the *duty* of the young man to love her daughter and desire her.

Joy somehow felt humiliated. It was not merely that she should be the centre of such a discussion—for, after all, it was through rescuing her that he was there at all; but she was hurt and disappointed that this particular man should be discussed in any way. She had seen no fault in him; nothing to discuss in his conduct or his bearing or his words or his person. She herself had admired him immensely. He was somehow different from all the other men she had ever seen.... Then pride came to her rescue. Not pride for herself, but for him. In her heart he was her man, and she had to protect his honour; and she would do so, if necessary. This idea at once schooled her to restraint, and steeled her to endure. With an unconscious shrug she remained silent.

But Judy's keen eyes had been on her, and both her natural sympathy and the experience of her own heart allowed her to interpret pretty well. She saw that for Joy's sake—either now or hereafter—some opposition to the Colonel's idea was necessary. She had noticed the settled look—it had not yet become a frown—which came over his face when his wife spoke of his looking at Joy. In just such moments and on subjects as this it is that a father's and a mother's ideas join issue. Whilst the mother expects the singling out of the daughter for devotion, the father's first impulse is to resent it. Colonel Ogilvie's resentment had all his life been habitually expressed with force and rapidity; even in a tender matter of this kind the habit unconsciously worked.

"All the more reason, Sarah, for his being candid about himself. For my own part I can understand one attitude or the other; but certainly not both at once!"

Joy began to get seriously alarmed. The mere use of her mother's formal name was a danger-signal of rare use. By its light she could realise that her father had what he considered in his own mind to be a real cause of complaint. She did not like to speak herself; she feared that just at present it might complicate matters. So she looked over appealing at Judy, who understood and spoke:

"What two attitudes? I'm afraid I for one, don't understand. You *are* talking in riddles to-night!" She spoke in a gay debonair manner so like her usual self that her brother-in-law was unsuspicious of any underlying intent of opposition. This was just the opportunity for which he was waiting. With a sardonic smile he went on, singling out Joy as before:

"Your mother, my dear, has told us one of them. Perhaps the young man did look at you. There's little wonder in that. Were I a young man and a stranger I should look at you myself; and I would also have looked at any other man who dared to look at you too. If this is a man's attitude he should be more genial—more explicit—more open—less constrained to her relatives. That my dear Judy,"—he turned to her as he spoke "is the other attitude." Mrs. Ogilvie answered—the conversation to-night was decidedly oblique:

"Really, Colonel, I can't agree with you. For my own part I thought his attitude towards her relatives was all that was courteous and respectful. Certainly to her mother!" She bridled, and Joy grew more serious. Her mother calling her husband "Colonel" was another danger-signal; and she knew that if once her father and mother got to loggerheads over him—"him" was her way of thinking of Mr. Hardy—it might keep him away from her. She summoned up her courage and said with all the affectionate raillery which was usually so effective with her father:

"Daddy dear do you remember Æsop's fable about the Boy and the Frogs?"

"I suppose I ought to, little girl; but I'm afraid I have forgotten. What was it about?"

"The Boys were throwing stones at the Frogs, and when the Frogs remonstrated the Boys said they were doing it for fun. So the Frogs answered: 'It may be fun to you; but it is death to us!'" Colonel Ogilvie puckered up his eyebrows:

"I remember, now, my dear; but for the life of me I don't see its application here." Joy said with a preternatural demureness:

"It means Daddy, that you are the Boy and I am the Frog!" Her father's gravity became intensified:

"That does not help me much, daughter!"

"Well, you see, Daddy, here are you and mother commenting on how a man looked at me—and—so forth. But you don't take into consideration the sensitiveness of a woman's heart—let alone her vanity. I think you've forgotten that I am not now 'merely a child emerging into womanhood'—don't you remember on the *Cryptic*—but a staid woman to whose waning attractions everything relating to a man is sacred. One who looks on man, her possible rescuer from the terrors of old maidhood with the desperation of accomplished years." As she had spoken unthinkingly the word "rescuer" a hot tide of blood had rushed to her face, but she went bravely on to the end of her sentence. There was not one of the three who did not understand the meaning. Her mother and aunt were concerned at the self-betrayal. Her father's face grew fixed, now to sternness. With a faint heart Joy felt that she had made a terrible mistake, and inwardly condemned herself for its foolishness. Colonel Ogilvie now went on with grave deliberateness, he was determined that there should be no error regarding his disapprobation. All the time he was inwardly fuming against Mr. Hardy whom he held responsible:

"As I was saying, that fellow's attitude, as it appeared to me, was wanting in both openness and that confidence which underlies respect." Here Joy quivered. Judy, watching her, noticed it and for a moment was scared. But the girl at once forced herself into calm, and Judy's anxiety quite disappeared. She knew that Joy was now quite master of herself, and would remain so. The Colonel, accepting the dejected silence as a request to continue, went on:

"Of course there is no need for me to say that he is a very gallant fellow and a superb horseman, and that his manners are those of a polished gentleman. Nor, further still, that I and mine are under a deep debt of gratitude to him. But there are some things which a man can do, or what is worse which he can leave undone, that show distrust."

"What things, for instance?" It was Judy who asked the question falteringly; but it was to Joy that the answer was directed:

"Well, my dear, I shall illustrate. When I, wishing to show that we all took an interest in him and his surroundings, mentioned Airlville and spoke of clubs and such matters he did not proffer me any information. Still, thinking that his reserve might be that usually attributed to the stand-off-ness of the English as often accepted here—that it was due to habit rather than intent—I asked him where he lived in London. He wrote an address on one of his cards—which by the way has no address graven on it—and handed it to me, saying: 'That is only a lodging. I have not got a house yet.' Then I asked what clubs he belonged to; and he simply said 'Several' and began to ask me questions about what sport we usually have in Kentucky.

Now my dear, I am not usually inquisitive; and as this man was my guest I could not proceed in face of such a—a snub." He winced at the word. "But as I was really anxious that we should see more of one who had rendered us so signal a service, I expressed a hope that when we were in England in the summer we might have the pleasure of seeing him. I am bound to say that he reciprocated the wish very eagerly. He asked me a host of questions as to our plans; and I told him what we had arranged about the Lake Country and the Border of which we have such traditions in our family. He certainly has a very winning way with him, and I quite forgot at the time his want of trust about his residence and his clubs!"

"Perhaps he may have no home; he may be a poor man," suggested Aunt Judy. The Colonel answered her, this time directly:

"He may not be a rich man, but he is certainly not a poor one. You and I" this to Joy "saw him pay three thousand for that horse. And he is free with his money too in other ways. That police sergeant who was with me this morning—and who, my dear, asked me to convey his gratitude to you; I gave it for you—told me that the gentleman had given him on the Viaduct a hundred dollars for himself, and then another hundred for the officer who was run down."

"How generous!" said Judy. Joy said nothing; but she leaned forward, gladness in her eyes. There is some chord in a woman's heart which sounds to any touch of generosity or even of liberality. It is some survival of conditions of primitive life, and a permanent female attribute. Judy, anxious to propitiate her brother-in-law, and to preserve the absent man's character, said as though it were the conclusion of some process of reasoning:

"He must be some important person who is here on private business." Ogilvie smiled genially:

"Our dear Judy will find a romance in everything—even in a man's distrust!" Judy, somewhat nettled, felt like defending her own position. This had nothing to do with Joy so she felt she could argue freely about it:

"It needn't be a romance, Lucius, only fact!"

"My dear Judy, I don't see why a man should give so extravagantly merely because he is on private business. Why, it is the very way to attract attention." Judy was made more obstinate by the apparent appositeness of the remark and by the tolerant tone of the speaker.

"I don't mean that he gives *because* he is on private business, surely you know that; but that he may be an important man who gives handsomely as a habit. He may be keeping his identity concealed."

"How do you mean exactly. How keep his identity concealed? He never told me; and he has been my guest!" Colonel Ogilvie had a puzzled look on his face.

"Well, for instance by taking another name for the occasion. Perhaps—" Here she caught sight of the look of positive horror on Joy's face and stopped short. Joy had seen in what direction the conversation was drifting, but was afraid to interfere lest she should bring on the very catastrophe which she dreaded. She had never forgotten her father's expressions regarding an alias; and she had reason to fear that should his suspicions be in any way directed towards the new friend whose accidental acquaintanceship already promised so much, some evil or hindrance must ensue. But her hypothetical concern was lost in a real one. As Judy spoke, the Colonel started to his feet, his manner full of suppressed fury. He was bristling all over, preliminary of his most dangerous mood.

Joy rose to the occasion. It was now or never. It was apparent that her father had taken that form of offence which is generally expressed in idiom or slang. Cornishmen call it a "scunner," Cockneys "the hump," Irishmen "an edge," Americans "shirty." It is a condition antecedent to active offence; a habitat of the germ of misunderstanding; a searchlight for cause of quarrel. Joy felt cold, into the very marrow of her bones; well she knew that her father would never forgive any such offence to him as was implied in an assumed name. His remarks on the subject flamed before her like fiery handwriting on the walls of her memory. Moreover Judy's incautious remark had but echoed her own thought. All day she had been dreaming of this man who had plunged so gallantly into her life. Naturally enough to a young woman, she had been weaving romances in various forms round that very identity which, even to her, had been unexpressed if not hidden. Naturally her dreams had in them some element of concealment; romances always have. She had in her secret heart taken it for granted that this man must be distinguished—how could he be otherwise; and now her father's suspicion might result in some breach which might result in her never seeing him again. . . . It was a possible tragedy! To her, grim and real from her knowledge of her own heart; and none the less a real tragedy or less potent because its bounds were lost in the vagueness of mist and fear. . . . She was pale and inwardly trembling; but, all the same, her light laugh rang true; she was desperate and fighting for her man, and so was strung up to nature's pitch:

"Why, Daddy, if you're going to kill anyone it will have to be dear Aunt Judy. She's the one who has made the alias. The poor man himself—who by the way is not here to answer for himself and explain—hasn't done any conceivable thing wrong that we know of—even you Daddy know that; except not having a house and not bragging of his clubs!"

This seemed to strike her father; it touched him on the point of Justice. The lightness of his daughter's laugh reassured him.

"True!" he said. "That is quite true. I was too hasty. And he saved my little girl's life!" He rose from the table and putting his arm round her shoulders kissed her. Then they went into the drawing-room.

Joy bore up bravely for the rest of the evening. But when she was in bed and assured that she was alone, the reaction came. She was as cold as a stone and trembled all over. Putting her face down into her pillow she pulled the sheet over her head and wept her very heart out.

"Oh what it might have been if all went well. But what might be if Daddy took some queer idea . . . and quarrelled . . . !"

CHAPTER VIII

"LOOK AT ME!"

WHEN on Tuesday afternoon "Mr. Hardy" visited at the Holland House he found only the single ladies at home. Colonel Ogilvie had gone out in the morning to see after several matters of business, both in connection with Air and relating to the forthcoming visit to Europe. He had said he would probably not be back till dinner time. Mrs. Ogilvie had gone out after lunch for a drive and would pay some visits before returning home. Joy pleaded headache as an excuse for remaining at home. Indeed her excuse was quite real; no one can pass so melancholy a part of a night as she had done without suffering the next morning. As the day wore on, however, the headache insensibly departed; something else had taken its place. Joy would not admit to herself what that something was; but that afternoon she took unusual pains with her toilet. Judy noticed it with her usual acute observation, understood it with her understanding sympathy; with her wonted discretion she remained silent. She felt, and rightly, that the time had not yet come when she could either be serious with Joy or jest with her on the subject nearest to her heart. One thing she did which can never be out of place, especially when it is true: she showed pleasure in her niece's looks, taking care, however to put her own reason for it on a non-offensive basis.

"Joy," she said "that terrible experience of Sunday has not told on you a bit. You are looking simply lovely." Ordinarily Joy would have known it, and would not have shrunk from admitting it to herself, or possibly even to her aunt; but to-day she was full of self doubting. Her very flush of happy excitement when her aunt spoke would have betrayed her secret to a much less sympathetic or experienced person than Judy.

It is love more than any other cause or emotion or feeling which creates self-distrust with the young. And sometimes with the old, for the matter of that.

When she found that Aunt Judy did not "chaff" her or ask her questions, which she rather feared would happen, Joy beamed.

Indeed it looked to Judy's loving eyes as if she visibly blossomed. Judy spoke of her dress, remarking how well the dark full-coloured green silk became her slender figure; but she was careful not to overdo her praise, or to suggest any special cause for so elaborate a toilet.

But Judy was of a distinctly practical nature. She took care to send a message to the hall that if any visitors should come, though both Colonel and Mrs. Ogilvie were out, Miss Ogilvie and Miss Hayes were at home.

Athlyne found both ladies busily idle. Joy was reading a novel; which by the way she put down hurriedly without as Judy noticed, marking the place. Judy was knitting; that sort of heavy uninteresting knitting which is manifestly for the poor! She was used to say that such was the proper sort of occupation for an old maid. She, too, put down the cause of her occupation, but deliberately; thereby giving time for the guest to salute her niece without the need of interruption. It did not matter, then, if Joy's hand did remain an instant longer in his than formality demanded, nor if—when released—it was white in patches as when extra force is applied to delicate flesh. For a few minutes Judy joined in the conversation with her usual brilliancy. But to-day she was distinctly restless, sitting down and jumping up again; moving out of the room quietly and coming back noisily—the proper way as she said on an after occasion for all old maids to move. Whenever she came back she would join in the conversation in a sort of butterfly fashion till she flitted away again.

In one of these trios when Mr. Hardy happened to remark that he would like to know what the movements of the Ogilvies would be, and what address they gave for letters when they were away, Joy answered:

"Daddy always has our letters sent to Brown Shipleys in Pall Mall. But we shall be moving about a good deal I expect. Mother has to take baths at Ischia again, and one of us will stay with her; but Daddy wants to go about a bit and see something of England. He is set on seeing the Border counties this summer."

"Then how am I to know where you are?" he asked impulsively. With a bright smile Joy nodded over to Miss Hayes:

"You had better ask Aunt Judy. She might keep you advised. She's the letterwriter of the family!"

When in her turn Joy had moved away on some little domestic duty he turned to Judy and said:

"Won't you let me know the moves on the board, Miss Hayes. It would be very kind of you." He looked so earnest over it that she felt her heart flutter. She said at once:

"Of course I shall, if you will let me have an address to write to." He had evidently thought over this part of the matter, for he took from his pocketbook a card on which he had written below his printed name: care Jonathan Goldsworth, Solicitor. 47B Lincoln's Inn Fields, London, W. C. That will always find me. I may be away or travelling; but my letters are sent on every day."

Judy thanked him, and seeing that Joy was out of earshot added on her own account:

"It is only right that you, who did so much for my dear niece—and so for us all—should know at least where she is."

"Thank you very, very much!" said Athlyne impulsively. He had all an Irishman's instinctive knowledge of woman's character and felt that Judy was to be trusted, that she was heart-wholly devoted to her niece. On her part Judy *knew* that he could be trusted to the full, especially where Joy was concerned. And from that moment she began to take an interest in the love affair; an interest quite personal to herself and independent of her love for the girl. She felt that she was a participant in all schemes which were to be; and that, she came to the conclusion, was about all the real romance that an old maid could share in. "Thank God there's that left at any rate!" was her prayer of gratitude.

Athlyne felt a powerful impulse to make a *confidante* of her. This was the first chance he had of disclosing the reality of things, and he was just about to begin when Joy returned. Once again did that self-distrust, incidental to his state of mind, cramp him. He fancied that it might be premature. Not knowing how deeply Joy cared for him already, he was unwilling to take any chance which might militate against his ultimate success. There was also another hampering feeling coincident with the self-distrust: he thought it might be possible that a confidence made to Judy might be embarrassing to her with her own folk. Already his devotion was deep enough and pure enough to prevent his doing intentionally anything which might cause her pain. Could Aunt Judy have looked into his heart, as she could and would have done had he been a woman, she would have been satisfied of the genuineness of his affection; and so she would have had no doubts at all as to the end of Joy's love affair.

Joy's return, however, brought somehow a sense of restraint. She had herself originated or initiated a mechanism of correspondence and she feared that Mr. Hardy might notice that she had done so. In her present state of feeling towards the man, the very idea of such a thing was fraught with humiliation. It is extraordinary how much people take to heart the belief on the part of others of that they have intended. Truth, truly, is a bright weapon; even the flash of it has its own terrors!

Judy did not comprehend exactly what the trouble was. She could see that there was restraint on both sides, and was wondering whether it had been possible that he had been speaking too impulsively—"going too quick" was the way she put it to herself—and that Joy had resented or feared it. Not the fact but the rapidity. Well Judy knew that in her youth a woman most holds back when the wildest desire of her heart is to rush forward; that the instinct of woman being to draw man on, she will spend the last ounce of her strength in pushing him back. Judy had once said:

"A woman wants a man to be master, and specially to be her master. She wants to feel that when it comes to a struggle she hasn't got a chance with him, either to fight or to run away. That's why we like to make a man follow when in truth we are dying to run after him—and to catch him up!" Some of her circle to whom the heterodox saying had been repeated professed to be very indignant as well as horrified. This was chiefly noticeable in such of the most elderly of the good ladies as had a lurid past or a large family, or both.

If, however, Judy had any doubts as to the cause she had none whatever of the fact. There was no mistaking the droop of Joy's eyes, or the sudden lifting and quick dropping of the lids which makes the densest man's heart flutter; no mistaking his eager look; the glowing eyes ranging over face and form when the windows of her soul were closed, and entranced in their light when they were open. Judy herself knew the power of those gray, deep eyes. Even when her niece had been a baby there seemed something hypnotic about them. They could disarm anger, or change the iron of theory into the water of fact. Often and often after some such episode when she had thought the matter over she had said to herself:

"Lord! if she's like that as a baby with me, what will she be with a man when she's a woman!" Judy who was a self-observer knew instinctively that in Joy was an inherent influence over men. There was some very subtle, delicate force which seemed to emanate from her; some force at once compelling and tranquillizing, for the explanation of which mere will-power was insufficient. The power was now in active exercise; but it was turned inwards. Joy was in love! Judy knew it as well as if she had herself acknowledged it; indeed better, for the acknowledgment of such a secret, except to the man himself, is given with reserve. And so she made up her mind to further the affair; but to prevent Joy betraying herself unduly during such furtherance. By "unduly" Judy really meant "unwisely" as to ultimate and most complete efficacy.

She had an idea that Joy herself would approve, at present, of such discretion. It seemed a direct confirmation of such idea when presently the girl said to her in a faint whisper:

"Don't go away again Aunt Judy!"

When, however, in the course of conversation as the three sat chatting together happily, Mr. Hardy mentioned that his ship sailed in the early morning and she saw the colour leave the girl's cheeks for a moment, just as a white squall sweeps a sunlit sea, Judy's heart softened. She understood that retreating wave of colour. Nature has its own analogies to its own anomalies; there is a white blackbird, why not a white blush! So when the time drew near for the departure of the visitor Judy slipped away for a minute. When she had gone the two sat still. Athlyne's eyes were on Joy, eager, burning. Her eyes were down, the black lashes curling against her cheeks. In a voice rather husky he said in a low tone:

"Won't you think of me sometimes till we meet again?" Her answer was given in what she wished to be a matter-of-fact tone, but the slight quaver in it told another story:

"Of course I shall! How can I help it? You saved my life!" There was an entrancing demureness in the downcast eyes. But it was not enough for the man. He wanted to see the eyes, to gaze in them, to lose himself in them once again. There is for each individual nature some distinctive way of expressing itself. Sometimes it is the mouth which tells the story; sometimes it is by simple existence such as the lines of the nose or forehead, by the shape and movement of the hands; sometimes by a characteristic habit. Joy's nature spoke through the eyes; perhaps it is, that intention is best given by the eyes. Anyhow the lover wanted to see them.

In a low voice—not a whisper—that thrilled with intensity he said:

"Joy, look at me!" He spoke her name, though it was for the first time, quite unconsciously. As she heard it Joy's heart beat so that she feared he would notice it, and all the self-protective instincts of womanhood rose at the thought. For an instant her face glowed; then it grew pale again. She did not hesitate, however. She raised her eyes and looked him full in the face. Her cheeks were flaming now, but she did not heed it. In the face of nature what, after all, is convention. As Athlyne lost himself in those wonderful eyes he had a wild almost over-mastering desire to take her in his arms and kiss her straight on the beautiful mouth. He was bending towards her for the purpose, she was swaying towards him, he believed; but for long afterwards he could not be sure of the matter.

But suddenly he saw a change in the girl's face, a look of something like terror which seemed in an instant to turn her to stone. It was but a momentary change, however. The spasm passed, and, just as though it was to his eyes as if he had waked from a dream, she was her easeful self again. At the same moment the outer door of the *piece* opened and Mrs. Ogilvie's voice was heard as she entered:

"Judy, I am so glad! I am told he has not gone yet. I should have been so sorry if I had not seen him!" When she entered the room, three seconds later, she found the two young people talking quietly according to the demure common-place of convention.

Mrs. Ogilvie was very hearty in her manner; a little more hearty than usual, for she had a sort of feeling as if something extra in the way of civility was due to him after the way her husband had spoken of him. This was illustrative of two things. First the woman's unconscious acceptance of an unfavourable criticism of an absent person, as if it had been made to and not merely of him; second the way the sternness of a man's judgment is viewed by the females of his family. She insisted that Mr. Hardy should stay for tea and asked Joy to ring and order it.

Joy had been at once relieved and disappointed by the sudden entry of her mother. The maidenhood in her was glad of the postponement of the necessity for her surrender; the womanhood in her was disappointed by it. She was both maid and woman; let the female reader say, and the male reader guess, which feeling most predominated. She was glad that *he* was staying a little longer; for so she might at least feast her eyes on him again; but it was at best a chastened gladness, for well she knew that that thrilling moment would not come again—during that interview. And he was going away next morning!

Athlyne, too, was ill at ease. He, too, knew there would be no more opportunity now to follow up his declaration. The chagrin of his disappointment almost made him cross, such being the nature of man. Here, however, both his breeding and the kindliness of his nature stood to him; the shadow quickly passed. Later on in the evening, when he was thinking the matter over, he came to the conclusion that the interposition, though he did not attribute it to any divine origin, was after all perhaps best. It could not, or might not, suit him to declare himself so quickly. He felt that under the circumstances of his false name it would be necessary, or at any rate wise, to take Colonel Ogilvie into his confidence before declaring himself to his daughter.

It is thus that we poor mortals deceive ourselves. He had been just about to declare himself in the most passionate and overt way a man can; by taking the girl in his arms and kissing her, without even a passing thought of her father. But now, from some other cause, quite outside the girl and not even within her knowledge, he found his duty. One might with this knowledge easily differentiate the values of "necessary" and "wise" in his mind regarding his confession to her father.

Joy found a very distinct, though shy, pleasure in handing him tea and cake. Judy as usual presided at the tea-table. She did not interfere unduly with her niece's ministrations, but she took care that she had plenty of opportunities. "Joy dear won't you see if Mr. Hardy will take more tea?"—"has Mr. Hardy enough sugar?" and so forth. She had noticed those sudden liftings of the girl's eyes, and knew what they meant to a woman—and to a man. Athlyne did not as a rule make tea a "square" meal, but this time he got in that direction. He refused nothing she offered. He would have accepted death at her hands now, if it would have pleased her; and it was only the girl's discretion which saved the situation.

In due time he made his adieux and took his leave. With Joy there was no more than a handshake. It was perhaps part of a second longer than customary, but the force with which the squeeze was given lingered long in her memory. Perhaps it was the pain inflicted in the operation which made her often during the evening, when she was alone, caress the possibly wounded hand! That night she went to sleep with her right hand pressed to her heart.

Judy had a wild impulse to tell Joy to go to the door with the departing guest, but in the presence of her mother she did not dare to suggest it. Had she been alone she would probably have done so.

Athlyne walked away with his mind in a whirl. In his heart was ever surging up through all other thoughts that one sublime recognition which comes to every man at least once in his life: that which Sir Geraint voiced:

"Here, by God's rood is the one maid for me!" To this all other thoughts gave way. It obsessed him. When he came to Forty Second Street he did not turn towards the hotel but kept straight on up Fifth Avenue till he reached Central Park. He felt the need of movement. He wanted to be alone in the open. At Central Park his steps took him seemingly of their own accord towards the Riverside Drive. When he came to a place amongst trees seeming to hang over the river he sat on a seat and gave way to his thoughts. There was no one near him. Below him was the quiet river with its passing life; beyond, the Jersey shore so distant that details of life were not apparent. He took off his hat, more in reverence than for ease, as he thought of the beautiful girl who had so strangely come into life. Over and over again he said to himself in endless repetition:

"Joy! Joy! Joy! Joy!" He sat till the light began to fail and for long after the sudden darkness of the American night had swooped down. Then he went home.

In the hotel he found a visitor waiting for him. Mr. Breckenridge had come to say good-bye. He did so with so much heartiness that Athlyne could not bear to be aught but hearty himself. Though he longed to be alone he insisted on the young fellow coming up to his own rooms. The boy was not quite at ease so Athlyne said to him:

"There is something on your mind. What is it?"

"Well, look here, sir," he answered gravely. "You have treated me like a comrade, and I want to treat you like one!"

"Go on, old chap. I'm listening." Not without some nervousness the other proceeded:

"I saw in the *Journal* last evening that you had dined on Sunday evening in the Holland with Colonel Ogilvie."

"Those damned reporters!" interrupted Athlyne, but at once told him with a wave of his hand to proceed:

"That hung in my mind from something you said to me the other evening. That confidence which I shall always value." Athlyne nodded. He went on:

"I know something of that family. I'm from Kentucky myself; and I was there for a while—that time of the nigger disturbance you know—and I was quartered not far from Airlville. I have met Colonel Ogilvie; but it was on duty and amongst a good many others so he would not remember me. I never met any of his family; but I need not tell you that I fell in love with Miss Ogilvie. No fellow could help that; one glimpse of her is enough—— However—— I heard a lot down there about the old man, and as I was keen about the girl I took it all in and remembered it. I want to tell you this, because he is a very peculiar man. He is a splendid old chap. As brave as a lion, and as masterful as Teddy Roosevelt himself. But all the same he has his ideas which are hardly up to date. He is as stern as Fate in matters of—of—well, social matters. They told me a story of him which when I recalled it has troubled me since I saw you. It was about a man whose identity he mistook and who for a jest allowed the error to go, and kept it up. He was a Northern of course, for a Southern would have understood, and our boys are sometimes very keen on a joke. But it was no joke when the old man tumbled to it. He called it an unforgivable outrage and insisted on fighting over it. I tell you it nearly cost the joker his life. He was drilled right through, and only escaped death by a miracle. I tell you all this, sir, because of your confidence in me. If I might make a suggestion—you won't think it beastly presumptuous of me will you?" Athlyne held out his hand; the other after shaking it, went on: "I would venture to suggest that—of course if you have not done so already—you should take him into your confidence before leaving here. It might be awkward if the old man were to find out for himself. He would think it a want of trust, and he might never forgive it. I am sure you would like to meet him and his again—you know you can't save the life of a girl like that every day——" He stopped there, confused and blushing.

Athlyne was touched by the young man's kindly frankness and sincerity. He thanked him heartily but in a regretful way added:

"Unfortunately I didn't tell him. It was all so quick, and there was no opportunity when we did meet; and now I may not have the chance for some time. It would not do to write; I must see him and explain. And I go away early to-morrow. But be sure of this: the very first chance I get I shall tell him. I do wish for the friendship of him and his; and I should be main sorry if any foolishness hindered it. I shall have to do it carefully, I can see from what you tell me that he may construe my accepting his hospitality in my assumed name as an offence." He went to the door with his friend, but before parting he said:

"By the way I should like you to do something for me if you don't mind. I have asked the Horse Exchange people to get me another mount of the same strain as my black, a mare this time. I have given them full instructions, and if you will, I shall tell them that they must have your approval. I want some one who knows a good horse; and as I have given them carte blanche as to price it is right I should have some one to refer to. They are to send it to England for me."

When Breckenridge was gone he set about his preparations for his early start. Strange to say he never thought of dinner at all that day; the omission may have been due to his hearty tea! As he worked he thought gravely over what his young friend had told him. He could see good cause for concern. Colonel Ogilvie's attitude towards misrepresentation only echoed his own feeling. He came to the conclusion that there lay before him much thought; and possibly much action.

But all the same this branch of the subject did not monopolise his thoughts that night. As he lay awake he kept repeating to himself again, and again, and again:

"Joy! Joy! Joy! Joy!" He fell asleep with the words on his lips. The thought continued in his heart!

CHAPTER IX

THE CAR OF DESTINY

ATHLYNE did not feel safe till the French vessel was dipping her nose into the open Atlantic seas, and the Long Island Hills were a faint blue line on the western horizon. The last dozen hours of his stay in New York had been as though spent in prison. He knew well now that he really loved Joy; that this was no passing fancy, no mere desire of possession of a pretty woman. All phases of the passion of love, from the solely physical to the purely spiritual, have their own forces commanding different sets of nerves. Any one of these many phases may be all-compelling—for a time. But it is rather the blind dogged reckless pursuit of an immediate purpose than the total abandonment to a settled conviction. All the passions—or rather the phases of one passion—are separate and coordinate. Inasmuch as they are centred in one physical identity they are correlated. Nature has its own mysteries; and the inter-relations of various functions of a human being form not the least of them. As there are broad divisions of them—Christians accept three, the ancient Egyptians held to eight—so must we accept their uses and consequences. "Body and soul," so runs the saying of the illiterate, not seldom used in objurgation. "Body, mind and soul" says the quasi-thinker who believes that he has grasped the truth of the great parcelling-out of qualities. "Heart, soul and flesh" says the lover who knows that he understands. The lover alone it is who knows as distinguished from believing. For his world is complete; in it there is no striving after knowledge, no vain desire of many things, no self-seeking. For the true lover's one idea is to give. In such a world there can be no doubting, no fearing, no hoping. Before its creation Pandora's box has been emptied to the last. It may be that the lover's world is only a phantasm, a condition. It may be that it is a reality which can only be grasped by those who have been gifted with special powers. It may be that it is an orb as real as our own world, whirling in space in darkness, and can only be seen by those who have a new sense of vision. Surely it is not too much to believe, following the great analogies, that the soul as well as the body has eyes, and that all eyes of all sorts and degrees have vision of one kind or another; that there may be even a power of choice. We know that in the great manifestation which we call Light are various rays, each with its own distinctive powers and limitations. When these are all classified and understood, then science may take breathing time for its next great effort at investigation. Why, then, may not certain visual organs be adapted to specific purposes! We know through our sensoria that there is response in various ways to seekings of our own; whatever be the means of communication; whatever it be—electrical or magnetic, or through some other of the occult root forces, the message is conveyed. Why may it not be, again following the great analogies, that two forces of varying kind coming together are necessary for creation of any kind. We know it of lightning, we know it of protoplasm, and of whatever lies between them of which we know anything. We find or have ground for believing that the same conditions hold in all the worlds which germinate and increase and multiply. May it then not be that in love—"creation's final law"—the meeting of the two forces of sex may create a new light; a light strange to either sex alone; a light in which that other world, spinning in the darkness through ether, swims into view in that new-created light.

In physical life when flesh touches flesh the whole body responds, provided that the two are opposite yet sympathetic. When ideas are exchanged, mind come forth to mind till each understands with a common force. When soul meets soul some finer means of expression comes into play. Something so fine and of condition so rare that other senses can neither realise nor conceive.

But in the lover all the voices speak, and speak simultaneously; the soul and the mind and the body all call, each to its new-found mate. What we call "heart" gives the note for that wonderful song of love; that song of songs whose music is as necessary in a living world as light or air, and which is more potent in the end than the forces of winds or seas.

To Athlyne this new world had dawned. In the light which made it visible to him other things looked small; some of them base. And this, though the consciousness of love was still wanting; it had only spoken instinctively. The completeness only comes with that assurance of reciprocity which need not be spoken in words.

Athlyne had been very close to it. The yearning of his own nature had spoken in that call out of the depths of his heart: "Joy look at me!" And if there had been time for the girl's new-wakened love to surge up through the deep waters of her virgin timidity his happiness might have been by now complete. As yet he only believed that there might yet be happiness for him; he did not know! Had he seen in Joy's beautiful eyes the answering look which he hoped for, he would have been justified in a change of his plans. He would then have spoken to her father at the earliest possible opportunity, have told him the entire story of his visit to America under an assumed name, and trusted to his good feeling to understand and absolve him. As it was he had to accept existing circumstances; and so he prepared himself for the future. First he would get rid of his alias; then he would try to see Joy again and form some idea of his fate. After that he would make his confession to Colonel Ogilvie; and if the latter still remained friendly he would press his suit.

If some impartial reasoner, like Judy for instance, had been summing up the matter for him the same would have said: "What are you troubling yourself about. You are as good as he is, you are a suitable match for the girl in every way. You have a title, a large estate, a fine social position personally. You have a more than good record as a soldier. You are young, handsome, strong, popular. You saved the girl's life at the risk of your own. Then why, in the name of common sense, are you worrying? The old man is not an ass; he will understand at once that you had a good reason for assuming another name. He will see that the circumstances of your meeting were such that you had no time to undeceive him. He owes you already the deepest debt of gratitude that a father can owe. The girl owes you also her life. What in the world better chance do you want? You love the girl yourself . . ."

Aye! there it was. He loved the girl! That hampered him.

During the whole time of the voyage he kept to himself. He made no new friends, not even acquaintances; he had begun to feel that so long as he remained under the shadow of that accursed alias each momentarily pleasant episode of his life was only the beginning of a new series of social embarrassments. When the ship arrived at Havre he got off and went at once to London. There he stayed for a few days in the lodgings which he had taken in the name of Hardy.

He set himself gravely to work to wipe out from his belongings every trace of the false name. It was carefully cut or scraped from the new luggage, obliterated from the new linen and underclothes by the simple process of scissors. The cards and stationery were burned. It was with a sigh of relief that, having discharged all his obligations, he drove to his chambers in the Albany and resumed his own name and his old life. He was, however, somewhat restless. He tried to satisfy himself with long rides, but even the speed of the Kentucky horse who got more than his share of work did not satisfy him. There was some new uneasiness in his life; an overwhelming want which nothing of the old routine, no matter how pleasant it might be, could fill.

When "Mr. Hardy" had said good bye to her, Joy's new life began. New life indeed, for Love is a new birth, a re-creation. Whenever she thought of herself she seemed to be leading a double life. All the routine, the cares and the duties of the old life remained unchanged; but superimposed on it was quite a new existence, one of self-surrender, of infinite yearning, of infinite hope, of endless doubting as to whether she was worthy of all that which she shyly believed really existed. She was all sweetness to those around her, to whom she seemed happy—but with a tinge of sadness. Both her father and mother believed that she was feeling the reaction from the shock of the Riverside adventure. Her mother possibly had at first an idea that she had given some thought to the handsome young man who had saved her; but when she herself reviewed in her mind how quietly, not to say unconcernedly, the young man had taken the whole episode she was content to let it take a minor place in both her concern and her recollection.

In due course the Ogilvie family set out on their European journey, and in due course without any occurrence of note they arrived at their destination.

Hotel Bellevue,
Casamicciola, Ischia.

Dear Mr. Hardy:

As I promised to write to you I now try to keep my word. I dare say you will think that an old maid is glad to get a chance of writing to a man! Perhaps she is! But I may say a word in your ear: the habit of personal reticence begins younger and lingers longer than you would think. However this is not the time or place—or weather for philosophising. The scenery is far too lovely to think of anything unpleasant. We got here all right after a voyage which was nice enough, though rather dull, and with no opportunities of making new friends. We can't have runaway horses on shipboard! My sister will remain here for some weeks and I shall stay with her as it wouldn't do to leave her all alone. It brought the whole caboodle of us hurrying over from America through a blizzard the last time! No, thank you! And Colonel Ogilvie doesn't care to travel by himself. He is set on going up to Westmoreland which he says is the original Country of his branch of the Ogilvies. He is complaining of getting no riding here; and yet he says that when he gets to London he will hire a motor. Men are queer things, aren't they? The rest of us are quite well and looking forward to our English visit where we may meet some friends. How are you? I suppose spending your time as usual galloping about like a knight-errant on a big black horse rescuing distressed ladies. And writing letters to a pack of women not *all* old maids! I suppose you will spare a moment to write to one in answer to this, just to say where you are and where you will be in the next few weeks. My brother's section of our party leaves here next week. As I am an old maid I am shy of telling my sister, and most of the rest of us, that I am writing to a gentleman; but if they knew it they too would send their love. For my own part I must confine myself to kind remembrance.

Believe me,
Yours faithfully,
JUDITH HAYES.

P. S.—By the way, I forgot to say that the first contingent will after a few days in London go on to Cumberland or Westmoreland—I know it is the "Lake" country!

Athlyne read the letter eagerly; but when he had finished he dropped it impatiently. There was not a thing in it that he wanted to know—not once the name he wanted to see. He sat for a while thinking; then he took it up again saying to himself:

"She's no fool; it must have taken her some pains to say so little." As he read it the second time, more carefully this time and not merely looking for what he wished to find, the letter told its own story, and in its own way. Then he smiled heartily as he sat thinking it over and commenting to himself:

"Not a word about her; not even her name! And yet she must know that it would be of *some* interest to me to hear of her. I wonder if it would do to run over to Ischia. There seems to be a party of them . . ." He read over the letter again with a puzzled look, which all at once changed to a smile. "Good old Judy! So that's it is it! That's not the first letter Miss Judy has written with a double meaning in it. She hasn't those fine eyes and that quick wit for nothing. Why it's as clever and as secret as that sent to Basing at Pretoria." For a good while he pondered over it, making notes on the back of the envelope. Then he read these over:

"We are at Ischia.

"I am writing because I promised.

"The habit of personal reticence (that means not saying a thing for yourself) is for both young and old.

"Our voyage was dull, no adventure, no meeting any one like you.

"Mrs. Ogilvie and Judy remain at Ischia some weeks.

"Colonel Ogilvie doesn't like going alone and goes to the Lake Country (who is to be with him but Joy?)

"He wants to go motoring (seems more in this—think it over).

The rest of us—(that can only mean Joy) are looking forward to meeting friends in England—(that proves she is going with her father).

"Let me know where you will be during the coming weeks.

"My brother's section of our party—(He and Joy)—leave here next week.

"I haven't told Mrs. Ogilvie *or most of the rest of us* (Besides Mrs. O. there are only two so that *most* of them must mean the bigger—that is Colonel Ogilvie—she has not told that one of the two—then she *has* told the other. And the other is Joy!)

"If any of those kept in ignorance knew they *too* would send their love!

"'*Too!*' Then one does. Judy sends her own 'kind remembrance.' The only other one, Joy, sends her love—to me.

"Joy sends her love to me!"

He sat for a moment in an ecstasy, holding the letter loosely in his hand. Then he raised it to his lips and kissed it. Then he kissed it a second time, a lighter kiss, murmuring:

"That's for Aunt Judy!" He proceeded with his comment:

"The postscript: 'After a few days in London—will go on to Cumberland or Westmoreland.' No address in either place, what does that mean? She has been so clever over the rest that she can't be dull in this. She *must* know the London address . . . she thinks it best not to tell it to me—why?"

That puzzled him. He could not make out any reason from her point of view. He was willing to accept the fact and obey directions, but Judy had been so subtle in the other matter that he felt she must have some shrewd design in this. But the simple fact was that in this matter she had no design whatever. She intended to write to him again on hearing from him and to give him all details.

But for his own part Athlyne had several reasons for not seeing Colonel Ogilvie in London. Knowing that the father might make some quarrel out of his coming to his home in a false name he wanted to make sure of the daughter's affection before explaining it to him. Besides there was the matter of continuing the fraud—even to Judy. Until things had been explained, meeting and any form of familiarity or even of hospitality on either side was dangerous. He could neither declare himself nor continue as they knew him. He was known in London to too many people to avoid possible *contretemps*, even if he decided to continue the alias with them and take chance, until he could seize a favourable opportunity. And as he could not introduce the old gentleman to his friends and his clubs it would be wiser not to see him at all. When all was said and done the pain of patient waiting might be the least of many ills.

All the morning and afternoon he thought over the letter which he was to write to Judy. He despaired of writing anything which could mean so much; and beyond that again he felt that he could say nothing which would be so important to its recipient as the message of Judy's letter had been to him. How could he hope for such a thing!

The letter, which just before the time of collection he posted with much trepidation, ran:

"My Dear Miss Hayes:

"Thank you very much for your most kind letter and for all that you have said and left unsaid. I too had a dull journey from New York and found London duller still. As a town it seems to have fallen off; but it will brighten up again I am sure before long! I am glad you are all well. I suppose your party will re-unite after Mrs. Ogilvie's cure has been completed. It is strange how we are all taking to motor cars. I am myself getting one, and I hope in the early summer to have some lovely drives. I am looking out for a companion. But it is a difficult thing to get exactly the one you want, and without such it is lonely work. Even going the utmost pace possible could not keep one's mind away from the want. When I went to America that time I was feeling lonely and dull; and I have felt lonelier and duller ever since. But when I get my motor I hope all that will shortly cease. I hope that when you arrive—if you and Mrs. Ogilvie do come over—that you will honour my car by riding in it. I shall hope to have some one with me whom you must like very much—you seem to like nice people and nice people seem to be fond of you. I greatly fear it will not be possible for me to see Colonel Ogilvie in London, for I have to be away very shortly on some business, and I probably shall not be back in time; but I am going up North in a few weeks—in my new car if it is ready—and I shall hope to see my friends. Perhaps Colonel Ogilvie and some of his friends will come for a drive with me. Won't you let me know where he will be staying after he leaves London. Please give, if occasion serves, my warm remembrance to all. I have not forgotten that delightful conversation we had before tea the day I called. Tell Miss Joy that I wish we could renew and continue it. Miss Ogilvie must be a very happy girl to have, in addition to such nice parents who love her so much, an aunt like you so much her own age, so sympathetic, so understanding. I cannot tell you how much I am obliged to you for writing. I look eagerly for another letter.

"Believe me,
"Yours very sincerely."

There he hesitated. He had meant never to write again the name Richard Hardy. Here the letter seemed to demand it. He had already thought the matter over in all ways and from all points of view and had, he thought, made up his mind to go through with the fraud as long as it was absolutely necessary. There was no other way. But now when he had to write out the lie—as it appeared to him to be—his very soul revolted at it. It seemed somehow to dishonour Joy. Since he had looked into the depth of her eyes, scruples had come to him which had not ever before troubled him. It was unworthy of her, and of himself, to continue a lie. And so with him began again the endless circle of reasoning on a basis of what was false.

A lie, little or big, seems gifted with immortality. At its creation it seems to receive that vitality which belongs to noxious things. The germs which preserve disease survive the quick lime of the plague-pit and continue after the seething mass of corruption has settled into earthly dust; and when the very bones have been resolved into their elements the waiting germs come forth on disturbance of the soil strong and baneful as ever.

Sometimes Athlyne grumbled to himself of the hardness of his lot. It was too bad that from such a little thing as taking another name, and merely for the purpose of a self-protective investigation of a lie, he should find himself involved in such a net-work of deceit. Other people did things a hundred times worse every day of their lives. He had often done so himself; but nothing ever came of it. But now, when his whole future might depend upon it, he was face to face with an actual danger. If Colonel Ogilvie quarrelled with him about it that would mean the end of all. Joy would never quarrel with her father; of that he felt as surely as that he loved her. All unknown to himself Athlyne had an instinctive knowledge of character. Any one who had ever seen him exercise the faculty would have been astonished by the rapidity of its working. The instant he had seen Joy he had recognised her qualities. He had understood young Breckenridge at a glance; otherwise he was too shrewd a man to trust him as he had done. It is not often that a man will entrust the first comer in a crowd with a valuable horse. To this man, too, an utter stranger, he had entrusted his secret, the only person who now knew it on the entire American continent. So also with Colonel Ogilvie. He was assured in his inner consciousness that that old gentleman would be hard to convince of the necessity for disguise. There was something about his fine stern-cut features—so exquisitely modified in his daughter—and in his haughty bearing which was obnoxious to any form of deceit.

One of these grumbling fits came on him now, and so engrossed him that he quite forgot to sign the letter. It was in the post box when he recollected the omission. He rejoiced when he did so that he had not written the lie. It was queer how sensitive his conscious was becoming!

One immediate effect of the awakened conscience was that he went about a motor car that very afternoon. He had said to Miss Judy that he was getting one, and his words had to be made good. Moreover he had, in addition to the train of reasons induced by Miss Judy's mention of Colonel Ogilvie's getting a car, a sort of intuition that it would be of service to him. Of service to him, meant of course, in his present state of mind with regard to Joy—of service in furthering his love affair. He had wished for a horse and got one, and it had brought him to Joy. Now he wanted a motor . . . The chain of reasoning seemed so delightfully simple that it would be foolish to dispute it. Sub-conscious intuition supplied all lacunæ.

The logic of fact seemed to support that of theory. He looked in at his club to find the name of a motor agency. There in the hall he met an old diplomatic friend, who after greeting him said:

"This is good-bye as well."

"How so?" he asked.

"I am off for Persia. Ballentyre got a stroke just as he was starting and they sent for me in a hurry and offered me the post. It is too good to refuse, so I am booked for another three years. I was promising myself a long rest, or a spell in a civilised place anyhow. It is too bad, just when I was expecting home my new Delaunay-Belleville car which has been nearly a year in hand."

"Do you take the car with you?" asked Athlyne feeling a queer kind of beating of his heart.

"No. It would be useless there; at all events until I see what the country and the roads are like. I was just off to the agents to tell them to sell it for me."

"Strange we should meet. I came here to look up the address of an agent. I want to buy a car."

"Look here, Athlyne; why not take over this? I shall have to sell it at a sacrifice, and why shouldn't you have the advantage. I'll let you have it cheap; I would rather clear it all up before I go."

"All right, old chap. I'll take it. What's the figure?"

"I agreed to pay £1,000. You may have it at what you think fair!"

"All right. Can we settle it now?"

"By all means." Athlyne took out his cheque-book and wrote a cheque which he handed to the other.

"I say," said Chetwynd. "You have made this for the full sum."

"Quite so! What else could I offer. Why man, do you think I would beat you down because you are in a hurry. If there is any huckstering it is I who should pay. I get my car at once, the very car I wanted. I should have to wait another year."

Three days after, the car arrived. Athlyne had spent the time in getting lessons at a garage and learning something of the mechanism. He was already a fair mechanic and a fine driver of horses; so that before another week was out he had learned to know his car. He got a good chauffeur so that he would always have help in case of need; and before the next letter arrived from Miss Judy he was able to fly about all over the country. The new car was a beauty. It was 100-110 h. p. and could do sixty miles an hour easily.

The next letter which he received from Miss Hayes was short and devoid, so far as he could discern after much study, of any cryptic meaning whatever. She thus made allusion to the fact that he had not signed his letter:

"By the way I notice that you forgot to sign your letter. I suppose you were thinking at the time of other things." The later sentence was underlined. The information in the letter was that Colonel Ogilvie and "his daughter" expected to be in London on the Saturday following her letter and would stay at Brown's Hotel, Albemarle Street, "where I have no doubt they will be happy to see you if you should chance to be in London at the time. I think Lucius intends to write you."

The latter sentence was literally gall to him. He knew that he must not be in London during their stay there. To be away was the only decent way of avoiding meeting them. He must not meet Colonel Ogilvie until he had made certain of Joy's feeling towards him, for he could not make his identity known till he had that certainty. He could then explain his position . . . The rest of the possibilities remained unspoken; but they were definite in his own mind.

As he had to go away he thought it would be well to study up the various branches of the Ogilvy as well as of the Ogilvie family. He would then make a tour on his own account to the various places where were their ancient seats. As Colonel Ogilvie was interested in the matter some knowledge on his part might lead . . . somewhere.

CHAPTER X

A LETTER

BEFORE he set out for London, Colonel Ogilvie wrote a letter to "Mr. Hardy" which he sent to the address given on the card handed to him at New York. He had thought over the matter of writing with the seriousness which he always gave to social matters. Indeed he was careful to be even more punctilious than usual with this young man; firstly because he had got the idea that his overtures had not been cordially received and he wished to be just, secondly because he felt he must not forget the great service rendered to his daughter and himself. In his letter he apprised Mr. Hardy that with his daughter he was coming to London for a week or more, that they would be staying at Brown's Hotel, Albemarle Street, and that they would be very pleased to see him there if he would honour them with a visit, and that perhaps he would make it convenient to dine with them any evening which he himself might select. He also told him that Mrs. Ogilvie and her sister were to remain some weeks longer in Italy, and that they would join him in the North of England, whence they would go all together to some bracing part of Scotland, to be decided later on when the time came for the after-cure. Of course, as he did not know that Athlyne was already in correspondence with Miss Judy, and was particular to give details of his future movements. Before posting it he showed the letter to Joy so that he might have her opinion as to whether all was correct. Joy was secretly fluttered, but she preserved admirably her self-control and came well through the ordeal, leaving no suspicion in the mind of her father as to the real state of things. She was now very deeply in love; the days that had passed had each and all fed the flame of her incipient passion. Time and the brain working together have a period of growth of their own which the physiopsychists have called "unconscious cerebration," a sort of intellectual process whereby crude thoughts are throughout the darkness of suspended effort developed into logical results. Again, one of Nature's mysterious workings; again one of her analogies to the inner and outer worlds of growth. As the hibernating seed, as the child in the womb, so the thought of man. Growth without ceasing, in light or darkness. Logical development, from the gates of Life to the gates of Death.

Joy was so deeply in love that all her thoughts, all her acts, all her hopings and fearings were tinged by it. Dreams need a physical basis somewhere; and whatever is the outward condition of man or woman so will be the mind. Whatever the inward, so will be the outward; each is the true index to the other. Her father, though an acute enough man in other respects, was sublimely unconscious of any change in his little girl; indeed he held her in his mind as but a child to whom the realities of life had not yet presented themselves. And yet even as a father he was feeling the effects of her developed affection. All the sweetness of her childhood had ripened. Somehow her nature had become more buoyant, more elastic. Sweetness and thoughtful understanding of his wishes seemed to breathe from her. Now and again were languorous moments when her whole being seemed to yield itself involuntarily to a wish outside her own. To a woman these are times of danger. For when the will ceases, passivity is no longer negative; it is simply a doubling of the external domination—as though an active spirit had been breathed into inertness. There are many readings to any of the Parables. When certain devils have been cast out and the house has been swept and garnished may it not be that spirits other than devils may find place therein. May it not also be that there is a virtue in even selfishness; if only that its protective presence keeps out devils that would fain enter the house where it abides.

With a spirit of meekness Joy waited the coming of the friend who had been bidden. She had every confidence that he would come. True that he had not written to her; but she had seen his unsigned letter to Judy, and into its barrenness had read meanings of her own. How could he *not* come to her when she would have so gladly flown to him? Besides there was always with her the memory of that rapturous moment when he had spoken her name: "Joy look at me!" It was not hard to remember that; it was the only time she had heard her name upon his lips. As the weeks had gone by, that little sentence impulsively spoken had arrived at the dignity of a declaration of passion. It had grown in her mind from a request to a command; and she felt the sweetness of being commanded by a man she loved. In that moment she had accepted him as her Master;

and that acceptance on a woman's part remains as a sacred duty of obedience so long as love lasts. This is one of the mysteries of love. Like all other mysteries, easy of acceptance to those who believe; an acceptance which needs no doubting investigation, no proof, no consideration of any kind whatever. She had faith in him, and where Faith reigns Patience ceases to be a virtue.

Her father waited also, though not in the same meekness of spirit. Indeed his feeling was fast becoming an exasperation in which the feeling of gratitude was merging. He felt that he had done all that was right and correct with regard to the young man. He had gone out of his way to be nice to him; but with only the result of insult—that was the way in which he was beginning to construe the silence of Mr. Hardy. Insult to his daughter as well as himself; and that was a thing which could not be brooked from anyone no matter how strong or how numerous were his claims for leniency! Joy saw that there was some cause of displeasure with her father, and with a sinking heart had to attribute it to the real cause. She knew—which her father did not—from his letter to Judy that Mr. Hardy would have to be away from London just at the time of their visit; but she was afraid to speak lest she should precipitate catastrophe. It was not that she had fear in the ordinary sense. Much as she loved her father she would face him if necessary. But she felt that it would be unwise to force the issue prematurely; her father was a man of such strong prejudices—he called them convictions!—that once they were aroused they mastered his judgment. What might happen if he should give them scope on this occasion! Her heart sank more deeply still at the very thought.

In her anxiety she took what was probably the wisest course; she kept him perpetually busy, trotting about with her to see the sights of London. This was a pleasure which she had long promised herself with—since the adventure with the run-away horse—the added interest of having present a nice Englishman to point out and explain. This special charm had now to be foregone; and the denial made her secretly sad. However, the best anodyne to pain is pain; her anxiety regarding her father's case was a counteractant to her own. Father and daughter were so busy, morning noon and night, and the girl appeared to be so tired when the day's programme as laid down had been exhausted, that occasion was lacking for consideration of a disagreeable subject. Towards the end of the first week, however, Colonel Ogilvie's patience began to fail. He felt that he must speak of his annoyance to some one, and there was no choice. Joy felt that the moment had come, and she did not flinch. She had a grim foreboding that there would be something said which would give her pain to hear. Her hands were tied. She could not even mention that Mr. Hardy was away; her father would be sure to ask how she knew it. If he did so, she would not dare to tell him; for she knew well that if he learned that the man who had not even answered his own letter was in secret correspondence with the ladies of his own family—that is how he would put it—the fact would add fuel to the flame, would change chagrin to fury. And so she steeled herself to the quiet endurance of suffering.

The blow fell at breakfast time when her father had looked through the few letters which lay beside his plate.

"Well, I do think that that young man's rudeness is unpardonable!"

Joy looked up with a pleasant smile which belied the chilly feeling about her heart. She felt that she must pretend ignorance; her father might, later on, hold a too ready acceptance as suspicious:

"What, Daddy? Who? Whose rudeness?"

"That—that gentleman whom I asked to dine with us. Mr. Hardy."

"Perhaps he may not have got your letter."

"How do you mean, daughter? He must have got it; I directed it to the address he gave me himself."

"But Daddy, he may be away. You remember he told you at dinner that day in the Holland that he had important business. It may have been prolonged you know. He may not even be in London."

"Then he should see that his letters are duly sent on to him."

"Certainly he ought. But perhaps Daddy he's not as careful as we are. He may not be a man of business!" Colonel Ogilvie smiled:

"I'm afraid that is a very bad argument my dear. You have just used the opposite!"

"How so, Daddy?" she asked wrinkling up her brows.

"You said he might be away on business!" He was so pleased with his combating of her argument that her purpose was effected; he abandoned the subject—for a time.

The next morning, however, he renewed it again under similar circumstances:

"I think, my dear, that we had better give up any idea of keeping that young man on the list of our friends. It is quite evident that he does not care to continue our acquaintanceship!" Joy suffered much this time; all the more because there was nothing that she could say which would be wise. She had to content herself with a commonplace acceptance of his views. So she answered with as steady a voice as she could manage:

"Of course, Daddy! Whatever you think right!" The answer pleased her father; he showed it in his reply:

"I am sorry about it, my dear; for he seemed a fine young fellow, and he saved you very bravely. However we cannot help it. We did all we could to make him welcome; but we can't force him to come to us. It isn't an occasion for wain-ropes!" After a pause she ventured to say meekly:

"Yes. It would be a pity if we had to quarrel with a man who did so much for us. I suppose if he *could* show that he did not get your letter, then it would be—you could forgive him."

"Of course I would, my dear. But these English are so stand-off that there is no understanding them. I wanted to be friends with the man who saved my little girl . . . But there, it is no use wishing anything when people are pig-headed . . ."

His words somehow made Joy's heart glow. It might be all right yet, if only . . .

But the present was sadly un-right. The suspense, the uncertainty, the waiting in the dark were hard to bear. It was little wonder that in the middle of the following week her father noticed that she had grown pale and listless. Deep down in his mind he connected it somehow with "that damned fellow" but he took care not to betray his thought to his daughter in any way. His present wish was that even the existence of the fellow should fall out of the memory of his family. As for himself he never let a grievance fall out of his memory; there had to be a day of reckoning for all concerned in such.

He quietly made preparations for their northern tour, and when all was ready told Joy who joined with alacrity in the move. London was now growing hateful to her.

In the meantime Athlyne, living either in his castle of Ceann-da-Shail—which he had long looked on as his home—as a centre, was flying about in his new motor, learning each day fresh mysteries of driving. The speeds of the motor are so much above those of other vehicles that a driver, howsoever experienced he may be in other ways, seems here to be dealing with a new force. The perspective changes so fast as the machine eats up the space that the mind requires to be practised afresh in judging distances and curves. It had been a bitter regret to him that he had to keep out of London just when Joy had come to it. His mind was always running on what a delight it would be to be with her when all the interesting things came before her; to note the sudden flushes of delight, to see the quick lifting of the beautiful eyes, to look into their mysterious, bewildering depths. At first when such ideas took him whilst driving, he nearly ran into danger. Unconsciously his hands would turn the wheel for speed, and in his eagerness he would make such swerves and jumps that undesirable things almost happened. However, after a few such experiences his nerves learned their own business. It is part of the equipment of a chauffeur to be able to abstract and control his driving senses from all other considerations; and such dual action of the mind requires habit and experience for its realisation. The constant watchfulness and anxiety had at least this beneficent use: that for a part of the day at all events his mind was kept from brooding over his personal trouble.

The arrival of Colonel Ogilvie's letter, sent on to him from London, made in a way a new trouble for him; for whilst he was delighted to get so friendly an overture it was he saw but another difficulty ahead of him. He must either reply in his false name, which was now hateful to him; or he must leave the letter, for the present, unanswered. This latter alternative would be dangerous with a man so sensitive and so punctilious; but, all told, it was the lesser evil. He had had opportunity to make up his mind on the subject before the letter came, for Aunt Judy had said in her last letter that Colonel Ogilvie had spoken about writing to him before they should arrive in London. Still it was a sore trial to him to be so discourteous, with the added chagrin that it might—probably would—stand in his way with the one man in the world whom he wished to propitiate.

As he did not know anything about the history of Colonel Ogilvie's family he went to the peerage books and made lists of the bearers of that name in its different spellings; and then as he decided to go to many of the places named, he made runs into Perthshire and Forfar. He came to the conclusion that he must have misunderstood Colonel Ogilvie in alluding to the "Border Counties." He laid up, however, a good deal of local information which might be pleasing to his prospective father-in-law.

One morning he had a letter which quite fluttered him. It was from Aunt Judy telling him that Colonel Ogilvie had announced his intention of starting on the then coming Thursday for the north, and that he had given as the direction of his letters till further notice the "Inn of Greeting," Ambleside. The unqualified pleasure which he received from this news was neutralised by the postscript:

"By the way—this of course in your private ear, now and hereafter—Colonel Ogilvie is vastly disappointed that you have not been to see him in London, and that you have not even replied to his letter. Surely there must be some mistake about this. I sincerely hope so, for he looks on any breach of courtesy, or any defect in it, as an unpardonable sin. I know from the fact of his mentioning it to his womenkind that he has taken it to heart. Do, do my dear friend, who have done so much for us and whose friendship we wish to hold, repair this without delay. He is an old man and may possibly expect more from a younger man than from one of his own standing. I am sure that if there has been any omission there is on your part a good reason for it. But do not lose any time. If you wish to please us *all*—and I am sure you do—you would do well to go up to Ambleside—if you have not seen him already—and call on him there. And do like a dear man drop me a line at once to say you have received this and telling me what you intend to do."

He sat for a while quite still, putting his thoughts in order. It was now Monday so that Colonel Ogilvie would have been already some days at Ambleside. He took it for granted that Joy was with him, but he could not help a qualm of doubt about even that. Aunt Judy had not mentioned her in the matter. The only possible allusion was in the underlining of the word "all." Otherwise the letter was too direct and too serious for any cryptic meaning.

He came to the conclusion that his best plan would be to go at once to some place on Windermere, and from there go quietly to Ambleside and find out for himself how things lay. The best place for him to stay at would, for his purposes, be Bowness. There he would leave his car with the chauffeur and drive in a carriage to Ambleside. When there he would contrive to meet if possible Joy alone. He would surely be able to form from her attitude some opinion of her disposition towards him. If he were satisfied as to this he would at once go to her father, tell him the whole story, and place himself in his hands.

But then he thought that if he were so near, his name might become known to Colonel Ogilvie; that infernal alias seemed to be always standing in his way! He was so obsessed by the subject that at times he quite overlooked the fact that neither the Colonel nor any of his family knew anything whatever of the matter. It took him an hour's hard thought before this idea presented itself to him. It took a weight off his mind. If by any chance Colonel Ogilvie should hear that an individual called Lord Athlyne was in the neighbourhood it would mean nothing to him. Nothing except the proximity of one more of that "bloated aristocracy," which one class of Americans run down—and another run after.

He was then up in Ross. As he did not wish to "rush" matters he decided to start next day. When that time came he had fully made up his plan of action. As the Ogilvies were at Ambleside he would go to Bowness. As there was a service of public coaches he could go between the places mentioned—without even the isolation of a carriage for his sole use. He would go quietly to the Inn of Greeting and learn what he could about their movements. The rest must depend on circumstances. But there must be no hurry; the matter was too serious now and the issue too important to take any risk. But when he should have seen Joy and knew, or believed, or understood . . . Then he would lose not a moment in seeing her father. But he might not get a chance of seeing him alone and under circumstances favourable to his purpose. He must be ready. All at once an idea struck him . . .

All these weeks Athlyne had now and again had a vague feeling of uneasiness which he could not understand: a sort of feeling that he would some time wake and wonder what he had been fretting and fuming about. Why could he not have written to Colonel Ogilvie at any time? Even before he had left New York, or whilst he had been on board ship, or whilst the American family had been in Italy, or even when the Colonel had been in London? Why not now? After all, there was nothing in any way wrong; nothing to be ashamed of. He was of good social position; at least as good as Joy's father was. He was himself rich and wanted no fortune with his wife. He had won certain honours—a man to whose name had been suffixed V.C. and D.S.O. must be considered personally adequate for ordinary purposes. And so on. Vanity and self-interest, in addition to the working of the higher qualities, supplied many good reasons.

And yet! . . . He was always being brought up against one of two things: Colonel Ogilvie's peculiar views and character, or his own position towards him with regard to the alias. He could always find in either of these something which might cause pain or trouble to Joy. Moreover there was another matter which was a powerful factor in his conclusions, although it was one which he did not analyse or even realise. It was one that worked unconsciously; a disposition rather than an activity; a tendency rather than a thought. Lord Athlyne was Scotch and Irish; a Celt of Celts on his mother's side. He had all that underlying desire of the unknown which creates sentiment, and which is so pronounced a part of the Celtic character. This it is whence comes that clinging to the place of birth which has made the peasantry of the Green Isle for seven hundred years fight all opposing forces, from hunger to bayonets, to hold possession of their own. This it is which animated a race, century after century, to suffer and endure from their Conquerors of a more prosaic race all sorts of pain and want, and for reasons not understandable by others. Those who have lived amongst those Celts of the outlying fringes, amongst whom racial tendencies remain unaltered by changing circumstances, and by whom traditions are preserved not by historical purpose but by the exercise of faith, know that there is a Something which has a name but no external bounds or limitations, no quick principle, no settled purpose. Something which to an alien can only be described by negatives; if any idea can at all be arrived at by such—any idea however rudimentary, phantasmal or vague—it can only be acquired at all by a process of exclusions. The name is "The Gloom"; the rest is a birthright. Those who can understand it need no telling or explaining; others can no more understand it than those born without eyes can see. It is a quality opposed to no other; it can exist with any. It can co-exist with fighting, with song, with commerce. It makes no change in other powers or qualities of the children of Adam. Those who possess it can be good or bad, clever or silly, heroic or mean. It can add force to imagination, understand nature, give quiet delight or spiritual pain. And the bulk of those who have it do not think of it or even know it: or if they do, hardly ever speak of it.

Athlyne had his full share of it. Being young and strong and of a class in life which seldom lacks amusement he had not been given to self-analysis. But all the same, though he did not think of it, the force was there. In his present emotional crisis it brought the lover in him up to the Celtic ideal. An ideal so strangely saturated with love that his whole being, his aims and ambitions, his hopes and fears, his pleasures and pains yielded place to it and for the time became merged in it. To him the whole word seemed to revolve round Joy as a pivotal point. Nothing could be of any use or interest which did not have touch of her or lead to her. So, he wanted to know beyond the mere measure of intellectual belief if Joy loved him or was on the way to doing so. When he was satisfied as to this he would be free to act; but not before.

On the journey he had allowed the chauffeur to drive, as he wanted to think over the whole matter without fear of interruption. He had sat in the tonneau and made from time to time notes in his pocket-book. He had now made up his mind that he would write a letter to Colonel Ogilvie telling him the whole circumstances. This he would keep in his pocket so that at the first moment when he was satisfied as to Joy's views he could post it, in case he could not have the opportunity of a personal explanation. After dinner the second night of the journey and then in his bedroom he sat up writing the letter and then copying it out on his own note paper of which he had for the purpose brought a supply with him. When it was completed it left nothing that he could think of open to doubt. When he had got this off his mind sleep came to him.

Next day he took the wheel himself; and that day when there was fitting opportunity the car hummed along merrily at top speed. Before sunset they arrived at Bowness. There he left the car in charge of the chauffeur, on whom he again impressed the necessity for absolute silence. The man was naturally discreet, and he saw that he was in a good situation. Athlyne was satisfied on leaving him that his orders would be thoroughly carried out.

In the forenoon of the next day he took the steamer which plies along the Lake, and in due course landed at Ambleside. His heart beat quickly now and his eyes searched keenly all around him as he moved. He would not miss a chance of seeing Joy.

CHAPTER XI

THE BEAUTIFUL TWILIGHT

The first couple of days at Ambleside were a delight to Joy. In the change from the roar and ceaseless whirl of London was such a sense of peace that it influenced even the pain of her heart-hunger. Here in this lovely place, where despite the life and movement of the little town nature seemed to reign, was something to calm nerves overstrung with waiting and apprehension. It was a relief to her at first, a pleasure later, to walk about the pleasant roads with her father; to take long drives beneath shady trees or up on the hillside where the lake lay below like a panorama; to sit on the steamer's deck and drift along the beautiful lake.

Her father was now and again impatient, not with her but because of the non-arrival of the motor which he had ordered in London. It had not been quite ready when they left and so it was arranged that it should follow them. He wanted to have it in possession so that they could fly all over the region; the American in him was clamorous for movement, for speed and progress! He kept up an endless telegraphing with the motor people in London, and when at last they wired that the car was nearly ready he got a map and traced out the route. Each day he marked out a space that he thought it ought to have covered, crediting it for every hour of daylight with top speed. After all, no matter what our ages may be, we are but children and the new toy but renews the old want and the old impatience; bringing in turn the old disillusionment and the old empty-hearted discontent. And the new toy may be of any shape: even that of a motor-car—or a beating human heart.

Partly out of affection for her father and so from sympathy with him, and partly as a relief to herself, Joy looked eagerly for the coming of the car. She used to go with him to the post office when he was sending his telegrams. Indeed she never left him; and be sure he was glad of her companionship. Now and again would come over her an overwhelming wave of disappointment—grief—regret—she knew not what—when she thought of the friendship so romantically begun but failing so soon. The letters from Aunt Judy used to worry and even humiliate her. For Judy could not understand why there was no meeting; and her questions, made altogether for the girl's happiness but made in the helplessness of complete ignorance, gave her niece new concern. She had to give reasons, invent excuses. This in itself, for she was defending the man, only added fuel to her own passion. Joy's love was ripening very fast; all her nature was yielding to it. Each day seemed to make her a trifle thinner. Her eyes seemed to grow bigger and at times to glow like lamps. Whenever she could, she kept looking out on the road by which He might come. Walking or driving or in the hotel it was all the same. In the sitting-room her seat was near the window, her place at table where she could command a view. All this added to her beauty and so her father took no concern from it. He thought she was looking well; and as she was hearty and always, whilst with him, in good spirits and vivacious and even eager in her movements, he was more than satisfied.

One morning as she was sitting alone close to the window, presumably reading for she had a book in her lap, she caught sight with the tail of her eye of a figure that she knew. There was no mistaking on her part that tall, upright man with the springy step; the image was too deeply burned into her heart for that. For a fraction of a second her heart stood still; and then the wave of feeling went over her. Instinctively she drew back and kept her head low so that only her eyes were over the line of the window sill. She did not wish to be recognised—all at once. With the realisation of her woman's wishes came all the instinctive exercise of her woman's wiles. He was walking so slowly that she had time to observe him fully, to feast her eyes on him. He was looking up at the hotel, not eagerly she thought, but expectantly. This, though it did not chill her, somehow put her on guard. She slipped behind the window curtain and peeped cautiously. As he came closer to the hotel he went still more slowly. He did not come to the door as she expected, but moved along the street.

This all puzzled her; puzzled her very much. She knew that Judy had written to him of their coming to London, she had seen his reply to her letter; and Judy with her usual thoughtful kindness had mentioned—as though by chance, for she was the very soul of kindly discretion—that when she knew what locality and hotel had been fixed on for the visit to the Lakes she would tell him. It was evident, that he knew they were there and in the hotel; why, then, did he not come to see them. How she would have hurried, she thought, had she been the man and loved as she did! She had no doubting whatever of his good faith. "Perfect love casteth out fear." And doubt is but fear in a timid form. She accepted in simple good faith that he had some purpose or reason of his own. Her manifest duty to him, therefore, was not to let any wish or act of hers clash with it. So she set herself to think it all out, feeling in reality far happier than she had done for many weeks. It was not merely that she had, after long waiting, seen the man; but she was now able to do something for him—if indeed it was only the curbing of her own curiosity, her own desires.

She rose quietly and went to her bedroom which was at another side of the house—on the side towards which He had passed. Her father was writing letters and would not want her; he had said at breakfast that he would not be able to go out for an hour or two. In her room she went cautiously to her window and, again hiding behind the curtains, glanced into the street. She felt quite sad when she only saw his back as he walked slowly along. Every now and again he would stop and look round him as though admiring the place and the views as the openings between the houses allowed him to see the surrounding country. Once or twice she could see him look out under his eyebrows as though watching the hotel without appearing to do so. Presently he turned the corner of the next street to the left, moving as though he wished to go all round the hotel.

She sat down and thought, her heart beating hard. Her face was covered with both her hands. Forehead and cheeks and neck were deeply flushed; and when she took away her hands her eyes were bright and seemed to glow. She seemed filled with happiness, but all the same looked impossibly demure; as is woman's nature, playing to convention even when alone.

Before she left her room she had changed her clothes, putting on after several experiments the frock which she thought the most becoming. She did not send for her maid, but did everything for herself; even to hanging up the discarded frocks. Then she went back to the sitting room and took as before her seat at the window, keeping however a little more in the background. She wanted to see rather than to be seen. With her eyes seemingly on her book, but in reality sweeping under her lashes the approaches to the hotel like searchlights, she sat quite quietly for some time. At length the eyes suddenly fell for an instant under an uncontrollable wave of diffidence; she had seen Him pass into the garden opposite to the hotel and go secretively behind some lilac bushes opposite the doorway. But after that one droop of the eyes, there was scarce even the flicker of an eyelid; she did not want to lose a single glimpse of him.

Sitting by the window, where he could see her, for a full hour until her father appeared, she thought over the new phase of the matter. If she had ever had any real doubt as to whether Mr. Richard Hardy loved her it was all resolved now. For certain he loved her— and as much, she hoped, as she loved him! He had sought her out at Ambleside; for even in her own secret mind she never went through the pretence of trying to persuade herself that it may have been some one else that he was looking for.

But why was he so secret? Why did he not come at once into the hotel and ask to see her father. He had been invited to come; he had been made a welcome guest at the Holland. He knew their movements; he had written to Judy. But why did he keep so aloof? If he wanted to avoid them altogether he had only to keep away. Why then did he keep coming round the house and looking at it secretively? She was absolutely at a standstill every time her thinking led her to this *impasse*. But, all the same, she never questioned or doubted the man. In her own mind she was sure that he had some good reason for all he did; and it was her duty not to thwart but to help him.

She had already accepted the position of a true wife, a true lover: The man's will was law!

Then her thoughts turned as to how best she could help him. Here all her brains as well as all the instincts of her womanhood came into play; and this is a strong combination in a man's service. Her arguments ran:

As he evidently wishes his presence to be unknown she must not seem to know of it.

As he evidently wanted to know something about her she would take care that he knew what he wished, so far as she could know or effect it.

As (perhaps) he wished to see her (from afar, or at all events without proclaiming himself) she would take care that he would have plenty of opportunities.

But as he did not want Daddy to see him—at present (this last qualification she insisted on to herself) she would have to be careful that her father did not notice his presence. This she felt would be difficult, and might be dangerous; she feared that if the two men should meet just at present (another qualification equally insisted on) her father might make some quarrel or trouble.

As Daddy might make trouble this way, she must keep very close to him. She might thus be able to smooth matters, or do *something* if any occasion came.

And she must be careful that he did not notice that she saw him. This argument came straight out of her sex-artfulness. Every instinct of her being told her that such would be the most effective way of bringing the man to her. And Oh! but she did long to see him, close to her where they could see each other clearly. "Look at me!" seemed to throb through her every nerve, and make a clang of great music in her brain.

When presently Colonel Ogilvie, having finished his letters, asked her what she would like to do that morning she said she would like to go for a drive. She knew that there would be more security in the isolation of a carriage than when walking, where a chance meeting might occur at any moment.

When Athlyne, who was watching the hotel from the garden where the shrubs gave him cover, saw the landau at the door he thought he would wait and see if by any chance it might be for the Ogilvies' use. His hopes were justified when he saw Joy follow her father from the doorway. She looked radiantly beautiful; so beautiful that all his love and passion surged up in him till he felt almost suffocated. He had quite a good view of her, for she stood for a minute or two in front of the horses giving them lumps of sugar and stroking their noses. He heard the voices of both father and daughter. Colonel Ogilvie's was strong and resonant; Joy's was sweet and clear. Moreover, she spoke on purpose a little more loudly than usual; she knew that He was listening and would like to hear her voice.

"Tell him where you would like to go, little girl."

"Anywhere you think best, coachman; provided we get a good view. We had better be back here in about an hour. Then, Daddy, we shall keep quiet after lunch—if that will suit you, dear. After tea we can go out again and have a long drive and come back in the lovely English twilight. Of course if you would like to, Daddy. I must say there is one institution that I wish we had in America."

"And what is that daughter?"

"The twilight! Since I have seen it, our own night seems very cruel! It shuts down too fast. For my own part if ever I fall in love—" here the words became indistinct; she was entering the carriage.

She had chosen her words on purpose. She wished to let Him know the plans for the day. She knew well that at the end of the hour he would be waiting, hidden in the garden, to see their return. Thus he would see her again, and she by going quickly to the window would perhaps see him again. She had spoken of not going out again till after tea, because she did not wish to keep him all day at his post; she knew that this would happen if he were in ignorance of her movements. He, poor fellow! would have to get lunch. . . . She was exercising for him already the solicitude of a wife for a husband. As to the remarks about twilight, that had a double origin. Firstly it was quite true; she had long had it in her mind. Secondly it was a sort of *ballon d'essai;* it might point or lead somewhere. Where that might be she knew not; but she had a vague hopeful feeling that there was an answer—somewhere.

As to the remark about ever loving. Well! she could not have explained that herself. All she knew was that she had a sudden desire to mention the word. . . .

Athlyne profited by the lesson; but his acts were not quite what Joy had anticipated. She, thinking from the feminine standpoint, had taken it that he would remain at his post until the return and then avail himself of the longer period for rest and food. But Athlyne was a soldier and had as such long ago learned the maxim that in route marching the camp should be set beyond the bridge. Moreover in the strenuous life of the Boer war he had superadded the wisdom of taking his meal at the first opportunity. As soon as the carriage had disappeared from view he went straight into the hotel and ordered his lunch in the Coffee-room. He was really hungry, and the lamb and salad were excellent; but had he not been hungry, and had the food been poor, he would have enjoyed it without knowing its inferiority. Everything was good to him this morning; he had seen Joy!

He was out in the garden in good time. Fortunately so, from his point of view. For Joy, believing that he would be still waiting, kept the coachman up to time. It might well have been that they had met in the hall.

The drive had increased the girl's loveliness, if such were possible. Her eyes were bright, there was fine colour in her cheeks, and her voice and manner were full of vivacity. The bright sun and the sweet, strong air had braced her; and perhaps some inward emotion had exercised the same effect. One quick glance under her eyelashes as they drove towards the hotel had shewn her the outline of a tall figure close to the lilacs in the garden. As her father helped her from the carriage with all his habitual gallantry of manner she said in a clear voice—Athlyne across the street heard every word:

"That drive was exquisite! Wasn't it Daddy? Thank you so much for it! The lights and shadows on the hills were simply divine. It would be nice to go again to-morrow in something of the same direction. We might go about the same hour, if it would suit you, and see the same effects again!"

When they had gone in Athlyne waited a little while in the garden. He sat in the sunshine on a garden seat placed in the centre of the grass plot. He was not afraid of being seen at present, and as he knew that Joy and her father were in the house he did not even try to look for them. Had he chosen a position for the purpose of giving Joy pleasure he could not have done better than this. From behind her window curtain she could see him plainly. To her he made a beautiful picture, of which the natural setting was complete: the background of sweet pale lilac, the dropping gold of the laburnum and the full red of scarlet hawthorn; his feet in the uncut grass starred with daisies. She had a long, long view of him, watching every movement and expression with eager eyes. One thing he did which she could not understand. He took from his breast pocket an envelope; this he opened and took from it a letter. Instead of reading it, however, he sat for a long time with it in his hand. Then with a quick movement he put it back in the envelope, moistened the flap with his lips and closed it. Joy's idea had been that it might have been

Judy's letter which he had intended to re-read; but this could not be. For an instant a spasm of pain had gripped her heart as the thought came that it might have been from some other woman. But that idea she swept aside imperiously. Now she knew that it was some letter of his own, and the questioning of her brain began to assail her heart:

Whom could he be writing to? What could he be writing about? Why did he have a finished letter in his pocket, not even sealed up?

If she had known the truth she would have sat quiet, not with perturbation but in a silent ecstasy. Athlyne had made up his mind that if occasion did not serve for his seeing Joy alone he would send the letter to Colonel Ogilvie and risk being refused. In such case he would have to take another course, and try to obtain her consent in spite of her father's wishes. He did not, however, intend to send the letter yet. His first hope was too sweet to abandon without good cause. His closing the letter was but an impulsive expression of his feeling.

Suddenly he stood up and moved out of the garden. This did not puzzle her, but awoke all her curiosity. She had a wild desire to see where he was going; but as she could not follow him she made up her mind to present patience. She watched from her window till he had passed out of sight. She was glad that she was concealed behind the curtain when she saw him at the furthest point of sight turn and give a long look back at the hotel. Then she went to her room to get ready for lunch.

Athlyne felt that he must do something to let off steam. Movement of some kind was necessary in his present frame of mind. For his pleasure was not unmixed. He had seen Joy, and she was looking more radiantly beautiful than ever. But she had said one thing that sent a pang through him: "if I ever fall in love." There could hardly be any doubt of her sincerity; she was talking to her father quite alone and unconscious that he of all men was within earshot. "If I ever fall in love," that meant that she had not yet done so. It would be wise to wait before sending the letter so that he might see if that happy time had come or had even begun to peep above the horizon. Unconsciously he took from his pocket the letter and his pocket-book, put the former into the latter and returned it to its place.

Athlyne was no fool; but he was only a man, and as such took for gospel every word spoken by the woman he loved. Had Joy been present and known his difficulty, and had cared to express herself then as she would have done later, she would have smiled at him as she said:

"Why you dear old goose how could I fall in love with you when I had done that already!"

Had Aunt Judy been commenting on the comment she would have said in her genial cynicism:

"A woman—or a man either—can only fall in love once in a life time; with the same person!"

Athlyne telephoned his chauffeur to whom he had already sent a wire to be prepared, and in a time to be computed by minutes met him outside Ambleside. There he took the wheel himself, telling the man to meet him a little before five o'clock. He felt that he must be alone. He went slowly so long as he was near the town; but when he found himself on a clear road, over which he could see for a long way ahead, the index went round to "speed" and as the car swept over the ground its rush kept pace with his own thoughts.

He went about a hundred miles before he regained anything like calm. Trying afterwards to recall the sequence of his thoughts he never could arrive at any sort of conclusion regarding them.

The only thing definite in his mind was that he wanted to see Joy again, and soon. He knew they would be starting out after tea time which meant, he knew, something after five o'clock; and not for a world of chrysolite would he miss being there. Outside Ambleside he met the chauffeur whom he sent back to Bowness; he did not want his car to be too much *en evidence* at Ambleside at present. He had a wash and a cup of tea at another hotel; and at five strolled back to his nook in the garden.

By this time Joy had made up her mind that he *might* come back that evening though—with still her protective instinct, partly for herself but more for him—she had quite made up her mind that even if he should not come she would not be disappointed. He was not to be blamed in any way, now or hereafter. How could he be? It would not be fair. A few minutes before five she took her place at the window, but sitting so far back this time that she could not be seen from without. She herself could see out, but only by raising her head high. This she did now and again, but very cautiously. She felt a sort of diffidence, a certain measure of shamefacedness lest he should see her again and suspect anything. We are very sensitive as to the discovery of truth by others when we are ourselves trying to deceive ourselves! The few minutes passed slowly, very slowly. Then when once more she looked out a great thrill of joy shook her. He *had* come. If doubt there had been, it could no longer exist. Her heart beat, her face flushed, she trembled with a sort of ecstasy; the waves of high passion swept her. She was half inclined to stand boldly in the window and let him see her; to let him see that she saw him; to run out to him and fall into his arms. There is no boldness that love will not commit when it is true! She felt this, though not consciously. There was no need for consciousness, for thought, for argument. She knew!

It was perhaps just as well that her father came into the room. He brought a sense of sanity with him; she felt that consciously enough. Her mere faint sigh of regret was sufficient proof.

Joy did not walk down the staircase; she floated, as though matter had ceased to exist and the soul was free. She stood for a minute on the step looking out at the view; but presently kept changing her pose so that her face might be seen with both profiles, as well as the full face. If He had come there to see her He should not be disappointed—if she could help it.

That drive was a dream, an ecstasy. At first there was a miserable sense that each turn of the wheels took them farther apart; but shortly this was lost in the overwhelming sense of gladness. She could have sung—danced—shouted. She wanted some physical expression of her feeling. Then the excitement settled down to a quiet tingling happiness, a sense of peace which was ineffable and complete.

> ". . . if that all of animated nature
> Be but organic harps diversely framed
> That tremble into thought as o'er them sweeps
> Plastic and vast one intellectual breeze
> At once the soul of each and God of all."

So sung, a century before, a poet of that sweet cult of the school centred in the very area in which she moved; and if his thoughts were true there was a true act of worship that sunny afternoon on the rising hills beyond the lakehead. For happiness is not merely to be at rest. It is to be with God, to carry out to the full His wish that His children should appreciate and enjoy the powers and good things given them by His hands. And when that happiness is based on love—and there is no true happiness on aught that is not high—the love itself is of the soul and quivers with the flapping of its wings. Then indeed can we realize that marvellous promise of the words of the Master:

"Blessed are the pure in heart for they shall see God." Wordsworth and those who held with him saw God and worshipped Him in those myriad beauties of the lake they loved; and as the beauty and its immortal truth soothed and purified their souls, so was the spirit of the love-sick girl cleansed of all dross. How at such a time, when the soul swam free in grateful worship, was there place for anything that was not clean? Her father thought, as he looked at her and heard the ring of her voice, that he had never seen her look better or happier. She was full of spirits, gay, sweet, tender; and yet there was over her such a grace of gentle gravity that the old man felt himself saying to himself:

"My little girl is a woman!"

That mellow afternoon was to her lovely; the trees and shrubs, the flowers, the fields. The singing of the birds was ethereal music; the lights and shadows were the personal manifestation of Nature's God. Her heart, her sympathy, her nature were at full tide; all overflowing and in their plenitude full.

The long summer afternoon faded into the softness of twilight during the homeward journey. Perhaps it was the yielding to its mysterious influence which made Joy so still; perhaps it was that she was drawing nearer to the man whom she adored. Her father neither knew nor took note of it. He saw that his little girl was silent in an ecstasy of happiness in that soft twilight of which she had spoken so tenderly; and he was content. He too sat silent, yielding himself to the influence of the beauty around him.

When they reached the hotel Joy seemed to wake from a dream; but she lost none of her present placidity, none of her content.

One form of happiness had given way to another, that was all. As she stood on the steps, waiting whilst her father was giving the coachman his instructions for the morrow, she tried to peer into the lilac bushes in the garden. She had a sort of intuition—nay more that an intuition, an actual certainty—that He was again behind them. And once more she so stood and moved that he might see her face as he would. When her father turned to come in she took his arm and pointed to the sky:

"Oh look, Daddy, the beautiful twilight! Is it not exquisite!" Then impulsively she put her hand to her lips and threw a kiss to it—over the square by way of the lilacs. Her voice was languishing music as she said softly, but clearly enough to heard in the garden:

"Good night; Good night beloved! Good night! Good night!"

And Athlyne peering through the bushes heard the words with a beating of his heart which made his temples throb. His only wish at the moment was that it might have been that the words had been addressed to him.

That evening before going to dress for dinner Joy went to the window and pulled aside the blind so that she stood outside it. The dusk was now thick; the day had gone, but the moon had not yet risen. It was impossible to see much; only the outline of the trees, and out on the grass the shadowy form of a man seated. There was one faint red spark of brightness, face high, such as might be the tip of a cigar.

When she came back into the room her father raised his face from his book:

"Why how pale you are little girl. I am afraid that long drive must have tired you. You were quite rosy when we arrived home. You had better sleep it out in the morning. If mother sees you pale she will blame me, you know. And Judy—well Judy will be Judy in her own way."

CHAPTER XII

ECHO OF A TRAGEDY

ATHLYNE had one other day almost similar to the last. This time he came to Ambleside a little earlier; fortunately so, for Joy had got up early. When he came into the square she was standing in the window looking out. Not in his direction; did a woman ever do such a stupid thing when at the first glance she had caught sight of the man far off. No, this time she appeared to be eagerly watching two tiny children toddling along the street hand in hand. He had time for a good look at her before she changed her position. This was only when the children had disappeared—and he had gained the shelter of the lilacs.

Love is a blindness—in certain ways. It never once occurred to Athlyne that Joy might have seen him, might have even known of his being at Ambleside or in its neighbourhood. Any independent onlooker or any one not bound by the simplicity and unquestioning faith of ardent love would at least have doubted whether there was not some possible intention in Joy's movements. His faith however saved him from pain, that one pain from which true love can suffer however baseless it may be—doubt. Early morning took him to Ambleside; he only went back to Bowness when those windows of the hotel which he knew were darkened for the night.

The second day of waiting and watching was just like the first, with only the addition that the hearts of both the young people were more clamant, each to each; and that the rising passion of each was harder to control. The same routine of going out and returning was observed by the Ogilvies, and each of the lovers had tumultuous moments when the other was within view. More than once Athlyne was tempted to put his letter in the post or to leave it at the hotel; but each time Joy's chance phrase: "If I ever fall in love" came back to him as a grim warning. He knew that if he once declared himself to Colonel Ogilvie the whole truth must come out, and then his title and fortune might be extraneous inducements to the girl. Whenever he came to this point in his reasoning he thrust the letter deeper into his pocket and his lips shut tight. He would win Joy on his mere manhood and his manhood's love—if at all!

By the post next morning Colonel Ogilvie and Joy both got letters from Italy. That of the former was from his wife who announced that they were just starting for London where they wished to remain for a few days in order to do some shopping. When this was done she would wire him and he could run up to London and bring them down with him. This pleased him, for he was certain that by then he would have his automobile. He felt in a way that his pride was at stake on this point. He had told his women folk that the car would be ready, and he wished to justify. He wired off at once to the agents, in even a sterner spirit than usual, as to the cause of delay. For excuses had come in a most exasperating way. Long after it had been reported that the car had started and had even proceeded a considerable distance on the way he was told that there had been an error and that by some strange mistake the progress made by a car long previously ordered by another customer had been reported; but that Colonel Ogilvie's esteemed order was well in hand and that delivery of the car was daily—hourly—expected; and that at once on its receipt by the writer it would be forwarded to Ambleside either with a trusty chauffeur or by train as the purchaser might wish. Colonel Ogilvie fumed but was powerless. He wanted the car and at once; so it was useless for him to cancel the contract. He could only wait and hope; and console himself with such attenuated expressions of disapproval as were permissible in the ethics of the telegraphic system.

Joy's letter was from Judy. It was in her usual bright style and full of affection, sympathy and understanding, as was customary in her letters to her niece. Judy had of late been much disturbed in her mind about the future, and as she feared Joy might be taking to heart the same matters as she did and in the same way, she tried to help the other. She knew from Colonel Ogilvie's letters to his wife which they talked over together that he was seriously hurt and pained by the neglect of Mr. Hardy. Indeed in his last letter he had declared that in spite of the high opinion he had formed of him from his brave and ready action he never wished to see his face again. To Judy this meant much, the most that could be of possible ill; Joy's happiness might be at stake. The aunt, steeped through and through with knowledge of the world and character—a knowledge gained from her own heart, its hopes and pains and from bitter experience of the woes of others—knew that her niece would suffer deeply in case of any rupture between her father and the man who had saved her life. It was not merely from imaginative sympathy that she derived her belief. She had had many and favourable opportunities of studying Joy closely, and she had in her own mind no doubt whatever that the girl's affections were given beyond recall to the handsome stranger. So in her letter she tried to guard her from the pain of present imaginings and yet to prepare her subtly for the possibility of disappointment in the future. Her letter in its important part ran:

"Your father is undoubtedly very angry with Mr. Hardy; and though I believe that his anger may have a slight basis it is altogether excessive. We do not know yet what Mr. Hardy's limitations of freedom may be. After all, darling, we do not know anything as yet of his circumstances or his surroundings. He may have a thousand calls on his time which we neither know nor understand. For all we can tell he may have a wife already—though this I do not believe or accept for a moment. And you don't either, my dear! Of course this is all a joke. We *know* he is free as to marriage, though I don't believe his heart is—Eh! Puss! But seriously if you ever get a chance tell him to try to be very nice to your father. Old men are often more sensitive in some things that young ones, more sensitive than even we women are supposed to be. So when he does come to see you both—for he *will* come soon (if he hasn't come already)—don't keep him all to yourself, but contrive somehow that your father can have a little chat with him. You needn't go altogether away you know, my dear. Don't sit so far away that he can't see you nor you him (this is a whisper expressed in writing) and I dare say you will like to hear all they say to each other. But if he says a word about seeing your daddy alone for a moment, if he begins to look ill at ease or to get red and then pale and red again, or stammers and clears his throat do you just get up quietly and go out of the room without a word in the most natural way in the world, just as if you were doing some little household duty. I suppose I needn't tell you this; you know it just as well as I do, though I have known it by experience and you can not.

You know how I know it darling though I never told you this part of it. Women are Cowards. *We* know it though we don't always say so, and we even disguise it from others now and then. But in such a time as I have mentioned we are *all* Cowards. We couldn't stay if we would. We *want* to get away and hide our heads just as we do when it thunders. But what an awful lot of *rot* I am talking. When Mr. Hardy and your father meet they will, I am sure, have plenty to talk about without either you or me being the subject of it. They are both sportsmen and fond of horses—and a lot of things. It is only if they don't meet that I am afraid of. I am writing by the way to Mr. Hardy this post to know where he is at present and where he has been. I shall of course write you when I hear; or if there be anything important I shall wire. We are off to London and it is possible that whilst we are there we may have unexpected meetings with all sorts of friends and calls from them. I hope, darling, that by the time we reach Ambleside we shall find you *blooming*, full of happiness and health and freshness, the very embodiment of your name."

The letter both disquieted Joy and soothed her. There were suggestions of fear, but there was also a consistent strain of hope. Judy would never have said such things if she did not believe them. Moreover she herself knew what Judy did not; her aunt hadn't peeped from behind window blinds at a tall figure behind lilac bushes or sitting in the darkness with only a fiery cigar tip to mark his presence. Poor Judy! The girl's sympathetic heart, made more sympathetic by her own burning love, ached when she thought of the older woman's lonely, barren life. She too had loved—and been loved; had hoped and feared, and waited. The very knowledge of how a woman would feel when the man was asking formally for parental sanction disclosed something of which the girl had never thought. She had always known Judy in such a motherly and elderly aspect that she had never realised the possibility of her having ever been in love; any more that she had given consideration to the love-making of her own mother. Now she was surprised to find that she too had been young, had loved, and had pleasures and heart-pains of her own. This set her thinking. The process of thought was silent, but its conclusion found outward expression; the girl understood now. The secret of her life—the true secret was unveiled at last:

"Poor Aunt Judy. Oh, poor Aunt Judy!"

Athlyne's letter reached him a day later, having been sent on from London. It was a fairly bulky one, with a good many sheets of foreign post, written hastily in a large bold hand.

"My Dear Friend:

I have been, and am, much concerned about you. I gather from his letters that Colonel Ogilvie has been much disappointed at not having heard from you. And I want, if you will allow me to take the liberty, to speak to you seriously about it. You will give me this privilege I know—if only for the fact that I am an old maid; for the same Powers that made me an old maid have made me an old woman, and such is entitled, I take it, to forbearance, if not to respect. You should—you really should be more considerate towards Colonel Ogilvie. He is an old man—much older than you perhaps think, for he bears himself as proudly as in his younger days. But the claim on you is not merely from his years; that claim must appeal to all. From you there is one more imperative still, one which is personal and paramount: he is under so very deep an obligation to you. A matter which from another would pass unconsidered as an act of thoughtfulness must now, when it is due to you, seem to him like a studied affront. I put it this way because I know you are a man of noble nature, and that generosity is to such even a stronger urge than duty—if such a thing be possible. In certain matters he is sensitive beyond belief. Even to a degree marked in a place where men still hold that their lives rest behind every word and deed, every thought or neglect towards another. I have some hesitation in mentioning this lest you should think I am summoning Fear to the side of Duty. But you are above such a misunderstanding, I am sure. Oh my dear friend do think of some of the rest of us. You have saved the life of our darling Joy—the one creature in whom all our loves are centred. Naturally we all want to see you again—to make much of you—to show you in our own poor way how deeply we hold you in our hearts. But if Colonel Ogilvie thinks himself insulted—that is how he regards any neglect however trivial—he acts on that belief, and there is no possible holding him back. He looks on it as a sacred duty to avenge affront. You must not blame him for it. In your peaceful English life you have I think no parallel to the ungovernable waves of passion that rage in the hearts of Kentuckians when they consider their honour is touched. Ah! we poor women know it who have to suffer in silence and wait and wait, and wait; and when the worst is made known to us, to seal up the founts of our grief and pretend that we too agree with the avenging of wrong. For it is our life to be silent in men's quarrels. We are not given a part—any part. We are not supposed to even look on. It is another world from ours, and we have to accept it so. Please God may you never know what it is to be in or on the fringe of a Feud. Well I know its dread, its horror! My own life that years ago was as bright and promising as any young life can be; when the Love that had dawned on my girlhood rose and beat with noonday heat on my young-womanhood made it seem as if heaven had come down to earth. And then the one moment of misunderstanding—the quick accusation—the quicker retort—and my poor heart lying crushed between the bodies of two men whom I loved each in his proper way. . . Think of what I say, if only on account of what I have suffered.

"Forgive me! But my anxiety lest any such blight should come across a young life that I love far far beyond my own is heavy on me. I have lost myself in sad thoughts of a bitter past. . . Indeed you must take it that my earnestness in this matter is shown in the lurid light of that past. I have been silent on it always. Never since the black cloud burst over me have I said a word to a soul—not to my sister—nor to Joy whom I adore and whose questioning to me of my 'love affair'—as they still call it when they speak of it—is so sweet a tightening bond between us. I have only said to her: 'and then he died,' and my heart has seemed to stop beating. Be patient with me and don't blame me. You are a man and can be tolerant. Think not of me or any gloom of my life but only that makes me sadly, grimly, terribly in earnest when I see similar elements of tragedy drawing close to each other before my eyes. You may be inclined to laugh at me—though I know you will not—and to put down my thinking of possible great quarrels arising from such small causes as 'an old maid's' fears. But when I have known the awful effect of a mere passing word, misunderstood to such disastrous result, no wonder that I have fears. It is due to that very cause that my fears are those of an old maid. I suppose I need not ask you to be sure to keep all this locked in your own breast. It is my secret; I have shared it with you because I deem such necessary for the happiness of—of others. I have kept it so close that not even those nearest and dearest to me have even suspected it. The rowdiness of spirit—as it seems to me—which other friends call fun and brightness and high spirits and other such insulting terms—has been my domino as I have passed through the hollow hearted carnival of life. Judge then how earnest I am when I put it aside and raise my mask for you a stranger whom I have seen but twice; I who even then was but an accessory—a super on the little stage where we began to act our little—comedy or tragedy which is it to be?

"There! I have opened to you my memory, not my heart. That you have no use for. After such a letter as this I shall not pretend to go back to the Proprieties, the *Convenances*. If I am right in my surmise—you can guess what that is or why have you written to the old rowdy aunt instead. . . there is every reason why I should be frank. But remember that I hold—and have hitherto held—what I believe to be your secret as sacredly as I hope you will hold mine. And if I am right—and from my knowledge and insight won by past suffering I pray to God that I am—you have no time to lose to make matters right, and possibly to save the world one more sorrowful heart like my own. It is only a word that is wanted—a morning call—a visit of ceremony. Anything that will keep open the doors of friendship which you unlocked by your own bravery. We are going in a day or two to Ambleside. In the meantime we shall be in London at Brown's Hotel Albemarle Street where my sister, and incidentally myself, shall be glad to see you. . . .

"Won't you let me have a line as soon as you can after you get this. I am torn with anxiety till I know what you intend to do about visiting Colonel Ogilvie. Again forgive me,

Your true friend,
JUDY.

"P. S.—I shall not dare to read this over, lest when I had I should not have courage to send it. Accept it then with all its faults and be tolerant of them—and of me."

Athlyne read the letter through without making a pause or even an internal comment. That is how a letter should be read; to follow the writer's mind, not one's own, and so take in the sequence of thoughts and the general atmosphere as well as the individual facts. As he read he felt deeply moved. There was in the letter that manifest sincerity which showed that it was straight from the heart. And heart speaks to heart, whatever may be the medium, if the purpose is sincere. It was a surprise to him to learn that Miss Judy's high and volatile spirits rested on so sad a base. His appreciation of her worthiness came in his unconscious resolution that when he and Joy were married Aunt Judy should be an honoured guest in the house, and that they would try to lighten, with what sympathy and kindness they could, the dark shadows of her life.

He sat with the letter in his hand for some time. He was sitting in the window of the hotel at Bowness looking out on the lake. It was still early and the life of the day had hardly begun. At Bowness the life was that of the tourists and visitors and it would still be an hour or more before they began to move out on their objectives. He had very many various and whirling thoughts, but supreme amongst them was one: Time was flying. He must not delay, for every hour was more and more jeopardising his chance of winning the woman he loved. He realized to the full that his neglect of Colonel Ogilvie, for so it was being construed, was making—had made—a difficulty for him. Each day, perhaps each hour, was widening the breach; if he did not take care he might end with the door permanently closed against him. As he came to the conclusion of his reasoning he drew once more from his pocket the sealed letter to Colonel Ogilvie, and stood up. He fancied that his determination was made that he would see Colonel Ogilvie as soon as possible and broach the subject to him. As however he went towards the boat—for he was going to Ambleside by water—he postponed the intention of an immediate interview. He would wait this one day and see what would turn up. If nothing happened likely to further his wishes he would whilst at Ambleside the next morning put the letter in the post. Then he would hold himself ready for the interview with Joy's father for which the letter asked.

At Ambleside he took his place behind the lilacs in the garden and kept watch on the window where Joy was wont to appear. A little before breakfast-time she appeared there for a brief space, and then moved back into the room. He waited with what patience he could till nearly eleven o'clock when the same carriage which they used drove up to the door; waiting became then an easier task. Presently Colonel Ogilvie came out and stood on the steps. Athlyne wondered; this was the first time that Joy had not been before him. Throwing his eyes around in vague wondering as to the cause he saw Joy standing in the window dressed and pulling on her gloves. She was radiantly beautiful. Her colour was a little heightened and her lovely grey eyes shone like stars. Her gaze was fixed so that her eyes seemed to look straight before her but beyond him. The look made him quiver as though he felt it were directed at him, and his knees began to tremble with a mighty, vague longing. For quite a minute she stood there, till her eyes falling she caught sight of her father standing by the carriage below. She drew back quickly and almost immediately appeared at the hall-door, saying:

"I am so sorry, Daddy. I hope I did not keep you waiting too long!"

"Not a bit little girl. It is a pleasure to me to wait for you; to do anything for you, my dear. Whatever else is the use of being a father."

"You dear! May we go to-day up the mountain road where we can look over the lake. I want you to have a nice glimpse of it again before you go."

Here Athlyne's heart sank for an instant. This was the first idea he had of any intention of moving, and it actually shook him. Joy had as usual a handful of sugar for the horses. She went to the off side horse first and gave him his share. Then when she stood at the head of the other, her face toward the lilacs, she turned to her father and said in a low, thrilling tone:

"Daddy, am I nice to-day? *Look at me!*" She stood still whilst the old man looked at her admiringly, proudly, fondly.

"You are peerless, little girl. Peerless! that's it!" She was evidently pleased at the compliment, for her colour rose to a deep flush. Her grey eyes shone through it like two great grey suns. Whilst her father was speaking to the coachman she gave the other horse, now impatient, his share of the sugar and stood looking across the road. Athlyne could hardly contain himself. The few seconds, although flying so fast, were momentous. Past and present rushed together to the creation of a moment of ecstasy. The sound of the words swept him; the idea and all it rewoke and intensified, transfigured his very soul. And then he heard her say in a low, languorous voice which vibrated:

"Thank you Daddy for such a sweet compliment. I am glad I said 'Look at me!'" As she spoke it seemed to Athlyne that her eyes fixed across the road sent their lightnings straight into his heart. And yet it did not even occur to him at the moment that the words could have been addressed to him.

During the drive Joy kept her father interested in all around them. He saw that she was elated and happy, and it made his heart glad to that receptive mood which is the recrudescence of youth. In the girl's mind to-day several trains of thought, all of them parental of action, went on together. She did not analyze them; indeed she was hardly conscious of them. The mechanism of mind was working to a set purpose, but one which was temperamental rather than intentional—of sex and individual character rather than of a studied conclusion. For that morning was to her momentous. She knew it with all her instincts. Unconsciously she drew conclusions from facts without waiting to develop their logical sequence.

A telegram had arrived from Mrs. Ogilvie saying that she and Judy were now ready to leave London and, as her husband had said that he wished to escort them to Ambleside, they would be prepared on his coming to leave on the next morning or whatever later time he might fix. After a glance at the time-table he had wired back that he would go up on that night, and that they would all start on the following morning. Joy had offered to accompany him, but he would not have it: "No, little girl," he said. "Travel at night is all very well for men; but it takes it out of women. I want your mother to see the bright, red-cheeked girl that has been with me for the last week, and not a pale, worn-out draggled young woman with her eyes heavy with weariness. You stay here, my dear, and get plenty of air and sunshine. You will not be afraid to be here alone with your maid!" Joy smiled:

"Not a bit, Daddy! I shall walk and drive all day and perhaps go down the Lake in a boat. If I do the latter I shall take Eugenie with me and we shall lunch down at Newby Bridge. We shall be home here in good time to drive over and meet you all at the station at Windmere."

From that moment Joy hardly left her father out of her sight. Instinctively she knew that the chance of her life had come. She had a conviction—it was more than a mere idea or even a belief—that if she were alone whilst her father was up in London or on the way down, that figure which even now was hidden by the lilacs would abandon secretive ways and come out into the open where she could see him close, and hear the sound of his voice—that voice whose every note made music in her ears. It was the presence of her father which kept him hidden. It was imperative, both in accordance with his wishes as well as from her own apprehensions of what might happen if they should meet unexpectedly before she had time to warn him, that no mischance should prevent an early meeting, free from any suspicion between herself and Mr. Hardy. When Daddy was well on his way. . . . Here she would close her eyes; definite thought was lost in a languorous ecstasy. The coming day would mean to her everything or . . . .

The drive was a fairly long one and they did not get back till nearly one o'clock. Colonel Ogilvie had said to Joy:

"I shall have a good time to-day, have plenty of fresh air and be ready for sleep when I get into the train. As I shall arrive early in the morning I shall have time to express my opinions on their conduct to those automobile people. They won't expect my coming and be able to get out of the way. I fancy it will do me good to say what I feel; or at any rate enough to give them some indication of what I could say, and shall say if there is any further delay in the matter."

When they arrived Joy went at once into the hotel leaving her father to tell the coachman at what hour to be ready for the afternoon drive. She went straight to the window and, keeping as usual behind the curtain, looked over at the lilac bushes. She could see through the foliage that there was *some one* there, and that satisfied her. She would have liked to have instructed the driver herself so that she would have been sure that he knew; but on this occasion a wave of diffidence suddenly overwhelmed her. Times were coming when she would not be able to afford the luxury of such an emotion, so she grasped it whilst she could.

Colonel Ogilvie was to catch the train from Windermere at nine o'clock, so the second drive should come after lunch and not after tea; and when she was in her own room, Joy feared that He might miss them. When, however, before going downstairs she looked out of the window she saw that he was still at his post. Athlyne's campaigning experience had had its own psychology. Seeing that there was some change in the Ogilvie day he had arranged his own plans to meet it. Whilst they had been taking their morning drive he had provided himself with some sandwiches; he had determined not to leave his post until he knew more. Joy's words had all day rung in his ears, and he was now and again distracted with doubts. Was it possible that there had been any meaning or intention in her words more than was apparent? Was the spontaneity consequent on some deep feeling which evoked memory? Could he believe that she really. . . . He would wait now before sending the letter, whatever came. In that he was adamant.

During the drive Joy was mainly silent. It was not the silence of thought; it was simply spiritual quiescence. She knew that the rest of the day was so laid out that it was unlikely it could be marred by an untoward accident. There was this in His persistent waiting that she had come to trust it. There was some intention, so manifest, though what it was was unknown to her, that it was hardly to be disturbed by any sudden exigency. She lived at the moment in a world of calm, a dream-world of infinite happiness. Now and again she woke to the presence of her father and then poured on him in every way in which a young woman can all the treasures of her thought and affection. This made the old man so happy that he too was content to remain silent when she ceased to speak.

When they got back to the hotel, she spoke to the driver: "You will be here at eight o'clock please, as you will have to drive Colonel Ogilvie to the station at Windermere in good time to catch the nine o'clock train. I shall not want you in the morning as I intend to take a walk; but you must be at Windermere to meet my father at five o'clock. If to-morrow afternoon there is any change in his plans he will wire the hotel people and they will let you know. Perhaps you had better call here on your way to Windermere as I may go over in the carriage. But if I am not here do not wait for me; I may possibly walk over. When you have left Colonel Ogilvie at Windermere to-night you will have to leave me back here. I am going to the depot with him."

Then she went into the doorway, and hurried to the sitting-room where she looked out into the garden—where the lilacs grew.

CHAPTER XIII

INSTINCTIVE PLANNING

Man's unconscious action is a strange thing. Athlyne had just heard words which took from him a strain under which he had suffered for a whole week of waiting and watching; words which promised him the opportunity for which he had longed for many weeks. His nerves had been strung to tension so high that now it would seem only natural if the relief sent him into a sort of delirium. But he quietly lit a cigar, taking care that it was properly cut and properly lit, and smoked luxuriously as he moved across the garden and into the street. Joy from her window saw him go, and her admiration of his ease and self possession and magnificent self-reliance sent fresh thrills through her flesh.

When Athlyne went out of the garden he had evidently made up his mind, consciously or unconsciously, to some other point in connection with the motor for he visited such shops as were open and made some purchases—caps, veils, cloaks and such like gear suitable for the use of a tall young lady. These he took with him in a hired carriage to the hotel at Bowness, where he added them to certain others already sent from London. Then he told the chauffeur to give the car a careful overhauling so that it be in perfect order, and went for a stroll up the Lake.

Shortly he was in a mental and physical tumult; the period which had elapsed since he heard the news of Colonel Ogilvie's coming departure had been but the prelude to the storm. At first he could not think; he had no words, no sequence of ideas, not even vague intentions. He had only sensations; and these though they moved and concentrated every nerve in his body were without even physical purpose. He went like one in a dream. But in the background of his mind was a fact which stood out firm and solid like the profile of a mountain seen against the glow of a western sunset. Joy would be alone to-morrow; the opportunity he waited for was at last at hand! The recognition of this seemed to pull him together, to set all his faculties working simultaneously; and as each had a different method the tumult was in reducing them to unison—in achieving one resultant from all the varying forces. Gradually out of the chaos came the first clear intent: he must so master the whole subject that when the opportunity had come he should be able to avail himself of it to the full. From this he proceeded to weigh the various possibilities, till gradually he began to realise what vague purpose had been behind his wish to have his automobile in perfect working order. It did not even occur to him that with such machinery at his command he might try to carry her off, either without her consent or with it. All that he wanted in the first instance was to have fitting opportunity of discovering how Joy regarded him. The last twenty-four hours had opened to his mind such glorious possibilities that every word she had said, every look on her eloquent face (though such looks had manifestly not been intended for him) had a place in a chain which linked her heart to his. "Look at me!" "I am glad I asked you to look at me!" though spoken to her father seemed to have another significance. It was as though an eager thought had at last found expression. "Good night! Good night, beloved!" though ostensibly spoken to the twilight was breathed with such fervour, with such languishing eyes and with such soft pouting of scarlet lips that it seemed impossible that it should have other than a human objective. These thoughts swept the man into a glow of passion. He was young and strong and ardent, and he loved the woman with all his heart; with all his soul; with all the strength of human passion. It is a mistake to suppose—as some abstract thinkers seem to do always, and most people at some moment of purely spiritual exaltation—that the love of a man and a woman each for the other is, even at its very highest, devoid of physical emotion. The original Creator did not manifestly so intend. The world of thought is an abstract world whose inner shrine is where soul meets soul. The world of life is the world of the heart, and its beating is the sway of the pendulum between soul and flesh. The world of flesh is the real world; wrought of physical atoms in whose recurrent groupings is the elaborated scheme of nature. Into this world has been placed Man to live and rule. To this end his body is fixed with various powers and complications and endurances; with weaknesses and impulses and yieldings; with passions to animate, with desires to attract, and animosities to repel. And as the final crowning of this wondrous work, the last and final touch of the Creator's hand, Sex for the eternal renewing of established forces. How can souls be drawn to souls when such are centred in bodies which mutually repel? How can the heart quicken its beats when it may not come near enough to hear the answering throb? No! If physical attraction be not somewhere, naught can develop. Judy, the outspoken, had once almost horrified a little group of matrons who were discussing the interest which a certain young cleric was beginning to take in one of the young female parishioners. When one of them said, somewhat sanctimoniously, that his interest was only in the salvation of her immortal soul, that he was too good a man to ever think of falling in love as ordinary men do, the vivacious old maid replied:

"Not a bit of it, my dear! When a man troubles himself about an individual young woman's soul you may be quite certain that his eyes have not neglected her body. And moreover you will generally, if not always, find that she has a pair of curving red lips, or a fine bust, or a well-developed figure somewhere!"

Athlyne loved Joy in all ways, so that the best of his nature regulated the standard of his thoughts. His love was no passing fancy which might or might not develop, flame up, and fade away. He had, he felt, found the other half of him, lost in the primeval chaos; and he wanted the union to be so complete that it would outlive the clashing of worlds in the final cataclysm. Healthy people are healthy in their loves and even in their passions. These two young people were both healthy, both red-blooded, both of ardent, passionate nature; and they were drawn together each to each by all the powers that rule sex and character. To say that their love was all of earth would be as absurd as to say that it was all of heaven. It was human, all human, and all that such implies. Heaven and earth had both their parts in the combination; and perhaps, since both were of strong nature and marked individuality, Hell had its due share in the amalgam.

Athlyne thought, and thought, and thought; till the length of his own shadow recalled the passing of time. He postponed the thinking over his plans for to-morrow—the active part of them, and hastened back to his place behind the lilacs.

He was just in time. The carriage stood at the door with Colonel Ogilvie's "grip-sack" at the driver's feet. Then the Boots ran down the steps and held the carriage door open. Joy came holding her father's arm. They got into the carriage and drove away. Athlyne waited, sitting on the seat on the grass lawn smoking luxuriously. He forgot that he was hungry and thirsty, forgot everything except that he would before long see Joy again, this time *alone*. His thoughts were evidently pleasant, for the time flew fast. Indeed he must have been in something like a waking dream which absorbed all his faculties for he did not notice the flight of time at all. It was only when, recalled to himself by the passing of a carriage, he looked up and saw Joy that he came back to reality. To his disappointment her head was turned away. When within sight of the garden, she had noticed him and as she did not wish him, just yet, to know that she knew of his presence, she found her eyes fixed on the other side of the street. It was the easiest and most certain way of avoiding complexities. He slipped over to the lilacs to see her alight. When she had done so she turned to the coachman and said:

"You understand I shall not want you in the morning as I shall be out walking; but if I don't send for you in the afternoon, or if you don't get any message you will meet my father at Windermere station at a quarter to five."

She went to the front of the carriage and stroked the horses' noses and necks after her usual fashion. He had as good a view of her profile as the twilight would allow. Then with a pleasant "Good evening!" to the coachman she tripped up the steps and disappeared. For more than a quarter of an hour Athlyne watched the windows; but she did not appear. This was natural enough, for she was behind the curtains peeping out to see if he went back to his seat on the lawn.

When she saw that he did not return Joy, with a gentle sigh, went to her room.

That sigh meant a lot. It was the reaction from an inward struggle. All day she had been suffering from the dominance of two opposing ideas, between which her inward natured swayed pendulum-wise. This "inward nature" comprised her mind, her reason, her intelligence, her fears, her hopes, her desires—the whole mechanism and paraphernalia of her emotional and speculative psychology. She would fain have gone out boldly into the garden and there met Mr. Hardy face to face—of course by pure accident. But this vague intention was combated by a maiden fear; one of those delicious, conscious apprehensions made to be combated unless thoroughly supported by collateral forces; one of those gentle fears of sex which makes yielding so sweet. Following this came the fixed intention of that walk to be taken in the morning. The morning was still far off and its apprehensive possibilities were not very dreadful. Indeed she did not really fear them at all for she had privately made up her mind that, fear or no fear, she was going on that walk. The only point left open was its direction. The hour was positively settled; an hour earlier than that at which for the past few days she had driven out with Daddy! Even to herself she would not admit that her choice of time was in any way controlled or influenced by the fact that it was the same hour about which Mr. Hardy made his appearance in the garden.

But all the same her thoughts and her intentions were becoming conscious. For good or evil she was getting more reckless in her desires; passion was becoming dominant—and she knew it.

This is perhaps the most dangerous phase of a woman's trial. She knows that there is at work a growing desire for self-surrender which it is her duty to combat. She knows that all contra reasons which can be produced will be—must be—overcome. She knows with all the subtle instincts of her sex that she is deliberately setting her feet on a slope down which some impulse, perhaps but momentary, will carry her with resistless force. It is the preparatory struggle to defeat; the clearing away of difficulties which might later be hampering or even obstructive; the clamant *wish* for defeat which makes for the conquered the satisfaction if not the happiness of finality. To all children of Adam, of either sex, this phase may come. To the strongest and most resolute warrior must be a moment when he can no more; when the last blow has been struck and the calling of another world is ringing in his ears; to the resolute amongst men this moment is the moment of death. To women it is surrender of self; surrender to the embrace of Death—or to the embrace of Love. It is the true end of the battle. The rest is but the carrying out of the Treaty of Peace, the Triumph of the Victory in which she is now proud to have a part—if it be only that of captive!

There was no sleep for Joy that night. She heard the hours strike one after the other, never missing one. She was not restless. She lay still, and quiet, and calm; patient with that patience which is an acceptance that what is to come is good. In all the long vigil she never faltered in her intention to take that walk in the forenoon. What was to happen in it she did not guess. She had a conviction that that tall figure would follow her discreetly; and that when she was alone they would somehow meet. It might be that she would hear his voice before she saw him; that was most likely, indeed almost certain, for she would not turn till he had spoken . . . or at any rate till she knew that he was close behind her. . . . Here her thoughts would stop. She would lie in a sort of ecstasy . . . whatever might come after that would be happiness. She would see Him . . . look into His eyes. . . . "Look at me, Joy!" seemed to sound in her ears in sweet low music like a whisper. Then she would close her eyes and lie motionless, passive, breathing as gently as a child; high-strung, conscious, awake and devoid of any definite intent.

When she was dressing for the day she put on one of the simplest and prettiest of her dresses, one which she had directed over night to be got ready; a sort of heavy gauze of dull white which fell in long full folds showing her tall slim figure to its perfect grace. Her maid who was a somewhat silent person, not given to volubility unless encouraged, looked at her admiringly as she said:

"I do think miss that is the most becoming of all your frocks!" This pleased her and sent a red glow through her cheeks. Then, fearing if she seemed to think too much of the matter it might seem suspicious as to some purpose, she said quietly:

"Perhaps then it would be better if I put on one of the lawn dresses. I am going for a walk this morning and as it may be dusty a frock that will not catch the dust may be better."

"It does seem a pity miss to wear such a pretty frock and spoil it when there is no one here to see it; not even your father." This gave Joy an opening of which she quickly availed herself. She had not the least intention of changing the frock or of looking, if she could avoid it, one whit below her best.

"Fie, Eugenie! one doesn't put on frocks to attract. If you think that way, I shall wear it; even if it is to get dusty." The Abigail who was a privileged person answered gravely:

"That's quite true, Miss, exactly as you say it. *One* doesn't put on nice frocks to attract; and that one is yourself. But all the rest do!" Joy's merry laugh showed the measure of her ebullient happiness.

"Dear me! Eugenie. You are quite an orthoëpist—indeed a precisionist. I shall have to polish up my grammar. However I'll keep on the frock if only in compliment to your sense of terminological exactitude!"

A little after breakfast, when the time for starting on the walk drew nigh, Joy did not feel so elated. Woman-like she was not anxious to begin. It was not that she in any way faltered in her purpose, but merely that she was suffering from the nervousness which comes to those of high strung temperaments in momentous crises. Humming merrily she put on her hat and finished her toilet for her walk. In the sitting room from the shelter of the curtain she looked out of the window, as she tried to think, casually. Her eyes turned towards the lilac bushes, but caught no indication of the tall figure that she sought. Her heart fell. But a second later it leaped almost painfully as she saw Mr. Hardy sitting out openly on the seat, and strange to say—for she had come to identify that seat with the practice—not smoking. He evidently had no present thought of being concealed. Why? The answer to her own question came in a rush of blood to her face, a rush so quick and thorough that it seemed for the moment to deplete her heart which beat but faintly . . . When she looked again he had risen and was moving toward the lilacs.

Without a word she walked downstairs and out through the hall-door.

Athlyne had not slept either that night. But the manner and range of his thoughts showed the difference between the sexes. Both his imagining and his reasoning were to practical purpose. He wanted to see Joy, to speak with her, to prove to himself if his hoping was in any way justified by fact. He had for so long been concentrating his thoughts on one subject that doubts at first shadowy had become real. It seemed therefore to him that in his planning for the morrow he was dealing with real things, not imaginative ones. And, after all, there is nothing more real than doubt—so far as it goes. Victor Cousin took from its reality his subtlest argument for belief: "At this point scepticism itself vanishes; for if a man doubt everything else, at least he cannot doubt that he doubts." So with Athlyne. By accepting doubt as reality he began the experiment for its cure.

In the silence of the night, with nerves high-strung and with brain excited he tried in those most earnest hours of his life, when for good or ill he was to organise his intellectual forces, to arrange matters so that at the earliest time he might with certainty learn his fate. He had an idea that in such a meeting as was before him he must not be over-precipitated. And yet he must not check impulsiveness as long as its trend was in the right direction. He knew that a woman's heart is oftener won by assault than by siege. For himself he had plenty of patience as well as a sufficiency of spirit; his task at present therefore was one of generalship alone: the laying out of the battle plans, the disposition of his forces. As he thought, and as his ideas and his intentions came into order, he began to understand better the purpose of those two preparations of his which were already complete: the overhauling of his automobile, and the supplying it with female wraps. He intended by some means or other, dependent on developing opportunity, to bring her for a ride in the motor. There, all alone, he would be able to learn, perhaps at first from her bearing and then from her own lips, how she regarded him.

Athlyne was a young man, a very young man in his real knowledge of the sex. There are hundreds, thousands, of half-pulseless boys, flabby of flesh, and pallid with enervating dissipation, who would have smiled cynically—they have not left in them grit enough for laughter—at his doubting.

He would not frighten her at first. Here for a time he took himself to task for seeming to plot against the woman he loved. Surely it would be better to treat her with perfect fairness; to lay his heart at her feet; tell her with all the passionate force that swept him how he loved her—tell it with what utterance he had. Then he should wait her decision. No, not decision! That was too cold a word—thought. If indeed there was any answering love to his, little decision would be required. Had *he* made any decision! From the first moment he had looked in her beautiful grey eyes and lost himself in their depths, his very soul had gone out to her. And it might be that she too had felt something of the same self-abandonment. He could never forget how on that afternoon visit at the Holland she had raised her eyes to his in answer to his passionate appeal: "Joy, Look at me!" Then at that memory, and at the later memory when she had spoken the words herself only the day before—the sweetness of her voice was still tingling in his ears, a sort of tidal wave of lover's rapture swept over him. It overwhelmed him so completely that it left him physically gasping for breath. He was in a tumult; he could not lie in bed. He leaped to his feet and walked to and fro with long, passionate strides. He threw up the lower sash of the window and looked out into the moonlight, craning his neck round to the right so that his eyes were in the direction of Ambleside as though the very ardour of his gaze could pierce through distance and stone walls and compel Joy's white eyelids to raise so that he might once more lose himself in those grey deeps wherein his soul alone found peace.

In this passion of adoration all his doubts seemed to disappear, as the sun drinks up the mist. He felt as though uplifted. At the very idea of Joy's loving him as he loved her he felt more worthy, more strong, and with a sense of triumph which had no parallel in his life. He stood looking out at the beauty of the scene before him, till gradually it became merged in his thoughts with Joy and his hopes which the morrow might realise. He never knew exactly how long he stood there. It must have been a long time, for when he realised any sense of time at all he was cramped and chill; and the forerunner of the morning light coming from far away behind him was articulating the fields on the hill-slopes across the lake.

He was then calm. All the thinking and reasoning and planning and passion of the night had been wrought into unity. His mind was made up as to the first stage of his undertaking. He would bring the car to Ambleside and leave it with the chauffeur outside the town. Then he would take his place in the garden and wait till she came out for that walk of which she had told her father. He would cautiously follow her; and when there was a fair opportunity for uninterrupted speech would come to her. If he found there was no change in her manner to him—and here once again the memory of those lifting eyes made him tremble—he would try to get her to come for a ride in his car. There, wrapped in the glory of motion and surrounded by all the grandeur of natural beauty, he would pour out his soul to her and put his fate to the touch. Then if all were well he would send on the letter to her father and would pay his formal visit as soon as might be. He would take care to have ready a luncheon basket so that if she would ride with him they might have together an ethereal banquet.

It is strange that even those who are habitually cautious, whose thoughts and deeds alike are compelled and ruled by reason, will in times of exaltation forget their guiding principle. They will refuse to acknowledge the existence of chance; and will proceed calmly on their way as though life was as a simple cord, with Inclination pulling at one end of it and Fact yielding at the other.

CHAPTER XIV

A BANQUET ON OLYMPUS

ON this occasion Athlyne did not continue to sit out on the lawn. Now that he wished to overtake Joy unawares he was as careful to hide his presence from her as he had previously hidden it from her father. He had hardly ensconced himself in his usual cover when Joy came out on the steps. Her maid was with her and together they stood on the steps speaking. As she turned to come down the steps Joy said:

"Perhaps I had better arrange to come back after a short walk; there might be some telegram from father to be attended to. If there is not, I can then go for a real, long walk." She did not say more but moved briskly down the roadway without ever turning her head. Athlyne slipped through the gate of the garden, following at such distance that he could easily keep out of view in case she should turn. When she had cleared the straggling houses which made the outskirts of the little town she walked slowly, and then more slowly still. Finally she sat on a low wall by the roadside with her back partially turned to Ambleside and looked long at the beautiful view before her where, between the patches of trees which here shut out the houses altogether and heightened the air of privacy of the bye road, the mountain slopes rose before her.

This was the opportunity for which Athlyne was waiting. He had hardly dared to hope that it would be in a spot so well adapted to his wishes. Dear simple soul! he never imagined that it had been already chosen—marked down by a keener intellect than his own, and that intellect a woman's!

Joy knew that he was coming; that he was drawing closer; that he was at hand. It was not needed that she had now and again thrown a half glance behind her at favourable moments as she went. There was at work a subtler sense than any dealing with mere optics; a sense that can float on ether waves as surely as can any other potent force. Nay, may it not be the same sense specialised. The sense that makes soul known to soul, sex to sex; that tells of the presence of danger; that calls kind to kind; and race to race, from the highest of creation to the lowest. And so she was prepared and waited, calm after the manner of her sex. For when woman waits for the coming of man her whole being is in suspense. Though in secret her heart beat painfully Joy did not look round, made no movement till the spoken words reached her:

"Miss Ogilvie is it not!"

Slowly she turned, as to a voice but partly heard or partly remembered. Athlyne felt his heart sink down, down as he saw the slowness of the movement and realised the absence of that quick response which he had by long and continuous thinking since last night encouraged himself to expect. The quick gleam of pleasure in the face as she turned, the light in her marvellous grey eyes, the gentle blush which despite herself passed like an Alpenglow from forehead to neck did not altogether restore his equanimity or even encourage him sufficiently to try to regain that pinnacle of complacent hope on which up to then he had stood.

"Why Mr. Hardy," she said warmly as she rose quickly to her feet. "This is real nice. I was afraid we were not going to see you whilst we were in England."

It was beautifully done; no wonder that some women can on the stage carry a whole audience with them, when off it so many can deceive intellects more powerful than their own. And yet it was not all acting. She did not intend it as such; not for a moment did she wish or intend to deceive. It was only the habit of obedience to convention which was guiding natural impulse into safe channels. For who shall say where nature—the raw, primeval crude article—ends or where convention, which is the artfulness necessitated by the elaboration of organised society, begins. A man well known in New York used to say: "All men are equal after the fish!" Kipling put the same idea in another way: . . . "the Colonel's Lady an' Judy O'Grady are sisters under their skins!"

When Athlyne looked into Joy's eyes—and there was full opportunity for so doing—all his intentions of reserve went from him. He was lover all over; nothing but lover, with wild desire to be one with her he loved. His eyes began to glow, his knees to tremble, then every muscle of his body became braced; and when he spoke his voice at once deepened and had a masterful ring which seemed to draw Joy's very soul out towards him. Well it was for her main purpose that her instinct had given that first chill of self-possession; had the man been able to go on from where he had first started nothing that she knew of reserve or self-restraint could have prevented her from throwing herself straightway into his arms. Had Athlyne not begun with that same chill, which to him took the measure of a repulse, he would have caught her to him with all the passions of many kinds which were beginning to surge in him.

But what neither of them could effect alone, together they did. The pause of the fraction of a second in the springing of their passion made further restraint possible. There is no fly-wheel in the mechanism of humanity to carry the movement of the crank beyond its level. Such machinery was not invented at the time of the organisation of Eden.

"I have longed for this moment more than I can say; more than words can tell!" His voice vibrated with the very intensity of his truth. Joy's eyes, despite her efforts to keep them fixed, fell. Her bosom rose and fell quickly and heavily with the stress of her breathing. Her knees trembled and a slow pallor took the place of the flush on her face. Seemingly unconsciously she murmured so faintly that only a lover's ear could hear or follow it:

"I have longed for it too—oh so much!" The words dropped from her lips like faint music. Instinctively she put her hand on the wall beside her to steady herself; she feared she was going to faint.

Athlyne, seeing and hearing, thrilled through to the very marrow of his bones. His great love controlled, compelled him. He made no movement towards her but looked with eyes of rapture. Such a moment was beyond personal satisfaction; it was of the gods, not of men. And so they stood.

Then the tears welled over in Joy's eyes beneath the fallen lids. They hung on the dark, curly lashes and rolled like silver beads down the softness of her cheeks. Still Athlyne made no sign; he felt that the time had not yet come. The woman was his own now, he felt instinctively; and it was his duty—his sacred privilege to protect her. Unthinkingly he moved a step back on the road he had come. Instinctively Joy did the same. It was without thought or intention on the part of either; all instinctive, all natural. The usage of the primeval squaw to follow her master outlives races.

Then he paused. She came up to him and they walked level. Not another word had been spoken; but there are silences that speak more than can be written in ponderous tomes. These two—this man and this woman—*knew.* They had in their hearts in those glorious moments all the wisdom won by joy and suffering through all the countless ages since the Lord rested on that first Sabbath eve and felt that His finished work was good.

When, keeping even step, they had taken a few quiet paces, Athlyne spoke in a soft whisper that thrilled:

"Joy, look at me!"

Without question or doubt of any kind she raised her shining eyes to his. And then, slowly and together as though in obedience to some divine command, their lips met in a long, loving kiss in which their very souls went out each to the other.

When their mouths parted, with a mutual sigh, each gave a quick glance up and down the road; neither had thought of it before.

The tree of the Knowledge of Good and Evil did not die in Eden bower. It flourishes still in even the most unlikely places all the wide world over. And they who taste its fruit must look with newly-opened eyes on the world around them.

Together, still keeping step, not holding each other, not touching except by the chance of movement, they walked to where the bye-road joined the main one. As yet they had spoken between them less than threescore words. They wondered later in the day when they talked together how so much as they had thought and felt and conveyed had been packed into such compass. Now, as they paused at the joining of the roads, Athlyne said—and strange to say it was in an ordinary commonplace voice:

"Joy won't you come with me for a ride. I have my motor here, and we can go alone. There is much I want to say to you—much to tell you, and the speed will help us. I want to rush along—to fly. Earth is too prosaic for me—now!" Joy looking softly up caught the lightning that flashed from his eyes, and her own fell. A tide of red swept her face; this passed in a moment, however, leaving a divine pink like summer sunset on snowy heights. Her voice was low and thrilling as she answered with eyes still cast down.

"I'll go with you where you will—to the end of the world—or Heaven or Hell if you wish—now!"

And then as if compelled by a force beyond control she raised her eyes to his.

"Shall you come with me to the car; or shall I bring it to the hotel?" He spoke once more in something like his ordinary voice.

"Neither!" she answered with her eyes still fixed on his unflinchingly. He felt their witchery run through him like fire now; his blood seemed to boil as it rushed through his veins. Love and passion were awake and at one.

"I must go back to see if there is any wire from Daddy, and to leave word that I am going for a drive. I shall tell my maid that I shall return in good time. Father and Mother and Aunt Judy are to arrive at Windermere at five o'clock unless we hear to the contrary. You bring up the motor to—to there where we met." Her eyes burned through him as without taking them from his she raised an arm and pointed gracefully up the bye-road, towards where they had sat.

"Don't come with me," she said as he moved with her. "It will be sweeter to keep our secret to ourselves."

And so, he raising his cap as he stood aside, she passed on after sending one flashing look of love right through him.

At the hotel she found a wire from her father to the effect that they would not be able to leave Euston at 11.30 as intended but that they hoped to reach Windermere at 7.05. This pleased her, for it gave her another two hours for that motor drive to which she looked forward with beating heart. She told her maid that she would be out till late in the afternoon as she was going motoring with a friend; and that she, Eugenie, could please herself as to how she would pass the time. When the maid asked her what she wished as to lunch she answered:

"I shall not want any lunch; but if we feel hungry we can easily get some on the way."

"Which way shall you be going, Miss, in case any one should ask."

"I really don't know Eugenie. I just said I would join in the drive. I daresay it is up somewhere amongst the lakes. That is where the fine scenery is."

"And what about wraps, miss? You will want something warm for motoring. That dress you have on is rather thin for the purpose."

"Oh dear; oh dear!" she answered with chagrin. "This will do well enough, I think. We shall not, I expect, be going very far. If I find I want a wrap I can borrow one." And off she set for the rendezvous.

In the meantime Athlyne had found the car, and had given instructions to the chauffeur to remain at an inn at Ambleside which he had already noted for the purpose and where a telegram would find him in case it might be necessary to give any instructions. He had made sure that the luncheon basket which he had ordered at Bowness was in its place. Then he had driven back to the bye-road and waited with what patience he could for the coming of Joy.

She came up the bye-road walking fast enough. Up to that point she had walked leisurely, but when she saw the great car all flaming magnificently in scarlet and gold she forgot everything in the way of demureness, and hurried forward. She had also seen Mr. Hardy. That morning he had put on his motor clothes, for he knew he had to look forward to a long spell of hard work before him—work of a kind which needs special equipment. More than ever did he look tall and lithe and elegant in his well-fitting suit of soft dark leather. When he caught sight of Joy and saw that she was still in her pretty white frock he began to lift from the bottom of the tonneau a pile of wraps which he spread on the side. Joy did not notice the things at first; her eyes were all for him. He stepped forward to meet her and, after a quick glance round to see that they were alone, took her in his arms and kissed her. She received the kiss in the most natural way—as if it was a matter of course, and returned it. It is surprising what an easy art to learn kissing is, and how soon even the most bashful of lovers become reconciled to its exacting rules!

Then she began to admire his car, partly to please him, partly because it was really a splendid machine admirably wrought to its special purpose—speed. He lifted a couple of coats and asked:

"Which will you wear?"

"Must I wear one? It is warm enough isn't it without a coat?"

"At present, yes! But when our friend here" he slapped the car affectionately "wakes up and knows who he has the honour of carrying you'll want it. You have no idea what a difference a fifty or sixty mile breeze makes."

"I'll take this one, please," she said without another word; a ready acquiescence to his advice which made him glow afresh. One after another she took all the articles which his loving forethought had provided, and put them on prettily. She felt, and he felt too, that each fresh adornment was something after the manner of an embrace. At the last he lifted the motor cap and held it out to her. She took it with a smile and a blush.

"I really quite forgot my hat," she said "'Tis funny how your memory goes when you're very eager!" This little speech, unconsciously uttered, sent a wave of sweet passion through the man. "Very Eager!" She went on:

"But where on earth am I to put it? I think I had almost better hide it here behind the hedge and retrieve it when we get back!" Athlyne smiled superiorly—that sort of affectionate tolerant superiority which a woman admires in a man she loves and which the least sentimental man employs unconsciously at times. He stooped into the tonneau and from under one of the seats drew out a leather bonnet-box which ran in and out on a slide. As he touched a spring this flew open, showing space and equipment for several hats and a tiny dressing bag.

"Why, dear, there is everything in the world in your wonderful car."

How he was thrilled by her using the word!—the first time her lips had used it to him. It was none the less sweet because spoken without thought. She herself had something of the same feeling. She quivered in a languorous ecstasy. But she did not even blush at the thought; it had been but the natural expression of her feeling and she was glad she had said it. Their eyes searched each other and told their own eloquent tale.

"Darling!" he said, and bending over kissed again the rosy mouth that was pouted to meet him.

In silence he opened the door of the tonneau. She drew back.

"Must I go in there—alone?"

"I can't go with you, darling. I must sit in the seat to drive. Unless you would rather we had the chauffeur!"

"You stupid old . . . *dear!*" this in a whisper. "I want to sit beside you—as close as I can . . . *darling!*" She sank readily into the arms which instinctively opened.

True love makes its own laws, its own etiquettes. When lovers judge harshly each the conduct of the other it is time for the interference or the verdict of strangers. But not till then.

Athlyne took the wheel, feeling in a sort of triumphant glory; in every way other than he had expected. He thought that he would be ardent and demonstrative; he was protective. The very trustfulness of her reception of his caresses and her responsiveness to them made for a certain intellectual quietude.

Joy too was in a sort of ecstatic calm. There was such completeness about her happiness that all thought of self disappeared. She did not want anything to be changed in the whole universe. She did not want time to fly betwixt now and her union with the man she loved. That might—would—come later; but in the meanwhile happiness was so complete as to transcend ambition, hope, time.

Athlyne, who had made up his mind as to the direction of the drive, came down on the high road and drove at moderate speed to Ambleside; he thought that it would be wise to go slowly so as not to be too conspicuous. He had given Joy a dust-veil but she had not yet adjusted it. The present pace did not require such protection, and the idea of concealing her identity did not even enter into her head. When they were passing the post-office a sudden recollection came to Athlyne, and he stopped the car suddenly. Joy for an instant was a little alarmed and looked towards him inquiringly.

"Only a letter which I want to post!" he said in reply as he stepped down on the pavement. He opened his jacket and took from his pocket a letter which he placed in the box. Joy surmised afresh about the letter; she vaguely wondered if it was the same that she had seen him close and put into his pocketbook. The thought was, however, only a passing one. She had something else than other people's letters to think about at present.

Just as he was turning back from the post box Eugenie, who was taking advantage of her freedom, passed along the pavement. She stopped to admire the tall chauffeur whom she thought the handsomest man she had ever seen. She did not know him. Her service with Miss Ogilvie had only commenced with the visit to London: up to the time of her leaving Italy Mrs. Ogilvie's maid had attended to Joy. She stood back and pretended to be looking in at a window as she did not care to be seen staring openly at him. Then she saw that he was no ordinary chauffeur. It was with a sigh that she said to herself:

"*Voila! Un vrai Monsieur!*" Her eyes following him as he turned the starting handle and took his seat behind the wheel, she saw that his companion was her mistress. Not wishing to appear as if prying on her either, she instinctively turned away.

As Athlyne was arranging himself to his driving work he said quietly to Joy:

"Sorry for delaying; but it was a most important letter, which I want to be delivered to-night. It might be late if it was not posted till Carlisle." This was the first knowledge Joy had of the direction of the journey. Eugenie heard only the last word as the car moved off.

The pace was comparatively slow until the outskirts of Ambleside had been passed; then he told Joy to put on her spectacles and donned his own. When they were both ready he increased the pace, and they flew up to the shores of Rydal Water. At Joy's request they slowed down whilst the lake was in sight; but raced again till the road ran close to the peaceful water of Grasmere. But when Grasmere with its old church and Coleridge's tomb lay away to their left they flew again up the steep road to Thirlmere. Athlyne was a careful driver and the car was a good hill climber. It was only when the road was quite free ahead that they went at great speed. They kept steadily on amongst the rising mountains, only slackening as they passed to Thirlmere and dropped down to Keswick. They did not stop here, but passing by the top of Derwentwater drew up for a few minutes to look down the lake whose wooded islands add so much to the loveliness of the view. Then on again full speed by the borders of Bassenthwaite Lake and on amongst the frowning hills to Cockermouth.

Joy was in a transport of delight the whole time. Her soul seemed to be lifted by the ever-varying beauty of the panorama as they swept along; and the rushing speed stirred her blood. She was silent, save at ecstatic moments when she was quite unable to control herself. Athlyne was silent too. He had been over the ground already, and besides such driving required constant care and attention. He was more than ever careful in his work, for was not Joy—his Joy!—his passenger.

They did not stop at Cockermouth but turned into the main road and, passing Bride-kirk—and Bothel, flew up to Carlisle. As he slowed down at the city wall Athlyne looking at his watch said quietly:

"An hour and a half and some fifty miles. Let us go on and eat our lunch in Scotland."

"Oh do! Go on! Go on—darling! I forgot to tell you that I have had a wire; they don't get in till seven; so we have two more hours," cried Joy enthusiastically. This time she used the word of endearment instinctively and without a pause. "Practice makes perfect" says the old saw.

Athlyne controlled himself and went at quiet pace through the Cumberland capital. He would like to have put the engine at full speed; the last word had fired him afresh. However, he did not want to get into police trouble. When he came out on the Northern road and climbed the steep hill to Stanwix he felt freer. The road was almost a dead level and there was little traffic, only a stray cart here and there. Then he let go, and the car jumped forward like an eager horse. Athlyne felt proud of it, just as though it had an intention of its own—that it wanted to show Joy how it loved to carry her. Joy almost held her breath as they swept along here. The wind whistled around her head and she had to keep her neck stiff against the pressure of the fifty-mile breeze. They slowed at the forking of the road beyond Kingstown; and at the Esk bridge and its approaches; otherwise they went at terrific speed till they reached the border where the road crossed the Sark. Then, keeping the Lochberie road to the right, they rushed away through Annan towards Dumfries.

Joy did not know that at that turning off to Annan they were almost in touch with Gretna Green. Athlyne did not think of it at the time. Had the knowledge or the thought of either been engaged on the subject the temptation it would have brought might have been too much for lovers in their rapturous condition . . . and the course of this history might have been different.

The run to the outskirts of Dumfries, where the traffic increased, was another wild rush which wrought both the occupants of the car to a high pitch of excitement.

To Joy it seemed a sort of realisation. On the drive to Carlisle, and from that on over the Border, the fringing hills of the Solway had been a dim and mystery-provoking outline. But now the hills were at hand, before them and to the north; whilst far across the waste of banks and shoals of Solway Frith rose the Cumberland mountains, a mighty piling mass of serrated blue haze. It was a convincing recognition of the situation; this was Scotland, and England was far behind! Instinctively she leaned closer to her companion at the thought.

Between Dumfries and Castle Douglas was a long hill to climb within a stretch of seven miles. But the Delaunay-Belleville breasted it nobly and went up with unyielding energy. Then, when the summit at Crocketford was reached, she ran down the hill to Urr Water with a mighty rush which seemed to carry her over the lesser hill to Castle Douglas. From thence the road to Dalry was magnificent for scenery. At Crossmicheal it came close to the Ken whose left bank it followed right up by Parton to "St. John's Town of Dalry" where it crossed the river. Athlyne had intended to rest a while somewhere about here; but the old coach road, winding with the curves of the river, looked so inviting that he ran a few miles up north towards Carsphairn. Coming to a bye-road where grew many fine trees of beech and stone pine which gave welcome shade, he ran up a few hundred yards to where the road curved a little. Here was an ideal spot for a picnic, and especially for a picnic of two like the present.

The curving of the road made an open space, which the spreading trees above shaded. Deep grass was on the wide margin of the flat road which presently dipped to cross a shallow rill of bright water which fell from a little rocky ledge, tinkling happily through the hum of summer insect life. Wildflowers grew everywhere. It was idyllic and delightful and beautiful in every way, even to where, towering high above a Druidic ruin in the foreground, the lofty hills of Carsphairn rose far away between them and the western sky. In itself the scene wanted for absolute perfection some figures in the foreground. And presently it had them in a very perfect form. Joy clapped her hands with delight like a happy child as she glanced around her. Athlyne drew up sharp, and jumping from his seat held out his hand to Joy who sprang beside him on the road. As they stood together when Joy's wrap had been removed they made a handsome couple. Both tall and slim and elegant and strong. Both straight as lances; both bright and eager; with the light of love and happiness shining on them more notably than even the flicker of sunlight between the great stems and branches of the trees. His brown hair seemed to match her black; the brown eyes and the grey both were lit with a "light that never came from land or sea!" Joy's eyes fell under the burning glances of her lover; the time had not yet come for that absolutely fearless recognition which, being a man's unconscious demand, a woman instinctively resists. Athlyne recognised the delicacy and acquiesced. All this without a single spoken word. Then he spoke:

"Was there ever such a magnificent run in the world. More than a hundred miles on end without a break or pause. And every moment a lifetime of bliss—to me at all events—Darling!"

"And to me!" Joy's eyes flashed grey lightning as she raised them for a moment to his, and held them there. Athlyne's knees trembled with delight; his voice quivered also as he spoke:

"And all the time I never left my duty once for an instant. I think I ought to get a medal!"

"You should indeed, darling. And I never once distracted you from it did I?"

"Unhappily, no!" His eyes danced.

"So I ought to get more than a medal!"

"What? What should you get—now?" His voice was a little hoarse. He drew closer to her. She made no answer in words; but her eyes were more eloquent. With a mutual movement she was in his arms and their mouths met.

"And now for lunch!" he said as after a few entrancing seconds she drew her face away. "I am sure you must be starving."

"I *am* hungry!" she confessed. Her face was still flushed and her eyes were like stars. She bustled about to help him. He took the seats and cushions from the tonneau and made a comfortable nest for her, with a seat for himself close, very close beside her. He lifted off the luncheon basket and unstrapped it. Whilst she took out the plates and packets and spread the cloth he put a bottle of champagne and one of fizzy water in the cool of the running stream.

They may have had some delightful picnics on Olympus in the days of the old gods who were so human and who loved so much— and so often. But surely there was none so absolutely divine as on that day that under the trees, looking over at the grey piling summits of the mountains of Carsphairn. The food was a dream, the wine was nectar. The hearts of the two young people beat as one heart. Love surely was so triumphant that there never could come a cloud into the sky which hung over them like a blue canopy. Life and nature and happiness and beauty and love took hands and danced around them fairy-like as they sat together, losing themselves and their very souls in the depths of each other's eyes.

CHAPTER XV

"STOP!"

Under the shading trees the time flew fast. It is ever thus in the sylvan glades where love abides:

> ". . . The halcyon hours with double swiftness run
> And in the splendour of Arcadian summers
> The quicker climb the coursers of the sun."

Athlyne and Joy sat in a gentle rapture of happiness. She had made him draw up his cushion close to her so that she could lean against him. They sat hand in hand for a while, and then one arm stole round her and drew her close to him. She came yieldingly, as though such a moment had been ordained since the beginning of the world. Her hand stole inside his arm and held him tight; and so they sat locked together, with their faces so close that their mouths now and again met in long, sweet kisses. More than once was asked by either the old question of lovers—which has no adequate or final answer: "Do you love me?" And at each such time the answer was given in the fashion which ruled in Eden—and ever since.

Presently Athlyne, drawing Joy closer than ever to him, said:

"Joy darling there is something I want to say to you!" He paused; she drew him closer to her, and held him tighter. She realised that his voice had changed a little; he was under some nervousness or anxiety. This woke the protective instinct which is a part of woman's love.

"We love each other?"

"I do!" As she spoke she looked at him with her great gray eyes blazing. He kissed her:

"And I love you, my darling, more than I have words to say. More than words can express. I am lost in you. You are my world, my hope, my heaven! Beyond measure I love you, and honour you, and trust you; and now that I feel you love me too . . . My dear! . . . my dear! the whole world seems to swim around me and the heavens to open . . ."

"Dear, go on. It is music to me—all music—that I have so longed for!"

"Darling! It seems like sacrilege to say anything just now—but—but—You know I love you?"

"Yes!" The simple word was stronger than any embellishment; it was of the completeness, the majesty, of sincerity in its expression.

"Then there is no need to say more of that now. But before I say something else which I long to hear—in words, dear, for its truth is already in my heart . . ."

"Darling!" she spoke the word lingeringly as though grudging that its saying must end . . .

"Before such time I must speak with your father!" He spoke the words with a gravity which brought a chill to her heart; her face blanched suddenly as does liquid in the final crystallization of frost. Her voice was faint—she was only a girl after all, despite her pride and bravery—as she asked:

"Oh, I hope it is nothing. . . ."

"Nothing, darling" he said as he stroked tenderly the hand that lay in his—he had taken his arm from her waist to do it—"except the courtesy which is due to an old man . . . and one other thing, small in itself—absolutely nothing in my own mind—which makes it necessary in respect to his . . . his . . . his convictions that I should speak to him before . . ." He stopped suddenly, remembering that if he went on he must betray the secret which as yet he wished to keep. Not on his own account did he wish to keep it. But there was Joy's happiness to be considered. Until he knew how Colonel Ogilvie would take the knowledge of his having introduced himself under a false name he must not do or say anything which might ultimately make difference between her and her father.

Joy erred in her interpretation of his embarrassment, of his sudden stopping. Again the pallor grew over her face which had under her lover's earlier words regained its normal colour. More faintly even than before she whispered: "It is nothing I hope that would keep us . . ." He saw her distress and cut quickly into her question:

"No! No! No! Nothing that could ever come between you and me. It is only this, Joy darling. Your father belongs to another country from my own and an older generation than mine. His life has been different, and the ideas that govern him are very masterful in their convention. Were I to neglect this I might make trouble which would, without our wish or part, come between us. Believe me, dear, that in this I am wise." Then seeing the trouble still in her eyes he went on: "I know well, Joy, that it is not necessary for me to justify myself in your eyes." Here she strained him a little closer and held his arm and his hand harder "but my dearest, I am going to do it all the same. I want to say something, but which I mustn't say yet, so that you must be tolerant with me if I say unneeded things which are still open to me. Truly, darling, there is absolutely nothing which could possibly come between you and me. I have done no wrong—in that way at all events. There should be no more difference between you and me for anything that is now in my mind than there is between your soul and the blue sky above us; between you and heaven. . . ." She put her hand over his mouth:

"Oh hush, hush, dear. . . . By the way what am I to call you—darling?" For the moment he was taken aback. To give her his own name as yet would be to break the resolution of present secrecy; to give her a false name now would be sacrilege. His native Irish wit stood him in good stead:

"That is the name for to-day—darling. There can be none like that—for to-day. We began with it. It took me on its wings up to heaven. Let me stay there—for to-day. For to-day we are true husband and wife—are we not?"

"Yes dear!" she answered simply. He went on:

"To-morrow . . . we can be grave to-morrow; and then I can give you another name to use—if you wish it!"

"I do!" she said with reverence. She accepted and returned, the kiss which followed. This closed the incident, and for a little space they sat hand in hand, his arm again round her whilst again she had linked her arm in his. Presently he said:

"And now Joy dear, won't you tell me all about yourself. You know that as yet you and I know very little about each other's surroundings. I want specially to know to-day dear, for to-morrow I want to see your father and it will be better to go equipped." Joy felt quite in a flutter. At last she was going to learn something about the man she loved. She would tell him everything, and he would . . . Her thoughts were interrupted by her companion going on:

"And then to-morrow when we have talked I can tell you everything...."

"Everything!" then there was something to conceal! Her heart fell. But as the man continued, her train of thought was again interrupted:

"When you see him to-night you had better..."

Suddenly she jumped to her feet in a sort of fright. Seeing her face he too sprang up, giving, with the instinct of his campaigning a quick look around as though some danger threatened:

"What is it Joy? What is wrong?..." She almost gasped out:

"My father! He will be home by seven! It must be late in the afternoon now and we are more than a hundred miles from home!..." Athlyne in turn was staggered. In his happiness in being with Joy and talking of love he had quite overlooked the passing of time. Instinctively he looked at his watch. It was now close on four o'clock.... Joy was the first to speak:

"Oh do let us hurry! No one knows where I am; and if when Daddy gets home and finds I am not there he will be alarmed—and he may be upset. And Mother and Aunt Judy too!... Oh do not lose a moment! If we do not get home before they arrive... and Daddy finds I have been out all day with you... Oh, hurry, hurry!"

Athlyne had been thinking hard whilst she spoke, and his thoughts had been arranging themselves. His intelligence was all awake now. He could see at a glance that Joy's absence might make trouble for all. Colonel Ogilvie was a man of covenance, and his daughter's going out with him in such a way was at least unconventional. She *must* get back in time! His conclusion was reached before she had finished speaking. His military habit of quick action asserted itself; already he was replacing the things in the carriage. Joy saw, and with feverish haste began to help him. When he saw her at work he ran to the engine and began to prepare for starting. When that was ready he held Joy's coat for her and helped her into her seat. As he took the wheel he said as he began to back down the road which was hardly wide enough to turn in:

"Forgive me, dear. It was all my selfish pleasure. But we shall do all we can. Bar accident we may do it; we have over three hours!" He set his teeth as he saw the struggle before him. It would be a glorious run... and there was no use forestalling trouble.... Joy saw the smile on his face, recognised the man's strength, and was comforted.

They backed into the road and sprang southward. Without taking his eyes off his work, Athlyne said:

"Tell me dear as we go along all that I must bear in mind in speaking to your father of our marriage...."

There! It was out unconsciously. Joy thrilled, but he did not himself seem to notice his self-betrayal. He went on unconcernedly:

"It may be a little uphill at first if we do not get in line in time." Joy looked under her lashes at the strong face now set as a stone to his work and kept silence as to the word. She was glad that she could blush unseen. After a little pause she said in a meek voice:

"Very well, dear. I shall tell you whenever we are on a straight bit of road, but I will be silent round the curves." They were then flying along the old coach road. The road was well-made, broad and with good surface and they went at a terrific pace. Athlyne felt that the only chance of reaching Ambleside was by taking advantage of every opportunity for speed. Already he knew from the morning's journey that there were great opportunities as long stretches of the road were level and in good order and were not unduly impeded with traffic. The motor was running splendidly, it seemed as if the run in the morning had put every part of it in good working order. He did not despair of getting to Ambleside in time. The train was not due at Windmere till seven. And it might be a little late. In any case it would take the arriving party a little while to get their things together and then drive to Ambleside. As they were sweeping down towards the bridge at Dalry he said to Joy without looking round:

"It will be all right. I have been thinking it over. We can do it!"

"Thank God!" she exclaimed fervently. She too had been thinking.

"Stop!"

The voice rang out imperiously; and a policeman, stepping from behind the trunk of a great beech, held up his hand. Instinctively Athlyne began to slow. He shouted back "All right!" He had grasped the situation and as they were out of earshot of the policeman said quickly to Joy:

"We are arrested! Oh, I am sorry darling. If they won't let me pay a fine and go at once you must take the car on. I shall try to arrange that. But do be cautious dear—you are so precious to me. If you are delayed anywhere and can't make it in time wire to your father tell him you are motoring and have been delayed. It will soften matters, even if he is angry. I shall go on by train in the morning. And darling if you are not getting on as you wish, take a train the best you can—a special. Don't stop at any expense. But get on! And don't tell your name to any one, under any circumstances. Don't forget the telegram if delayed." As he was speaking the car was slowing and the panting policeman was coming up behind. When the car stopped, Athlyne jumped out and walked towards the officer; he wanted to be as conciliatory as possible.

"I am very sorry, officer. That beautiful bit of road tempted me; and being all quite clear I took a skim down it?"

"Ye did! Man, but it was fine! But I hae to arrest ye all the same. Duty is duty!"

"Certainly. I suppose the station is across the bridge?"

"Aye sir." The policeman, who at first sight had from his dress taken him for a chauffeur, had by now recognised him as a gentleman.

"Will you come in the car? It's all right. I'll go slow."

"Thank ye sir. I've had a deal o' walkin' the day!" When the man was in the tonneau Athlyne who had been thinking of what was to be done said to him affably:

"It was silly of me going at such a pace. But I wanted my wife to see how the new car worked." He had a purpose in saying this: to emphasise to Joy the necessity of not mentioning her name. It was the only way to keep off the subject when they should get to the station. Joy turned away her head. She did not wish either man to see her furious blushing at hearing the word. She took the hint; silence was her cue.

At the station Joy sat in the car whilst Athlyne went inside with the officer. The sergeant was a grave elderly man, not unkindly. He too recognised, but at once, that the chauffeur was a gentleman. There was an air of distinction about Athlyne which no one, especially an official, could fail to appreciate. He was not surprised when he read the card which Athlyne handed to him. He frowned a little and scratched his head.

"I fear this'll be a bit awkward my lord. Ye come frae o'er the Border and ye'll hae to attend the summons at New Galloway. I dinna want to inconvenience you and her ladyship but . . ."

"Will it not be possible to let the car go on. My wife has to meet her father and mother who are coming up to Ambleside to-night, and they will be so disappointed. Her mother is an invalid and is coming from Italy. I shall be really greatly obliged if it can be managed."

The sergeant shook his head and said slowly:

"'Tis a fine car. A valuable commodity to take out of the jurisdiction and intil a foreign country." Athlyne had already taken out his pocket-book. Fortunately he had provided himself well with money before coming north.

"I paid a thousand pounds for the car. Will it not suit if I leave that amount in your custody." The official was impressed.

"Losh! man what wad I be daen wi' a thoosan poons in a wee bit station like this, or carryin' it aboot in me claes. Na! na! if ye'll de-po-sit say a ten poon note for the guarantee I'm thinkin' 'twill be a' reet. But how can the leddy get ava; ye'll hae to bide till the morn's morn."

"Oh that's all right, officer, she's a licensed driver. Unhappily she has not got her license with her. She left it in Ambleside as I was driving myself and had mine." He said this to avert her being questioned on the neglect; in which case there might be more trouble about the pace.

"Ooh! aye. Then that's a' reet! A maun ax her masel forbye she mayn't hae the license aboot her. Wimmen is feckless cattle anyhow!"

"Do you think sergeant she may get away at once. It is a long drive, and the day is getting on. I shall be very grateful indeed if you can manage it!" The sergeant was still impressed by the pocket book.

"Weel A'll see what A can dae!" He went outside with Athlyne to the automobile, and touching his cap said:

"Yer pardon ma leddy, ye're the wife o' the defender?" Joy was glad that she had put on the motor veil attached to her cap.

"Yes! My husband told you, did he not?" she said. The thrill that came to her with the speaking of the word "husband" she kept for later thought. The sergeant answered respectfully:

"He did ma leddy. But as an offeecial o' the law I hae to make sure as ye're aboot to travel oot o' the jurisdiction. He says ye hae left yer licence at hame; but as ye hae answered me that ye are his wife I will accept it, an' ye may go. The defender remains here; but I'm thinkin' there's a chance that he may no hae to remain so lang as he's fearin! Ma service to ye ma leddy." He touched his cap and went back into the station.

Athlyne came forward and said in a low voice, for the policeman who had effected the arrest was now standing outside the door:

"You will be careful darling. You may be able to do it. But if you are late and your father be angry say as little as you can. Unhappily I must remain here, but I shall do all I possibly can to settle things quietly. I shall follow in the morning; but not too early. Don't forget to wire your father if you are delayed anywhere, or are certain to be late. For my own part I shall leave proof everywhere of my own presence as we shall be in different countries!" He said this as it occurred to him that if she should be delayed it might later avert a scandal. Then he spoke up for the benefit of the policeman:

"As the time is so short, and we have learned the lesson of the danger of going too fast, you might ask when you get to Carlisle whether it is not quicker to return by Penrith and Patterdale. That way is some miles shorter." The policeman who had heard—and had also seen the pocket-book—came close and said with a respectful touch of his cap:

"If A may make sae bold, the leddy can save a wheen o' miles by takin' the road to Dumfries by Ken Brig an' Crocketford up yon. A saw ye the morn comin' up there." Athlyne nodded and touched his pocket; the man drew back into the station. One last word to Joy:

"I wish you knew the machine darling. But we must take chance for all going well." As he spoke he was turning the starting handle. Joy in a low voice said:

"Good bye my darling!" Resolutely she touched the levers, and the car moved off quietly to the "God bless you!" of each.

Athlyne watched the car as long as it was in sight; then he went back into the station. He spoke at once to the sergeant.

"Now sergeant is there nothing that can possibly be done to hasten the matter. You see I have done all I can to obey rules—once having broken them. I am most anxious to get back home as I have some very important business in the morning. I shall of course do exactly as is necessary; but I shall be deeply obliged if I can get away quietly, and double deeply to you if you can arrange it."

"Well ma lord I dinna think ye'll hae much trouble or be delayed o'er lang neither. For masel A canna do aught; but A'm thinkin that the Sheriff o' Galloway himsel will be here ony moment. He nearly always rides by when the fair at Castle Douglas is on, as it is to be in the morn. A'll hae a sharp look oot for him. He's a kind good man; an A'm thinkin that he'll no fash yer lordship. He can take responsibeelity that even a sargeant o' polis daurn't. So it's like ye'll get ava before the nicht."

Athlyne sat himself down to wait with what patience he could muster. Once again nature's pendulum began to swing in his thoughts; on one side happiness, on the other anxiety. The delight of the day wherein he had realised to the full that Joy indeed loved him, even as he loved her; the memory of those sweet kisses which still tingled on his lips and momentarily exalted him to a sort of rapture; and then the fear which was manifold, selfish and unselfish. She might get into any one of many forms of trouble if only from her anxiety to reach home before the arrival of her parents. She was, after all, not a practiced driver; and was in control of the very latest type of machine of whose special mechanism she could know nothing. If she should break down far from any town she would be in the most difficult position possible: a girl all alone in a country she did not know. And all this apart from the possibility of accident, of mischance of driving; of the act of other travellers; of cattle on the road; of any of the countless mishaps which can be with so swift and heavy a machine as a motor. And then should she not arrive in time, what pain or unpleasantness might there not be with her father. He would be upset and anxious at first, naturally. He might be angry with her for going out on such a long excursion with a man alone; he would most certainly be angry with him for taking her, for allowing her to go. And at such a time too! Just when everything was working—had worked towards the end he aimed at. He knew that Colonel Ogilvie was and had been incensed with him for a neglect which under the circumstances was absolute discourtesy. And here he bitterly took himself to task for his selfishness—he realised now that it was such—in wanting to make sure of Joy's love before consulting her father, or even explaining to him the cause of his passing under a false name. Might it not be too late to set that right now. . . . And there he was, away in Scotland, kicking his heels in a petty little police station, while she poor girl would have to bear all the brunt of the pain and unpleasantness. And that after a long, wearying, wearing drive of a hundred miles, with her dear heart eternally thumping away lest she might lose in her race against Time. And what was worse still that it would all follow a day which he did not attempt to doubt had been, up to the time of the arrest, one of unqualified happiness.

> ". . . nessun maggior dolore
> Che ricordasi del tempo felice
> Nella miseria."

("A sorrow's crown of sorrow is remembering happier things.")

The contrast would be terrible. He knew what the thought of it was to him; what would it be to her! Her sweet, gentle, loving heart would be hurt, crushed to the very dust.

He sprang to his feet and walked about the room, till noticing the sergeant was watching him with surprise and suspicion, he controlled himself.

He talked with the sergeant for a while genially. It was positively necessary that there should not be any doubt in the mind of the latter when the Sheriff should arrive. This episode took the strain from his mind—for a time. He expressed to the officer how anxious he was to get on and interested the worthy man so much that he sent over to the hotel to borrow a time-table. There Athlyne learned that it would be practically impossible for him to get on to Ambleside that night. Not even if he could get a special train at Carlisle—there was no possibility of getting one from a nearer place. When he asked the sergeant his opinion, that grave individual condescended to smile:

"Losh! man they don't run specials on these bit lines. 'Tis as much as they can do to run a few trains a day. A'm thinkin' that if ye asked the stationmaster anywheer along the Dumfries and Kircudbright line for a special he'd hae ye in the daft-hoose, or he'd be there himsel!" Athlyne went back to his seat; once again the pendulum of his thoughts swung to and fro.

He was now face to face with one certainty amongst many possibilities: Whatever befel he could not give any immediate help to Joy. She, poor dear, must fend for herself and if need be, fight her battle alone. He could only try to make it up to her afterwards. And yet what could he do for her, what more give to her who had already all that was his! And here again he lost himself in memories of the immediate past; which presently merged into dreams of the future which has no end.

But again swung the pendulum with the thought of what he was next day to do which might help Joy. He began to realise out of the intensity of his thought, which was now all unselfish, in what a danger of misconception the girl stood already and how such might be multiplied by any accident of her arrival. In the eyes of her friends her very character might be at stake! And now he made up his mind definitely as to how he would protect her in that way. He could prove his time of leaving Ambleside by his chauffeur, the time of that swift journey would be its own proof; the time of his arrest was already proved. Likewise of Joy's departure for home. Henceforward till he should meet her father he would take care that his movements were beyond any mystery or suspicion whatever. In any case—even if she did not arrive at home till late—Joy would be actually in another country from that which held him, and the rapidity of her journey would in itself protect. He would stay in some hotel in a place where he could get a suitable train in the morning; and would arrange that his arrival and departure were noted.

Naturally the place he would rest for the night, if he should succeed in getting away, would be Castle Douglas; for here lines from Kirkcudbright, from Stranraer, and from Glasgow made junction so that he had a double chance of departure. If he were detained at Dalry the police themselves would be proof of his presence there.

He felt easier in his mind after this decision, and was able to await with greater patience the coming of the Sheriff.

CHAPTER XVI

A PAINFUL JOURNEY

Joy started on her long journey in a very agitated frame of mind; though the habit of her life and her concern for her lover enabled her to so bear herself that she appeared calm. To start with, she was full of fears; some of them natural, others of that class which is due to the restrictions and conventions of a woman's life. She was by no means an expert driver. She merely had some lessons and was never in an automobile by herself before. Moreover she was not only in a country strange to her, but even the road to Dumfries on which she was started was absolutely new to her. In addition to it all she was—as an American—handicapped by the difference in the rules of the road. In America they follow the French and drive on the off side: in England the "on" rule is correct.

She had no option, however; she dared not make any difficulty or even ask advice or help, for such might betray her and she might not be allowed to proceed at all. So with as brace a face and bearing as she could muster, but with a sinking heart, she started on her journey, praying inwardly that she might not meet with any untoward accident or difficulty. For she did not know anything about mechanism; the use of the wheel and the levers in driving was all that had been embraced in her lessons.

At first all went well enough. The road was clear and she felt that she had the machine well in hand. As far as Balmaclellan she went slowly, carefully, climbing laboriously up the steep *zigzag* road; and presently she began to feel in good heart. She did not know the name of the place; had never heard of it. But it was somewhere; one stage at least on the way home. When the village lay behind her she began to put on more speed. With the apprehension gone of not being able to get on at all, she began to think of her objective and of how long was the journey before it could be revealed. With increased speed, however, came fresh fears. The importance of the machine began to be manifest; such force and speed needed special thought. The road changed so rapidly that she felt that she wanted another pair of eyes. The wheel alone, with its speed and steering indices, took all attention. She hardly dared to look up from it. And yet if she did not how could she know the road to take; how could she look out for danger. Happily the mere movement was a tonic; the rush through the air braced her. Otherwise she would have been shortly in a state of panic.

Very soon she began to realise the difficulty of driving on an unknown road, when one is not skilled in the art. So many things have to be considered all at once, and the onus of choosing perpetually is of nightmare shadow. The openings of bye-roads and cross-roads are so much more important than is suspected that there is a passing doubt as to direction; and country roads generally wind about so that distant land-marks, which can guide one in general direction, come and go with embarrassing suddenness. At first every cart-track or farm-road made such doubts, and even when she got to understand such minor trends she got confused over bye-roads of more importance. Crossroads there were before long, right or left making shortcuts for those who knew. These she had to pass; she could judge only of her course by the excellence of the main road—not always a safe guide in remote agricultural districts. One thing told in her favour: the magnificent bracing air of that splendid high-hung moor through which she passed. By the time she got to Corsock, however, she was beginning to feel the strain severely. She was hot and nervous and wearied; only the imperative need of getting on, and getting on quickly, enabled her to keep up at all. At Corsack she stopped to ask the way, but found it hard to understand the Lowland Scotch in which directions for her guidance were given. The result was that she started afresh with a blank despair gripping at her heart. Already she felt that her effort to reach home in time was destined to failure. The time seemed to fly so fast, the miles to be so long. She even began to feel a nervous doubt as to whether she should even be able to send word to her father. East of Corsock the nature of the road is confusing to a stranger. There are bye-roads leading south and up northwards into the mountains; and Urr Water has to be crossed. Joy began to lose the perspective of things; her doubts as to whether she was on the right road became oppressive. Somehow, things were changing round her. Look where she would, she could not see the hill tops that had been her landmarks. A mist was coming from the right hand—that was the south, where was Solway Firth.

Then she gave up heart altogether. There came to her woman's breast the reaction from all the happy excitement of the day. It was too bright to last. And now came this shadow of trouble worse even than the mist which seemed to presage it . . . Oh, if only He were with her now . . . He! . . . Strange it was that in all that day she had not once spoken to him by name. "Dear" or "Darling" seemed more suitable when her hand was in his; when he was kissing her. She closed her eyes in an ecstasy of delightful remembrance . . . She was recalled to herself by a sudden jar; in her momentary forgetfulness she had run up a bank.

It was a shock to her when her eyes opened to see how different were her surroundings from her thoughts. Those hours when they sat together where the sunbeams stole through the trees would afford her many a comparison in the time to come. All was now dark and dank and chill. The mist was thickening every instant; she could hardly see the road ahead of her.

However, she had to go on, mist or no mist; at least till she should reach some place whence she could telegraph to her father. With a pang she realised that she must not wire also to Him as she would have loved to have done. It would only upset and alarm him, poor fellow! and he had quite anxiety enough in thinking of her already! . . . With a heavy heart she crawled along through the mist, steering by the road-bed as well as she could, keeping a sharp lookout for cross-roads and all the dangers of the way.

The time seemed to fly, but not the car; the road appeared to be endless. Would she never come to any hospitable place! . . . It was a surprise to her when she came on straggling cottages, and found herself between double rows of houses. Painted over a door she saw "Crocketford Post-Office." In her heart she thanked God that she was still on the right road, though she had only as yet come some dozen or more miles. It seemed as if a week had passed since she left Dalry . . . and . . . She drew up to the post-office and went in. There she sent a wire:

"Went out motoring caught here in mist am going on however but must arrive very late so do not be anxious about me. Love to Mother and Aunt Judy and dear Daddy. Joy."

When she had handed it in she looked at her watch. It was only half-past five o'clock!

It was still therefore on the verge of possibility that she might get back in time. She hurried out. Several people had gathered round the motor, which was throbbing away after the manner of motors, as though impatient to get to real work. A policeman who was amongst them, seeing that she was about to go on, suggested that she should have her lamps lit as it would be a protection as well as a help to her in the mist. She was about to say that she thought it would be better not; for she did not know anything about acetylene lamps and feared to expose her ignorance, when he very kindly offered to light them for her: "'Tis no wark for a bonny leddy!" he said in self-justification of bending his official dignity to the occasion. She felt that his courtesy demanded some explanation, and also that such explanation would, be accounting for her being all alone, avoid any questioning. So said sweetly:

"Thank you so much, officer. I really do not know much about lamps myself and I had to leave my . . . my husband, who was driving, at Dalry. He was going too fast, and your people had a word to say to him. However, I can get on all right now. This is a straight road to Dumfries is it not?" The road was pointed out and instructions given to keep the high road to Dumfries. With better heart and more courage than heretofore she drove out into the mist. There was comfort for her in the glare of the powerful lights always thrown out in front of her.

All went well now. The road was distinctly good, and the swift smooth motion restored her courage. When in about half an hour she began to note the cottages and houses grouping in the suburbs of Dumfries she got elated. She was now well on the way to England! She knew from experience that the road to Annan, by which they had come, was fairly level. She did not mind the mist so much, now that she was accustomed to it; and she expected that as it was driving up northwards from the Firth she would be free from it altogether when she should have passed the Border and was on her way south to Carlisle.

In the meanwhile she was more anxious than as yet. The mist seemed to have settled down more here than in the open country. There were lights in many windows in the suburbs, and the street lamps were lit. It is strange how the perspective of lines of lamps gets changed when one is riding or driving or cycling in mist or fog. If one kept the centre of the road it would be all right; but as one keeps of necessity to the left the lines between the lamps which guide the eye change with each instant. The effect is that straight lines appear to be curved; and if the driver loses nerve and trusts to appearances he will soon come to grief. This was Joy's first experience of driving in mist, and she naturally fell into the error. She got confused as to the right and wrong side of the road. She had to fight against the habit of her life, which instinctively took command when her special intention was in abeyance. She knew that from Dumfries the road dropped to the south-east and as the curve seemed away to the left from her side of the road she, thinking that the road to the left was the direct road, naturally inclined towards the right hand, when she came to a place where there were roads to choose. There was no one about from whom to ask the way; and she feared to descend from the car to look for a sign-post. The onus of choice was on her, and she took the right hand thinking it was straight ahead. For some time now she had been going slow, and time and distance had both spun out to infinitude; she had lost sense of both. She was tired, wearied to death with chagrin and responsibility. Everything around her was new and strange and unknown, and so was full of terrors. She did not know how to choose. She feared to ask lest the doing so might land her in new embarrassments. She knew that unless she got home in something like reasonable time her father would be not only deeply upset but furiously angry—and all that anger would be visited on Him. Oh she must get on! It was too frightful to contemplate what might happen should she have to be out all night ... and after having gone out with a man against whom her father had already a grievance, though he owed him so much!

The change in the road, however, gave her some consolation; it was straight and smooth, and as the wind was now more in heir face she felt that she was making southward. But her physical difficulties were increasing. The wind was much stronger, and the mist came boiling up so fast that her goggles got blurred more than ever. Everything around her was becoming wet.

For a few miles—she could only guess at the distance—all went well, and she got back some courage. She still went slowly and carefully; she did not mean to have any mischance now if she could help it. It would not be so very long before she was over the Border.

Then most likely she would be out of the mist and she could put on more speed.

Presently she felt that the car was going up a steep incline. When it had been running swiftly she had not felt such, but now it was apparent. It was not a big hill, however, and the run down the other side was exhilarating, though the fear of some obstacle in front damped such pleasure as there was. Even then the pace was not fast; ordinarily it would have been considered as little better than a rapid crawl. For a while, not long but seeming more than long, the road was up-and-down till she saw in the dimness of the mist glimpses of houses, then a few gleams of light from the chinks of shut windows. Here she went very slowly and tooted often. She feared she might do some harm; and the slightest harm now might mean delay. She breathed more freely when she was out in the open again. That episode of the arrest and the prolonged agitation which followed it had unnerved her more than she had thought; and now the mist and the darkness and the uncertainty were playing havoc with her. It was only when she was long past the little place that she regretted she had not stopped to ask if she was on the right road. There was nothing for it, however, but to go on. The road was all up and down, up and down; but the surface was fairly good, and as the powerful lamps showed her sufficient space ahead to steer she moved along, though it had to be with an agonising slowness. How different it all was, she thought, from that fairy-chariot driving with Him in the morning. The road then seemed straight and level, and movement was an undiluted pleasure! For an instant she closed her wearied eyes as she sighed at the change—and ran off the road-bed.

Happily she was going slowly and recovered herself before more than the front wheels were on the rough mass of old road-scrapings. In a couple of seconds she had backed off and was under way again. She was preternaturally keen now in her outlook. She felt the strain acutely; for the road seemed to be always curving away from her. Moreover there was another cause of concern. Night was coming on. Even in the densest mist or the blackest fog the light or darkness of the sky is to some degree apparent. Now the sense came on her that over the thick mist was darkness. She stopped a moment and getting out looked at her watch in the light of the lamps.

Her heart fell away, away. It was now close to *eight* o'clock. There was no use worrying she felt; nothing to be done but to go on, carefully for the present. When she made up her mind to the worst, her courage began to come back and she could think. She felt that as the wind was now strongly in her face she must be nearing the Firth, and that in time she would pass the Border and be heading for home and father. She jumped into her seat and was off again.

The fog—she realised now that it was not mist but fog—was thicker than ever; the wind being strongly in her face, it seemed above the glare of the powerful lamps, to come boiling up out of the roadway which she could see but dimly. Fear, vague and gaunt, began to overshadow her. But there was no use worrying or thinking of anything except the immediate present which took the whole of her thought and attention. In the face of her surroundings she dared not go fast, dared not stop. And so for a time that seemed endless she pressed on through the fog. Presently she became aware that the wind was now not so much in her teeth. As she was steering by the road-bed she did not notice curves; there was no doubt as to her route, as there did not seem to be any divergent roads at all. On, on, on, on! A road full of hills, not very high nor especially steep but enough to keep a driver on constant watch-out.

At last she felt that she was close to the sea. The wind came fiercely, and the drifting fog seen against the luminous area round the lamps seemed like a whirlpool. There was a salt smell in the air. This gave her some hope. If this were the Firth she must be close to the Border and would soon be at the bridge over which they had entered Scotland. Instinctively she went forward faster. And at last there surely was a bridge. A narrow enough bridge it was; as she went slowly across it she wondered how it was that they had seemed to fly over it in the morning.

However she could go on now in new hope. She was in England and bye and bye she would come through the fog-belt, and having passed Carlisle would drop down through the Lake roads to Ambleside. Though the fog was dense as ever she did not feel the wind so much; she crowded on—she did not dare go much faster as yet and as she was now climbing a long steep hill she ceased to notice it. After a while, when there came a stronger puff than usual, she noticed that it was on her back—the high hood of the car had protected her for some time past. After a little however the old fear came back upon her. At the present rate of progress to reach home at any time, however late, seemed an impossibility. And all was so dark, and the fog was so dense; and the road didn't seem a bit like that they had come by between Carlisle and the Border. All at once she found that she was crying—crying bitterly. She did not want to stop the car, and so dared not take her hands from the wheel, even to find her pocket-handkerchief. She wept and wept; wept her heart out, whilst all the time mechanically steering by the light of the lamps on the road. Her weeping aided the density of the fog, and with her eyes set on the road and the driving wheel in her hands she did not notice that she was going between houses. She came to a bridge, manifestly of a little more importance than the one she had already passed, and crossed it. The road swayed away to the left; presently this was crossed by another almost at right angles, but she kept straight on. There was no one from whom to ask the way; and had there been anyone she probably would not have seen him. A little way on there was another cross-road but of minor importance; then further on she came to a place of difficult choice. Another cross-road, again almost at right angles; but the continuance of the road she was on showed it to be but a poor road ill-kept. So, too, was that to her left; but the road to the right was broad and well kept. It was undoubtedly the main road; and so keeping to the rule she had hitherto obeyed, she followed it.

She was now feeling somehow in better heart; the fit of crying had relieved her, and some of her courage had come back. She wanted comforting—wanted it badly; but those whose comfort only could prevail were far away; one behind her in Scotland, the others still far away at Ambleside. The latter thought made her desperate. She put on more speed—and with her thoughts and anxieties not in the present but the future, ran up a steep bank. There was a quick snap of something in front of the car; the throbbing of the engine suddenly ceased. With the shock she had been thrown forward upon the wheel, but fortunately the speed had not been great enough to cause her serious injury. The lamps made the fog sufficiently luminous for her movements, and she scrambled out of the car. She knew she could do nothing, for she was absolutely ignorant of the mechanism, and she had no mechanical skill. The only thing she could do was to go along the road on the blind chance of meeting or finding some one who could help her, or who might be able to assist her in finding better help. And so with a heavy heart, and feet that felt like lead, she went out into the fog. It was a wrench for her to leave the car which in the darkness and the unknown mystery of the fog seemed by comparison a sort of home or shelter. It was an evidence of the mechanical habit of the mind, which came back to her later, that through all her weariness and distress she thought to pin up her white frock before setting out on the dusty journey.

It was astonishing how soon the little patch of light disappeared. When she had taken but a few steps she looked back and found all as dark as it was before her. One thing alone there was which saved her from utter despair: the fog seemed not to be so absolutely dense. In reality it was not that the fog had lessened, but that her eyes, so long accustomed to the glare of the lamps which had prevented her seeing beyond the radius of their power, had now come back to their normal focus. Though the darkness seemed more profound than ever, since there was no point of light whatever, she was actually able to see better. After all, this fog was a sea mist unladen with city smoke, and its darkness was a very different thing from the Cimmerian gloom of a city fog. To her, not accustomed to winter fogs, it was difficult and terrifying. When, however, she began to realise, though unconsciously, that the nebulous wall in front of her fell back with every step she took, her heart began to beat more regularly, and she breathed more freely. It was a terrible position for a delicately nurtured girl to be in. Though she was a brave girl with a full share of self-reliance her absolute ignorance of all around her—even as to what part of the country she was in—had a somewhat paralysing effect upon her. However she had courage and determination. Her race as well as her nature told for her. Her heart might beat hard and her feet be heavy but at any rate she would go on her set road whilst life and strength and consciousness remained to her. She shut her teeth, and in blind despair moved forward in the fog.

In all her after life Joy could never recall the detail of that terrible walk. Like most American girls she was unused to long walks; and after a couple of miles she felt wearied to death. The long emotional strain of the day had told sorely on her strength, and the hopeless nerve-racking tramp on the unknown road through the gloom and mystery of the fog had sapped her natural strength. Looking back on that terrible journey she could remember no one moment from the other, from the time that she lost sight of the lamps until she found herself in a dip in the road passing under a railway bridge. The recognition of the fact reanimated her. It was an evidence that there was some kind of civilisation somewhere—a fact that she had begun in a vague way to doubt. She would follow that line if she could, for it must lead her to some place where she might find help; where she could send reassuring word to her father, and where there would be shelter. Shelter! At the first gleam of hope her own deplorable position was forced upon her, and she realised all at once her desperate weariness. She could now hardly drag herself along.

Beyond the railway there was a branch road to the left; and this she determined to follow, rather than the main road which went away from the line. She stumbled along it as well as she could. The time seemed endless. In her weariness the flicker of hope which her juxtaposition to the railway had given her died soon away. The fog seemed denser, and the darkness blacker than ever.

The road dipped again under the line; she was glad of that; manifestly she was not straying from it. She hurried on instinctively; found the road wider, and rougher with much use. Her heart beat hard once again, but this time it was with hope.

And then, right in front of her, was a dim gleam of light. This so overcame her that she had to sit down for a moment on the road side. The instant's rest cheered her; she jumped to her feet as though her strength had been at once restored. Feeling in her heart a prayer which her lips had not time to utter, she climbed over a wire fence between her and the light; stumbled across a rough jumble of sleepers and railway irons. Then the light was over her head—the rays were manifest on the fog. She called out:

"Hullo! Hullo! Is there any one awake?" Almost instantly the window through which the light shone was opened and a man looked out:

"Aye! A'm awake! Did ye think A'd be sleepin' on a nicht like this. 'Tis nae time for a signal-man to be aught but awake A'm tellin' ye."

"Thank God, oh thank God!" Joy's heart was too full for the moment to say more. The man leaned further out:

"Is yon a lassie? What are ye daein' here a nicht like this? Phew! A canna see ma ain hond!"

"Yes, I'm a girl and I'm lost. Will you let me come in?" The man's voice became instantly suspicious.

"Na! na! A canna let ye in. 'Tis no in accord wi' the Company's rules to let a lassie intil the signal-box. Why don't ye go intil the toon?"

"Oh do let me in for a moment," she pleaded. "I have been lost in the fog, and my motor broke down. I have had to walk so far that I am wearied and tired and frightened; and the sight of a light and the hope of help has finished me!" She sat right down on the ground and began to cry. He heard her sob, and it woke all the man in him. This was no wandering creature whose presence at such a time and place might make trouble for him. He knew from the voice that the woman was young and refined.

"Dinna greet puir lassie!—Dinna greet. A canna leave the box for an instant lest a signal come. But go roond to the recht and ye'll find a door. Come recht up! Rules or no rules A'm no gangin' to let ye greet there all by yer lanes. There's fire here, and when ye're warmed A can direct ye on yer way intil the toon!"

With glad steps she groped her way to the door. A flood of light seemed to meet her when she opened it, and she hurried up the steep stairs to where the signal-man held open the upper door.

"Coom in lassie an hae a soop o' ma tea. 'Tis fine and warrm! . . . Coom in and let me offer ye some refreshment, an' if A may mak sae bold may A offer ye all A hae that'll warm ye? Coom in ma'am. Coom in ma leddie!" he said in a crescendo of welcome and respect as he saw Joy's fine motor coat and recognised her air of distinction.

Glad indeed was Joy to drink from the worthy fellow's tin tea-bottle which rested beside the stove; glad to sit down in front of the fire. Then indeed she felt the magnitude of her weariness, and in a minute would have been asleep.

But the thought of her father, and all that depended on her action and his knowledge, wakened her to full intellectual activity. She stood up at once and said quickly:

"What place is this?"

"The signal-box of Castle Douglas Junction."

"And where is that? I think I have heard the name before."

"Tis a toon as they ca' it here. The junction is o' the Glasgie an' South Western, the Caledonian, the Port Patrick an' Wigtownshire, the London an' North Western, an' the Midland lines. But for short there are but twa. One frae Kirkcudbright, an' th' ither frae Newton Stewart."

"In what country are we?" Seeing the astonishment in his face she went on: "I am an American, and not familiar with the district. We came from England this morning—from Westmoreland—from Ambleside—and I am confused about the Border. I had to drive myself because my—we got into trouble for driving fast, and I had to come on alone. And then the fog overtook me. I went along as well as I could. Are we anywhere near Carlisle?" Her face fell as she saw the shake of his head:

"Eh ma leddie but ye're mony a mile frae Carlisle. 'Tis over fifty miles be the line. Ye maun hae lost yer way sair. Ye're in Kirkcudbrightshire the noo." Her heart sank:

"Oh I must send a telegram at once."

"Ye canna telegraph the nicht ma leddie! The office is closed till eight the morn's morn."

"My God! What shall I do. My father arrived from London to-night and he does not know where I am. I came out for a drive and thought to be back in good time to meet him. He will be in despair. Is there no way in which I can send word? It is not a matter of expenses; I shall pay anything if it can be done!" She looked at him in an agony of apprehension. The man was stirred by the depth of emotion and by her youth and beauty; and his clever Scotch brain began to work. His mouth set fast in a hard line and his rough heavy brows began to wrinkle. After a pause he said:

"A'll do what A can, ma leddie; though A can't be sure if 'twill wark. The telegraphs are closed. Even if we could find an operator it wouldn't be possible to get the wires. Our own lines are closed, for we'll hae no traffic till morn." Here an idea struck Joy and she interrupted him:

"Could I not get a special train? I am willing to pay anything?"

"Lord love ye, ma leddy, they don't have specials on bit lines like this. Ye couldn't get one nigher than Glasgie, an' not there at this time o' day. Let alone they'd no send in such a fog anyhow. But I'm thinkin' that A can telephone to Dumfries. The operator o' oor line there is a freend o' mine, an' if he's on dooty he'll telephone on to Carlisle wheer there's sure to be some one at the place. An' mayhap the latter'll telephone on till Ambleside. So, if there be any awake there, they'll send to the hotel. Is it a hotel yer faither'll be in?"

"Oh thank you, thank you," said Joy seizing his hand in a burst of gratitude. "I'll be for ever grateful to you if you'll be so good!"

"A'm thinkin'" he went on "that perhaps 'twill cost yer ladyship a mickle—perhaps a muckle; but A dar say ye'll no mind that . . ."

"Oh no, no! It will be pleasure to pay anything. See, I have plenty of money!" She pulled out her purse.

"Na! na! Not yet ma leddie. 'Tis no for masel—unless yer ladyship insists on it, later on. 'Tis for the laddies that will do what they can. Ye see there may be some trouble o'er this. We signal-men and offeecials generally are not supposed to attend to aught outside o' the routine. But if it should be that there is trouble to us puir folk, A'm sure yer ladyship an' some o' yer graan' freens'll no see us wranged!"

"Oh no indeed. My father and Mr.—— and all our friends will see to it that you shall never suffer, no matter what happens."

"Well now, ma leddy—if ye'll joost write down your message A'll do what A can. But 'twill be wiser if ye gang awa intil a hotel an' rest ye. A can send the message better when A'm quit o' ye. Forbye ye see 'tis no quite respectable to hae a bonny lassie here ower lang. Ma wife is apt to be a wee jalous; an' it's no wise to gie cause where nane there is."

"But I do not know where to go—" she began. He interrupted her hastily:

"There's a graan hotel i' the toon—verra fine it is; but A'm thinkin' that yer ladyship, bein' by yer lonesome, may rather care to go to a quieter house. An' as A'd recommend ye to seek the 'Walter Scott' hotel. 'Tis kep by verra decent folk, an' though small is verra respectable an' verra clean. Say that yer kent by Tammas Macpherson an' that will vouch for ye, seein' that ye're a bit lassie by yer lanes.

'Tis a most decent place entirely, an' A'm tellin' ye that the Sheriff o' Galloway himsel' aye rests there when he comes to the toon."

Joy wrote her message on the piece of paper which he had provided whilst speaking:

"To Col. Ogilvie, Inn of Greeting, Ambleside: Dearest Daddy I have been caught in a heavy fog and lost, but happily found my way here. I shall return by the first train in the morning. Love to mother. I am well and safe. Joy."

Then the signal man gave her explicit directions as to finding the house. As she was going away he said with a diffident anxiety:

"To what figure will yer ladyship gang in this—this meenistration? A'd joost like to ken in case o' neceesity?" She answered quickly:

"Oh anything you like—twenty-five dollars—I mean five pounds—ten pounds—twenty—a hundred, anything, anything so that my father gets the message soon." He looked amazed for a moment. Then as he held open the door deferentially he said in a voice in which awe blended with respect:

"Dinna fash yersel' more ma leddie. Yer message will gang for sure; an' gang quick. Ye may sleep easy the nicht, an' wi'out a thocht o' doobt. An'll leave wi' ma kinsman Jamie Macpherson o' the Walter Scott ma neem an' address in case yer ladyship wishes me to send to yon the memorandum o' the twenty poons."

Joy found her way without much difficulty to the Walter Scott. The house was all shut up, but she knocked and rang; and presently the door was unchained and opened. The Boots looked for a moment doubtful when he saw a lady alone; but when she said:

"I am lost in the fog, and Mr. Thomas Macpherson of the railway told me I should get lodging here," he opened the door wide and she walked in. He chained the door, and left her for a few minutes; but returned with a young woman who eyed her up and down somewhat suspiciously. Joy seemed to smell danger and said at once:

"I got lost in the fog, and the motor met with an accident. So I had to leave it on the road and walk on."

"An' your shawfer?" asked the doubting young woman.

"He got into trouble for driving too fast, and had to be left behind."

"Very weel, ma'am. What name shall A put down?" Joy's mind had been working. Her tiredness and her sleepiness were brushed aside by the pert young woman's manifest suspicion. She remembered Mr. Hardy's caution not to give her own name; and now, face to face with a direct query, remembered and used the one which had been given to her on the *Cryptic*. It had this advantage that it would put aside any suspicion or awkwardness arising from her unprotected position, arriving as she did in such an unaccredited way. So she answered at once:

"Athlyne. Lady Athlyne!" The young woman seemed impressed. Saying: "Excuse me a moment" she went into the bar where she lit a candle. She came back in a moment and said very deferentially:

"It's all recht yer ladyship. There's twa rooms, a sittin'-room an' a bed-room. They were originally kept for the Sheriff, but he sent word that he was no comin'. So when the wire came frae th' ither pairty the rooms were kept for him. When no one arrived the name was crossed aff the slate. But it's a' recht! Shall I light a fire yer Leddyship?"

"Oh no! I only require a bedroom. I must get away by the first train in the morning. I shall just lie down as I am. If you can get me a glass of milk and a biscuit that is all I require. If it were possible I should like the milk hot; but if that is not convenient it won't matter." As they went upstairs the girl said:

"Ye'll forgie me yer Leddyship, but I didna ken wha ye were. Mrs. Macpherson was early up to bed the nicht, when the fog had settled doon and she knew there was no more traffic. To-morrow is a heavy day here, and things keep up late; and she wanted to be ready for it. An' she's michty discreet aboot ony comin' here wi'oot—wi'oot—"

She realised that she was getting into deep water and turned the conversation. "There is yer candle lit. The fire in the kitchen is hearty yet, an' I'll bring yer milk hot in the half-o' two-twos. I'll leave word that ye're to be called in good time in the morn."

Within a few minutes she came back with the hot milk. Joy was too tired and too anxious to eat; and refusing all proffers of service and of help as to clothing, bade the girl good night. She just drank the milk; and having divested herself of her shoes and stockings which were soiled with travel and of all but her under-clothing, crept in between the sheets. The warmth and the luxury of rest began to tell at once; within a very few minutes she was sound asleep.

CHAPTER XVII

THE SHERIFF

It was late in the afternoon when the Sheriff rode into Dalry. The police sergeant spoke to him, and he kindly came into the station. There the sergeant put the matter before him. He was an elderly man, hearty and genial and with a pleasant manner which made every man his friend. When he heard the details of the case, regarding which the policeman asked his advice, he smiled and took snuff and said pleasantly to the officer:

"I don't think ye need be uneasy in your mind. After all 'tis only a matter of a fine; and as the chauffeur is ready to pay it, whatever it may be; and is actually in your custody having as you say more than sufficient money upon him to pay the maximum penalty hereto inflicted for furious driving in this shire, I think you will not get much blame for allowing the lady to go away in the car to a 'foreign country,' as you call it. I suppose sir" turning to Athlyne "you can get good bail if required?"

"I think so" said Athlyne smiling. "I suppose a Deputy Lieutenant of Ross Shire is good enough;" whereupon he introduced himself to the Sheriff. They chatted together a few minutes and then, as he went to his horse which a policeman was holding at the door, he said to the sergeant:

"I must not, as Sheriff, be bail myself. But if any bail is required I undertake to get it; so I think you needn't detain his lordship any longer. You'd better serve the summons on him for the next Session and then everything will be in order."

Athlyne walked down the village with him, he leading his horse. When he knew that Athlyne was going to walk to Castle Douglas so as to be ready to catch his train to the south he said:

"To-morrow is a busy day there and you may find it hard to get rooms at the Douglas, especially as the fog will detain many travellers. Now I had my rooms reserved at the Walter Scott, kept by an old servant of mine, where I always stay. An hour gone I wired countermanding them as I am going to stay the night with Mulgrave of Ennisfour where I am dining; so perhaps you had better wire over and secure them. I shall be there myself in the morning as I have work in Castle Douglas, but that need not interfere with you. If you go early you may be off before I get there."

"I do not want to go South very early; so I hope you will breakfast with me if I am still there." The genial old Sheriff shook his head:

"No, no. You must breakfast with me. I am in my own bailiwick and you must let me be your host."

"All right!" said Athlyne heartily. The old man who had been looking at him kindly all the time now said:

"Tell me now—and you won't think me rude or inquisitive; but you're a young man and I'm an old one, and moreover sheriff—can I do anything for you? The Sergeant told me you were in a state of desperate anxiety to get away—or at any rate to let the lady get off; and I couldn't help noticing myself that you are still anxious. The policeman said she was young, and much upset about it all. Can I serve you in any way? If I can, it will I assure you be a pleasure to me."

He was so frank and kind and hearty that Athlyne's heart warmed to him. Moreover he was upset himself, poor fellow; and though he was a man and a strong one, was more than glad to unburden his heart to some one who would be a sympathetic listener:

"The fact is, sir, that the young lady who was with me came for a drive from Ambleside and we came on here on the spur of the moment. Her father had gone to London and returns this evening; and as no one knew that I—that she had gone out motoring he will be anxious about her. Naturally neither she nor I wish to make him angry. You will understand when I tell you that she and I are engaged to be married. He does not know this—though" here he remembered the letter he had posted at Ambleside "he will doubtless know soon. Unhappily he had some mistaken idea about me. A small matter which no one here would give a second thought to: but he is a Kentuckian and they take some things very much to heart. This was nothing wrong—not in any way; but all the same his taking further offence at me, as he would do if he heard from someone else that she had been motoring with me without his sanction, might militate against her happiness—and mine. So you can imagine Mr. Sheriff, how grateful I am to you for your kindness."

The sheriff paused before replying. He had been thinking—putting two and two together: "They are engaged—but her father doesn't know it. Then the engagement was made only to-day. No wonder they were upset and anxious. No wonder he drove fast. . . . Ah, Youth! Youth!" . . .

"I understand, my lord. Well, you did quite right to get the lady away; though it was a hazardous thing for her to start off alone in the mist."

"It hadn't come on then, sir. Had it been so I should never have let her go alone—no matter what the consequences might be! But I hope she's out of it and close to home by this time."

"Aye that's so. Still she was wise to go. It avoids all possibility of scandal. Poor bairn! I'm hoping she got off South before the fog came on too thick. It's drifting up from the Firth so that when once she would have crossed the Border most like it would have been clear enow. Anyhow under the circumstances you are right to stay here. Then there can be no talk whatever. And her father will have had time to cool down by the time ye meet.

"We're parting here, my Lord. Good-bye and let me wish ye both every form of human happiness. Perhaps by morn you will have had some news; and I'm hoping ye'll be able to tell me of her safe arrival."

At the cross roads the men parted. The Sheriff rode on his way to Ennisfour, and Athlyne went back to Dalry. He ordered his dinner, and then went out to send a telegram at the little post office. His telegram ran:

To Walter Scott Hotel Castle Douglas
    Keep rooms given up by Sheriff for to-night.
                                   Athlyne.

He had written the telegram through without a pause. The signature was added unhesitatingly, though not merely instinctively. He had done with falsity; henceforth he would use his own name, and that only. He felt freer than he had done for many a day.

He ate his dinner quietly; he was astonished at himself that he could take matters so calmly. It was really that he now realised that he had done all he could. There was nothing left but to wait. In the earlier part of that waiting he was disturbed and anxious. Difficulties and dangers and all possible matters of concern obtruded themselves upon his thought in endless succession. But as time wore on the natural optimism of his character began to govern his thinking. Reason still worked freely enough, but she took her orders from the optimistic side and brought up arrays of comforting facts and deductions.

It was with renewed heart and with a hopeful spirit that he set out on his road to Castle Douglas. He had deliberately chosen to walk instead of taking a carriage or riding. He did not want to arrive early in the evening, and he calculated that the sixteen miles would take him somewhere about four hours to walk. The exercise would, whilst it killed the time which he had to get through, give him if not ease of mind at least some form of mental distraction. Such, he felt, must be his present anodyne—his guarantee of sanity. As he had no luggage of any kind he felt perfectly free; the only addition to his equipment was a handful of cigars to last him during the long walk.

He had left Dalry some miles behind him when he began to notice the thickening of the mist. After a while when this became only too apparent he began to hesitate as to whether it would not be wiser to return. By this time he realised that it was no mere passing cloud of vapour which was driving up from the south, but a sea fog led inward through the narrowing Firth; he could smell the iodine of the sea in his nostrils. But he decided to go on his way. He remembered fairly well the road which he had traversed earlier in the day. Though a rough road and somewhat serpentine as it followed the windings of the Ken and the Dee, it was so far easy to follow that there were no bifurcations and few cross-roads. And so with resolute heart—for there was something to overcome here—and difficulty meant to him distraction from pain—he pushed on into the growing obscurity of the fog.

On the high ground above Shirmers he felt the wind driving more keenly in his face; but he did not pause. He trudged on hopefully; every step he took was bringing him closer to England—and to Joy. Now it was that he felt the value of the stout walking cudgel that he had purchased from a passing drover. For in the fog he was like a blind man; sight needed the friendly aid of touch.

But it was dreadfully slow work, and at the end of a few hours he was wearied out with the overwhelming sense of impotence and the ceaseless struggling with the tiniest details of hampered movement. Being on foot and of slow progress he had one advantage over travelling on horseback or in a vehicle: he was able to take advantage of every chance opportunity of enlightenment. From passing pedestrians and at wayside cottages he gathered directions for his guidance. It was midnight—the town clock was striking—when he entered Castle Douglas and began to inquire his way to the Walter Scott hotel.

After repeated knocking the door was opened by the Boots—a heavy, thick-headed, sleepy, tousled man, surly and grudging of speech. Athlyne pushed past him into the hall way and said:

"I wired here in the afternoon to have kept for me the Sheriff's rooms. Did my telegram arrive."

"Aye. It kem a'recht. But that was all that kem. Ye was expectit, an' the missis kep the rooms for ye till late; but when ye didna come she gied ye up an' let anither pairty that was lost i' the fog hae the bedroom. All that's left is the parlour, an that we can hae an ye will. Forbye that ye'll hae to sleep on the sofy. A'm thinkin' it's weel it's o'er long than ordinair', for ye're no a ween yersel. Bide wheer y' are, an' A'll fetch ye a rug or two an' a cushion. Ye maun put up wi' them the nicht for ye'll git nane ither here." He left him standing in the dark; and shuffled away down a dim stairway, to the basement.

In a few minutes he re-appeared with a bundle of rugs and pillows under his arm; in his hand was a bottle of whiskey, with the drawn cork partly re-inserted. With the deftness of an accomplished servitor he carried in his other hand, together with the candle, a pitcher of water and a tumbler. As he went up the staircase he said in a whisper;

"Man, walk saft as ye gang; an' dinna cough nor sneeze or mak' a soond in the room or ye'll maybe waken th' ither body. Joost gang like a man at a carryin'. An' mind ye dinna snore! Lie ye like a bairn! What time shall A ca'ye?"

"I want to catch the morning train for the south."

"That'll be a'recht. A'll ca' ye braw an' airly!"

"Good night!" said Athlyne as he softly closed the door.

He spread one rug on the sofa, which supplemented by a chair, was of sufficient length; put the other ready to cover himself, and fixed the cushions. Having stripped to his flannels he blew out the candle, and, without making a sound, turned in. He was wearied in mind and nerve and body, and the ease of lying down acted like a powerful narcotic. Within a minute he was sound asleep.

CHAPTER XVIII

PURSUIT

Colonel Ogilvie found his wife in excellent health and spirits. The cure had been effective, and the prospect of meeting Joy so filled her with delight that her youth seemed to be renewed. He could see, when the morning light was admitted to their bedroom, that her eyes were bright and her cheeks rosy; and all her movements were alert and springy. Judy too, when they went to breakfast, looked well and was in good spirits; but there was something about her which he could not understand. It was not that she was quick of intellect and speech, for such had been always her habit; it was not that she was eager, for she was not always so; it was not that she was exuberantly fond of Joy—she had never been anything else. But there seemed now to be some sort of elusive background to all her thoughts. He began to wonder in a vague way if it were possible that she had fallen in love. She asked, after her usual manner, a host of questions about Joy and about the visit to the Lakes; where they had been and who they had seen; and of all the little interests and happenings during the time of separation. Colonel Ogilvie felt a little wearied of it all. He had already covered the ground with the girl's mother, for arriving in the grey of the dawn, he had gone straight to his wife's room where he had rested till breakfast time. There he had told her all that he could remember. With, however, the patient courtesy which had not as yet in his life failed him with women he went over all the ground again with Judy. He could not but be struck with Judy's questioning on one subject: whether they had met at Ambleside any special acquaintance. He concluded that she meant Mr. Hardy, and asked her if such were the case. She blushed so brightly when she admitted it that he conceived the idea that the peccant Englishman was the object of her affection. Then, as she dropped that subject of questioning, he, in order to draw her out, went on:

"But my dear Judy it was not possible that we could have seen him. He has not seemed particularly anxious to meet us; and even if he was anxious he could not have done it as he did not know where we were."

"Oh, yes he did!" The Colonel was surprised; the tone of her words carried conviction of truthfulness. He answered quickly:

"He did! How on earth do you know that?" Judy in her emotional interest answered without thinking.

"Because I told him so!"

"Oh, you saw him then?" Again she answered without thought:

"No, but I wrote to him."

"How do you know that he got your letter?"

"Because he answered it!" She would have given all she possessed to have been silent or to have answered more discreetly when she saw her brother-in-law's face wrinkle into a hard smile, and noted the cruel keenness of his eyes and the cynical smile on his mouth. She answered sharply; and, as is usual, began the instant after, to pay the penalty for such sharpness. His voice seemed to rasp her very soul as he said:

"I am glad to hear that the gentleman has consideration for some one—even a lady—who writes to him. But to my mind such but emphasises his rudeness—if for the moment I may call it so—of his conduct to others. As for myself when I meet the gentleman—should I ever have the good fortune to do so—I shall require him to answer for this insult—amongst others!"

"Insult?" murmured Judy in a panic of apprehension.

"Yes, my dear Judith. There is no stronger word; had there been I should have used it. When the same man who does *not* answer my letters, or write even to accept or decline my proffered hospitality carries on at the same time a clandestine correspondence with ladies of my family he shall have to answer to me for it. By God he shall!" Judy thought silence wiser than any form of words, and remained mute. Colonel Ogilvie went on in the same cold, rasping voice:

"May I ask you, Miss Hayes,"—"Miss Hayes, my God!" thought poor Judy trembling. He went on: "if my daughter has had any meeting or correspondence with him?"

"No! No! No!" cried Judy. "I can answer for that."

"Indeed! May I ask how you can speak with certainty on such a subject. I thought you were in Italy and that my daughter had been with me." In despair she spoke impulsively:

"I don't *know*, Lucius. How could I—I only think so."

"Exactly! Then you are but giving your opinion! For that my dear Judith I am much obliged; but it has been for so long my habit to judge for myself in matters of those mutual relations between men which we call 'honour' that I have somehow come to trust my own opinion in preference to that of any one else—even you my dear Judith—and to act upon it." Then, seeing the red flush of anger and humiliation in her cheeks whilst the tears seemed to leap into her eyes, he felt that he had gone too far and added:

"I trust that you will forgive me, my dear sister, if I have caused you unnecessary pain. Unhappily pain must follow such dereliction of duty as has been shown by that young man, and by you too; but believe me I would spare you if I could. But I can promise—and do so now—that I shall not again forget myself and speak bitterly, out of the bitterness of my heart as I have done. I pray your forgiveness, and trust that it may be extended to me." The cynical words and tone of his apology, however it may have been meant, only added fuel to her anger. Words were inadequate, so she sought refuge in flight. As she went out of the door she heard Colonel Ogilvie say as if to himself:

"I may not know how to speak to women; but thank God, I do know how to deal with that damned fellow!"

Judy threw herself on her bed in a storm of futile passion. She could not but feel that she had been brutally treated; but she was powerless to either resent or explain. But well she knew that she had helped to leave matters worse for poor Joy than they had been. All the anger that Colonel Ogilvie had been repressing had now blazed out. He had expressed himself, and she had never known such expression of his to fail in tragic consequences. He would now never forgive Mr. Hardy for his double sins of omissions and commission. She was sorry for the young man's sake; but was in anguish for the sake of the poor girl who had, she felt and knew, set her heart upon him. Joy's romance in which her heart—her whole being and her future happiness—had been embarked was practically over, though she did not know it as yet. All the life-long brightness that even her father had ever hoped for her was gone. Henceforth she would be only a poor derelict, like Judy herself, wrecked on a lee shore! Judy had always pitied herself, but she had never realized the cause of that pity as she did now, seen as it was through the eyes of loving sympathy.

> "I pitied my own heart,
> As if I held it in my hand,
> Somewhat coldly,—with a sense
> Of fulfilled benevolence,
> And a 'Poor thing' negligence."

Colonel Ogilvie went out in a very militant humour to interview the motor-agent. He felt angry with himself for having lost his temper—and to a lady; and his anger had to be visited on some one. In any case he considered that the motor people had treated him scurvily and should suffer accordingly. In reality he was in a reaction from great happiness. He was an affectionate husband who had been deeply concerned at his wife's long illness, and lonely and distraught in her long absence. Only that morning he had met her again and had found her quite restored to health and as though she had regained her youth. He had shared in her pleasure at the good account he had to give of Joy. It was, after all, perhaps natural to a man of his peculiar temperament to visit heavily his displeasure on the man who had, to his mind, ill-used him, and on all concerned with him in the doing. Mr. Hardy it was who had jarred the wheels of his chariot of pleasure; and Mr. Hardy it was who must ultimately answer to him for so doing.

The expression of his opinions as to the moral and commercial worth of the motor-agent and of the manufacturer with whom he dealt seemed to relieve his feelings to some degree; he returned to Brown's in a much milder frame of mind than that in which he had gone out. He was kept pretty busy till the time of departure, but in his secret heart—made up to action during the time of his work—he determined to try to make amends to Judy for the pain he had given her. He rejoiced now that his wife had not been present at that scene which it already pained him to look back upon.

He was somewhat incensed that as he could not leave by his intended train he would have to postpone the journey by several hours. He could not now arrive at Ambleside till nearly midnight.

In the train he took the first opportunity of making the *amende* to Judy. Mrs. Ogilvie had fallen asleep—she had been awake since very early in the morning, so the Colonel said quietly to his sister-in-law:

"Judy I want you to forgive me, if you can." She thrilled with pleasure as he spoke her name in the familiar form. It seemed some sort of presage of a change for the better, a sort of lifting of the ban which had all day lain so heavy on her. As he went on her hopes grew; there were possibilities that, after all, Joy was not yet finally doomed to unhappiness. At all times Colonel Ogilvie was impressive in his manner; the old-fashioned courtesy on which he had long ago founded himself was permeated with conscious self-esteem. Now when the real earnestness of the moment was grafted upon this pronounced manner he seemed to the last degree dignified—almost pompous:

"I cannot tell you how sorry I am that I caused you pain this morning, or how ashamed I am for having so lost my temper before you. For more than twenty years I have honestly tried, my dear, to make you happy." Here she interrupted him: "And you succeeded Lucius!" He rose and bowed gravely:

"Thank you, my dear. I am grateful to you for that kindly expression. It does much, I assure you, to mitigate the poignancy of my present concern. It was too bad of me to let my bitterness so wound you. It shall not occur again. Moreover I feel that I owe you something; and I promise you that if I should be so—so overcome again by anger I shall try to obey you to the best of my power. You shall tell me what you wish me to do; and if I can I shall try to do it." Here a look of caution, rare to him, overspread his face: "I won't promise to give up a purpose of my life or brook any interference with the course of honour—that I can promise to no one, not even to you my dear. But if I can grant any consideration—or—or favour I shall certainly try to do so!"

Judy was not so well satisfied with the end of the promise as with the beginning. But it was hopeful of better things for the future; so she meekly and gratefully accepted it *en bloc*.

When they arrived at Ambleside it was dark and the lamps of the station lent but a dim light. It became evident to Mrs. Ogilvie and Judy that Colonel Ogilvie was disappointed at not finding

Joy awaiting them on the platform. He had, during the journey, explained to them with some elaboration that they were not to expect her as he had said there was no need of her coming; but, all the same, he had himself expected her. As the train drew up he had leaned out of the window looking carefully along the whole range of the platform. When, however, he ascertained that she was not there, he turned his attention to Judy whom he observed prolonging the search. His mind at once went back to his original concern that there was something between her and Mr. Hardy. She heard him say to himself fiercely under his breath:

"That damned fellow again!" She did not of course understand that it was with reference to herself, and took it that it presaged ill to Joy. She knew from Colonel Ogilvie's expression and bearing that the man he had now grown to hate was in his mind, and with a heavy heart she took her place in the waiting landau.

When the carriage arrived at the hotel Colonel Ogilvie jumped out and ran up the steps. This was so unlike his usual courtesy that it not only pained the two ladies but made them anxious. When Colonel Ogilvie forgot his habitual deference to women something serious indeed must have been in his mind! When they followed, which they did as quickly as they could, they found him in the hall reading a telegram. A railway envelope lay on the table, and beside it a little pile of letters. When he had finished reading the first telegram he opened the second and read it also. All the time his face was set in a grim frown, the only relief from which was the wrinkling of his forehead which betrayed an added anxiety. He handed the two transcripts to his wife, saying as he did so:

"I have put them in order; one is a few hours earlier than the other!" Mrs. Ogilvie read in silence and handed the forms to Judy, the Colonel remaining grimly silent.

Mrs. Ogilvie said nothing. When Judy had turned over the last and looked at the back of it in that helpless manner which betrays inadequate knowledge, Colonel Ogilvie said:

"Well?"

"I trust the poor child is not in any danger!" said the mother.

"How thoughtful of her to have sent twice. She knew you would be so anxious about her!" said the aunt, wishing to propitiate the angry father. For fully a minute no more was said. Then the Colonel spoke:

"She went motoring. In whose car? I have not yet got my own!" As he was speaking the hotel proprietor came into the hall to pay his respects, as he usually did with incoming guests. He heard the last remark and said:

"Pardon me, Colonel Ogilvie. But your car has arrived. The chauffeur who had charge of it and came in the same train with it to Kirkby Stephen drove it here some time ago!" Colonel Ogilvie bowed a slight acknowledgment and turning to Judy said:

"Then it could not be in that car she went. If not, whose car was it? Whom did she go with? We know no one here who owns a car; and we did not make any new acquaintances during our stay. Indeed none even of our old acquaintances did us the honour of calling. But perhaps my dear Judy," he spoke with manifest and comforting self-restraint—"you can enlighten us. Do you know if your friend Mr. Hardy whom you informed of our being here has a motor car?" Judy feared to precipitate disaster, and not knowing what to say answered feebly with a query:

"Why Colonel?" The storm cloud of the father's wrath instantly broke:

"Why, madam 'why'" he almost roared whilst the discreet proprietor withdrew closing the inner door of the hall behind him—the luggage was being taken in by the basement door:

"I'll tell you why if you wish—though perhaps you know it already. Because I want to know under what circumstances my daughter has gone out motoring with some stranger—though indeed it may be that he is not quite a stranger—the moment my back was turned. Let me tell you that it is not usual for unmarried young ladies to go out motoring into far away places with men, unchaperoned. My honour—*my* honour through my daughter—is here concerned. And it is like that damned fellow to take her away in such an underhand manner. You need say nothing of him. It's no use trying to palliate his conduct. True enough I don't know for certain that it is he, or that she is alone with any man; but I have a conviction that it is so; and I tell you I shall lose no time in putting my convictions to the test. I mean to take no chances with regard to that damned fellow. I don't trust him! He has already affronted me, and has been tampering with the women of my family. I have borne even that with what temper I could because I was under obligation to him. But if, as it would seem, he has run away with my daughter, I shall brook his insolence no longer. He shall render me a full account of his doings with me and mine!" He crammed his letters into his pocket and strode upstairs. There he rang the bell in such a violent manner that the proprietor himself attended to it. Colonel Ogilvie asked him to have the chauffeur sent up to him, and requested the proprietor to come also himself as he wished to ask him some questions on local matters. He had by now his temper in hand, and was all the more dangerous because cold. In a few minutes the proprietor brought in the chauffeur, a stolid, hard-featured, silent man; manifestly one to obey orders and to stand any amount of fatigue. When Colonel Ogilvie had looked at his credentials and asked him some questions, all of which he did with perfect self-control and courtesy, he turned to the proprietor and asked:

"Can you tell me whereabout is a place called Castle Douglas?"

"In Scotland, Colonel. In Galloway—the part of Scotland just beyond the Firth of Solway. It is I think in Kirkcudbrightshire."

"How far from here?"

"Something over a hundred miles I should say." The father started:

"Good God!" Judy's heart sank at the exclamation and the tone; his voice was laden with horror and despair. The new chauffeur's mouth opened. He spoke as if every word was grudgingly shot out:

"It is exactly ninety-one and a half miles." Colonel Ogilvie turned to him quickly:

"How do you know so accurately; have you driven it?"

"Never sir!"

"Then how do you know?"

"In the train coming down I spent my time looking over the maps and the distance as given in the books of the Motorists' Touring Club. I noted that."

"Had you any reason for examining that particular route?" asked the Colonel suspiciously. He was obsessed by an idea that the "damned fellow" was corrupting everybody so as to work against him, Colonel Ogilvie.

"None special; I was only trying to do my business well. I thought it likely that you might want me to stay with you a short time until you and your permanent chauffeur should become acquainted with the mechanism of your new car. You see, I was told you were an American, and the American makes differ somewhat from our own. And as I am myself looking out for a permanent situation where I should be well paid, made comfortable, and treated with whatever consideration is due to a first-rate *mechanicien* and driver I thought that if I showed zeal in your temporary service you might wish to retain me permanently. In a certain sense I took, I may say, special note of at least part of that particular route."

"Why?" Colonel Ogilvie's suspicions came up afresh at the admission.

"Simply because I took it that you might want to drive into Scotland, and Galloway is perhaps the most promising region for motoring on this side of that country. All the motor roads from this side of England run through Carlisle. Then you cross the Border close to Gretna Green. . . ."

"To where?" The Colonel's voice was full of passion. The chauffeur went on calmly and explicitly:

"Gretna Green. That is where run-away marriages used to be made. That place was usually chosen because it was the first across the Border where Scotch law ruled. The simplifying of our marriage laws and the growth of sanity amongst parents of marriageable daughters generally has done away with the necessity of elopement. Now we go by there without stopping, as Galloway is the modern objective. Indeed in going there you do not go into Gretna at all; you pass it by on the right when you have crossed the bridge over the Sark and are making for Annan. And as to my knowledge of mileages that is a part of my trade. It is my business to arrange for the amount of petrol necessary for the run I am ordered to make. I don't think that you need disturb yourself about that one small item of my knowledge. It may set you more at ease if I tell you that it is one hundred and thirty-six and a half miles to Glasgow; a hundred and one to Abbotsford; seventy-five and a half to Dumfries; a hundred and thirty-five and a half to Edinburgh; two hundred and seventy-four and a half to Aberdeen; one hundred and fifty-eight and three quarters to. . . ."

"Stop! stop!" cried Colonel Ogilvie. "I am obliged to you for your zeal in my service; and I think I can promise you that if in every way you suit, you may look on the permanent post as your own. I shall want you to begin your duties this very night. But this is a special job; and with special reward, for it is difficult and arduous."

"I am willing sir, whatever it may be."

"That is well said. You are the sort of man I want."

"My orders sir?"

"I want you to take me to Castle Douglas to-night—now—as soon as you can get ready. I wish to get there as soon as I can. You will want to have everything right, for we must have no break-down if we can help it. And you must have good lamps."

"'Twill be all right, sir. We shan't, I expect, break down. But if we do—the motor is a new one and I did not make it—I shall put it right. I am a first-rate *mechanicien* and an accomplished driver...."

"All right; but don't talk. Get the car ready, and we shall start at once."

"We can start at once, so far as the car and I are concerned. But we lack something as yet. We must have a pilot."

"A pilot! I thought you knew the way."

"On paper, yes; and I doubt not I could get there all right—in time. But you want to go quick; and we would lose time finding out the way. Remember we are going in the dark." Then turning to the proprietor he said:

"Perhaps you can help us here, sir. Have you any one who can pilot?"

"Not a chauffeur; but I have a coachman who knows all round here for a couple of days' journey. I have no doubt that he knows that road amongst the others. He could sit beside you and direct you how to go!"

"Right! Can you get him soon?"

"At once. He lives over the stables. I shall send for him now." He rang the bell and when the servant came gave his message. And so that matter was settled and the journey arranged. The chauffeur went to have a last look over the motor car, and to bring it round to the door.

All the time of the interview Colonel Ogilvie stood silent, keeping erect and rigid. He was so stern and so master of himself that Judy wished now that he had less self-control. She feared the new phase even more than the old. Then care for what had still to be done took hold of her. She took her sister away to prepare a little basket of food and wine for Colonel Ogilvie and the men with him; they would need some sustenance on their long, arduous journey. Those kindly offices kept both women busy whilst Colonel Ogilvie was putting on warm clothes for the night travelling. Presently Mrs. Ogilvie joined him. When they were alone she said to him somewhat timidly:

"You will be tender, dear, with Joy? The child is young, and a harsh word spoken in anger at a time when she is high-strung and nervous and tired and frightened might be a lasting sorrow to her!" She half expected that he would resent her speaking at all. She was surprised as well as pleased when, putting his hands kindly on her shoulders, he said:

"Be quite easy in your mind on that subject, wife. Joy has all my love; and, whatever comes, I shall use no harsh word to her. I love her too well to give her pain, at the moment or to think of afterwards. She shall have nothing but care and tenderness and such words as you would yourself wish spoken!" The mother was comforted for the moment. But then came a thought, born of her womanhood, that the keenest pain which could be for the woman would be through her concern for the man. She had little doubt as to what her husband's action would be if his surmises as to Mr. Hardy should prove to be correct. And such would mean the blighting of poor Joy's life. She would dearly have loved to remonstrate with her husband on the subject; and she would have done so, whatever might have been the consequences to herself, but that she feared that any ill-timed expostulation might be harmful to her daughter. All the motherhood in her was awake, and nerved her to endure in silence. The only other words she said as she kissed her husband were:

"Good-bye for a while, dear. God keep you in all dangers of the road—and—and in all the far greater dangers that may come to you at the end of it. My love to Joy! Be good to her, and never forget that she can suffer most through any one dear to her. Bring her home to me, safe and—and happy! I . . ." Her voice broke and she wept on his shoulder. Colonel Ogilvie was a determined man, and in some ways a harsh and cruel one; but he was a man, and understood. He took his wife in his arms and kissed her fondly, stroking her dark hair wherein the silver threads were showing. Then he passed out in silence.

By the door of the car he found Judy who said:

"I have put in your supper—you will want it dear—and also supper for the men. And oh! Lucius, don't forget, for poor Joy's sake, that this day you hold her heart—which is her life—in your hand!"

This added responsibility filled the cup of Colonel Ogilvie's indignation. Already his conscience was quickening and his troubles—the agitation to his feelings—were almost more than he could bear. He would have liked to make some cynical remark to Judy; but before he could think of anything sufficiently biting, the motor which had been throbbing violently started.

Before the angry man could attempt to get back his self-possession he was gazing past the two shrouded figures before him and across the luminous arc of the lamps out into the night. The darkness seemed to sweep by him as he rushed on his way to Scotland.

When he had gone Judy turned to her sister and said: "I was going to give him Joy's dressing bag and a change of dress to take with him. She will want them, poor dear, after a long day of travel and a night in a strange place. But I have thought of a better plan."

"And that?" asked the anxious mother.

"To take them myself! Moreover it won't be any harm my being present in case the Colonel gets on the rampage. It will restrain him some. Now you go and lie down, dear. Don't say anything—except your prayers—in case you feel you must say something. But sleep will be your best help in this pretty tough proposition. I'll go and get a hustle on that Dutch landlord. He's got to find an automobile and a chauffeur, and a pilot if necessary, for me too!"

CHAPTER XIX

DECLARATION OF WAR

Joy Ogilvie was so tired out that her body lay like a log all night. How her mind was occupied she only knew afterwards. For the memory of dreams is an unconscious memory at the time; it is only when there is opportunity of comparison with actualities that dreams can be re-produced. Then, as at first, the dreams are real—as they are forever whilst memory lasts. Indeed regarding dreams and actualities, one might almost appeal to scientific analogy; and in comparing the world of imagination—which is the kingdom of dreams—with the material world, might adduce the utterance of Sir Oliver Lodge in comparing the density of æther with that of matter in the modern scientific view: "Matter is turning out to be a filmy thing in comparison with æther."

This might well serve as a scientific comparison. Nay more, it might well be an induction. The analogies of nature are so marvellously constant, as exemplified by the higher discoveries in physics, that we might easily wander farther than in taking the inner world of Thought as compared with the outer world of Physical Being, as an analogy to the Seen and Unseen worlds.

In the meantime we may take it that Joy's dreams that night were in some way reflective of the events of the day. No girl of healthy emotional power could fail to be influenced by such a sequence of experiences of passion and fear as she had gone through. The realized hoping of love, the quick-answering abandonment of expressed passion; long, long minutes of the bliss of communion with that other soul—minutes whose sweetness or whose length could not be computed until the leisure of thought gave opportunity. Unconscious cerebration goes on unceasingly; and be sure that with such data as she had in her mind, the workings of imagination were quick and by no means cold. Again she lived the moments of responsive passion; but so lived them that she had advanced further on the road to completed passion when the unconsciousness to physical surroundings began to disappear and on the senses the actualities began to consciously impress themselves. The dawn, stealing in between the chinks of the folded shutters, made strange lines on the floor without piercing through the walls of sleep. The myriad sounds of waking life from distant field and surrounding street brought no message to the closed eyes of weariness. The sun rose, and rose, and rose; and still she lay there unmoving.

At last that unaccountable impulse which moves all living things to sentience at the ending of sleep, stirred her. The waking grew on her. At first, when her eyes partially opened, she saw, but without comprehending, the dim room with its low ceiling; the wide window, masked in with shutters whose edges were brilliant with the early light; the odd furniture and all the unfamiliar surroundings. Then came the inevitable self-question: "where am I?"

The realization of waking from such dreaming as hers is a rude and jarring process, and when it does come, comes with something of a shock. For what seemed a long time Joy lay in a sort of languorous ecstasy whilst memory brought back to her those moments of the previous day which were sweeter even than her dreams. Again she heard the footsteps of the man she loved coming up rapidly behind her. Again she saw as she turned, in obedience to some new impulse which swayed her to surrender, the face of the man looking radiant with love and happiness. Again she felt the sweet satisfaction of living and loving when his arms closed round her and her arms closed round him and they strained each other strictly. Again there came to her the thrill which seemed to lift her from her earthly being as his mouth touched hers and they kissed each other in the absolute self-abandonment of reciprocated passion—the very passing memory of which set her blood tingling afresh; the thrill which set her soul floating in the expanse of air and made all conventions of the artificial world seen far below seem small and miserable and of neither power nor import. Again she was swept by that tide of wild desires, vague and nebulous as yet, inchoate, elusive, expansive, all-absorbing, which proclaimed her womanhood to herself. That desire of wife to husband, of sex to sex, of woman to man, which is the final expression of humanity—the love song of the children of Adam. It was as though memory and dreaming had become one. As if the day had merged in the night, and the night again in the coming day; each getting as it came all the thoughts and wishes and fancies and desires which follow in the train of the all-conquering Love-God.

In such receptive mood Joy awoke to life. When she realized where she was; and when the import of her new surroundings had broken in upon her, all the forces of her youth and strength began at once to manifest themselves. She slid softly from her bed—the instinct of self protection forbade noise or else she would have jumped to the floor. Doing must follow dreaming! The attitude of standing, once again helped to recall the previous evening, and she remembered that she had thought then that she must not open the windows in the morning because they faced directly other windows across a narrow street.

She remembered also that the next room, through which she had entered, had windows on two sides. Those on one side opened as did her own; but those on the other side looked out on an open space. And so, without further thought, she opened the door between and passed into the outer room. It too, like her own, was dark from the closed shutters. Instinctively she went softly, her bare feet making no sound on the carpet. With the same instinctive caution she had opened the door noiselessly; when the self-protective instinct has once been awakened, it does not easily relapse to sleep. She went over to one of the windows and tried to look out through the chinks. The day was bright outside and the sun was shining; the fog had entirely disappeared. In the sudden desire to breathe the fresh morning air, and to free in the sunlight her soul cramped by the long darkness of fog and night, she threw open the heavy shutters.

Athlyne slept so soundly that he never stirred. He lay on the sofa on his left side with his face out to the room. He too had been dreaming; and to his dreams the happiness of the day had brought a vivifying light. Through all his weariness of mind and body came to his spirit the glow of those moments when he knew that his love was reciprocated; when his call to his mate had been answered—answered in no uncertain voice. And so he, too, had lain with bodily nature all quiescent, whilst the emotional side of his mind ranged freely between memory and expectation. And in due process the imaginative power of the mind had worked on the nerves—and through them on the body—till he too lay in a languorous semitrance—the mind ranging free whilst the abnormally receptive body quivered in unison. It was a dangerous condition of being in which to face the situation which awaited him.

The sound of the opening shutter wakened him, fully and all at once. The moment his eyes opened he saw a figure between him and the window; and at the knowledge that some stranger was in his room the habit of quick action which had prevailed in his years of campaigning re-asserted itself. On the instant he flung aside his blanket and sprang from his bed.

At the sound of a step on the floor Joy turned. The light streaming in through the unshuttered window showed them in completeness each to the other. The light struck Athlyne full in front. There was instant recognition, even in the unaccustomed garb, of that tall lithe form; of those fine aquiline features, of those dark flashing eyes. As to Joy, who standing against the light made her own shadow, Athlyne could have no doubt. He would have realized her presence in darkness and silence. As she stood in her fine linen, the morning light making a sort of nimbus round the opacity of the upper part of her body, she looked to him like some fresh realization—some continuation in semi-ethereal form—of the being of his dreams. There was no pause for thought in either of the lovers. The instant of recognition was the realization of presence—unquestioning and the most natural thing in the world that the other should be there. Delight had sealed from within the ears of Doubt. Unhesitatingly they ran to each other, and before a second had passed were locked tightly in each other's arms.

In the secret belief of the Conventional world—that belief which is the official teaching of the churches of an artificial society, and not merely the world of Adam and Eve (and some others)—the ceremony of Marriage in itself changes the entire nature of the contracting parties. Whatever may have been the idiosyncrasies of these individuals such are forthwith changed, foregone, or otherwise altered to suit that common denominator of Human Nature which alone is officially catalogued in the records of the Just. It were as though the recorded promise of two love-stricken sufferers, followed by the formal blessings of the Church in any of its differentiations— or of the Registrar—should change baser mortals to more angelic counterpart; just as the "Philosopher's Stone" which the mediæval alchemist dreamed of and sought for, was expected to change baser metals to gold.

Perhaps it is because this transmutation is so complete that so many of those marriages which the Church does sanctify turn out so differently from the anticipations of the contractors and blessors!

But Dame Nature has her own church and her own ritual. In her case the Blessing comes before the Service; and the Benediction is but the official recognition that two souls—with their attendant bodies—have found a perfect communion for themselves. Those who believe in Human Nature—and many of them are seriously minded people too—realize and are thankful for the goodness of, God who showers the possibilities of happiness with no stinting and no uncertain hand. "After all" they say "what about Eden?" There was no church's blessing there—not even a Registrar; and yet we hold that Adam and Eve were united in Matrimony. Nor were their children or their children's children made one with organized formality. What was it then that on these occasions stood between fornication and marriage? What could it be but the Blessing of God! And if God could make marriage by His Blessing in Eden, when did He forego that power. Or if indeed there be only a "Civil Contract"—as so many hold to-day—what proofs or writings must there be beyond that mere "parole" contract which is recognized in other matters by the Law of the Land.

So, the believers in natural religion and natural law—those who do not hold that personal licence, unchecked and boundless, is an appanage or logical result of freedom. To these, freedom is in itself a state bounded on all sides by restrictive laws—as must ever be, unless Anarchy is held to be the ultimate and controlling force. And in the end Anarchy is the denial of all Cosmic law—that systematised congeries of natural forces working in harmony to a common end.

But law, Cosmic or Anarchic, (if there be such a thing, and it may be that Hell—if there is one—has its own laws—) or any grade between these opposites, is a matter for coolness and reflection. *Inter arma silent leges* is a maxim of co-ordinate rulings in the Court of Cosmic law. And the principle holds whether the arms be opposed or locked together in any form of passion. When Love lifts the souls, whose bodies are already in earthly communion, Law ceases to be. From the altitude of accomplished serenity the mightiest law is puny; just as from a balloon the earth looks flat, and even steeples and towers have no perspective.

So it was with the two young people clasped in each other's arms. The world they lived in at the moment was *their* world, bounded only by the compass of their arms. After all what more did they want—what could they want. They were together and alone. Shame was not for them, or to them, who loved with all their hearts—whose souls already felt as one. For shame, which is a conventional ordering of the blood, has no place—not even a servitor's—in the House of Love: that palace where reigns the love of husbandhood and wifehood, of fatherhood and motherhood—that true, realized Cosmos—the aim, the objective, the heaven of human life.

Their circumstances but intensified the pleasure of the embrace. Athlyne and Joy had both felt the same communion of spirits when they embraced at their first meeting out of Ambleside when their souls had met. This had been intensified when they sat in close embrace after lunch beyond Dalry, when heart consciously beat to heart. Now it was completed in this meeting, unexpected and therefore more free and unhampered by preparatory thoughts and intentions, when body met body in a close if tentative communion. The mere paucity of raiment had force and purpose. They could each feel as they hung together closely strained, the beating of each other's heart; the rising and falling of each other's lungs. Their breaths commingled as they held mouth to mouth. In such delirious rapture—for these two ardent young people loved each other with a love which both held to be but the very beginning of an eternal bond and which took in every phase, actual and possible, of human beings—there was no place for forethought or afterthought. It was the hour of life which is under the guidance of Nature; to be looked forward to with keen if ignorant anticipation; and which is to be looked back on for evermore as a time when the very heavens opened and the singing of the Angelic choir came through unmuffled.

For seconds, in which Time seemed to stand still, they stood body to body and mouth to mouth. The first to speak was the man:

"I thought you were in England by late in the evening—and you were there all the time!" He indicated the direction by turning his eyes towards her room. His words seemed to fire her afresh. Holding him more closely to her, she leaned back from her hips and gazed at him languorously; her words dropped slowly from her opened lips:

"Oh-h! If we had only known!" What exactly was in her mind she did not know—did not think of knowing—did not want to know. Perhaps she did not mean anything definite. It was only an expression of some feeling, of some want, some emotion, some longing—some primitive utterance couched in words of educated thought, as sweet and spontaneous as the singing of a bird in its native woods at springtime.

Somehow, it moved Athlyne strangely. Moved the manhood of him in many ways, chiefest among them his duty of protection. It is not a commonly-received idea that man—not primitive man but the partially-completed article of a partially-completed cosmic age—is scrupulous with regard to woman. The general idea to the contrary effect is true *en gros* but not *en detaille*. True of women; not true of a woman. An educated man, accustomed to judgment and action in matters requiring thought, thinks, perhaps unconsciously, all round him, backward as well as forward; but mainly forward. Present surroundings form his data; consequences represent the conclusion. Himself remains neutral, an onlooker, until he is called on for immediate decision and consequent action.

So it was with Athlyne. His instant ejaculation:

"Thank God we didn't know!" would perhaps have been understood by a man. To a woman it was incomprehensible. Woman is, after all, more primitive than man. Her instincts are more self-centred than his. As her life moves in a narrower circle, her view is rather microscopic than telescopic; whilst his is the reverse. Inasmuch then as he naturally surveys a larger field, so his introspective view is wider.

Joy loved the man; and so, since he had already expressed himself, considered him as already her husband; or to speak more accurately considered herself as already his wife. It was, therefore, with something like chagrin that she heard his disavowal of her views. She did not herself quite understand what those views were, but all the same it was a disappointment that he did not really acquiesce in them; nay more that he did not press them on his own account—press them relentlessly, as a woman loves a man to do, even when his wishes are opposed to her own.

A woman's answer to chagrin is ultimate victory of her purpose; and the chagrin of love is perhaps the strongest passion with a purpose that can animate her.

When Joy became conscious, as she did in a few seconds, that her lover following out his protective purpose was about to separate himself from her—she quite understood without any telling or any experience both motive and purpose—she opposed it on her part. As the strictness of his embrace lessened, so in proportion did hers increase. Then came to the man the reaction—he was only a man, after all. His ardour redoubled, and her heart beat harder with new love as well as triumph as he drew her closer to him in a pythonic embrace. Then she, too, clung to him even closer than before. That embrace was all lover-like—an agony of rapture. In its midst they were startled somewhat by the rumbling of a motor driven fast which seemed to stop close to them. Instinctively Joy tried to draw away from her lover; such is woman's impulse. But Athlyne held her all the tighter—his embrace was not all love now, but the protection which comes from love. She understood, and resigned herself to him. And so they stood, heart to heart, and mouth to mouth, listening.

There was a clatter of tongues in the hall. Joy thought she recognised one voice—she could not be sure in the distance and through the closed door—and her heart sank. She would again have tried to draw away violently but that she was powerless. Her will was gone, like a bird's tinder the stare of the snake. Athlyne, too, was in suspense, his heart beating wildly. He had a sort of presage of disaster which seemed in a way to paralyse him.

There were quick steps on the stairs. A voice said: "There" and the door rattled. At this moment both the lovers were willing to separate. But before they could do so, the door opened and the figure of Colonel Ogilvie blocked the entrance.

"Good God!" The old man's face had grown white as though the sight had on the instant frozen him. So pallid was he, all in that second, that Joy and Athlyne received at once the same idea: that his moustache, which they had thought of snowy whiteness, was but grey against the marble face.

The father's instinct was protective too, and his action was quick. In the instant, without turning his face, he shut the door behind him and put his heel against it.

"Quick, daughter, quick!" he said in a whisper, low but so fierce that it cut the air like a knife, "Get into that room and dress yourself. And, get out if you can, by another way without being noticed!" As he spoke he pointed towards the open door through which in the darkened room the bed with clothing in disarray could be dimly seen. Joy fled incontinently. The movements of a young woman can be of extraordinary quickness, but never quicker than when fear lends her wings. It seemed to Athlyne that she made but one jump from where she stood through the door-way. He could remember afterwards the flash of her bare heels as she turned in closing the door behind her.

"Now Sir!" Colonel Ogilvie's voice was stern to deadliness as he spoke. Athlyne realised its import. He felt that he was bound hand and foot, and knew that his part of the coming struggle would have to be passive. He braced himself to endure. Still, the Colonel's question had to be answered. The onus of beginning the explanation had been thrust upon him. It was due to Joy that there should be no delay on his part in her vindication. Almost sick at heart with apprehension he began:

"There has been no fault on Joy's part!" The instant he had spoken, the look of bitter haughtiness which came on Colonel Ogilvie's face warned him that he had made a mistake. To set the error right he must know what he had to meet; and so he waited.

"We had better, I think, leave Miss Ogilvie's name out of our conversation. . . . And I may perhaps remind you, sir, that I am the best judge of my daughter's conduct. When I have said anything to my daughter's detriment it will be quite time for a stranger to interfere on her behalf. . . . It is of *your* conduct, sir, that I ask—demand explanation!"

Athlyne would have liked to meet a speech of this kind with a blow. In the case of any other man he would have done so: but this man was Joy's father, and in all circumstances must be treated as such. He felt in a vague sort of way—a background of thought rather than thought itself—that his manhood was being tested, and by a fiery test. Come what might, he must be calm, or at least be master of himself; or else bitter woe would come to Joy. Of course it would come—perhaps had come already to himself; but to that he was already braced.

Colonel Ogilvie was skilled in the deadly preliminaries to lethal quarrel. More than once when a foe had been marked down for vengeance had he led him on to force the duel himself. In no previous quarrel of his life had he ever had the good cause that he had now, and be sure that he used that knowledge to the full. There was in his nature something of that stoical quality of the Red Indian which enables him to enjoy the torture of his foe, though the doing so entails a keen anguish to himself. Perhaps the very air of the "dark and bloody ground" of Kentucky was so impregnated with the passions of those who made it so that the dwelling of some generations had imbued the dwellers with some of the old Indian spirit. As Athlyne stood face to face with him, watching for every sign of intention as a fencer watches his opponent, he realised that there would be for him no pity, no mercy, not even understanding. He would have to fight an uphill contest—if Joy was to be saved even a single pang. What he could do he would: sacrifice himself in any way that a man can accomplish it. Life and happiness had for him passed by! One of his greatest difficulties would be, he felt, that of so controlling himself that he would not of necessity shut behind him, by anything which he might say or do, the door of conciliation. He began at once, therefore, to practice soft answering:

"My conduct, sir, has been bad—so far as doing an indiscreet thing, and in not showing to you that respect which is your due in any matter in which Miss Ogilvie may be concerned." For some reason which he could not at the moment understand this seemed to infuriate the Colonel more than ever. In quite a violent way he burst out:

"So I am to take it that no respect is due to me in my own person! Such, I gather from your words. You hint if you do not say that respect is only my due on my daughter's account!" At the risk of further offence Athlyne interrupted him. It would not do for him to accept this monstrous reading of what he meant for courtesy:

"Not so, sir. My respect is to you always and for all causes. I did but put it in that way as it is only in connection with your daughter that I dared to speak at all." Even this pacific explanation seemed to add fuel to the old man's choler:

"Let me tell you, sir, that this has nothing whatever to do with my daughter. Miss Ogilvie is my care. Her defence, if any be required, is my duty—my privilege. And I quite know how to exercise—and to defend—both."

"Quite so, sir. I realise that, and I have no wish to arrogate to myself your right or your duty; for either of which I myself should be proud to die!" Athlyne's voice and manner were so suave and deferential that Colonel Ogilvie began to have an idea that he was a poltroon; and in this belief the bully that was in him began to manifest itself. He spoke harshly, intending to convey this idea, though as he did so his heart smote him. Even as he spoke there rose before his bloodshot eyes the vision of a river shimmering with gold as the sunset fell on it, and projected against it the figure of a frightened woman tugging at the reins of a run-away mare; whilst close behind her rode a valiant man guiding with left hand a splendid black horse to her side, his right hand stretched out to drag her to his saddle. Before them both lay a deadly chasm. In the pause Athlyne took the opportunity of hurriedly putting on his outer clothing.

But even that touching vision did not check the father's rage. His eyes were bloodshot and even such vision—any vision—could not linger in them. It passed, leaving in its place only a red splotch—as of blood; the emotion which the thought had quickened had become divergent in its own crooked way. But in the pause Athlyne had time to get in a word:

"Sir, whatever fault there has been was mine entirely. I acted foolishly perhaps, and unthinkingly. It placed us—placed me in such a position that every accident multiplied possibilities of misunderstanding. I cannot undo that now—I don't even say that I would if I could. But whatever may be my fate—in the result that may follow my acts—I shall accept it without cavil. And may I say in continuance and development of your own suggestion, that no other name should be mentioned in whatever has to be spoken of between us." As he finished he unconsciously stood upon his dignity, drawing himself up to his full height and standing in soldierly attitude. This had a strange effect on Colonel Ogilvie. Realising that he could rely implicitly on the dignity of the man before him, he allowed himself a further latitude. He could afford, he felt, to be unrestrained in such a presence; and so proceeded to behave as though he was stark, staring raving mad. Athlyne saw the change and, with some instinct more enlightening than his reason, realised that the change might later, have some beneficent effect. More than ever did he feel now the need for his own absolute self-control. It was well that he had made up his mind to this, for it was bitterly tested in Colonel Ogilvie's mad outpour:

"Do you dare, sir, to lecture me as to what I shall not say or shall say about my own daughter. What shall I say to you who though you had not the courtesy to even acknowledge the kindness shown you by her parents, came behind my back when I was far away, and stole her from my keeping. Who took her far away, to the risk even of her reputation. Risk? Risk! When I find you here together, alone and almost naked in each other's arms! God's Death! that I should have seen such a thing—that such a thing should be. . . ." Here his hot wrath changed to ice-cold deadly purpose, and he went on:

"You shall answer me with your life for that!" He paused, still glaring at the other with cold, deadly malevolence. Athlyne felt that the hour of the Forlorn Hope had come to him at last—he had been hot through all his seeming coolness at de Hooge's Spruit. His self-control, could, he felt never be more deeply tested than now; and he braced himself to it. He had now to so bear himself that Joy would suffer the minimum of pain. Pain she would have to endure—much pain; he could not save her from it. He would do what he could; that was all that remained. With real coolness he met the icy look of his antagonist as he said with all the grace and courtesy of which he was naturally master:

"Sir, I answer for my deeds with my life. That life is yours now. Take it, how and when you will! As to answering in words, such cannot be whilst you maintain your present attitude. I have tried already to answer—to explain."

"Explain sir! There is no explanation."

"Pardon me!" Athlyne's voice was calm as ever; his dignity so superb that the other checked the words on his lips as he went on:

"There is an explanation to be made—and made it must be, for the sake of . . . of another. I deny in no way your right of revenge. I think I have already told you that my life is yours to take as you will. But a dying man has, in all civilised places, a right to speak to the Court which condemns him. Such privilege is mine. I claim it—if you will force me to say so. And let me add, Colonel Ogilvie, that I hold it as a part of my submission to your will. We are alone now and can speak freely; but there must be a time—it will be for your own protection from the legal consequences of my death—when others, or at least one other, will know of your intention to kill. I shall speak then if I may not now!" Here the Colonel, whose anger was rising at being so successfully baffled, interrupted him with hard cynicism.

"Conditions in an affair of honour! To be enforced in a court of law I suppose." He felt ashamed of himself as he made the remark which he felt to be both ungenerous and untrue. He was not surprised when the other answered his indignant irony with scorn:

"No sir! No law! Not any more appeal to law in my defence than there has been justice in your outrageous attack on me. But about that I shall answer you presently. In the meantime I adhere to my conditions. Aye, conditions; I do not hesitate to use the word."

Colonel Ogilvie, through all the madness of his anger, realised at that moment that the man before him was a strong man, as fearless and determined as he was himself. This brought back his duty of good manners as a first installment of his self-possession. For a few seconds he actually withheld his speech. He even bowed slightly as the other proceeded:

"I have tried to explain. . . . My fault was in venturing to ask . . . a lady to come for a ride in my car. I had no intention of evil. Nothing more than a mere desire to renew and further an—a friendship which had, from the first moment of my knowing her—or rather from the first moment I set eyes on her, become very dear to me. It was a selfish wish I know; and in my own happiness at her consent I overlooked,—neglected—forgot the duty I owed to her father. For that I am bitterly sorry, and I feel that I owe to him a debt which I can never, never repay. But enough of that. . . . That belongs to a different category, and it has to be atoned for in the only way by which an honourable man can atone. . . . As I have already conceded my life to him I need . . . can say no more. But from the moment when that lady stepped into my car my respect has been for her that which I have always intended to be given to whatever lady should honour me by becoming my wife. Surely you, sir, as yourself an honourable man—a husband and a father, cannot condemn a man for speaking an honourable love to the woman to whom it has been given. When I have admitted that the making of the occasion was a fault I have said all that I accept as misdoing...." He folded his arms and stood on his dignity. For a few seconds, Colonel Ogilvie stood motionless, silent. He could not but recognise the truth that underlay all the dignity of the other. But he was in no way diverted by it from his purpose. His anger was in no way mitigated; his intention of revenge lessened by no whit. He was merely waiting to collect his thoughts so as to be in a position to attack with most deadly effect. He was opening his lips to speak when the other went on as though he had but concluded one section or division of what he had to say:

"And now sir as to the manifest doubt you expressed as to my *bona fides* in placing my life in your hands—your apprehension lest I should try to evade my responsibility to the laws of honour by an appeal in some way to a court of law. Let me set your mind at ease by placing before you my views; and my views, let me tell you, are ultimately my intentions. I have tried to assure you that with the exception of waiting to ask your consent to taking . . . a certain passenger for a drive, my conduct has from that moment been such as you could not find fault with. I take it for granted that you—nor no man—could honestly resent such familiarities as are customary to, and consequent on, a man offering marriage to a lady, and pressing his suit with such zeal as is, or should be, attendant on the expression of a passion which he feels very deeply!" Even whilst he was speaking, his subconsciousness was struck by his own coolness. He marvelled that he could, synchronously with the fearful effort necessary to his self-control and with despair gnawing at his heart, speak with such cold blooded preciseness. As is usual in such psychical stresses his memory took note for future reference of every detail.

His opponent on the contrary burst all at once into another fit of naming passion. Athlyne's very preciseness seemed to have inflamed him afresh. He thundered out:

"Familiarities sir, on offering marriage! Do you dare to trifle with me at a time like this. When but a few minutes ago I saw you here in this lonely place, at this hour of the morning after a night of absence, undressed as you were, holding in your arms my daughter undressed also. . . God's death! sir, be careful or you shall rue it!" He stopped almost choking with passion. Athlyne felt himself once more overwhelmed with the cold wave of responsibility. "Joy! Joy!

Joy!" he kept repeating to himself as a sort of charm to keep off evil. To let go his anger now might—would be fatal to her happiness. He marvelled to himself as he went on in equal voice, seemingly calm:

"That sir was with no intent of evil. 'Twas but a natural consequence of the series of disasters which fell on the enterprise which had so crowned my happiness. When I turned to come home so that. . . so that the lady might be in time to meet her parents who were expected to arrive at—at her destination, I forgot, in my eagerness to meet her wishes, the regulations as to speed; and I was arrested for furious driving. In my anxiety to save her from any form of exposal to publicity, and in my perplexity as to how to manage it, I advised her returning by herself in my motor, I remaining at Dalry. When she had gone, and I had arranged for attending the summons served on me, I wired over to this hotel to keep me rooms. I thought it better that as J . . . that as the lady had gone to England I should remain in Scotland. I started to walk here; but I was overtaken by a fog and delayed for hours behind my time. The house was locked up—every one asleep. The night porter who let me in told me that as I had not arrived, as by my telegram, the bedroom I had ordered was let to some one else who had arrived in a plight similar to my own. 'Another party' were his words; I had no clue to whom or what the other visitor was. The only place left in the house unoccupied—for there were many unexpected guests through the fog—was that sofa. There I slept. Only a few minutes ago I was waked by some one coming into the room. When I saw that it was . . . when I saw who it was—the woman whom I loved and whom I intended to marry—I naturally took her in my arms without thinking." Then without pausing, for he saw the anger in the Colonel's face and felt that to prolong this part of the narration was dangerous, he went on quickly:

"I trust that you understand, Colonel Ogilvie, that this explanation in no way infringes your right of punishing me as you suggest. Please understand—and this is my answer to your suggestion as to my appealing to law—that I accept your wish to go through the form of a duel!" He was hotly interrupted by the Colonel:

"Form of a duel! Is this another insult? When I say fight I mean fight—understand that. I fight *à l'outrance;* and that way only." Athlyne's composure did not seem even raffled:

"Exactly! I took no other meaning. But surely I am entitled to take it that even a real duel has the form of a duel!"

"Then what do you mean sir by introducing the matter that way?"

"Simply, Colonel Ogilvie, to protect myself from a later accusation on your part—either to me or of me—of a charge of poltroonery; or even a silent suspicion of it in your own mind!"

"How do you mean?"

"Sir, I only speak for myself. I have already said more than once that I hold my life at your disposal. From that I do not shrink; I accept the form of a duel for my execution."

"Your execution! Explain yourself, sir?" In a calm even voice came the answer.

"Colonel Ogilvie, I put it to you as man to man—if you will honour me with so simple a comparison, or juxtaposition whichever you like to consider it—how can I fight freely against the father of the woman whom I love. Pray, sir," for the Colonel made an angry gesture "be patient for a moment. I intend no kind of plea or appeal. I feel myself forced to let you know my position from my point of view. You need bear no new anger towards me for this expression of my feelings. I do so with reluctance, and only because you *must* understand, here and now, or it may make, later on, further unhappiness for some one else—some one whom we both hold in our hearts." Colonel Ogilvie hesitated before replying. The bitter scowl was once again on his face as he spoke:

"Then I suppose I am to take it, sir, that you will begin our meeting on the field of honour by putting me publicly—through the expression of your intention—in the position of a murderer."

"Not so! Surely you know better than that. I did not think that any honourable man could have so mistaken another. If I have to speak explicitly on this point—on which for your own sake and the sake of . . . of one dear to you, I would fain be reticent—let me reassure you on one point: I shall play the game fairly. For this duel is a game, and, so far as I am concerned at all events, one for a pretty large stake. If indeed that can be called a 'game' which can only end in one way. You need not, I assure you, feel the least uneasy as to my not going through with it properly. I am telling you this now so that you may not distort my intention yourself by some injudicious comment on my conduct, or speech, or action, made under a misapprehension or from distrust of me. Sir, your own honour shall be protected all along, so far as the doing so possibly rests with me."

Here, seeing some new misunderstanding in the Colonel's eye he went on quickly:

"I venture to say this because I am aware that you doubt my being able to carry out my intention. When I say 'rests with me,' I mean the responsibility of acting properly the role I have undertaken. I shall conduct my part of the duel in all seriousness. It must be in some other country; this for your sake. For mine it will not have mattered. We have only to bear ourselves properly and none will suspect. I shall go through all the forms—with your permission—of fighting *à l'outrance,* so that no one can suspect. No one will be able afterwards to say that you could have been aware of my intention. I shall fire at you all right; but I shall not hit!"

Instinctively Colonel Ogilvie bowed. He did not intend to do so. He said no word. The rancour of his heart was not mitigated; his intention to kill in no way lessened. His action was simply a spontaneous recognition of the chivalry of another, and his appreciation of it.

Athlyne could not but be glad of even so slight a relaxation of the horrible tension. He stood quite still. He felt that in some way he had scored with his antagonist; and as he was fighting for Joy he was unwilling to do anything which might not be good for her. He was standing well out in the room with his back to the door of the bedroom. As they stood he saw a look of surprise flash in Colonel Ogilvie's face. This changed instantly to a fixed one of horror. His eyes seemed to look right through his antagonist to something beyond. Instinctively he turned to see what it might be that caused that strange look. And then he looked horrified himself.

In the open door-way of the bedroom stood Joy.

CHAPTER XX

KNOWLEDGE OF LAW

ALL three stood stone still. Not a sound was heard except faint quick breathing. Athlyne tried to think; but his brain seemed numb. He knew that now was a crisis if not *the* crisis of the whole affair. It chilled him with a deathly chill to think that Joy must have heard all the conversation between her father and himself. What a remembrance for her in all the empty years to come! What sorrow, what pain! Presently he heard behind him as he stood facing her a sound which was rather a groan than an ejaculation—a groan endowed with articulated utterance:

"Good God!" Unconsciously he repeated the word under his breath:

"Good God!"

Joy, with a fixed high-strung look, stepped down into the room. She stood beside Athlyne who, as she came close to him, turned with her so that together they faced her father. Colonel Ogilvie said in a slow whisper, the words dropping out one by one:

"Have—you—been—there—all—the—time? Did—you—hear—all—we—said?" She answered boldly:

"Yes! I was there and heard everything!" Again a long pause of silence, ended by Colonel Ogilvie's next question:

"Why did you stay?" Joy answered at once; her quick speech following the slow tension sounded almost voluble.

"I could not get away. I wanted to; but there is no other door to the room. That is why I came out here when I woke. . . . I could not get my boots which the maid had taken last night, and I wanted to get away as quickly as possible. And, Father, being there, though I had to move about dressing myself, I could not help hearing everything!" Her father had evidently expected that she would say something more, for as she stopped there he looked at her expectantly. There was a sort of dry sob in his throat. Athlyne stood still and silent; he hardly dared to breathe lest he should unintentionally thwart Joy's purpose. For with all his instincts he realised that she had a purpose. He knew that she understood her father and that she was the most potent force to deal with him; and knowing this he felt that the best thing he could do would be to leave her quite free and unhampered to take her own course. He kept his eyes on her face, gazing at her unwinkingly. Her face was fixed—not stern but set to a purpose. Somehow at that moment he began to realise how well he understood her. Without more help than his eyes could give him, he seemed to follow the workings of her mind. For her mind was changing. At the first her expression was of flinty fixedness; but as she continued to look at the old man it softened; and with the softening her intentioned silence gave way. Her lover's thoughts translated thus:

"I will protect my—him against my father. He has threatened him; he is forcing him to death. I shall not help him by sparing him a pang, an awkwardness. And yet—why that? He is an old man—and my father! That white hair demands respect. He is angry—hard and untender now; but his life has been a tender one to me—and he is my father! Though I am determined to save my lover—my husband, I need not in the doing cause that white head to sink in shame; I can spare him the pang of what he may think ingratitude in me. And, after all, he has what must seem to him just cause of offence. He cannot—will not understand.... He is brave and proud, and has a code of honour which is more than a religion. And he my lover—my husband is brave too. And as unyielding as my father. And he is willing to die—for me. To die for me—*my* honour *my* happiness. Though his dying is worse—far worse than death to me.... But he is dying bravely, and I—that was to have been his wife—must die bravely, worthily too. If he can suffer and die in silence, so too must I...."

It seemed a natural sequence of thought when she said to her father:

"Daddy, do you know you have not said a word to me yet. What have I ever done in my life that you should not trust me now? Have I ever lied to you that you cannot trust me to answer truly when you ask me—ask me anything. Why don't you ask me now? I know that things do not look well. I realise that you must have been shocked, when you came into the room. But, Daddy dear, there are few things in the world that cannot be explained—at any rate in part. Don't forget that I am a woman now. I am no longer a child whose ignorance is her innocence. Speak to me! Ask me what you will, and I will answer you truly! Hear me, even as you would listen to one dying! For indeed it is so. If you carry out your intention, as I have heard it expressed, I shall no longer live; there will be nothing for me to live for."

"Do you mean that you will commit suicide?" said her father.

"Oh, no! I hope I have pluck enough to live—if I can. Do not fear for me, Daddy! I shall play the game full, as he will do." As she spoke, she pointed a finger at Athlyne. She felt now, and for the first time, acutely that she did not know what to call him before a third person—even her father. Athlyne looked relieved by her words. When she spoke of dying he had grown sadly white; he shared her father's apprehension. Colonel Ogilvie saw the change in his look, and took it ill. As may be surmised a part of his anger towards Athlyne arose from jealousy. Until this man had appeared upon the scene his "little girl" was his alone; no other man shared in her affection. As she was an only child all his parental affection had been centred in her. Though he might have been prepared to see her mate with a man of his own choosing—or at any rate of his acceptance, he was jealous of the man who had stepped in, unaccredited and wanting in deference to himself. It must have been a tinge of this jealousy which prompted his next question. Turning with a bitter formality to Athlyne he said:

"I suppose you are satisfied, now, sir. Whatever may come, my daughter is estranged from me; and it is your doing!" In answer Joy and Athlyne spoke together. Said the latter:

"Oh sir!" There he stopped; he feared to say more lest his anger should master him. But the protest was effective; the old man flushed—over forehead and ears and neck. Joy spoke in a different vein:

"There is no estrangement, Daddy dear; and therefore it can be no one's doing. Least of all could such a thing come from this man who loves me, and . . . and whom I love." As she spoke she blushed divinely, and taking her lover's right hand between both her hands held it tight. This seemed for some reason to infuriate her father afresh. He strode forward towards Athlyne as though about to strike him. But at the instant there came a quick rap on the door. Instinctively he drew away, and, having called out "Come!" stood expectingly and seemingly calm. The door opened slightly and the voice of the Sheriff was heard:

"May I come in? I am Alexander Fenwick, Sheriff of Galloway!" As he was speaking he entered the room with a formal bow to each in turn. He continued to speak to Colonel Ogilvie:

"You will pardon this intrusion I hope, sir. Indeed I trust you will not look upon it as an intrusion at all when you know the reason of my coming." Colonel Ogilvie's habit of old-fashioned courtesy came at once to the fore with the coming of a stranger. With a bow which to those reared in a newer and less formal school of manners seemed almost grandiloquent he spoke:

"I came here on some business, and on my arrival a few minutes ago was asked by our landlady—an old servant of my own—who on that account thought that she might ask what she thought a favour—to come up here. She thought, poor anxious soul, that some unpleasantness might be afoot as she heard high words, and feared a quarrel. All the more on account of a sudden arrival of a gentleman who seemed somewhat incensed. This I took from her description of the personality, to be you sir. Indeed, I recognise all the points, except that of the anger!" As he spoke he bowed with pleasant courtesy. The other bowed too, partly in answer to the implied question and partly in recognition of the expressed courtesy of the words and manner.

Whilst he had been speaking, the Sheriff had been watching keenly those around him. He had been for so long a time in the habit of forming his opinion rather by looks than words that the situation seemed to explain itself; young lovers, angry father. This opinion was justified and sustained by the confidence which had been given to him by Athlyne on the previous afternoon. He had been, on entering the room, rather anxious at the state of affairs; but now he began to breathe more freely. He felt that his experience of life and of law might really be here of some service. But his profession had also taught him wariness and caution; also not to speak on side issues till he knew the ground thoroughly. Joy he read like an open book. There was no mistaking her love, her anxiety, her apprehension. Athlyne he knew something of already, but he now saw in his face a warning look which bade him be silent regarding him. He diagnosed Colonel Ogilvie as a proud, masterful, vain, passionate man; something of a prig; tender, in a way he understood himself; faithful to his word; relentless to an expressed intention; just—according to his own ideas of right and wrong. Weighing these attributes for his own pacific purposes he came to the conclusion that his first effort at conciliation should be made with regard to the last-mentioned. So he began, speaking in a manner of courtly and deferential grace:

"I trust sir, you will yield to me the consideration often asked by, and sometimes granted to a well-intentioned man, however bungling the same might be in thought or method or manner." Colonel Ogilvie conceded the favour with a gracious bow. Thus emboldened, if not justified, he went on:

"I fain would ask that I might be allowed to make something in the nature of a short statement, and to make it without interruption or expostulation. You will understand why presently." Again the gracious acquiescence; he continued:

"You are, I take it, a stranger to this country; though, if I am not misled by name and lineament, claiming Scottish forbears?" Colonel Ogilvie's bow came more naturally this time. His in-lying pride was coming to the rescue of common sense. The Sheriff understood, and went on with better heart:

"The experience which I have had in the performance of my duties as sheriff has shewn me that such a group as I see before me—father, daughter and lover, if I mistake not—is not uncommon in this part of Scotland." No one answered his bow this time. All were grimly silent in expectancy. He felt that it was a dangerous topic; but the fact had been stated without being denied. He hurried on:

"Just across the Border, as we are, we have had very many occasions of run-away marriages; I have had myself in earlier days to explain for the good of all parties how the law stands in such matters. More than once the knowledge enabled those interested in it to spare much pain to others; generally to those whom they loved best. I trust that now I may use that knowledge in your behalf—as a friend. I am not here in my official capacity—or perhaps I might not be so free to advise as I am now without, I trust, offence to any one." Colonel Ogilvie's gracious bow here answered for all the party. The Sheriff felt more at ease. He was now well into his subject; and the most difficult part of his duty had been, he thought, passed. All three of his hearers listened eagerly as he went on:

"A knowledge of the law can hurt no one; though it may now and again disappoint some one—when expounded too late. Well, there is a common belief in South Britain—and elsewhere that the marriage law in Scotland is a very filmy thing, with bounds of demarcation which are actually nebulous. This doubtless arises from the fact that all such laws are based on the theory that it is good to help such contracting parties to the secure and speedy fulfilment of their wishes. But anyone who thinks that they are loose in either purpose or action is apt to be rudely enlightened. The Scots' Marriage laws demand that there be a manifest and honest intention of marriage on the part of the contractors. This intention can be proved in many ways. Indeed the law in certain cases is willing to infer it, when direct proof is not attainable, from subsequent acts of the parties. I may fairly say that in all such cases courts of law will hold that mutuality of intention is of the essence of marriage rite. This followed by cohabitation *is* the marriage; though the latter to follow close on the declaration is not always deemed necessary. In our law the marriage may be either of two kinds. The most formal is that effected by a minister or proper official after due calling of banns, or by notice given to sheriff or registrar. The other form is by what is known in the law as 'Irregular marriage.' This is in legal parlance—for which I make no apology as it is necessary that all married folk, or those intending to enter that honourable condition should understand it—is known as 'intention followed by copula.' Now you must know that either form of marriage is equally binding—equal in law and honour; and when the conditions attached to each form have been duly fulfilled such marriage is irrefragable. In old days this facility of marriage made Gretna Green, which is the first place across the Border, the objective for eloping lovers matrimonially inclined; and as till 1856 no previous residence in Scotland was required, romance was supposed to stop at the Border. That is, the marriage could be effected and parental objections—did such exist—were overborne. There were many cynical souls who held that repentance for the hasty marriage could then begin. I feel bound to say that this is an opinion in which I do not myself share.

"In 1856 an Act of Parliament, 20th Vict. Cap. 96, was passed, by which it became necessary for the validity of irregular marriage that at least one of the two contractors should have his or her usual residence in Scotland, or have been resident in Scotland for three full weeks next preceding the marriage.

"I thank you, Colonel Ogilvie, for having listened to me so patiently. But as I have no doubt that you three have much to say to each other I shall withdraw for the present. This will leave you free to discuss matters. And perhaps I may say, as an old man as well as a responsible officer of the Law, that I trust the effect will be to make for peace and amity. I am staying here in the hotel and I shall take it as a great pleasure and a great honour if you will breakfast with me in say an hour's time. All your family will be most welcome." With a bow, in which deference and geniality were mingled, he withdrew.

Each of the three left kept looking at each other in silence. Joy drew closer to Athlyne and took his hand. Colonel Ogilvie pretended not to notice the act—an effort on his part which made his daughter radiant with hope. The first words spoken were by the Colonel:

"That man is a gentleman!" The two others felt that silence was present discretion; to agree with Colonel Ogilvie in his present mood was almost as dangerous as to disagree with him. His next words were in no way conciliatory though the *arrière pensée* made for hope.

"Now sir, what have you to say for yourself in this unhappy matter? Remember I in no way relax my intention of—of punishment; but I am willing to hear what you have to say." Athlyne winced at the word "punishment," which was not one which he was accustomed to hear applied to himself. But for Joy's sake he made no comment. He even kept his face fixed so as not to betray his anger. He felt that any change of subject, or drifting off that before them, must be for the better; things, could, he felt, hardly be worse than at present. Moreover, it might smooth matters somewhat if Colonel Ogilvie could be brought to recollect that he was not himself an undesirable person for alliance, and that his intention of matrimony had been already brought before Joy's father. In this conviction he spoke:

"As in this country, sir, intention counts for so much, may I crave your indulgence for a moment and refer you back to my letter to you on the subject of a very dear wish of mine—a wish put before you with a very decided intention." Colonel Ogilvie's answer, given in manner of equal suavity, was disconcerting; the bitterness behind it was manifest.

"I think sir, there must be some error—which is not mine. I never received any letter from you! Your epistolary efforts seem to have been confined to the ladies of my family." With an effort Athlyne restrained himself. When he felt equal to the task he spoke, still with a manner of utmost deference:

"An error there surely is; but it is not mine either. I posted yesterday at the Ambleside post office a letter to you. . . ." He was interrupted by Colonel Ogilvie who said bluntly:

"I am not so sure, sir, that the fault of my not reading such a letter was not yours; though perhaps not in the direct manner you mean. When I arrived home last night and found the horrible state of things with regard to my daughter's rash act—due to you" this with a look of actual malevolence "I was so upset that I did not look at the pile of letters awaiting me. I only read Joy's messages." As he said this Athlyne's eyes flashed and there was an answering flash in the eyes of the woman who looked so keenly at him; this was the first time since his arrival that the father had condescended to even mention his daughter's name. There might be some softening of that hard nature after all. Then the old man continued:

"I put them in my pocket; here they are!"—Whilst he looked at the envelopes in that futile way that some people unused to large correspondence love, Joy said with an easy calmness which made her lover glance at her in surprise: "Daddy, hadn't you better read your letters now; we shall wait." The tone was so much that to which he was accustomed from her that he did not notice the compromising "we" which would otherwise have inflamed him afresh. Drawing a chair close to one of the windows he opened the letters and began to read. Athlyne and Joy, instinctively and with unity of thought, moved towards the other window which was behind him. There they stood hand in hand, their eyes following every movement of the old man. Joy did not know, of course, what was in the letter; but she had seen it before in the garden at Ambleside and when he had posted it before setting out on their motor ride. And so, piecing her information with the idea conveyed by her lover's recent words, she was able to form some sort of idea of its general import. A soft, beautiful blush suffused her face, and her eyes glistened as she stood thinking; in the effort of thought she recalled many sweet passages. She now understood in a vague way what was the restraining influence which had moved her lover to reticence during all those hours when he had tried to tell her of his love and his hopes without actually speaking words, the knowledge of which given without his consent would have incensed her father against him, and so wrought further havoc. So moved was she that Athlyne, whose eyes were instinctively drawn to her from the observation of her father, was amazed and not a little disconcerted. There must be some strange undercurrent of feeling in her which he could not understand. Joy saw the look on his face and seemed to understand. She raised to her lips the hand that she so strongly clasped in hers and kissed it. Then she raised a finger of her other hand and touched her lips. Thus reassured of her love and understanding, Athlyne followed with his eyes the trend of hers; and so together they continued to watch her father, trying to gather from his bearing some indication of his thoughts. Indeed this was not a difficult matter. Colonel Ogilvie seemed to have lost himself in his task, and expressed his comments on what he read by a series of childlike movements and ejaculations. Athlyne who knew what the letter contained could apply these enlightening comments, and even Joy in her ignorance of detail could inferentially follow the text. Colonel Ogilvie did say a word of definite speech, but the general tendency of his comment was that of surprise—astonishment. When he had finished reading Athlyne's letter—it was the last of the batch—he sat for quite half a minute quite still and silent, holding the paper between finger and thumb of his dropped left hand. Then with a deep frown on his forehead he began to read it again. He was evidently looking for some passage, for when he had found it he stood up at once and turned to them. By this time Joy, warned by the movement, had dropped her lover's hand and now stood some distance away from him. The old man began:

"Sir . . . There is a passage in a letter here which I understand to be yours. So far I must acknowledge that I have been wrong. You evidently *did* send the letter, and I evidently received it. Listen to this: 'Having heard in a roundabout way that there was a woman in New York who was passing herself off as my wife I undertook a journey to that City to make investigation into the matter; and in order to secure the necessary secrecy as to my movements took for the time an assumed name—or rather used as Christian and surname two of those names in the middle of my full equipment which I do not commonly use.' What does all that mean? No, do not speak. Wait and I shall tell you. You say the lady—woman you call her—took your name. For saying such a thing, and for the disrespect in her description as a woman, you will have to answer me. Either of them will cost you your life." Athlyne answered with a quiet, impressive dignity which helped in some degree to reassure Joy who stood motionless in open-eyed wonder—her heart seeming to her as cold as ice at the horror of this new phase of danger. It was a veritable "bolt from the blue," incomprehensible to her in every way: "Colonel Ogilvie, I regret I shall be unable to meet your wishes in this respect!" As the old man looked astonished in his turn, he proceeded:

"I already owe you a life on another count; and I have but one. But if I had ten you should have them all, could they in any way assuage the sorrow which it seems must follow from my thoughtless act. I have told you already that I shall freely give my life in expiation of the wrong I have—all unintentionally—done to your daughter and yourself. And if any means could be found by which it could add to Joy's happiness or lessen her sorrow I should in addition and as freely give my soul!"

Colonel Ogilvie's reception of these words was characteristic of the man, as he took himself to be. He drew himself up to his full height and stood at attention. Then he saluted, and followed his salute with a grave bow. The soldier in him spoke first, the man after. Both Joy and Athlyne noticed with new hope that he allowed the speaking of her name to pass unchallenged as a further cause of offence. Presently, and in a new tone, he said:

"I have taken it for granted from the allusions in your letter that you are the writer; and from your mentioning an alias have not been surprised at seeing a strange name in the signature. But I have been and am surprised at the familiarity from a man of your years to a man of mine of a mere Christian name."

It was now Athlyne's turn to be surprised.

"A Christian name!" he said with a puzzled pucker of his brows. "I am afraid I don't understand." Then a light dawning on him he said with a slight laugh: "But that is not my Christian name."

"Then your surname?" queried the Colonel.

"Nor my surname either." His laugh was now more pronounced, more boyish.

"Oh I see; still another alias!" The words were bitter; the tone of manifest offence.

Athlyne laughed again; it was not intentional but purely spontaneous. He was recalled to seriousness by the look of pain and apprehension on Joy's face and by the Colonel's angry words, given with a look of fury:

"I am not accustomed to be laughed at—and to my face Mr.— Mr.—Mr. Richard Hardy Athlyne et cetera."

His apology for inopportune mirth was given with contrition— even humbly:

"I ask your pardon, Colonel Ogilvie, very deeply, very truly. But the fact is that Athlyne is my proper signature, though it is neither Christian name nor surname. I do hope you will attribute my rudeness rather to national habit than to any personal wish to wound. Surely you will see that I would at least be foolish to transgress in such a direction, if it be only that I aim at so much that it is in your power to grant." There was reason in this which there was no resisting. Colonel Ogilvie bowed—he felt that he could do no less. Athlyne wisely said no more; both men regarded the incident as closed.

With Joy it was different. The incident gave her the information she lacked for the completion of the circle of her knowledge. As with a flash she realised the whole secret: that this man who had saved her life and whom now her father wanted to kill was none other than the man whose name she had taken—at first in sport and only lately in order to protect herself from troubles of inquisitiveness and scandal. At the moment she was in reality the only one of the three—the only one at all—who had in her hand all the clues. Neither her father nor Athlyne knew that she had given to the maid at the hotel a name other than her own. She began to have also an unconscious knowledge of something else. Something which she could not define, some intuition of some coming change; something which hinged on her giving of the name. Now, for the first time she realised how dangerous it may be for any one to take the name of any other person—for any purpose whatever, or from any cause. She could not see the end.

But though her brain did not classify the idea her blood did. She blushed so furiously that she had serious thoughts of escaping from the room. Nothing but the danger which might arise from such a step kept her in her place. But something must, she felt, be done. Things were so shaping towards reconciliation that it would be wise to prevent matters slipping back. For an instant she was puzzled as to what to do; then an inspiration came to her. Turning to her father she said:

"Daddy, let us ask the old Sheriff to come in again!" She felt that she could rely on his discretion, and that in his hands things might slide into calmer waters. Her father acquiesced willingly, and a courteous message was sent through a servant.

CHAPTER XXI

APPLICATION OF LAW

WHILST the servant was gone there was a great clatter of arrival of a motor at the hotel; but all in Athlyne's room were too deeply concerned with their own affairs to notice it.

Presently there was a light tap at the door, and the Sheriff's "May I come in?" was heard. Colonel Ogilvie went himself to the door and threw it open. Beside the Sheriff stood a lady, heavily clad and with a motor veil.

"Joy! Joy!" said the veiled figure, and Aunt Judy stepping forward took the girl in her arms. In the meantime the Sheriff was explaining the situation:

"I was just coming from my room in obedience to your summons, when this lady entered the hall. She was asking for you, Colonel, and for Miss Ogilvie, as who she had learned at the railway station, was stopping here. I ventured to offer my services, and as she was coming up here, undertook to pilot her."

Joy was delighted to see Judy. She had so long been accustomed to look with fixed belief on her love and friending that she now expected she would be able to set matters right. Had she had any doubt of her Aunt's affection such must have soon disappeared in the warmth of the embrace accorded by her. When this was concluded—which was soon for it was short, if strenuous—she turned to Colonel Ogilvie and held out her hand:

"Good morning, Lucius. I see you got here all right. I hope you had a good journey?" Then turning to Athlyne she said, as if in surprise:

"Why, Mr. Hardy, how are you? And how do you come to be here? We thought we were never going to see you again." Then she rattled on; it was evident to Joy, and to Colonel Ogilvie also, that she was purposeful to baffle comment by flow of her own speech:

"Lucius, you must thank this gentleman who is, as the landlady whispered to me, the Sheriff of somewhere or other. He's a nice man, but a funny sort of Sheriff. When I asked him where was his posse he didn't know what I meant." Here she was interrupted by the Sheriff who said with a low bow to her:

"It is enough for any man, dear lady, to be in *esse* in such a charming presence!" Judy did not comprehend the joke; but she knew, being a woman, that some sort of compliment was intended; and, being a woman, beamed accordingly:

"Thank you, sir, both for your kindness in helping me and for your pretty talk. Joy, I have brought your dressing bag and a fresh rig out. You must need them, poor dear. Now you must tell me all your adventures. I told them to bring the things presently to your room. I shall then come with you whilst you are changing. Now, Mr. Sheriff, we must leave you for a little; but I suppose that as you have to talk business—you told me they had sent for you—you will doubtless prefer to be without us?"

"Your pardon," said the Sheriff gracefully. "I hope the time will never come when I shall prefer to be without such charming company!" This was said with such a meaning look, and in such a meaning tone, that Judy coloured. Joy, unseen by the others, smiled at her, rejoicing. The Sheriff, thinking they were moving off, turned to the Colonel saying:

"Now, Colonel Ogilvie, I am at your disposal; likewise such knowledge of law and custom as I possess." He purposely addressed himself to Colonel Ogilvie, evidently bearing in mind Athlyne's look of warning to silence regarding himself.

Whilst he had been speaking, Joy stood still, holding Judy by the hand and keeping her close to her. Judy whispered, holding her mouth close to her ear and trying to avoid the observation of the others:

"Come away dear whilst they are talking. They will be freer alone!" Joy whispered in return:

"No, I must not go. I must stay here, I am wanted. Do not say anything, dear—not a word; but stay by me." Judy in reply squeezed her hand and remained silent. Colonel Ogilvie, with manifest uneasiness and after clearing his throat, said to the Sheriff:

"As you have been so good sir, as to tell me some matters of law; and as you have very kindly offered us other services, may I trespass on your kindness in enlightening me as to some matters of fact." The Sheriff bowed; he continued:

"I must crave your indulgence, for I am in some very deep distress, and possibly not altogether master of myself. But I need some advice, or at any rate enlightenment as to some matters of law. And as I am far from home and know no one here who is of legal authority—except yourself," this with a bow, "I shall be deeply grateful if I may accept your kindness and speak to you as a friend." Again the Sheriff bowed, his face beaming. Colonel Ogilvie, with a swift, meaning glance at each of the others in turn, went on:

"I must ask you all to keep silent. I am speaking with this gentleman for my own enlightenment, and require no comments from any of you. Indeed, I forbid interruption!" Unpromising as this warning sounded, both Joy and Athlyne took a certain comfort from it. The point they both attached importance to was that Athlyne was simply classed with the rest without differentiation. The Sheriff, who feared lest the father's domineering tone might provoke hostilities, spoke quickly:

"Now, Colonel Ogilvie, I am at your disposal for whatever you may wish to ask me."

"I suppose Mr. Sheriff, I need not say, that I trust you will observe honourable silence regarding this whole painful affair; as I expect that all present will." This was said with a threatening smile. When the Sheriff bowed acceptance of the condition he went on:

"Since you spoke to us here a little while ago a strange enlightenment has come to me. Indeed a matter so strange and so little in accord with the experiences of my own life that I am in a quandary. I should really like to know exactly how I—how we all stand at present. From what you have said about the Scottish marriage laws I take it that you have an inkling of what has gone on. And so, as you are in our confidence, you will not perhaps mind if I confide further in you?"

"I shall be deeply honoured, Colonel Ogilvie."

"Thank you again, sir. You are a true friend to a man in deep distress and in much doubt . . . We are, as you perhaps know, Americans. My daughter's life was saved by a gentleman in New York. I think it right to say that it was on his part a very gallant act, and that we were all deeply grateful to him. He came to my house—at my own invitation; and my wife and her sister, Miss Judith Hayes"—the Sheriff turned to Judy and bowed as at an introduction;

she curtsied in reply—"were very pleased with him. But we never saw him again. He returned very soon afterwards to England; and though we were coming to London he never came near us. Indeed his neglect was marked; for though I invited him to call, he ignored us." As he said this he looked straight at Athlyne with hard eyes. "I have reason to know that my daughter was much interested in him. Ordinarily speaking I should not mention a matter of this kind. But as I have received from him—it has only been made known to me in the interval since our meeting—an assurance of his affection and a proffer of marriage, I feel that I may speak." He turned away and began walking up and down the room as though trying to collect his thoughts.

As Joy heard him speak of her own interest in the man and of his proposal of marriage she blushed deeply, letting her eyes fall. But when, by some of the divine instinct of love, she knew that he was looking ardently at her she raised them, swimming, to his. And so once more they looked deep into each other's souls. Judy felt the trembling of the girl's hand and held it harder with a sympathetic clasp, palm to palm and with fingers interlaced. She felt that she understood; and her eyes, too, became sympathetically suffused. The Sheriff had now no eyes except for Judy. Whilst the Colonel had been speaking he had looked at him of course—he knew well that it would be a cause of offence if he did not. But the walking up and down gave him opportunity for his wishes. Judy could not but recognise the ardour of his glance, and she too blushed exceedingly. Somehow, she was glad of it; she knew that blushing became her, and she felt that she would like to look her best to the eyes of this fine, kindly old man. When Colonel Ogilvie began to speak again there was a change in him. He seemed more thoughtful, more cautious, more self-controlled; altogether he was more like his old self. There was even a note of geniality in his voice.

"What I want to ask you in especial is this: How can we avoid any sort of scandal over this unhappy occurrence? My daughter has acted thoughtlessly in going out alone in a motor with a gentleman. Through a series of accidents it appears that that ride was unduly and unintentionally prolonged, and ended in her being caught in a fog and lost. By accident she came here, walking after the motor had broken down. She slept last night in that room; and the man, who had also found his way hither later, slept, unknowing of her proximity, in this. I need not tell you that such a state of things is apt to lead to a scandal. Now, and now only, is the time to prevent it" . . . He was interrupted by the Sheriff who spoke hurriedly, as one who had already considered the question and had his mind made up:

"There will be no scandal!" He spoke in so decided a way that the other was impressed.

"How do you know? What ground have you for speaking so decidedly?"

"It rests entirely on you—yourself, Colonel Ogilvie."

"What!" His tone was laden with both anger and surprise. "Do you think I would spread any ill report of my own daughter? Sir, you must——" Once more the Sheriff cut into his speaking:

"You misapprehend me, Colonel Ogilvie. You misapprehend me entirely. Why should I—how could I think such a thing! No! I mean that if you accept the facts as they seem to me to be, no one—not you, nor any one else, can make scandal; if you do not!"

"Explain yourself," he interrupted. "Nay, do not think me rude"—here he put up a deprecating hand—"but I am so deeply anxious about my daughter's happiness—her future welfare and happiness," he added as he remembered how his violent attitude had, only a few minutes ago imperilled—almost destroyed, that happiness. Joy had been, off and on, whispering a word to her aunt so that the latter was now fairly well posted in the late events.

"Quite so! quite so, my dear sir. Most natural thing in the world," said the Sheriff soothingly. "Usual thing under the circumstances is to kill the man; or want to kill him!" As he spoke he looked at Athlyne meaningly. The other understood and checked the words which were rising to his lips. Then, having tided over the immediate danger of explosion, the Sheriff went on:

"The fact is Colonel Ogilvie, that the series of doings (and perhaps misdoings) and accidents, which have led to our all meeting here and now, has brought about a strange conclusion. So far as I can see"—here his manner grew grave and judicial—"these two young people are at the present moment man and wife. Lawfully married according to Scottish law!"

The reception of this dictum was varied. Colonel Ogilvie almost collapsed in overwhelming amazement. Joy, blushing divinely, looked at her husband adoringly. Athlyne seemed almost transfigured and glorified; the realisation of all his hopes in this sudden and unexpected way showed unmistakably how earnest they had been. Judy, alone of all the party, was able to express herself in conventional fashion. This she did by clapping her hands and, then by kissing the whole party—except the Sheriff who half stood forward as though in hope that some happy chance might include him in the benison. She began with Joy and went on to her brother-in-law, who accepted with a better grace than she feared would have been accorded. When she came to Athlyne she hesitated for a moment, but with a "now-or-never" rush completed the act, and fell back shyly with a belated timorousness.

The Sheriff, having paused for the completion of this little domestic ceremony, went on calmly:

"Since I left you a few minutes ago I have busied myself with making a few necessary inquiries from my old servant Jane McBean, now McPherson. I made them, I assure you Colonel Ogilvie, very discreetly. Even Jane, who is in her way a clever woman, has no suspicion that I was even making inquiry. The result has been to confirm me in my original conjecture, which was to the effect that there has been executed between these two people an 'irregular' marriage!" At the mention of the words the Colonel exploded:

"God's death, sir, the women of the Ogilvies don't make irregular marriages!" The Sheriff went calmly on, only noticing the protest for the sake of answering it.

By this time Joy and Judith were close together, holding hands. Insensibly the girl drew her Aunt over to where Athlyne was standing and took him by the arm. He raised his other hand and with it covered the hand that lay on his arm, pressing it closer as he listened attentively to the Sheriff's expounding of the law:

"I gather that I did not express myself clearly when a short time ago I spoke of the Scottish marriage laws. Let me now be more precise. And as I am trying to put into words understandable by all a somewhat complex subject I shall ask that no one present will make any remark whatever till this part of my task has been completed. I shall then answer to the best of my power any question or questions which any of you may choose to ask me.

"Let me begin by assuring you all that what in Scottish law we call an 'irregular' marriage is equally binding in every way with a 'regular' marriage; the word only refers to form or method, and in no wise to the antecedents or to the result. In our law 'Mutual Consent' constitutes marriage. You will observe that I speak of marriage—not the proof of it. Proof is quite a different matter; and as it is formally to be certified by a Court it is naturally hedged in by formalities. This consent, whether proved or not, whether before witnesses or not, should of course be followed by co-habitation; but even this is not necessary. The dictum of Scots' law is *'Concensus non concubitus facit matrimonium.'* But I have a shrewd suspicion that the mind of the Court is helped to a declaration of validity when *concensus* has been followed by *concubitus*.

"Now let us take the present case and examine it as though testing it in a Court of Law; for such is the true means to be exact. This man and woman—we don't know 'gentleman' and 'lady' in the Law—declared in the presence of witnesses that they were man and wife. That is, the man declared to the police sergeant at Dalry that the woman was his wife; and the woman declared timeously to the police officer who made the arrest that the man was her husband. These two statements, properly set out, would in themselves be evidence not only of inferred consent by declaration *de præsenti* but of the same thing by 'habit and repute.' The law has been thus stated:

" 'It may be held that a man and a woman, by living together and holding themselves out as married persons, have sufficiently declared their matrimonial consent; and in that case they will be declared to be married although no specific promise of marriage or of *de præsenti* acknowledgement has been proved.'

"But there is a still more cogent and direct proof, should such be required. Each of these consenting parties to the contract of 'marriage by consent,' on coming separately to this hotel last night gave to the servant of the house who admitted them the name by which I hold they are now bound in honourable wedlock!" He spoke the last sentences gravely and impressively after the manner of an advocate pressing home on a jury the conclusion of an elaborate train of reasoning. Whilst speaking he had kept his eyes fixed on Colonel Ogilvie, who unconsciously took it that an exhortation on patience and toleration was being addressed to him. The effect was increased by the action of Joy, who seeing him all alone and inferring his spiritual loneliness, left Judith but still holding Athlyne's arm drew the latter towards him. Then she took her father's arm and stood between the two men whom she loved. Judy quietly took Athlyne's other arm, and so all stood in line holding each other as they faced the Sheriff. No one said a word; all were afraid to break the silence.

"We now come to further proofs if such be required. The woman, who arrived first, gave the name of Lady Athlyne." Here Joy got fearfully red; she was conscious of her father's eyes on her, even before she heard him say: "That foolish joke again! Did not I forbid you to use it daughter?" She felt it would be unwise to answer, to speak at all just at present. In desperation she raised her eyes to the face of her lover—and was struck with a sort of horrified amazement. For an instant it had occurred to him that Joy must have known his identity—for some time past at all events. The thought was, however, but momentary. Her eyes fell again quickly, and she stood in abashed silence. There was nothing to do now but to wait. The calm voice of the Sheriff went on, like the voice of Doom:

"The man arrived later. He himself had wired in his own name for rooms; but by the time he had arrived the possibility of his coming had, owing to the fog, been given up. The other traveller had been given the bedroom, and he slept on the sofa in the sitting-room—this room." As he spoke he went over to the door of communication between the rooms and examined the door. There were no fastenings except the ordinary latch; neither lock nor bolt. He did not say a word, but walked back to his place. Judy could not contain her curiosity any longer; she blurted out:

"What name did he give?" The Sheriff looked at her admiringly as he answered:

"The name he gave, dear lady, was 'Athlyne'!"

"Is that your name?" she queried—this time to Athlyne.

"It is!" He pulled himself up to his full height and stood on his dignity as he said it. His name should not be dishonoured if he could help it.

Colonel Ogilvie stood by with an air of conscious superiority. He already knew the name from Athlyne's letter, though he had not up to that moment understood the full import of it. He was willing to be further informed through Judy's questioning.

"And you are Lord Athlyne—the Earl of Athlyne?"

"Certainly!"

To the astonishment of every one of the company Judy burst into a wild peal of hysterical laughter. This closely followed a speech of broken utterance which only some of those present understood at all—and of those some only some few partly. "Athlyne!"—"kill him for it!"—"calling herself by his name,"—"oh! oh! A-h-h!" There was a prolonged screech and then hysterical laughter followed. At the first this unseemly mirth created a feeling of repulsion in all who heard. It seemed altogether out of place; in the midst of such a serious conversation, when the lives and happiness of some of those present were at stake, to have the train of thought broken by so inopportune a cachinnation was almost unendurable. Colonel Ogilvie was furious. Well was it for the possibilities of peace that his peculiar life and ideas had trained him to be tolerant of woman's weakness, and to be courteous to them even under difficulties. For had he given any expression to his natural enough feelings such would inevitably have brought him into collision—intellectual if not physical—with both Athlyne and the Sheriff; and either was to be deplored. Joy was in her heart indignant, for several reasons. It was too hard that, just as things were possibly beginning to become right and the fine edge of tragedy to be turned, her father's mind should be taken back to anger and chagrin. But far beyond this on the side of evil was the fact that it imperilled afresh the life of—of the man she loved, her . . . her husband. Even the personal aspect to her could not be overlooked. The ill-timed laughter prevented her hearing more of . . . of the man who it now seemed was already her husband. However she restrained and suppressed herself and waited, still silent, for the development of things. But she did not consider looks as movements; she raised her eyes to Athlyne's adoringly, and kept them there. He in turn had been greatly upset for the moment; even now, whilst those wild peals of hysterical laughter continued to resound, he could not draw any conclusions from the wild whirl of inchoate thoughts. There was just one faint gleam of light which had its origin rather in instinct than reason, that perhaps the interruption had its beneficial side which would presently be made manifest.

When Joy looked towards him there was a balm for his troubled spirit. In the depths of her beautiful eyes he lost himself—and his doubts and sorrows, and was content.

The only one unmoved was the Sheriff. His mental attitude allowed him to look at things more calmly than did those personally interested. With the exception of one phase—that of concern that this particular woman, who had already impressed her charming personality on his heart, should be in such distress—he could think, untroubled, of the facts before him. With that logical mind of his, and with his experience of law and the passions that lead to law-invoking, he knew that the realization of Athlyne's name and position was a troublesome matter which might have been attended with disastrous consequences. To a man of Colonel Ogilvie's courage and strong passion the presence of an antagonist worthy of his powers is rather an incentive to quarrel than a palliative.

As to poor Judy she was in no position to think at all. She was to all practical intents, except for the noise she was occasionally making—her transport was subsiding—as one who is not. She continued intermittently her hysterical phrenzy—to laugh and cry, each at the top note—and commingling eternally. She struggled violently as she sat on the chair into which she had fallen when the attack began; she stamped her heels on the floor, making a sound like gigantic castanets. The sound and restless movement made an embarrassing *milieu* for the lucid expression of law and entangled facts; but through it all the Sheriff, whose purpose after all was to convince Ogilvie, went on with his statement. By this time Joy, and Athlyne, whom with an appealing look she had summoned to help, were endeavouring to restore Judy. One at either side they knelt by her, holding her hands and slapping them and exercising such other ministrations as the girl out of her limited experience of such matters could, happily to soothing effect, suggest. The Sheriff's voice, as calm voices will, came through the disturbance seemingly unhindered:

"Thus you will note that in all this transaction the Earl of Athlyne had made no disguise of his purpose. To the police who arrested him he at once disclosed his identity, which the sergeant told me was verified by the name on his motor-driver's license. He telegraphed to the hotel by his title—as is fitting and usual; and he gave his title when he arrived. As I have already said, he stated to the police, at first on his own initiative and later when interrogated directly on the point, that the woman in the motor was his wife. And the identity of the woman in the motor and the woman in the hotel can easily be proved. Thus on the man's part there is ample evidence of that matrimonial purpose which the law requires. All this without counting the letter to the woman's father, in which he stated his wish and intention to marry her.

"Now as to the woman—and I must really apologise to her for speaking of the matter in her presence."—Here Athlyne interrupted his ministrations with regard to Judy in order to expostulate:

"Oh, I say Mr. Sheriff. Surely it is not necessary." But the Sheriff shut him up quite shortly. He had a purpose in so doing: he wished in his secret heart to warn both Athlyne and Joy not to speak a word till he had indicated that the time had come for so doing.

"There is nothing necessary, my Lord; except that both you and the young lady should listen whilst I am speaking! I am doing so for the good of you both; and I take it as promised that neither of you will say a single word until I have told you that you may do so."

"Quite right!" this was said *sotto voce* by Colonel Ogilvie.

"You, young madam, have taken upon yourself the responsibilities of wifehood; and it is right as well as necessary that you understand them; such of them at least as have bearing upon the present situation.

"As to the woman. She, when questioned by the police as to her status for the purpose of verification of Lord Athlyne's statement, accepted that statement. Later on, she of her own free will and of her own initiative, gave her name as Lady Athlyne—only the bearer of which could be the wife of the Defender; I mean of Lord Athlyne." The interruption this time came from Colonel Ogilvie.

"If Lord Athlyne is Defender, who is the other party?"

"Lady Athlyne, or Miss Ogilvie, in whichever name she might take action, would be the Pursuer!"

"Sir!" thundered the Colonel, going off as usual at half-cock, "do you insinuate that my daughter is pursuer of a man?" He grew speechless with indignation. The Sheriff's coolness stood to him there, when the fury of the Kentuckian was directed to him personally. In the same even tone he went on speaking:

"I must ask—I really *must* ask that you do not be so hasty in your conclusions whilst I am speaking, Colonel Ogilvie. You must understand that I am only explaining the law; not even giving any opinion of my own. The terminology of Scot's Law is peculiar, and differs from English law in such matters. For instance what in English law is 'Plaintiff and Defendant' becomes with us 'Pursuer and Defender.' There may be a female as well as a male Pursuer. Thus on the grounds of present consent as there is ample proof of Matrimonial Consent of either and both parties—sufficient for either to use against the other. I take it that the Court would hold the marriage proved; unless *both* parties repudiated the Intent. This I am sure would never be; for if there were any mutual affection neither would wish to cause such gossip as would inevitably ensue. And if either party preferred that the union should continue, either from motives of love or interest, the marriage could be held good. And I had better say at once, since it is a matter to be considered by any parent, that should there have been any valid ground for what you designate as 'scandal,' such would in the eyes of the law be only the proper and necessary completion of the act of marriage. And let me say also that the fact of the two parties, thus become one by the form of Irregular Marriage, having passed the night in this suite of rooms without bolt of fastening on the connecting door would be taken by a Court as proof of consummation. No matter by what entanglement of events—no matter how or by what accident or series of accidents the two parties came into this juxtaposition!

"There is but one other point to be considered regarding the validity of this marriage. It is that of compliance with the terms of Lord Brougham's Act of 1856. The man has undoubted domicile in Scotland for certain legal purposes. But the marriage law requires a further and more rigid reading of residence than mere possession of estates. The words are that one of the parties to the marriage must 'have his or her usual place of residence' in this Country. But as I have shown you that in Lord Athlyne's case his living in Scotland for several weeks in one or other of his own houses would be certainly construed by any Court as compliance with the Act, I do not think that any question of legality could arise. Indeed it is within my own knowledge that as a Scottish peer—Baron of Ceann-da-Shail—who declared Scottish domicile on reaching his majority and whose 'domicile of origin' was not affected by his absence as an officer in foreign service, his status for the purpose of Scottish marriage is unassailable.

"In fine let me point out that I am speaking altogether of *proof* of the marriage itself. The actual marriage is in law the consent of the parties; and such has undoubtedly taken place. The only possible condition of its nullity would be the repudiation of the implied Consent by both of the parties. One alone would not be sufficient!

"And now, Colonel Ogilvie, as I believe it will be well that you and the two young people should consider the situation from this point of view, will you allow me to withdraw—still on the supposition that you will join me later at breakfast. And if this merry lady"—pointing to Judy who had gained composure sufficiently to hear the end of his explanation—"will honour me by coming to my sitting-room, just below this, where breakfast will be served, it may perhaps be better. I take it that you will be all able to speak more freely, you and your daughter—and her husband!"

He withdrew gracefully, giving his arm to Judy who having risen bashfully had taken his extended arm. She was blushing furiously.

The door closed behind him, leaving Joy standing between her father and Athlyne, and holding an arm of each.

CHAPTER XXII

THE HATCHET BURIED

For a few minutes there was silence in the room; silence so profound that every sound of the street was clearly heard. Even the shutting of the Sheriff's door in the room below was distinct.

The first to speak was Colonel Ogilvie. Athlyne, who would have liked to break the silence refrained through prudence; he feared that were he to speak before Colonel Ogilvie did, that easily-irate gentleman might take offence. He knew that this might be disastrous, for it would renew the old strife in an acute form; as it was, there were distinct indications of coming peace. Joy, and Joy alone, was to be thought of now. By this time Athlyne was beginning to get the measure of Colonel Ogilvie's foot. He realised that the dictatorial, vindictive, blood-thirsty old man would perhaps do much if left to himself; but that if hindered or thwarted or opposed in any way his pride or his vanity—and they were united in him—would force him to keep his position at any cost.

"Well, sir?" The tone was so peremptory and so "superior" that any man to whom it had been used might well have taken offence; but Athlyne was already schooled to bear, and moreover the statement made by the Sheriff filled his heart with such gladness that he felt that he could bear anything. As Joy was now his wife he *could* not quarrel with her father—nor receive any quarrel from him. Still, all the same, he felt that he must support and maintain his own independent position; such would be the best road to ultimate peace. Moreover, he had his own pride; and as he had already made up his mind to die if need be for Joy's sake, he could not go back on that resolution without seeming to be disloyal to her. There would—could—be no hiding anything from her as she had already heard the whole of the quarrel and of his acquiescence to her father's challenge. No one, however, would have thought he had any quarrel who heard his reply, spoken in exquisitely modulated accents of respect:

"Need I say, Colonel Ogilvie, that I am equally proud and happy in finding myself allied with your House by my marriage with your daughter. For, sir, I love her with all my soul, as well as with all my heart and mind. She is to me the sweetest, dearest and best thing in all the universe. I am proud of her and respect her as much as I love her; and to you, her father, I hope I may say that I bless—and shall ever bless for so long as I live—the day that I could call her mine." As he spoke, Joy's hand on his arm, which had trembled at the beginning, now gripped him hard and firmly. Turning his eyes to hers he saw in them a look of adoration which made his heart leap and his blood seem on fire. The beautiful eyes fell for an instant as a red tide swept her face and neck; but in an instant more they were raised to his eyes and hung there, beaming with pride and love and happiness. This nerved and softened him at once, to even a gentler feeling towards the old man; those lovely eyes had always looked trustingly and lovingly into her father's, and he would never disturb—so he vowed to himself—if he could avoid it by any sacrifice on his part, such filial and parental affection. And so, with gentler voice and softened mien, he went on speaking.

"Now I must ask you to believe, sir, that with the exception of that one fault—a grave one I admit—of taking Miss Ogilvie out alone in my motor I have not willingly or consciously been guilty of any other disrespect towards you. You now understand, of course, that it was that unhappy assumed name which prevented my having the pleasure of visiting you and your family on this side of the Atlantic. No one can deplore more than I do that unhappy alias. The other, though I regret—and regret deeply—the pain it has caused, I cannot be sorry for, since it has been the means of making Joy my wife."

Here he beamed down into the beautiful grey eyes of the said wife who was still holding his arm. As he finished she pinched gently the flesh of his arm. This sent a thrill through him; it was a kiss of sorts and had much the same effect as the real thing. Joy noted the change in his voice as he went on:

"I so respected your wishes, sir, that I did not actually ask in words Joy to be my wife until I should have obtained your permission to address myself to her. If you will look at that letter you will see that it was written at Ceann-da-Shail, my place in Ross-shire—days before I posted it."

"Then if you did not ask her to marry you; how is it that you are now married—according to the Sheriff?" He thought this a poser, and beamed accordingly. Athlyne answered at once:

"When two people love each other, sir, as Joy and I do, speech is the least adequate form of expression. We did not want words; we knew!" Again Joy squeezed his arm and they stood close together in a state of rapture. The Colonel, with some manifest hesitation, said:

"With regard to what the Sheriff spoke of as 'real cause of scandal,' was there. . . . ?"

"That, sir," said Athlyne interrupting with as fierce and truculent an aspect as had been to the Colonel at any moment of the interview "is a subject on which I refuse to speak, even to you." Then after a pause he added:

"This I will say to you as her father who is entitled to hear it: Joy's honour is as clear and stainless as the sunlight. Whatever has taken place has been my doing, and I alone am answerable for it." Whilst he was speaking Joy stood close to him, silent and with downcast eyes. In the prolonged silence which ensued she raised them, and letting go Athlyne's arm stepped forward towards her father with flashing eyes:

"Father what he says is God's truth. But there is one other thing which you should know, and you must know it from me since he will not speak. He is justified in speaking of my honour, for it was due—and due alone—to his nobility of character that I am as I am. That and your unexpected arrival. For my part I would have——"

"Joy!" Athlyne's voice though the tone was low, rang like a trumpet. Half protest it was, half command. Instinctively the woman recognised the tone and obeyed, as women have obeyed the commands of the men they loved, and were proud to do so, from Eden garden down the ages.

"Speak on, daughter! Finish what you were saying." His voice was strangely soft and his eyes were luminous beneath their shaggy white brows. Joy's answering tone was meek:

"I cannot, father. My . . . Mr.—Lord Athlyne desires that I should be silent." She was astonished at his reply following:

"Well, perhaps he is right. Better so!" Then in *sotto voce* to Athlyne:

"Women should not be allowed to talk sometimes. They go too far when they get to self-abasement!" Athlyne nodded. Again silence which Colonel Ogilvie broke:

"Well, sir. I suppose we must take it that the marriage is complete in Scotch law. So far for the past. What of the future?" In a low voice Athlyne replied:

"Whose future?"

"Yours—yours and my daughter's." He was amazed at Athlyne's reply, spoken in a voice both low and sad: so too was Joy:

"Of that I cannot say. It does not rest with me."

"'Not rest with you, sir? Then with whom does it rest." Athlyne raised his eyes and looked him straight in the face:

"With you!"

"With me?" the Colonel's voice was faint with amazement.

"Yes, with you! What future have I, already condemned to death! What future has my wife, whose sentence of widowhood came even before the knowledge of her marriage! Do you forget Colonel Ogilvie that my life is pledged to you? On your own doing, I took that obligation; but having taken it I must abide by it. Such future as may be for either of us rests with you!" Colonel Ogilvie did not pause before answering. He spoke quickly as one whose mind is made up:

"But that is all over." Athlyne said quietly:

"You had not said so! In an affair of this kind the challenged man is not free to act. Pacific overture must be with the one who considering himself injured has sought this means of redress." Joy listening, with her heart sinking and her hand so trembling that she took it from his arm lest it should upset him, was amazed. He was at least as determined as her father. But she was rejoiced to see that his stiffness was having its effect; her father was evidently respecting this very quality so much that he was giving way to his opponent. Seeing this, and recognising in her woman's way for the first time in her life this fundamental force, she made up her mind that she too would on her side keep steadfastly to her convictions just as . . . as . . . He had done. In silence she waited for what would follow this new development going on before her eyes. Presently Colonel Ogilvie spoke:

"I suppose Lord Athlyne you are satisfied with the validity of the marriage?" He answered heartily:

"Of course I am! The Sheriff was quite clear about it; and what he says is sufficient for me."

"And your intention?"

"Sir, from the first moment when my eyes lit on your daughter I had only one intention, and that was to make her my wife. Be quite satisfied as to me! I am fixed as Fate! if there is any hindrance to my wishes it can only come from my wife. But understand this: that if for any cause whatever she may wish this marriage annulled, or consider that it has not been valid, she has only to indicate her wish and I shall take any step in my power to set her free."

"Father!" Colonel Ogilvie turned in astonishment at the sound of his daughter's voice, which was in such tone as he had never heard from her. It rang; her mind was made up:

"Father, a while ago when you seemed in some grave trouble I asked you why you did not ask me anything. I told you I had never lied to you and should not do so then; but you asked me nothing. Why don't you ask me now?"

"What should I ask you, little girl. You are married; and your duty is to some one else whose name you bear. Besides, I don't ask women questions which may be painful to answer. Such I ask of men!"

To this she spoke in a calm voice which made Athlyne uneasy. He could not imagine what she was coming at; but he felt that whatever it might be it was out of the truth of her nature, and that he must support her. Her love he never doubted. In the meantime he must listen patiently and learn what she had to say.

"Well father, as you will not ask I must speak unasked. It is harder; that is all. The Sheriff said that mutual intention was necessary for marriage. Let me tell you that I had not then such intention! I must say it. I have never lied to you yet; and I don't intend to begin now. Especially when I am entering on a new life with a man whom I love and honour. For if this marriage be not good we shall soon have one that is—if he will have me." Athlyne took her hand; she sighed joyfully as she went on:

"I certainly did intend to marry Mr. . . . Lord Athlyne when . . . when he should formally ask me; but I understood then that there was some obstacle to his doing so. This I now know to be that he was wanting to get your consent beforehand. But if I did not then intend that our coming for a run in the motor together was to be marriage, how can I by that act be married?" As she paused Athlyne realised what was the cause of that vague apprehension which had chilled him. Colonel Ogilvie was beset by a new difficulty by this new attitude of Joy. If she repudiated intention such would nullify the marriage, since Athlyne had signified his intention of letting her have her way. If there were no marriage, then there would be scandal. So before beginning to argue with his daughter on the subject of the validity of the marriage, he thought it well to bring to the aid of reason the forces of fear. He commenced by intimidation:

"Of course you understand, daughter, that if you and Lord Athlyne were not married through the accidents of your escapade, there will be scandal from it; there is no other alternative. In that case, such pacific measures as I have now acceded to will be abrogated; and the gentleman who was the cause of the evil must still answer to me for it." At this threat Joy grew ghastly pale, Athlyne, wrung to the heart by it, forgot his intention of discretion and said quickly and sharply:

"That is not fair, Colonel Ogilvie. She is a woman—if she *is* your daughter, and is not to be treated brutally. You must not strike at a man through a woman. If you want to strike a man do so direct! I am the man. Strike me, how and when you will; but this woman is my wife—at least she is until she repudiates our marriage! But till then by God! no man—not even her father himself—shall strike her or at her, or through her!" Both he and Joy were surprised at the meek way in which the old man received this tirade. But even whilst he had been uttering the cruel threat both his conscience and his courage had been against him. This, the man and the woman who heard could, from evidence, divine. But there was another cause of which they had no knowledge. The moment after speaking, when his blind passion began to cool, the last words of his wife came back to his memory: "Be good to her, and never forget that she can suffer most through any one dear to her." Furthermore, the recollection of Judy's words as he was leaving clinched the matter: "You hold poor Joy's life—which is her heart—in your hand!" He began his reply to

Athlyne truculently—as was usual to him; but melted quickly as he went on:

"Hey-day my young bantam-cock; you flash your spurs boldly.... But I don't know but you're right. I was wrong; I admit it! Joy my dear I apologise for it; and to you too, sir, who stand up so valiantly and so readily for your wife. I am glad my little girl has such a defender; though it is and will be a sad thought to me that I was myself the first to cause its evidence. But keep your hair on, young man! Men sometimes get hurt by running up against something that's quite in its right place.... It's my place to look after my little girl—till such time as you have registered your bond-rights. And see, doesn't she declare she had no idea she was being married. However, it's all right in this case. I don't mean her to give herself away over this part of the job any more than you did a while ago when you stopped her telling me something that it wouldn't have been wise to say. So, sir, guess we'll call it quits this time. Well, little girl, let me tell you that you've said all at once to me two different things. You said you *didn't* intend to marry Lord Athlyne that time, but that you *did* at some other. If that last doesn't make an intention to marry I'm a Dutchman. I think we'd better let it rest at that! Now as to you Lord Athlyne! You seem to want—and rightly enough I'll allow—that I make a formal retraction of my demand for your life. Well I do so now. There's my hand! I can give it to you freely, for you are a brave man and you love my little girl; and my little girl loves you. I'm right sorry I didn't know you at the first as I do now. But I suppose the fact is, I was jealous all along. You don't know—yet—what I know: that you were thrown at me in a lot of ways before I ever saw you, by the joke that my little girl and Judy put up on me. When I knew that my girl was calling herself by your name...."

"Daddy dear!" This was Joy's protest. "Yes, little girl, I won't give you away; but your husband should know this fact lest he keep a grudge in his heart against your old daddy—and I know you wouldn't like that. You can tell him, some of these days or nights, what you like yourself about the whole thing from the first. I dare say he'll want to know, and won't let you alone till you tell him. And I dare say not then; for he'll like—he's bound to—all you can say. Here, Athlyne—I suppose that's what I am to call you since you're my son now—at any rate my daughter's husband." As he spoke he held out his hand. Athlyne jumped forward and seized it warmly. The two men shook hands as do two strong men who respect each other. Joy stepped forward and took the clasped hands between her own. When the hands parted she kissed her husband and then her father; she had accepted the situation.

After a pause Athlyne said, quietly but with a very resolute look on his face:

"I understand, sir, that the hatchet is now buried. But I want to say that this must be final. I do so lest you should ever from any cause wish to dig it up again. Oh, yes I understand"—for the Colonel was going to speak "but I have had a warning. Just now when it seemed that Joy was going to repudiate—though happily as it turned out for only a time—our marriage as an existing fact, you reopened that matter which I had then thought closed. Now as for the future Joy's happiness is my duty as well as my privilege and my pleasure, I must take all precautions which I can to insure it. It would not do if she could ever have in her mind a haunting fear that you and I could quarrel. I know that for my own part I would be no party to a quarrel with you. But I also have reason to know that a man's own purpose is nothing when some one else wants to quarrel with him. Therefore for our dear Joy's sake——"

"Good!" murmured the Colonel. "*Our* dear Joy's sake!" Athlyne repeated the phrase—he loved to do so:

"For our dear Joy's sake will you not promise that you will never quarrel with me."

"Indeed I will give the promise—and more. Listen here, little girl, for it is for your sake. I find I have been wrong to quarrel so readily and without waiting to understand. If a nigger did it I think I'd understand, for I don't look for much from him. But I do expect much from myself; and therefore I'll go back a bit and go a bit farther. Hear me promise, so help me God, I'll never quarrel again! Quarrel to kill I mean of course. Now, sir, are you satisfied!" Joy flung herself into his arms cooing lovingly:

"Dear, dear Daddy. Oh thank you so much; you have made me so happy! That promise is the best wedding-gift you could possibly give me!" Athlyne took the hand extended to him and wrung it heartily:

"And I too, thank you, sir. And, as I want to share in all Joy's happiness and in her pleasant ways, I hope you will let me—as her husband—call you Daddy too?"

"Indeed you may, my boy; I'll be right glad!" It was a happy trio that stood there, the two men's right hands clasping, and Joy once more holding the linked hands between hers.

"We may go join the Sheriff and Judy I think, little girl!" said the Colonel presently. He felt that he wanted to get back to himself from the unaccustomed atmosphere of sentiment which encompassed him.

"Just one moment—Daddy!" said Athlyne speaking the familiar name with an effort and looking at Joy as he did so. The approval shining from her beautiful eyes encouraged him, and he went on more freely:

"Now that our dear Joy is my care I should like to make a proposition. The Sheriff's suggestion is good, and his reading of the law seems as if it were all right; but, after all, there is no accounting for what judges and juries may decide. Now I want—and we all want—that there be no doubt about this marriage—now or hereafter. And I therefore suggest that presently Joy and I shall again exchange Matrimonial Intention and Consent, or whatever is the strongest way that can be devised to insure a flawless marriage. We can even write this down and both sign it, and you and the Sheriff and Judy shall witness. So that whatever has been before—though this will not disturb it—will be made all taut and secure!" Joy's comment was:

"And I shall be married to my husband a second time!"

"Yes, darling" said Athlyne putting his arm round her and drawing her close to him. She came willingly and put her arms round him. They embraced and kissed each other and he said:

"Yes darling; but wait a moment, I have a further suggestion. In addition to this we can have a 'regular' marriage to follow these two irregular ones. I shall go to London and get a special license from the Archbishop of Canterbury, who is a connection of my own. With this we shall have a religious marriage to supplement the civil ones. We can be married, sir, in your own rooms, or in a church, just as Joy wishes—and, of course, as her mother and her Daddy wish. We can be married the third time, Joy darling, in Westminster Abbey if you so desire!"

"Anywhere you choose—darling!" she spoke the last word shyly "will be what I wish. I am glad I am to be married three times to you."

"Why darling?"

"Because darling" she spoke the word now without shyness or hesitation. "I love you enough for three husbands; and now we must have three honeymoons!" she danced about the room gaily, clapping her hands like a happy child.

When they were ready to go to breakfast Colonel Ogilvie instinctively offered his arm to Joy, but catching sight of Athlyne drew back and motioned to him to take the honourable place. The husband was pleased, but seeing a new opening for conciliation he said, heartily:

"No, no. I hope the time will never come when my wife won't love to go with her father!" The old man was pleased and called to his daughter:

"Come, little girl, you have got to take us both!" She took her husband's arm as well as her father's; and all three moved towards the door. When they got there, however, some change was necessary, for it was not possible to pass through three abreast. Each of the men was willing to give place to the other; but before either man could move, or indeed before either had his mind made up what to do, the quicker-witted woman slipped back behind them. There taking Athlyne's hand in hers she had placed it on her father's arm. As they both were about to protest against going in front of her she said hastily:

"Please, please Daddy and . . . Husband I would really rather you two went first, and arm in arm as father and son should go. For that is what it is to be from this on; isn't it? I would rather a thousand times see the two men I love best in all the world going so, than walk in front of them as a Queen."

"That's very prettily said!" was the comment of her father. Then with a fond look back at her he took the young man's hand from his own arm and placed his own hand on the other's arm. That's better!" he said, "Age leaning on Youth, and Beauty smiling on both!"

And in this wise they entered the Sheriff's room, in time to see him sitting at one end of the sofa and Judy sitting at the furthest corner away from him—blushing.

CHAPTER XXIII

A HARMONY IN GRAY

As the trio entered the room Judy jumped from the sofa vivaciously. The Sheriff followed with an agility wonderful in a man of his age; he bade them all welcome with a compelling heartiness. Judy was full of animation; indeed she out-did herself to a degree which made Joy raise her eyebrows. Joy was a sympathetic soul, and unconsciously adapted herself to her Aunt's supra-vivacity.

To Colonel Ogilvie, less enthusiastic by nature and concern, it appeared that she was as he put it in his own mind "playing up to the old girl." He seemed to realise that the Sheriff was ardent in his intentions; and, with the calm, business-like aptitude of a brother-in-law to a not-young lady, had already made up his mind to give his consent.

Judy flew to Joy and kissed her fervently. The kisses were returned with equal warmth, and the two women rocked in each other's arms, to the envy, if delight, of certain of the onlookers viewing the circumstance from different standpoints. Judy took her niece to the now-vacated sofa, and an animated whispering began between them. Joy's attention was, however, distracted; her senses had different objectives. Her touch was to Judy sitting beside her and holding her close in a loving embrace; her ears were to her father who was talking to the Sheriff. But her eyes were all with her husband, devouring him. There came a timid knock at the door, and in answer to the Sheriff's "Come in," it was partly opened. The voice of the landlady was heard: "May I speak with ye a moment, Sheriff?" He went over to the door, and a whispered colloquy ensued, all his guests turning their eyes away and endeavouring in that way, as usual, to seem not to be listening. Then the Sheriff, having closed the door, said:

"Our good hostess tells me that there will be a full half hour of waiting before we can breakfast, if she is to have proper time to do justice to the food which she wishes to place before us. So I must ask pardon of you all."

"Capital! Capital!" said Colonel Ogilvie, "that half hour is just what we want. Mr. Sheriff, we have a little ceremony to go through before we breakfast. The fact is we are going to have an Irregular Marriage. If you are able to take part in such a thing I hope you will assist us." Joy rose up and stood beside Athlyne. The Sheriff answered:

"Be quite easy on that point, sir. I am not in my own shrieval district, and so, even if such were contra to my duties at home, I am free to act as an individual elsewhere. But who are the contracting parties? You are married already; so too are your daughter and my Lord Athlyne. Indeed it looks, Miss Hayes, as if you and I are the only available parties left. But I fear such great happiness is not for me; though I would give anything in the wide world to win it!" He bowed to her gallantly and took her hand. She looked quite embarrassed—though not distressed, and giggled like a schoolgirl.

"Indeed, Mr. Sheriff!" she said, "this is very sudden. Affairs of the heart seem to move quickly in this delightful country!" As she spoke she looked at Joy and Athlyne who happened to be at the moment standing hand in hand. Joy came over and sat beside her and kissed her. Athlyne, in obedience to a look from his wife, kissed her too. Then the Colonel gallantly followed suit. There was only the Sheriff left, and he, after a pause, took advantage of the occasion and kissed her also. Then to relieve her manifest embarrassment he spoke out:

"I fear I have diverted your purpose, Colonel Ogilvie. I am not sorry for it"—this with a look at Judy which made her blush afresh "but I apologize. I take it that you were alluding to something in which I am to have a less prominent part than I have suggested."

"The marriage, sir, is to be between Lord Athlyne and my daughter." As he spoke Athlyne went to a side table whereon were spread the Sheriff's writing materials. He took a sheet of paper and began to write. Colonel Ogilvie went on:

"We have come to the conclusion; that, though the act of marriage which has already taken place between these two young people is in your view lawful and complete, it may be well to go through the ceremony in a more formal manner. There are, we all know, intricacies and pitfalls in law; and we are both agreed with the suggestion of my lord that it would be well not to allow any loophole for after attack. Therefore in your presence—if you will be so good," the Sheriff bowed, "they shall again pledge their mutual Matrimonial Consent. They will both sign the paper to that effect which I see Lord Athlyne is preparing; and we shall all sign it as witnesses. Then, when this new marriage is complete—and irrefragable as I understand from what you said awhile ago it will be—we shall be ready for breakfast. It will be more than perhaps you expected when you so kindly asked us to be your guests: a wedding breakfast!"

Judy whispered to her niece.

"Joy, you must come to your room and let me dress you properly. I have brought a dress with me."

"What dress dear?" she asked.

"The tweed tailor-made."

"But, Judy dear, I have on a white frock, and that is more suitable for my wedding."

"That was all right yesterday, dear. But to-day you shall not wear white. You are already a married lady; this is only a re-marriage." A beautiful blush swept over Joy's face as she looked at her husband writing away as hard as his pen could move.

"I shall wear white to-day!" she said in the same whisper, and stood up.

Just at that moment a fly drove quickly past the window. It stopped at the hotel door, and there was a sudden bustle of arrival. Voices raised to a high pitch were heard outside. Various comments were heard in the room.

"That's mother!"

"My wife!"

"Sally!"

"Why Aunt Judy that's the voice of Mrs. O'Brien!"

"My Foster-mother!"

The door opened, and in swept Mrs. Ogilvie who flew first to her husband's arms; and then, after a quick embrace, seemed to close round Joy and obliterate her. A similar eclipse took place with regard to Athlyne; for Mrs. O'Brien dashed into the room and calling out as though invoking the powers of earth and heaven: "Me bhoy! me bhoy!" fell upon him. He seemed really glad to see her, and yielded himself to her embrace as freely as though he had been a child again.

"Joy dear," said Mrs. Ogilvie "I hope you are all right. After your father and then Judy had gone, I was so anxious about you, that I got the north mail stopped and caught it at Penrith. Just as I was going to get ready for the journey Mrs. O'Brien came in. She had written to me in London that she would like to pay her respects, and I had said we were going on to Ambleside but would be glad if she would come and see us there and spend a few days with us." Mrs. O'Brien who was all ears, here cut into the conversation:

"Aye, an Miss Joy acushla,—my service to ye miss!—she sent me postal ordhers to cover me railway fare an me expinces. Oh! the kind heart iv her!"

She had by now released Athlyne and stood back from him pointing at him as she spoke:

"An comin' here through yer ladyship's goodness who do I find but me beautiful bhoy. Luk at him! Luk at him! Luk at him!" Her voice rose in crescendo at each repetition. "The finest, dearest, sweetest, bonniest child that ever a woman tuk to her breast. An now luk at him well. The finest, up-standinest, handsomest, dearest, lovinest man that the whole wurrld houlds. That doesn't forget his ould fosther mother an him an Earrll, wid castles iv his own, an medals on to him an Victory Crasses. An it's a gineral he ought to be. Luk at him, God bless him!" She turned to one after another of the party in turn as though inviting their admiration. Joy came and, putting her arms round the old woman's neck, hugged and kissed her. When she got free, Mrs. O'Brien said to Athlyne:

"An phwat are ye doin' here me darlin' acushla me lord—av I may make so bould as t' ask ye? How did ye come here; and phwat brung ye that yer ould nurse might have her eyes made glad wid sight iv ye?"

"I am here, my dear, because I am married to Joy Ogilvie, and we are going to be married again!"

Then the storm of comment broke, all the women speaking at once and in high voices suitable to a momentous occasion:

"What, what?" said Mrs. Ogilvie. "Married to my daughter! Colonel Ogilvie, how is it that I was not informed of this coming event?"

"Faith, my dear I don't know" he answered "I never knew it—and—and I believe they didn't know it themselves . . . till the moment before it was done." He added the last part of the sentence in deference to the Sheriff's direction as to 'intention.' Fortunately the Sheriff had not heard his remark.

"Do explain yourself, Lucius. I am all anxiety."

"My dear, yesterday Joy made an irregular marriage with Lord Athlyne!"

"Good God!" The exclamation gave an indication of the social value of "irregular" marriage to persons unacquainted with Scottish law. Her husband saw that she was pained and tried to reassure her:

"You need not distress yourself, my dear. It is all right. 'Irregular' is only a name for a particular form of marriage in this Country. It is equally legal with any other marriage."

"But who is Lord Athlyne, and where is he? That is the name of the man who Mrs. O'Brien told Joy was the only man good enough for her."

"Lord Athlyne" said Colonel Ogilvie "at present our son-in-law, is none other than Mr. Richard Hardy with whom you shook hands just now!"

"Lucius, I am all amazed! There seems to be a sort of network of mystery all round us. But one thing: if Joy was married yesterday how on earth can she be going to be married to-day?"

"To avoid the possibility of legal complications later on! It is all right, my dear. You may take it from me that there is no cause for concern! But there were certain things, usually attended to beforehand, which on this occasion—owing to ignorance and hurry and unpremeditation—were not attended to. In order to prevent the possibility of anything going wrong by any quibble, they are to be married again just now."

"Where? when?"

"Here, in this room!"

"But where's the clergyman; where is the license?"

"There is neither. This is a Scottish marriage! Later on we can have a regular church marriage with a bishop if you wish or an archbishop; in a church or a room or a Cathedral—just as you prefer." Mrs. Ogilvie perceptibly stiffened as he spoke. Then she said, with what she thought was dignified gravity, which seemed to others like frigid acidity:

"Do I understand, Colonel Ogilvie, that you are a consenting party to another 'irregular'"—she quivered as she said the word—"marriage? And that my daughter is to be made a laughing stock amongst all our acquaintances by *three* different marriages?"

"That is so, my dear. It is for Joy's good!"

"Her good? Fiddlesticks! But in that case I have nothing more to say!" Some of her wrath seemed to be turned on both Athlyne and Joy; for she did not say a single word to either of them. She simply relapsed into stony silence.

Mrs. O'Brien's reception of the news afforded what might be termed the "comic relief" of the strained situation. She raised her hands, as though in protest to heaven for allowing such a thing, and emitted a loud wail such as a "keener" raises at an Irish wake. Then she burst into voluble speech:

"Oh wirrasthrue me darlin' bhoy, is it a haythen Turk y' are becomin', to take another wife whin ye've got one already only a day ould. An such a wan more betoken—the beautifullest darlinest young cratur what iver I seen! Her that I picked out long ago as the only wan that ye was good enough for. Shure, couldn't ye rist content wid Miss Joy, me darlin'? It's lookin' forward I was to nursin' her childher, as I nursed yerself me lord darlin', her childher, an yours! An' now it's another woman steppin' in betune ye; an' maybe there'll be no childher at all, at all. Wirrasthrue!"

"But look here, Nanny," said Athlyne with some impatience. "Can't you see that you're all wrong. It is to Joy that I am going to marry again! There's no other woman coming in between us. 'Tis only the dear girl herself!"

"Ah, that's all very well, me lord darlin'; but which iv them is to be the mother? Faix but I'll go an ax her Ladyship this minit!" And go she did, to Athlyne's consternation and Joy's embarrassment. All in a hurry she started up and went over to the sofa where Joy sat, and with a bob curtesy said to her:

"Me lady, mayn't I have the nursin' av yer childher, the way I had their father before them? Though, be the same token, it's not the same nursin' I can give thim, wid me bein' ould an' rhun dhry!" Joy felt that the only thing to do was to postpone the difficulty to a more convenient season, when there should not be so many eyes—some of them strange ones—on her. To do this as kindly and as brightly as she could, she said:

"But dear Mrs. O'Brien, isn't it a little soon to think—or at any rate to speak—of such things?"

"Wasn't ye married yesterday?" interrupted the old woman. But looking at her lady's cheeks she went on in a different tone:

"But me darlin'—Lady, it's over bould an' too contagious for me to mintion such things, as yit. But I'll take, if I may, a more saysonable opportunity to ask ye to patthernise me. Some time whin ye're more established as a wife thin ye are now!"

"Indeed" said Joy kindly. "I shall only be too happy to have you near me. And if I—if we are ever blessed with a little son I hope you will try to teach him to be as like his———" she stopped, blushing, but after a short pause went on "as like my dear husband as ever you can!" There was a break in her voice which moved the old woman strongly. She lifted the slim fine young hand to her withered lips and kissed it fervently.

"Glory be to God! me Lady, but it's the proud woman I'll be to keep and guard the young Earrll. An' I'll give my life for him if needs be!"

"Come now!" said the Sheriff who had been speaking with Colonel Ogilvie and Athlyne, and who had read over the paper written by the latter. "Come now all you good people! All sit round the room except you two principals to this solemn contract. You two stand before me and read over the paper. You, my Lord, read it first; and then you too, my Lady, do the same!" They sat round as they wished. Joy and Athlyne stood up before the Sheriff, who was also standing. Instinctively they took hands, and Athlyne holding the paper in his left hand, read as fellows:

"We Calinus Patrick Richard Westerna Mowbray Hardy Fitzgerald, Earl of Athlyne, Viscount Roscommon and Baron Ceannda-Shail and Joy Fitzgerald or Ogilvie late of Airlville in the State of Kentucky, United States of America, agree that we shall be and are united in the solemn bonds of matrimony according to the Law of Scotland and that we being of one mind as to the marriage, are and hereby declare ourselves man and wife.

Witness of above

    We the undersigned hereby declare that we have in the presence of the above signatories and of each other seen the foregoing signatures appended to this deed by the signatories themselves in our presence and in the presence of each other.

    Alexander Fenwick (Sheriff of Galloway).

    Lucius Ogilvie (father of the bride).

    Mary Hayes Ogilvie (mother of the bride).

    Bedelia Ann O'Brien, widow (formerly nurse and foster mother to the bridegroom).

    Judith Hayes (aunt of the bride)."

When the document was completed by the signatures the Sheriff, having first scanned it carefully, offered it to Colonel Ogilvie, who raising a protesting hand said:

"No, no, Mr. Sheriff! I think we should all prefer that it should be kept in your custody, if you will so oblige us."

"With the greatest pleasure" he said; and Athlyne and Joy having consented to the scheme he folded the document and put it into his pocket. Just then the landlady, having knocked and being bidden to enter, came into the room followed by several maids and men bearing dishes.

"And now to breakfast" he went on. "Will the Bride kindly sit on my right hand, with her Husband next her. Mrs. Ogilvie, will you honour me by sitting on my left, with Colonel Ogilvie to support you on the other side. Miss Hayes will you kindly sit on Lord Athlyne's right."

"And Mrs. . . . Mrs. O'Brien," whispered Judy. He went on:

"Mrs. O'Brien will you sit on Colonel Ogilvie's left."

"'Deed an' I'll not!" said the Irishwoman sturdily.

"Do you mean" asked Colonel Ogilvie icily "that you do not care to sit next to me individually?"

"Faix an' I don't mane anything so foolish yer 'ann'r. Why should the likes o' me dar to object to the likes iv you? All I mane, sorr, is that an ould Biddy like me isn't fit to sit down alongside the quality—let alone an Earrll and his Laady whose unborn childer I'm to nurse. An', more betoken, on such an owdacious occasion—shure an I don't mane that but such a suspicious occasion."

"Mrs. O'Brien ma'am" said the Sheriff taking her hand "you're going, I hope, to take your place at the table that all these good friends wish you to take."

"In troth no yer"—whispering to Joy "what's a Sheriff called Miss Joy? Is he 'yer Majesty' or 'me lord' or 'yer ann'r' or what is he anyhow?" "I think he is ' yer honour'" said Joy. So Mrs. O'Brien continued: "Yer Ann'r. Don't ask me fur to sit down wid the quality where I don't belong. But let me give a hand to these nice girrls and byes to shling the hash. Shure it's a stewardess I am, an accustomed to shovin' the food."

"Nanny" said Athlyne kindly but in a strong voice "we all want you to sit at table with us to-day. And I hope you won't refuse us that pleasure."

"Certainly me darlin' lord!" she said instantly. "In coorse what plases ye!" The Master had spoken; she was content to obey without question. In the meantime Joy had been whispering to her mother who now spoke out:

"Mr. Sheriff, will you allow me to make a suggestion about the places at table?"

"With a thousand delights, madam. Pray make whatever disposition you think best. I am only too grateful for your help."

"Thank you, sir. Well, if you do not mind I should like my sister, Miss Hayes, placed next to you; then Colonel Ogilvie and myself. On the other side if you will place next to my son-in-law his old nurse, I am right sure that both will be pleased."

"Hear, hear!" said Athlyne. "Come along, Nanny, and sit next your boy! Joy and I shall be delighted to have you close to us. Won't you, darling." Joy's answer was quite satisfactory to him:

"Of course . . . Darling!" It was wonderful what a world of love she put into the utterance of those two syllables.

The breakfast was a great success, though but few of the party ate heartily. Neither Athlyne nor Joy did justice to the provender. They whispered a good deal and held hands surreptitiously under the table, and their eyes met constantly. The same want of appetite seemed to have affected both the Sheriff and Judy; but silence and a certain restraint and primness were their characteristics. Mrs. O'Brien, seated on the very edge of her chair, was too proud and too happy to eat. But she was storing up for future enjoyment fond memories of every incident, however trivial.

It was mid-day before any move was made. There were no speeches—in public, as all considered it would break the charm that was over the occasion if anything so overt took place. When all is understood, speech becomes almost banal. But there were lots of whisperings; whispers as soft in their tone as their matter was sweet. No one appeared to notice any one else at such moments; though be sure that there were words and tones and looks that were remembered later by the receivers, and looks and movements that were remembered by the others. Judy and the Sheriff had much to say to each other. Ample opportunity was given from the fact that the newly married pair found themselves occupied with each other almost exclusively. Occasionally, of course, Joy and the Sheriff conversed; but as a working rule he was quite content to devote himself to Judy who seemed quite able to hold up her end of the serious flirtation. When finally the party broke up, preparatory to setting out for the south, the Sheriff asked Colonel Ogilvie if it might be possible that he should join in travel with the party, as he wished to spend a few days in Ambleside—a place which he had not visited for many years. Colonel Ogilvie cordially acquiesced. He was pretty sure by now that the meeting of Judy and this new friend would end in a match, and he was glad to do anything which might result in the happiness of his sister-in-law of whom he was really fond. But it was not on this account only that he made him welcome. The reaction from his evil temper was on him. Conscience was awake and pricking into him the fact that he had behaved brutally. His mind did not yet agree in the justice of the verdict; but that would doubtless come later. He now wished to show to all that there was quite another side of his character. In this view he pressed that the Sheriff should be his guest. The other was about to object when he realised that by accepting he would be one of the household, and so much closer to Judy, and more and oftener in her society than would otherwise be possible. So he accepted gladly, and he and the Colonel soon became inseparable—except when Judy was speaking! In such case Colonel Ogilvie often felt himself rather left out in the cold. At the beginning of breakfast Athlyne had learned from Joy of the abandonment of the motor, and he had accordingly sent his father-in-law's chauffeur, with his pilot, to bring it back. They had to travel in a horse carriage; he could not drive two motors at once, and the pilot could not drive one. In due course the motor was retrieved, and having been made clean and taut by the "first-class *mechanicien* and driver" was ready for the road. Colonel Ogilvie's motor was also ready, and as the pilot could now be left to travel home by train, so that the owner could sit by his chauffeur, there would be room for the new guest to sit between the two ladies in the tonneau. When he mentioned this arrangement, however, the Sheriff did not jump at it, but found difficulties in the way of incommoding the ladies. At last he said:

"I hope you will excuse me, Ogilvie, but I had already formed a little plan which I hoped with your sanction and that of your wife, to carry out. Before breakfast I—Miss Hayes and I had been talking of the old manner of posting. Her idea had, I think, been formed by seeing prints of breakdowns of carriages in run-away matches to Gretna Green, and I suggested . . . In fact I ventured to offer to drive her in old-fashioned postal style to Ambleside, and let her see what it was like. I have in my house at Galloway a fine old shay that my father and mother made their wedding trip in. It has always been kept in good trim, and it is all right for the journey. As Sheriff I have post-boys in my employ for great occasions and I have good horses of my own. So when J . . . Miss Hayes accepted my offer . . . of the journey, I wired off to have the trap sent down here. Indeed it should arrive within a very short time. I have also wired for relays of horses to be ready at Dumfries, Annan, Carlisle and Patterdale, so that when we start we should go without a hitch. My boys know the road, and four horses will spin us along in good style—even if we cannot keep up with your motor." So it was arranged that the pilot could occupy his old place with the chauffeur; and the Colonel and Mrs. Ogilvie would travel in the tonneau, Darby and Joan fashion. This settlement of affairs had only been arrived at after considerable discussion. When her father had told Joy that she was to ride with her mother, she had spoken out at once—without arrangement with Athlyne or even consultation with him:

"Athlyne will drive me, and we can take Mrs. O'Brien with us. There is stacks of room in the tonneau, and we have no luggage. I am sure my husband would like to have her with us."

But when the arrangement was mentioned to the foster-mother she refused absolutely to obey any such order:

"What" she said "me go away in the coach wid the bride and groom! An ould corrn-crake like me wid the quality; an this none other than me own darlin' lord and Miss Joy that I'm going to nurse the childher iv her. No, my Lady, I'll do no such thing! Do ye think I'm goin' to shpoil shport when me darlin' does be drivin' wid his beautiful wife by him an' him kissin' her be the yard an' the mile an' the hour, an' huggin' her be the ton, as he ought to be doin', or he's not the man I've always tuk him for. Shure ma'am" this to Mrs. Ogilvie "this is their day an' their hour; an' iviry minit iv it is goold an dimons to them! I'm tellin' ye, I'd liefer put me eyes on Styx than do such a thing!" Mrs. Ogilvie, who recognised the excellence of her ideas, said:

"Then you must come with the Colonel and me. We've loads of room, and we are all alone."

"An' savin' yer presence, so ye should be ma'am whin ye're seein' yer daughter goin' aff wid her man. There's loads iv things you and your man will want to be talkin' about. Musha! if it's only rememberin' what ye said an' done whin ye was aff on yer own honeymoon. Mind ye, ma'am, it's not bad talkin' or rememberin', that's not! No motors for me, ma'am—to-day at any rate. I'll go by the thrain that I kem' by; an' when I get to yer hotel, if I'm before ye, I'll shtraighten out things for ye, an' have the rooms nice an' ready. For mind ye, ma'am, me darlin' Lord tould me that he's goin' to have a gran' weddin' to Miss Joy whin he gets his license! Be the way, does he get that, can ye tell me ma'am, from the polis or where the sheebeeners gits theirs? An' av there's goin' to be a weddin' wid flowers an' gowns an' veils an' things in church, I suppose they won't be too previous about comin' together. Musha! but's it's a quare sort iv ways the quality has! Weddin's here be the Sheriff, an' thin be bishops, an' wid licenses. An' him in Bowness—for that's where he tells me he's shtoppin'—an' his wife in Ambleside—on their weddin' night! Begob! Ireland's changin' fast, fur that usen't to be the way. I'm thinkin' that the Shinn-Fayn'll have to wake up a bit if that's the way things is going to go. Or else there'll be millea murther, from the Giant's Causeway to Cape Clear!" As Mrs. Ogilvie did not wish to discuss this part of the question herself, she beckoned over

Athlyne and told him that Mrs. O'Brien had refused to go in his motor.

"Not even if I ask you or tell you to?" he said to the old woman, having not the least intention of doing either.

"Not even thin, me Lord darlin'" she said with a cheery smile. "An' I'm thinkin' it's thankin' me—you an' yer lovely wife too—'ll be before ye're well out of sight of this place. Faix it's a nice sort iv ould gooseberry I'd be, sittin' in the carriage wid me arrums foulded, wid me darlin' Lord sittin' in front dhrivin' like a show-flure in a shute iv leather. An' his bride beside him, wid her arrums round him bekase both his own is busy wid the little wheel; an' her wondhrin', wid tears in her beautiful grey eyes, why he doesn't kiss her what she's pinin' fur. Augh! no! Not me, this time! I was a bride meself—wanst. An' I know betther nor me young Lady does now, what is what on the weddin' day afther the words is said. Though she'll pick up, so she will. She's not the soort that'll be long larnin'! Musha . . ." Her further revelations and prophesyings were cut short by Athlyne's kissing her and saying "Goodbye!"

If the journey up North had been Fairyland, the journey Southward was Heaven for both the young people. Athlyne felt all the triumph of a conqueror. If he had sung out loud, as he would like to have done, his song would have been a war-song rather than a love-song. There was the *élan* of the conqueror about him; the stress of love-longing and love-pining were behind him. The battle was won, and his conqueror's booty was beside him, well content to be in his train. Still even conqueror's love has its duties as well as its right, and he was more tender than ever to Joy. She, sitting beside him in all the radiancy of her new found wifehood, felt that their hearts were beating together; and that their thoughts swayed in unison. When her eyes would be lifted from the lean, strong, brown hands gripping the steering wheel—for in the rush of departure he had other things to think of than putting on the gloves which were squeezed behind him in his seat—and would look up into his face she would feel a sort of electric shock as his eyes, leaving for a moment their steering duty, would flash into hers with a look of love which made her quiver. But presently when his yielding to affection had been tested, and even her curiosity had been satisfied, she ceased such sudden looks. She realized his idea of the gravity of the situation when she saw, as his eyes returned to their necessary task, the hard look become fixed on his eagle face—the look which to one engaged in his task means safety to those under his care. She was all sympathy with him now. She was content that his will should prevail; that his duty should be the duty of both; that her service was to help him. And the first moment she realized this, she sighed happily as she sank back in her seat, her lover-rapture merged in wife-content. She had compensation for the foregoing in the exercise of her own pride. From her present standpoint all that came within the scope of her senses was supremely beautiful. The mountains grey and mysterious in their higher and further peaks; the dark woods running flame-like up into the glory of the mountain colouring; the scent of the new-mown hay, drifted across the track by the bracing winds sweeping over the hills; the glimmering sapphire of the water as they swept by lake or river, or caught flashes of the distant Forth through long green valleys. They went fast; Athlyne's wild excitement—the echo of the battle-phrenzy that had won him distinction on the field—found some relief in speed. He had thrown open the throttle of his powerful engine and swept along at such a speed that the whole landscape seemed to fly by the rushing car, giving only momentary glimpses of even the most far-flung beauty. He did not fear police traps now. He did not fear anything! Even the car seemed to have yielded itself like a living thing to the spell of the situation. Its wheels purred softly as it swept along, and the speed made a wind which seemed to roar in the ears of the two who were one.

Joy felt that she had a right to be content. This journey was of her own choosing entirely. The manner of it had been this: when the party had been arranged for starting her father had said to Athlyne:

"When you get to Ambleside, as I suppose you will do before us, will you give orders to have everything ready for our party. You can do this before you drive over to Bowness. You can come over to dinner if you like. I suppose you and Joy will want to see something of each other—all you can indeed, before the wedding comes off. That can be as soon as you like after you have got the license." To this he had replied:

"I should like to—and shall—do anything I can, sir, to meet your wishes. But I cannot promise to do anything now, on quite my own initiative. You see our dear girl has to be consulted; and I need not tell you that her wishes must prevail—so far as I am concerned!"

"Quite right, my boy! Quite right!" said the old man. "Then we shall leave the orders to her. Here, Joy!" she came over, and her father put his suggestion to her. She hesitated gravely, and paused before she spoke; she evidently intended that there should be no mistake as to her deliberate intention:

"No! Daddy, that won't do; I'm going with my husband!" She took his arm and clung to him lovingly, her finger tips biting sweetly into his flesh. "But, Daddy dear, we'll come over to-morrow and lunch or breakfast with you, if we may. Call it early lunch or late breakfast. We shall be over about noon. Remember we have to come from Bowness!"

Athlyne seemed to float in air as he heard her. There was something so sweetly—so truly wifely, in her words and attitude that it won to his heart and set him in a state of rapture.

The late breakfast at Ambleside next day, though ostensibly a mere family breakfast, was hardly to be classed in that category. It was in reality regarded by all the family at present resident in that town as a wedding breakfast. They had one and all dressed themselves for the occasion. Not in complete marriage costume, which would have looked a little overdone, but in a modified form which sufficiently expressed in the mind of each the prevailing spirit of rejoicing. A few seconds before noon the "toot toot" of Athlyne's powerful hooter was heard some distance off. All rushed to the windows to see the great red car swing round the corner. The chauffeur was driving; the bride and groom sat in the tonneau. As Athlyne was not driving he wore an ordinary morning dress—a well-cut suit of light grey which set out well his tall, lithe powerful figure. Joy was wrapped in a huge motor coat of soft grey, with her head shrouded in a veil of the same colour. In the hall they both took off their wraps, Athlyne helping his wife with the utmost tenderness. When they came into the room they made a grey pair, for with the exception of Athlyne's brown eyes and hair and a scarlet neck tie, and Joy's dark hair and a flash of the same scarlet as her husband's on her breast, they were grey—all grey. It would seem as if the whole colour-scheme of the couple had been built round Joy's eyes. She certainly looked lovely;

there was a brilliant colour in her cheeks, and between her scarlet lips her teeth, when she smiled, flashed like pearls. She was in a state of buoyancy, seeming rather to float about than to move like a being on feet. She was all sweetness and affection, and flitted from one to another, leaving a wake of beaming happiness behind her.

Athlyne too was manifestly happy; but in quieter fashion, as is the way of a man. He was not overt or demonstrative in his attention to Joy; but his eyes followed her perpetually, and his ears seemed to hear every whisper regarding her. Her eyes too, kept turning to him wherever she might be or to whom speaking. Judy at first stood beaming at the pair with a look of proprietary interest: but after a while she began to be a trifle nettled by the husband's absorption in her niece. This feeling culminated when as Joy tripped slightly on the edge of the hearth-rug her husband started towards her with a swift movement and with that quick intake of breath which manifests alarmed concern. Judy's impulsiveness found its expression in a semi-humorous, semi-sarcastic remark:

"Why Athlyne you seem to look on the girl as if she was brittle! You weren't like that yesterday when you flashed her away from us at sixty miles an hour!" For a moment there was silence and all eyes were fixed on Joy who looked embarrassed and turned rosy-red. Athlyne to relieve her drew their attention on himself:

"No, my dear Judy—I'm not ever going to call you anything else you know. She wasn't my wife then!"

"Wasn't she!" came the answer tartly spoken. "She was just as much your wife then. She had been married to you only twice! And the first marriage was good enough for anything. I know that is so, for my sheriff says so!—Oh . . ." The ejaculation was due to the shame of sudden recognition of her confession. She blushed furiously; the Sheriff, looking radiantly happy, stepped over to her, took her hand, raised it to his lips, and kissed it.

"I think my dear," he said slowly and quietly, "that constitutes a marriage—if you will have it so?" She looked at him shyly and said quietly:

"If you like to count it a step on the way—like Joy's first marriage, do so—dear! Then if you like we can make it real when Joy becomes a wife—in the Church!"

Everyone in the room was so interested in this little episode that two of them only noticed a queer note of dissent or expostulation, coming in the shape of a sort of modified grunt from the two matrons of the party. Said Athlyne, still mindful of his intent to protect Joy:

"All right, Judy. I'll remember: '*my* sheriff,' if there's any more chaffing. It seems that he'll be 'brittle' before long!" Judy flashed one keen happy glance at him as she whispered close in his ear:

"Don't be ungenerous!" For reply he whispered back:

"Forgive me—dear. I did not intend to be nasty. I'm too happy for anything of that sort!"

As breakfast wore on and the familiarity of domestic life followed constraint, matters of the future came on the tapis. When Mrs. Ogilvie asked the young couple if they had yet settled when the marriage—the church marriage—was to come off, Joy looked down demurely at the table cloth as her husband answered:

"I go up to town early in the morning to get the License. It is all in hand and there will be no hitch and no delay. I had a wire this morning from my solicitor about it; and also one from the Archbishop congratulating me. I shall be home by the ten ten train on Thursday and we can have the wedding late that afternoon, if you will have the church and the parson ready."

"But, my dear boy, isn't that rather sudden?"

"Not sudden enough for me! But really, so far as I am concerned, I shall wait as long as Joy wishes. Now that we are married already, I fancy it doesn't much matter. Only that anything which could possibly bind me closer to Joy will always be a happiness to me, I don't care whether we have a third marriage at all." Mrs. Ogilvie caught her daughter's eye and answered at once:

"So be it then! Thursday afternoon at six. I suppose there can be no objection as to canonical hours?" The Sheriff answered:

"I can tell you that. The License of the Archbishop goes through and beyond all canonical hours and all places—in South Britain of course. Armed with that instrument you can celebrate the marriage when and where you will." Joy and Athlyne were by this time holding hands and whispering.

"Of course Joy will stay with us till then—Athlyne." Mrs. Ogilvie spoke the last word with a pause; it was the first time she had used his name.

"Not 'of course.'" he answered. "She is the head of her house now and must be free to do as she please. But I am sure she will like to come to you." Joy made a protesting *"moue"* at him as she said:

"Of course I'd like to be with Mother and Daddy, and Judy— if I—if I am not to be with you—Oh, darling! you're hurting me. You're so frightfully strong!"

Breakfast being over, the party broke up and moved about the room. Joy was sitting on the sofa with her Mother when Mrs. O'Brien came sidling up by the wall. When she got close she curtsied and said:

"Won't ye tell me now, me Lady, if I'm to be the wan to nurse yer childher?"

"Oh dear! But Mrs. O'Brien, I said only yesterday that I'd tell you that some other time. You *are* previous!—Didn't you hear that I am to be married on Thursday. Later on . . ."

"No time like the prisint, me Lady. It was yistherday ye shpoke; an to-day's to-day. Mayn't I nurse yer ch . . ."

"Tell her, dear—" her Mother had begun, when Judy joined the group.

"What's all this about? Whose children are you talking of?" began the merry spinster. But her sister cut her short:

"Never you mind, Judy! You just go and sit down and try and get accustomed to silence so as to be ready to keep your Sheriff out of an asylum." Athlyne, too, with ears preternaturally sharp on Joy's account, had heard something of the conversation. Looking over at his wife, he saw her face divinely rosy, and with a troubled, hunted look in her eyes. He too instantly waded into the fray.

"I say, let her alone you all! I hope they're not teasing you darling?" Joy, fearing that something unpleasant might be said, on one side or the other, made haste to reassure him.

Then she closed his mouth in the very best way that a young wife can do—the way that seems to take his feet from earth and to raise him to heaven.

THE END.

Printed in the United States
99546LV00002B/133/A